THE SONG OF THE BUTCHER BIRD

Book I

BIGFELLA KIDMAN

Matt Smaller

Dedicated with love to Mum, Alice and Bea,
and to the countless millions of souls who didn't get a fair go,
especially my sister Emma Jane, Gillie, Louise, Chris, Rick and Teesa.

ISBN 978-1-9996278-0-5

First published by yella mickey limited 2018
www.yellamickey.com
info@yellamickey.com

Printed and bound in Great Britain by Clays Ltd, Elcograf S.p.A

September 1914

BOOMERANG

Not that it made much difference in the Queensland bush, but it was a Thursday morning early in the dry season when the big white man came out of his bark hut, shotgun first.

He was badly hungover and ready to belt the living daylights out of the lazy slut who should have been brewing him a billy of tea.

But as he half expected, there was no fire burning in the silent, empty clearing. No black gin cowering. No billy brewing. None of the muted noise and movement of morning among the cluster of shabby wurleys that normally housed his Aborigines.

Even the busybody mobs of galahs and parakeets that usually filled the gidgee trees with raucous squabbling had fled.

The big man shifted the shotgun into the crook of his right arm and walked across the clearing to the nearest deserted wurley.

Nothing remained to show that it had ever been occupied.

He swore and aimed a vicious kick at the side of the lopsided, flimsy structure, and he was opening his flies to piss into the hole he had made when he saw the skeleton emerging from the long morning shadows of the trees, just thirty yards or so from where he was standing.

For several seconds the white man stared in disbelief. A droplet of sweat ran down the side of his face into his beard. Rum-sweat stains flowered under his arms and down his back, spreading outwards to old tidemarks on his filthy shirt.

He spat and raised the shotgun to his shoulder, but before he could fire the skeleton lifted a long, thin arm and pointed down the treeline to the big man's right. The movement of another figure caught his eye and made him turn, the barrel of the shotgun swinging to this new target.

It was a smaller figure, indistinct but clearly visible, an Aborigine boy who also raised an arm and pointed accusingly at the white man, and then wavered and dissolved into the shifting pattern of the shadows and was gone.

The white man glared for a moment into the trees. Then he turned back to face the skeleton and the boomerang hit him right above the bridge of his nose.

The boomerang was not a lightweight wing designed for ritual fights or scaring birds. It was an ironbark-wood throwing club made for killing kangaroos, as heavy and long as the big man's thighbone. The force of its impact hurled him backwards, spreadeagled in the dust, the stock of the shotgun still gripped in his right hand and his eyes screwed shut against the dark, humming blur whirling towards him in the last millisecond of his conscious life.

There was no blood visible to show where the boomerang had hit him, only a deep concavity in the middle of his forehead, and he breathed stertorously through his open mouth.

He lay still long enough for the flies to settle on his face, long enough for the birds to make their first hesitant calls in the scrubby bushland that stretched away north and west from the ramshackle camp. Then the skeleton moved at the edge of the clearing and walked slowly towards the body.

In motion the skeleton became an Aborigine warrior, a tall, thin, almost naked figure painted in bone-white stripes caked and cracking on his dark skin, and he walked without a sound.

He nudged the big whitefella with a broad big toe and studied the slack, snoring face for some time. Then he placed the fire-hardened point of the spear on the man's chest, adjusted the position carefully, and leaned on the shaft.

The spear slid in discernible jerks through the sweatstained shirt, through the skin, through the membrane between the ribs, and the big body spasmed and shuddered as the hardwood point penetrated the muscle of the heart.

The warrior eased his weight off the shaft, took a step closer to the body, placed one foot on it and pulled the spear with some difficulty back out of the big white man's chest. He wiped the wet tip of the spear on the whitefella's shirt, stooped to retrieve the boomerang, turned away and disappeared among the trees.

In the eight years since he had first squatted on the abandoned Berrie Berrie outstation, Foley had never failed to appear at the Currawah grog shop on a Saturday afternoon.

When he missed two Saturdays on the trot, Shanghai Lo, the grog shop's proprietor, sent a message into Springvale to let the police know that the big white man must be crook or worse, and that a boundary rider from Seymour Creek coming in to blue his cheque at Currawah had seen a mob of blackfellas going walkabout from the Berrie Berrie direction.

So it was ten days after the incident that Senior Constable Cleary and his police detail arrived on the scene of the killing.

Ten days was more than enough time for the local wild pigs and dingoes to spread the dead man widely around the clearing, and it took Cleary and his men over an hour to assemble the remains. The body of evidence was incomplete, but they found the skull under a mulga bush, and as far as the senior constable was concerned the fist-sized depressed fracture in the forehead proved what he already knew.

This was not the first time there had been trouble between Foley and the Aborigines who still clung to this corner of their tribal homeland, and it was their scuffed trail the native trackers followed the next morning, hunting westwards with the two white policemen riding behind them.

The Berrie Berrie blackfellas had stopped at the creek that marked the edge of their tribal area, about eighty miles from the scene of the crime. It took the police detail two days to cover the same distance, so it was late on the third afternoon of his investigation when Cleary stopped as a single horseman emerged from the dense scrub to the north and trotted across the open ground to meet them.

It was a young stockman, his face shaded by a battered, broad-brimmed hat. A second horse carrying his swag and camp kit was tied by a long, greenhide lead-rope to his saddle. He touched his hat brim in greeting to the policeman. 'I got your message,' he said. 'You were right. They're at the creek. I can't get up too close but I counted them. Did you find him?'

'We did, what's left of him,' said Cleary. 'We knew his blackfellas had run for it and we tracked 'em all the way here, just to be sure.'

The stockman nodded and pushed his hat up on his forehead. He told the policeman there were fifteen adults in a straggling camp beside a tree-shaded billabong less than half a mile to the east. Six old men, nine women, and eight children including three infants. No dogs. Foley had hated dogs.

The billabong was bounded on the far side by a long limestone bluff a homesick English squatter had named the White Cliffs. The Aboriginal name for it was a thousand generations older and the rock wall was one of their most sacred sites, but today it formed a convenient barrier that helped the senior constable make his decision.

There was at least an hour of good daylight left, so Cleary followed the stockman in silence another quarter of a mile closer to the creek before swinging himself off his horse and issuing his orders. The three mounts, three spares and two police packhorses were hobbled and tied under the shade of a gidgee tree, and ten rounds of ammunition distributed to each of the six native trackers. The senior constable handed a police-issue revolver to the stockman and checked his own.

They formed a loose line with Cleary, his junior constable and the stockman at the centre, and then the three white men walked as quietly as their boots allowed through the bush towards the camp, the native trackers fanning out noiselessly on either side. The young stockman walked clumsily through the long grass, limping badly.

As they approached they could hear voices, the murmur of men, a woman calling and a child's laugh that echoed faintly against the bluff. The voices stopped abruptly when the cordon was fifty or sixty paces from the camp, and as the line of men emerged out of the trees onto the grass that covered the bank of the billabong, Cleary counted the fifteen adults, frozen in the commonplace acts of their evening routine.

Three of the women holding the infants were younger than the other adults, but to Cleary the adults all looked like the subhuman wreckage slumped in the dust behind the pub in Springvale. They were wearing the motley remnants of missionary cast-offs and third-hand charity scraps barely recognisable as proper clothing, and the camp was littered with the detritus they had salvaged from the outstation: fire-blackened old jam tins, broken baskets, badly patched sugar bags and flour sacks with makeshift twisted grass handles.

The senior constable was holding his revolver down by his side, half hidden in the loose flare of his khaki whipcord uniform breeches. He

4

picked out the oldest of the men, grey headed and bearded, holding a frond of eucalyptus over the frame of a half-built humpy shelter.

'You blackfellas from Berrie Berrie?' Cleary asked the elder.

The grey-headed man nodded. His face had turned grey, too, and he was shaking. 'Yiss, boss.'

'You the chief bigfella?'

The man nodded again. *'Yarala galamu galamu baringgala.'*

'Why'd you kill your boss at Berrie Berrie?' Cleary asked matter-of-factly.

The old man shook his head vehemently. 'We ain't kill 'im anytime, straight up boss. *Yamba yanigu wumbaragu.'* He waved the frond in agitation, and behind him two of the older women also shook their heads in emphatic denial. *'Dara,* boss. *Dhalibara,* boss.'

Cleary turned his head in his junior constable's direction but kept his eyes on the old man, who stood stock still, looking anxiously at the white *booliman.*

'Note the weapon in the suspect's hand, Constable Stannard.'

The Aborigines were standing or squatting as though they had been turned to stone, one of the infants motionless in the act of suckling.

'Note we are outnumbered and the suspects are showing signs of hostility.'

Cleary raised his revolver and shot the old man in the chest, and turned immediately to another target, an older woman, her mouth opening wide. He shot her in the chest too, and turned again as she slumped onto the grass. He shot an infant clinging to its mother squatting near the fire, and then stepped forward and shot the mother in the head as she struggled to rise, still clinging to her dead child, so the mother and her baby toppled sideways into the flames together.

On either side of the senior constable his men were firing into a huddle of panicking, screaming Aborigines. The outlying native trackers were firing as fast as they could reload at a handful of the older children attempting to escape along the bank of the billabong. Cleary saw one boy hit as he tried to jump through a turkey bush, punched sideways into the water by the force of the impact, and a half-grown girl backing slowly away from another grinning tracker, her hands held up like a talisman across her chest in defence against his Martini-Henri rifle.

On his other wing he could hear the young stockman snarling, 'Dirty fuckin' Abos,' over and over again as he fired, and Cleary shouted, 'Make sure. Make bloody sure,' as he fired his last shot at a small figure struggling to free itself from the crook of its dead mother's arm.

When his revolver clicked empty, Cleary stood and waited among the corpses in the middle of the camp until the carbine shots died away too, and his men began dragging scattered bodies out of the bushes and into the clearing.

There was one final, isolated shot from the trees to his left, and the junior constable started counting the bodies, pointing at them in turn and muttering the figures to himself. His face grew paler as he counted. The damage to a human body inflicted at close range by a blunt brass bullet capable of killing a bull at five hundred yards was devastating. One of the women had been almost broken in two by a shot that had exited through her spine.

'Fifteen adults, sir,' he said after a minute. He cleared his throat noisily. 'Five, six, seven... seven. Only seven young 'uns.' He spoke with a north country English accent barely altered by his two years in Queensland.

'Check again,' said Cleary, and the native trackers began pulling the bodies into rough lines.

There was a tangle of jumbled figures near the fire where the mother and her dead infant lay smouldering, and as they dragged the upper bodies away the young stockman bent down awkwardly. 'Eight!' he shouted and hoisted a small, struggling boy into view. 'Christ...' his voice died away. Under the dark film of his mother's blood that covered his chest, the toddler was the colour of milky coffee, with brown hair tipped with pale streaks bleached by the sun.

There was complete silence as the senior constable stared at the last survivor of his investigation. The boy was about a year old, his eyes enormous with shock. As they looked at him an arc of urine gleamed in the air, and the stockman stumbled backwards in an effort to avoid it, holding the small figure at arm's length and cursing.

One of the trackers laughed out loud, then covered his mouth apologetically with his hand. Cleary saw a sudden, vivid image of his own children back in their clean, neat home in Springvale. His youngest was about the same age, but this was a different species altogether. One of Foley's bastards, presumably, but he had the Aborigine nose and dark brown eyes. A black bastard, then.

The detail was looking at him, waiting for orders, and Cleary nodded. 'Get rid of it,' he said shortly.

The young stockman was holding the boy by one ankle and he handed him quickly to one of the native trackers. Cleary turned away, and if he heard the dull smack of the small body hitting a ghost gum trunk, he showed no sign. He carried on issuing orders to the trackers to collect their shell casings and move back to the horses. There was half an hour of daylight left, time enough for the trackers to find another waterhole and make camp a decent distance from this midden.

The trackers were chattering and laughing as they returned to the horses. The young stockman caught up with the senior constable and limped awkwardly alongside him. 'D'you reckon this lot did it?' he asked.

'Not at all,' said Cleary. He stopped for a moment and glanced briefly at the junior constable, who was walking alone, picking his way between the sparse tussocks of long, dry grass, his eyes on the ground.

'The bush blacks will have done it, but they're all in it together.' The senior constable cleared his throat and spat into the pale pink dust. It darkened as it absorbed his spittle to a deeper red.

The young stockman looked at him sideways. 'Won't there be trouble? I mean, we're on Milbourne here, aren't we? Won't Saltwood and the Gallaghers kick up a big stink about this? What about Kidman?'

Cleary stopped and turned to the younger man and smiled. 'Listen, Bluey, we got the nod for this from high places. How do you think these animals got permission to travel here?'

He jerked a thumb at the gaggle of trackers, then clapped the stockman on the back. 'That stuck-up pommie cockie and the Gallagher bitch have had it their way far too long, and they aren't here to squeal about it, are they now? They're all away to fight for the bastard English in their bloody war, so this is your chance to do the right thing for your country, Bluey, and you and me, we're going to make sure we get rid of these vermin once and for all.'

He nodded westwards. 'Tomorrow we'll head on out there and clean up those bush blacks, and then we're going to drop into Milbourne and sort out your jumped-up little mate.' He gestured at the young stockman's crook leg. 'Time for us both to get our own back, Bluey boy.'

Senior Constable Cleary walked on through the low rays of sunshine streaming through the trees, reloading his revolver as he went. Behind him, a thin trickle of smoke rose from the trees into the darkening blue of the sky, and from the far side of the billabong came the liquid, dissonant song of a butcher bird.

September 1908

1

The butcher birds were already calling as the first, fierce sunlight speared through the trees and touched the heads of two boys fighting behind the shed near the Warrigal station cattle yards.

There were no words, just the scuffling of their feet and explosive grunts and gasps for breath as they struggled in a jerky waltz across the bone-dry, ochre-coloured ground, hazed in the billows of fine dust their feet were churning into the suddenly sunlit air.

Then the bigger boy ripped his right arm free and hooked his fist up into his opponent's face, and the smaller of the two stumbled backwards and collapsed with the bigger boy on top of him.

As the dust drifted, the bigger boy straddled his opponent, jamming his knees painfully into the smaller boy's biceps, pinning him, and punched down hard. The smaller figure squirmed violently, trying to throw the much heavier boy off balance.

'Give up, ya stupid little yella bugger,' jeered the boy on top. Another boy ducked back from the corner of the lean-to where he had been keeping a lookout and hissed a warning. 'The men are coming, Bluey.'

The bigger boy leaned forwards and pushed his face down close to the face of the boy almost totally obscured beneath him. 'Stay away from the bloody horses. Ya don't bloody well belong here.'

He put a hand on the smaller boy's throat to keep him pinned to the ground and pushed himself upright. 'And stay away from me, ya yella bastard. Next time I'll break ya bloody neck, ya bloody nigger.'

As the voices of the stockhands moved closer, the bigger boy turned his back on the slight figure hauling himself unsteadily to his bare feet and swaggered away, slapping the dust out of his trousers as he went.

The third boy followed, looking back furtively at the loser, now bent double, his hands on his knees, his head hanging, the sunlit dust sifting out of the air above him onto his back.

Sitting on the long verandah at the back of the homestead twenty minutes later, an elderly stump-tailed blue heeler cattle dog lifted her nose and inhaled the familiar scents of an outback morning.

To the tall, dark-haired girl standing next to the dog, the smell of the stockmen's breakfast curry cooking in the kitchen just a few yards from the back of the house overpowered all the other scents in the morning air.

Underneath the smell of curry, the dog could detect the eucalyptus smoke of the cooking fires from the blackfellas' camp downstream by the creek. She registered the faint tang of ammonia in the dust stirred in the yards by the horses that had been driven in from the Teatree Creek outstation the day before, and the sharp scent of horse sweat from the saddle blankets left to dry overnight on the racks next to the tack shed.

The old dog was losing the best of her once bat-sharp hearing but in the clear stillness of this early morning both the dog and the girl could hear faint, familiar noises from the distant yards where drafting had begun in the cool dawn.

They could hear the drumming of running hooves, punctuated by occasional yells and the whistling crack of a stockwhip. They could hear the mournful complaint of the crows patrolling the nearby chook paddock in the hope of an unclaimed egg, and far off down by the creek the mad, metallic cackle of a kookaburra.

At the dog's eye height the view was limited, but from the verandah the girl could see the ghost gums that lined the creek half a mile away, and the top of the flame trees that shaded the yards. She could see the stockmen's quarters and the deep overhang of the meat-house roof, and between the laundry and the station stores she could see two older Aborigine women, leaning on their hoes in the vegetable garden they were supposed to be tending.

Life stirred early on a cattle station in Queensland at the start of the dry season, getting the hard yakka done before the temperature tipped into the high nineties and sucked the breath right out of your lungs.

The girl heard the women in the vegetable garden chuckling at something one of them had said and smiled. The dog noticed the smile and her almost non-existent tail twitched on the verandah boards.

Rachel Gallagher was twenty years old. She had been schooled away south in Brisbane but she had been born and had grown up on this Queensland station, and the shy, wheezy laughter of blackfella women was as deeply woven into her love of the outback as the kookaburra's lunatic laughter or the silver-green shimmer of eucalyptus leaves turning in an evening breeze.

She was still smiling when two figures appeared from behind the corner of the mudbrick stores, and her smile faded.

The dog's tail twitched again.

The larger of the two newcomers was a full-blooded Aborigine, her face creased by a deep frown. She was barefoot and shapeless in a man's ancient jersey pulled over a faded yellow shift, and she was pushing a reluctant boy along in front of her with insistent jabs of her forefinger.

It was Mickey and his mother, Sally, and the blood on the boy's face showed that he had been fighting again.

Although he was small for his age, Rachel knew that Mickey was twelve years old, and if she didn't also already know it as a fact, his much lighter colouring would have told her that his parentage was almost certainly mixed.

It would have been difficult for a stranger to tell what age Sally was. She didn't know exactly herself, but Rachel could remember her as a slim, young girl cradling her first baby when Rachel was just a little girl, which would put Sally in her early thirties now.

She also knew exactly why the pair were making their way to the back of the house, and her heart sank.

Sally looked up as they approached the verandah and shook her head at the girl. She jabbed her finger into the boy's shoulder one last time, so hard he stumbled forwards to the foot of the verandah steps. The bitch's stump of a tail wagged more noticeably.

'Bin fightin' longa dem big fellas agin,' said Sally. 'Blurry larrikin.'

'Already?' said Rachel. 'Strewth, Mickey, it's not even half past six! What happened this time?' As if she didn't know. The boy squinted up at the tall white girl standing at the top of the four steps, and his teeth gleamed suddenly through the dried blood and dust as he grinned at her. He didn't reply, but a casual one-shouldered shrug said it all.

'We'd better have a look at the damage,' said Rachel. Her long cotton skirt swirled as she took the verandah steps two at a time and strode across the space to the screen door that led into the sweltering heat of the kitchen. The old dog stayed where she was, watching the boy.

The two Aborigine women who were cooking breakfast for the stationhands looked up as Rachel swept into the kitchen and the younger one smiled shyly.

'Mickey's been fighting again,' said Rachel.

The younger black woman's smile disappeared instantly. She ducked her head and continued kneading out a mound of damper bread dough, but the older woman stopped stirring the copper curry pan and scowled in disapproval. She took the big metal spoon out of the pan and waved it in the general direction of the yards. 'Ain't Mickey makin' trouble, miss. Dem bigfella boys pickin' on 'im all longa time.'

'I know, Mella,' said Rachel. She half filled a small enamel bowl from the rainwater tap and picked out the cleanest cloth she could find on the washing table. 'I'm going to have to speak to my father about this again. Those boys need sorting out.'

'You kin do it, Miss Rachel, but it never make it better.' The older woman waggled the spoon in the white girl's direction and smacked it back into the curry.

Rachel bit her lip and pushed the sprung screen door open with her shoulder, careful not to spill any of the precious rainwater. The wire mesh door banged loudly behind her as she carried the bowl out into the already hot sunshine. She put the bowl down on the bottom step of the house verandah, pushed a lock of hair back behind her ear with the hand that held the cloth, and looked at the small, skinny boy standing stoically in front of her.

'Come on then, Mickey. Let's have a look at you.'

The boy raised his face and looked into her eyes as she bent down to examine his injuries, but as her face drew closer to his own, his eyes slid away from hers and he gazed up at the corrugated iron homestead roof over her right shoulder.

The girl soaked the cloth in the water, took a gentle hold of the boy's chin with her finger and thumb, and dabbed carefully at his nose and mouth. He flinched very slightly as the cloth moved across a split in his top lip, and Rachel winced in apology. *'Djindjin?* Sorry.'

The boy's eyes flickered back to hers momentarily, and she felt the Aborigines' deep distrust of any kindness a whitefella might show them. Even a whitefella like her who had grown up here among them, spoke their language and had fought their corner on the station ever since she was knee-high to a joey roo. 'Bluey did this to you again, didn't he?' she asked. Mickey gave another half shrug and there was another glint of amusement in his eyes.

'Just a bit of fun down the yards,' he said indistinctly through the cloth. The boy's mother cuffed him on the shoulder. 'Don't you give Miss Rachel no backchat, eh?'

The girl stopped dabbing for a second and turned the boy's face slightly towards hers. 'Doesn't look like much fun to me. You got another hiding from Bluey, didn't you?'

Another almost imperceptible shrug was all she knew she would get in reply. She finished wiping away the blood and dust. There was a large swelling rising over the boy's cheekbone, and she pressed around it as carefully as she could to see if there was any movement of broken bone. It was firm under the swelling. She let go of his chin and dropped the cloth back into the bowl.

'No loose pegs?' she asked. The boy shook his head and gave her a dazzling, exaggerated smile, showing two rows of large, even, very white teeth. He snapped them shut loudly a couple of times. 'Fights like a girl.'

His mother cuffed him again, but she was struggling not to laugh and when Rachel laughed aloud Sally too broke into the same wheezy giggle the girl had heard earlier from the veggie patch. The dog's stump tail brushed on the verandah planking.

'What are we going to do with you, Mickey?' Rachel put her hands on his shoulders and shook him gently. 'You have *got* to stop getting into scrapes with Bluey. One of these days he's going to break something, and then we'll have to haul you into Townsville and leave you with the Brothers at the Mission for a month. How'd you like that?'

The boy looked up at her with wary curiosity. He'd been told since the day he could walk that you could trust the whitefellas about as far as you could trust a grumpy old Brown Snake, but he had to admit that Miss Rachel had always been straight with him. 'Don't you worry miss,' he said seriously. 'I'm getting bigger. One of these days he's gonna be a *wumbararrgu.*'

There was a squeak of outrage behind him and he ducked as his mother's hand came down on the top of his head.

2

The clocks were striking six o'clock in the morning in London when Sid Kidman finally had to admit to himself that he was completely lost.

If he'd been set down blindfold anywhere in the fifty thousand square miles of the Australian bush that he owned or controlled at the time, he could have told you within seconds exactly where he was and found his way a thousand miles home.

But here in a maze of filthy East End alleyways he was as lost as he'd never been before in his life. He was in fact only four hundred yards from the broad open spaces of the Mile End Road that he was trying to find, but in the sunless and evil-smelling labyrinth of back streets that he'd hoped would offer him a shortcut he had lost his way and his sense of direction for the first time since he was a thirteen-year-old, minding sheep in the Barrier area for old Harry Raines, not long after he ran away from home.

At this crack-of-dawn hour in the morning there were people about, but they were a rough, suspicious lot and he was aware that he had strayed into an area where the quality of his clothes might invite unwanted attention. Of the three people he had passed most recently, two were clearly women of a certain age and calling who looked at him with predatory curiosity as he stood wondering which direction to take along a grim passage called, ironically, Flower Street. The other was a drunken man supported between them who had snarled at Sid as he'd been half-carried by.

The Australian hadn't felt that it would be diplomatic to ask any of them to show him the way.

Then the boys started to appear, materialising out of the walls and around invisible corners, hard-faced street urchins even filthier than the streets themselves, most of them in patched rags and tatters, some in bare feet and several showing the ricketty signs of under-nourishment. They gathered round him silently in a growing crowd.

Kidman automatically took a quick stockman's head-count and came up with a tally of nineteen, including two heads with only one pair of legs, which turned out to be a very small boy carried on a bigger boy's back. 'Hello lads,' he said. 'You're up early. Can you point me towards Stepney Green?'

There was no answer for a moment or two. All eyes turned to one of the bigger boys who was lighting the squashed remains of a cheroot in a broken pipe. He puffed hard, blew out a plume of smoke and squinted up at the tall stranger. 'Gizza shillin' and we'll show ya,' he said hoarsely. 'Gizza narf a crown an' we'll fuckin' carry ya.'

His acolytes erupted in shrieks of laughter, and two of the smaller boys started hooting and punching each other on the arm.

The bigger boys closed in on Kidman from all sides and bombarded him with questions.

'Where ya from, mister?'

'Why'd you talk funny like that?'

'What ya doin' 'ere then?'

'You rich, mister?'

'How much money you got on ya, mister?'

'That's my business, boys,' replied Sid. 'Come on now, you just point me towards Stepney and I'll be on my way.'

Kidman put his hands in his overcoat pockets and looked around over the boys' heads for some sort of adult help. The older boy moved a step closer. He was wearing an old cloth cap on the back of his head, and he pulled the peak of it forward suddenly with a forefinger and thumb.

'What's wrong with yer titfer?' he asked urgently, pointing at Kidman's wide-brimmed hat.

'My what?' said Kidman.

'Yer titfer tat, yer 'at,' shouted the boy as though Kidman's head had burst into flames, and Sid fell for it. He pulled his right hand out of his coat pocket and raised it to his head, then whipped it back smartly enough to grab the small paw sliding into his pocket from behind. There was a shrill yell of alarm from the would-be pickpocket and an outburst of vicious abuse from the swarm of juvenile delinquents now surrounding him.

'Get yer fuckin' 'ands off Sammy ya foreign fucka.'

'Who d'ya fuckin' think ya fuckin' are ya fucka?'

Sid Kidman made a point of never swearing himself, but he had

16

worked all his life among stockmen and drovers and goldrush miners who cursed as often and worse than this. But to hear it coming from these undergrown panhandlers made him blink.

He let the small hand go and turned at bay to find the gang leader close enough to poke the tall Australian hard in the diaphragm with his forefinger. 'That's assault that is, *mister*. You one of them queers wot likes boys, *mister*? We know the law, *mister*. You better pay up now before we get the fuckin' coppers on ya.'

There was another roar of approval and abuse from the now wildly overexcited crowd of boys, a hyena outcry of pack bloodlust that was cut off instantly and completely by an ear-splitting screech from the far end of the street.

For a second the boys were frozen where they stood, and then like a shoal of minnows flickering away from a pike they vanished, melting into the soot-encrusted brickwork and the shadows as suddenly as they had appeared.

Kidman stood in the middle of the narrow cobbled street and breathed a sigh of relief. He patted his pockets under his greatcoat to check that nothing was missing, and then turned towards the source of the screech. The two women he had passed just minutes before were hurrying back down the alley, minus their drunken cargo. They stopped far too close to the big Australian for his liking, and both of them looked him up and down like a pair of butchers examining one of his bullocks in the Adelaide auction ring.

The smaller of the two cocked her head speculatively and put one hand on her hip. Sid thought that on balance he would rather have dealt with the boys.

'Well now, Gloriana, what 'ave we here?'

She turned her head in mock enquiry to her friend, who put a finger to her chin. 'I do believe it's our posh gent agin, Theadora. What can he be doin' in these parts at this time of the mornin'? D'you think he's looking for something we can help him find?'

The smaller woman puckered her lips and made a thoughtful kissing noise. 'Ay'm sure Ay don't know, Gloriana, my dear. Ay think we should arst him.' She placed the backs of her hands under her cleavage and pushed upwards. 'What do you think, mister? Bit early in the day for a kneetrembler?'

Kidman took a half step backwards and put his own hands up in a gesture of surrender. He'd seen far worse sights in the goldmining camps, where the ladies of the night provided a twenty-four-hour, more or less open-air service and didn't bother doing up their corsets between customers. He'd gained a reputation even as a young drover for refusing the temptations of the bottle and the brothel, but he was off his patch here in the depths of the East End of London, and he wasn't sure how to handle this situation.

As it usually did, his sense of humour came to his rescue. For a big man he had a surprisingly gentle and disarming laugh, and he laughed now and raised his hat. 'Ladies, I owe you. Those jolly beggars had me tree'd and I reckon they'd have skinned me if you hadn't rescued me there. I'm very much obliged to you both.'

The women stared at Kidman for a moment, then looked at each other. 'Listen to 'im! What'd he say? Get away with ya.' They looked back at Kidman with more friendly curiosity. 'You're a foreign toff, ain't yer? Where you from then? What you doing in this shit-hole in yer fancy togs this time of the morning? You'll get yourself done like a kipper larkin' about on yer todd in this neck of the woods.'

Kidman understood the gist of this if not the detail, scratched his beard and laughed again in self-deprecation. 'Ladies, I'm in the wrong place and I hope you'll be good enough to show me the track out. I like to get around early like this before the place wakes up, so I've walked up from the hotel to try and find a place called Stepney Green, but I'm good and lost and I'm in your hands entirely. Is this Stepney?'

He was aware that more people were emerging into the alley as they spoke, but he jumped when the taller of the two women suddenly leaned sideways round him and let fly with another furious screech. 'Get out of it you little buggers or I'll tan your arses off you, starting with you,' she pointed at the leading boy. 'You cocky little runt, you give me any cheek I'll have your guts for fuckin' garters...'

She stopped in mid flow and shot Kidman a quizzical look. 'Pardon my French an' all but they don't take a blind bit of notice 'less you light into 'em good and proper. There, look at the little sods.' Sid looked round to see several of the small boys making lewd hand gestures at him and his rescuers from a safe distance.

'Where do they come from?' he asked. 'Why aren't they at home at this time in the morning? What are their parents doing? They look like they could use a good scrub and a better feed before they go off to school, the lot of them.'

The ladies laughed sourly. 'Lord love yer, that lot of little buggers don't go near no school. Most of 'em don't have no parents. They're just street rats, that lot. Used to be 'undreds of 'em all over the bleeding place, sleeping in coal holes, stables and the like or down the market they was, wasn't they, Theadora? On the streets all hours of the day and night until they started rounding 'em up a few years back and sticking them in that Barnardo place. Theadora nodded. 'Don't you feel sorry for the little so-and-sos. This is the hard lot that's kept out of the poorhouse. They're up to no good most of the time and you better keep a beady on them or they'll be on your back again before you can say boo to a goose.'

Two more, older women had shuffled closer and one of them nodded emphatically, pulling her shawl tighter in self-defence. 'Too right, sir. If you'd been here like this twenty years ago they would have snitched you to the gangs then, real bad'uns, half murdered you they would have, but this lot'll knock you down flat and thieve the shoes off your feet if you don't watch it.' She turned for approval to several more older women who were sizing up Kidman critically as though he was a freak-show exhibit. 'Wouldn't they just, eh? Little buggers.'

Gloriana turned on the old biddy with a warning finger. 'You be careful and get yer sticky beak out where it don't belong.' The older woman retreated, protesting wheezily that she was only trying to help the nice gentleman. 'Anyway, it's you better be careful...'

'You shut your trap, you old badger,' said Gloriana, 'and you lot can fuck off an' all,' she added loudly to the gathering audience of bystanders.

She turned her attention back to Kidman. 'Now, what was we saying? What did you say your name was and where you from then?'

'I didn't,' said Sid. 'My name's Kidman. Sidney Kidman. I'm visiting England from South Australia.'

The women looked at each other and the taller one gave the smaller a friendly push on the arm. 'Told you he was a foreigner, didn't I? There you are, Australian. I thought that's what he was.'

She turned back to Kidman again, who was beginning to enjoy

himself. 'So what you doing here in Whitechapel, then, Mr Sidney Kidman from Australia?'

Sid stared at her a moment. 'Whitechapel! I've heard of Whitechapel. Isn't that where those murders happened?'

The two women narrowed their eyes. 'Jack the Ripper. Yes, right here it was. We was here, wasn't we?' The one called Theadora waved her arm up Flower Street. 'We was working...' she glanced at her friend... 'working the halls mostly then, wasn't we, Gloriana, music halls all over Whitechapel and Spitalfields.'

Gloriana nodded. 'We was indeed. Halls and balls.' They both started laughing and then looked up at Kidman speculatively and became serious again. 'Yes, sir, the Ripper did his business round these streets, Mr Kidman. Twenty years ago now, it was, more or less. We was just starting out in the *theatrical* profession, wasn't we?'

They nodded in agreement. 'Mind you, it still happens regular in these parts. Got to watch your bleedin' step, don't yer? We can show you the gaff where he did poor little Mary Kelly if you like, just round the corner. What a sight that was, eh? Miller's Court, just up there off Dorset Street, blood everywhere. Only cost you...' The smaller woman glanced at her taller friend, '...what? Half a crown apiece?' The taller woman nodded. 'Half a crown apiece for the full works. You can still see the spot where he cut her up, bloodstains an' all. Another five bob on top if it makes yer feel frisky.'

Kidman held up his hands again. 'That's kind of you, ladies, but I was trying to find the house where Captain Cook used to live. I was told he lived in Stepney Green, and I fancied taking a look, but I have to be back in the City for a meeting at ten o'clock. How about half a crown apiece to show me the way out?'

He opened his greatcoat and pulled out his pocketwatch to check the time. It was ten minutes after six.

Theadora put her hand quickly over the silver half-hunter watch and hissed at him. 'God love yer, mister! You'll get yourself knocked on the bleedin' head flashing that round here.'

She bundled his hand and the watch back towards his waistcoat pocket and pulled the edges of his overcoat together smartly like a pair of tweed curtains.

'Who's this Captain Cook, then? We don't know no Captain Cook do we, Edie... I mean, Gloriana? There's that Captain thingummyjig in Saddler's Court but he's a Frenchie or whatnot and he ain't called Cook however you spell it, so he's no good to yer.'

Sid shook his head. 'No, Captain Cook, you know, who discovered Australia, over a hundred years ago. They told me at the hotel he lived in Stepney Green or thereabouts and I'd like to pay my respects.'

The two women stared at him blankly for a moment then bustled into action. 'Well, he'll be long gone by now but for five bob we can show you the way to Stepney alright, Mr Kidman.'

'Five bob *each* that is, Gloriana. Let's get you out of 'ere.'

They turned him round to face up the street and he caught sight of the boys' faces again, peering at him intently out of the shadows. He stopped for a moment and pushed a hand into his pocket, pulled out a coin and spun it in the direction of the boy in the cap. 'Get yourselves a bit of breakfast, boys, and get yourselves to school.' The lead urchin was holding up the half-crown coin in the middle of a scrum of boys, and Kidman's two self-appointed guardians were tutting in disapproval.

'Don't go encouraging those little b... so-and-sos, Mr Kidman. You don't know what they're like.'

'Well,' he said, 'I reckon some breakfast and a bit of schooling would do 'em a power of good. I didn't learn to read or write until my wife taught me, and I reckon it was the making of me, you know.'

The two women ranged themselves on either side of the tall Australian and hurried him away up Flower Street. They steered him off the street along a passageway barely wide enough for the three of them, past doorways that opened into shadow-worlds of Dickensian darkness, watched by people Kidman only glimpsed briefly by the whites of their eyes in the gloom.

Then suddenly they turned a corner and emerged onto a broader street lined with business premises, with purposeful people already at work or on their way to it. The light was brighter here and a hundred paces away to the east Kidman could see a major thoroughfare running at right angles to this street. The women stopped.

'There you are then,' said the taller of the two. They both looked up at him. In the stronger light they looked even tawdrier than in the alleyways and the lines around their eyes betrayed their age, but they had a certain self-reliant dignity, and they both smiled at him with genuine warmth, as though he was a large, exotic animal they had decided to adopt as a pet, rather than eat.

'That's the Mile End Road, there, and you turn left up that to get to Stepney Green. It's about twenty minutes' walk, so you'll have to get a move on to get up there and back to the City for your meeting. That's a bit grand for us, ain't it, Edie? Don't think we'd better show you the way to a posh bit like that. Might give 'em the wrong idea about you.'

'Well,' said Kidman, 'I was planning to catch a horse bus back down to the City. It's not too far, I reckon, and I like the horse buses. Remind me of home.' He leaned forward confidentially. 'Some of them let me drive, if I slip 'em a good tip.'

The two ladies agreed that a really good tip could get you a long way in London. The taller of the two coughed into her hand meaningfully and both of them looked hard at the spot on his overcoat that hid his pocketbook.

Sid slapped his hand on his chest and reached inside his coat.

'That reminds me.' He extracted two large, white five-pound notes. The women stared at them, more money than they could make in a good month.

'Thanks for getting me out of that pickle and steering me up here. You've done me a good turn and I won't forget you.' He grinned. 'Theadora and Gloriana? Well, good luck to you both, ladies, and thank you again for your help. Here's my card. You can get in touch with me at the hotel if there's anything I can do to help you. And call me Sid. My friends call me Sid.'

The two women glanced nervously behind them and tucked their five-pound notes hurriedly down the fronts of their shabby dresses. 'You're a proper gent, you are,' said the taller woman, 'even if you are from Australia. It's Lizzie and Edie to you, Mr Kidman. You come and look us up again sometime. Ask anyone for Lizzie and Edie. We'll be around here somewhere, won't we, Edie?' She grimaced. 'Open all hours, that's a fact, ain't it?'

They watched the Australian stride to the end of the street. The boy in the cloth cap also watched from a deep doorway in the alleyway as Sid turned and raised his wide-brimmed hat once more, and then disappeared round the corner onto the Mile End Road.

3

Half a mile further up the Mile End Road in Stepney, Charlie Downs pulled his coat collar gloomily up around his ears and headed down the Mile towards Gilroy's horse bus stables on White Horse Lane.

There were blurred figures moving in the glow of gaslight behind the steamed-up windows of the bakery on the corner of Cambridge Road, and in the chill of the September dawn the fleeting gust of warm, fresh bread that enveloped him as he passed lifted his spirits briefly.

At most times of the day or night on this stretch of the Mile End, the big Anchor Brewery and the Scottish Laundry next to it filled the air with an overpowering mixture of hops and carbolic soap. But the pervading smell of a London morning was the sulphurous acridity of coal burning in a million fireplaces and forges, stoves and steam engines, boilers, bread-ovens and kitchen ranges all over the biggest city in the world.

Looking down towards the Thames from the height of Stepney Green, Charlie could see thousands of tendrils of dark smoke already rising above the streets, spreading into the still air like a canopy of dirty foliage above a forest of chimneys. On a foggy autumn day the early morning mist might thicken this into a full-blown London Particular, a proper pea-souper smog, but today there was a promise that the autumn sunshine England had been enjoying was going to continue. Charlie pinched the last quarter inch of his Woodbine carefully between his finger and thumbnail, drew on it until the red glow stung his fingertips, and pitched the remaining fragment into the gutter.

At this time, just after dawn, he was one of the earlier birds on the streets of the waking city, but there were many others up and under way. Postmen and milkmen finishing their rounds. Servant girls in drab maid's uniforms, wrapped in threadbare shawls, hurrying to another thankless day of drudgery in dreary basement kitchens. Sales clerks with their breakfast in their hands, half-running along the pavement to beat the clock to the shop or the warehouse door.

Two years earlier, when he first started driving the Number 4 horse bus on Gilroy's Stepney to Oxford Circus route, this brisk walk to the stables and the camaraderie of the dawn workforce had put a skip in Charlie's step. It made him feel like a soldier in the unseen army that kept the wheels of the great city turning around the clock, and it was reassuring to see how many of those wheels bowling along the Mile were still horse-drawn.

Even at this time of the day when the traffic on the Mile End Road was as light as it would ever be, he could see the nodding heads of two great Shire horses leading a convoy of towering haywains rumbling in from the countryside close by to the north east. They would be making for the Whitechapel Haymarket with forage for thousands of other horses waiting patiently in barracks and bus depots and mews and jobbing stables all over the city.

Three of the country carts from the market gardens that ringed the city were heading the other way, their single ponies plodding homewards up the Mile past the brewery from Spitalfields market. A two-horse rail company carrier clattered past briskly on its way to catch a train raising steam at Kings Cross or Liverpool Street or Euston. And a couple of hackney cabs were trotting down the Mile from Bow on their way to pick up the first fares of a long and weary day.

It was still the horse that kept London supplied and on the move, and Charlie had been a horseman body and soul from the moment on his third birthday when his father had hoisted him onto the broad, warm back of a grey bus horse that had seemed to him then to be as gigantic and as mythical as an elephant.

But this morning the sight of horses and the sound of hooves on the Mile made Charlie feel even more downcast than he had been when he had left his young wife weeping in their lodgings ten minutes earlier.

Just two months back, Ted Gilroy had told him that the London General Omnibus Company had made an offer for Gilroy's one remaining route, and although the old man had shaken his head dismissively and patted Charlie on the back, the knowledge had cast a shadow of unease over the young driver that he hadn't been able to shake off since.

As if on cue to spite him, round the corner of Globe Road came one of the new London General motor buses, chuffing and spluttering past him down the Mile towards the city.

Charlie and his fellow horse bus drivers ridiculed these ungainly red monstrosities, but they could carry half a dozen more passengers than an old-fashioned two-horse bus and charge them less, and the LGOC was systematically squeezing the few remaining small operators off the streets and out of existence. He would scoff at the motorbuses with the other drivers, just as they scoffed at the horse trams and the electric trams, but deep down Charlie knew that the horse buses he drove were fighting a battle for survival, and the internal combustion engine was winning.

The motorbus left in its wake an alien stink of petroleum fumes that stayed in his nostrils all the way to the stables. In the good old days when his grandfather drove a mail coach, the outside passengers could smell London ten miles before they saw the first signs of its eastern sprawl, downwind on the Ipswich Road. That was the proper smell of old London, his dad had told him. '*Soot and shit, Charlie boy.*' Coal smoke, human and horse shit and, on hot summer days, the eye-watering sewage stench of the river Thames.

Charlie turned onto White Horse Lane, heading down towards the stables a hundred yards away, and walked quickly across the road and through the big double gates under their once-imposing wooden arch. Gilroy s Municipal Omnibus Service read the name on the arch. It was a flaking sign of the times, its missing apostrophe a recent symptom of the company's decline.

Charlie walked across the big cobbled stableyard to a scuffed green door in the corner nearest the road, and stepped into the low, dingy brick building that housed Ted Gilroy's office. It also served as a changing room and unofficial clubhouse for his dwindling team of drivers and conductors, and it greeted Charlie this morning with the reassuring fug of stale tobacco, damp gabardine overcoats, horse sweat and leather that he had associated with the horse bus business ever since he could remember.

There was a small fire burning in the grate, and a single gaslight cast a dim glow over the familiar, diminished ranks of assorted, battered chairs that lined the walls on either side of the fireplace. Fifteen years ago there had been forty-four drivers in Gilroy's London service. Today there were only twelve, but here in the sanctuary of this snug

Gilroy's drivers could still tell each other that they were the old guard, the immoveables, and although the golden days were badly tarnished, on their own turf they were still the lords of the White Horse stables.

Over the past six months since the baby had died, the busmen's room had become a bolthole for Charlie, but as if his day couldn't get any gloomier, the first object he clapped eyes on when he pushed open the door was the smirking face of Gilroy's teenage nephew and apprentice groom, Thomas Crawfurd, the crow turd.

Since he was the youngest and newest of the drivers, Charlie drove the first bus of the day and was always the first of the busmen to arrive for work. The stable staff were here at least an hour earlier, cleaning and feeding, preparing the horses and the buses for the day ahead, but other than Tiddler Taylor sidling in to light or tend the fire, not one of them other than Tommy Crawfurd would dream of setting foot over the threshold of the drivers' room.

Charlie glared at the youth. 'What the 'ell are you doing in 'ere?'

Crawfurd was perched sideways on the worn wooden arm of the chair nearest the fire, and he swung his leg to and fro to show how little he cared for Charlie's hostility.

'Your lot's 'arnessed up,' he said casually, staring back at Charlie with smug confidence. 'So I came to see if I could help Uncle Ted wiv anyfink in 'ere.'

The door to the empty office was wide open and Tommy Crawfurd knew full well his uncle was away at his farm near Romford, but this was typical of the way he threw his special status in the drivers' faces. Charlie gritted his teeth and nodded to the stable yard door. 'You should be minding the horses, Crawfurd, so fuck off out and do it.' Crawfurd swung his leg and smirked again. 'NOW,' shouted Charlie. The teenager waited a couple of seconds, then hauled himself off the chair and edged past Charlie out into the yard.

The crow turd had been given a job six months previously on the insistence of his mother, Gilroy's widowed half-sister. He had been started not as a stable lad as any other boy of his age but on a par with the more experienced and better-paid grooms, and although the timing was a coincidence, the staff at the White Horse Stables saw him as a Jonah whose arrival had put the tin lid on the company's slide, if not actually caused it. He was disrespectful to the drivers, cheeky to the senior grooms and ostlers, ignorant, stupid and worst of all, impatient and aggressive with the horses. It was something Gilroy would not have tolerated for ten seconds from any other groom, and of all his shortcomings, including his habit of chewing food noisily with his mouth open and his cocksure leeriness, it was this mishandling of the horses that most infuriated Charlie, and Crawfurd knew it.

That was partly why Charlie had taken to arriving at the yard half an hour earlier each morning. It gave him a guilty excuse to escape from Tilly's morning misery, but he also needed the extra time to check his harness and keep an eye on Crawfurd as his horses were being readied for the beginning of the day.

Crawfurd resented Charlie's special relationship with Gilroy and made a point of goading him by mistreating Samson, the big bay horse Charlie drove on his first route of the day three days a week. Most bus horses lasted five years at best on the unforgiving streets of London. Samson had done six already and showed no signs of weakening. He was tireless, honest and utterly reliable, 'a Christian and a gentleman,' as Gilroy described him, maybe the best he had ever bred in fifty years on his Essex farm. So Tommy's sly viciousness to this horse in particular never failed to bring Charlie as close to the boil as he could rise without losing his temper and his job together.

This morning, Tommy slouched behind Charlie as the young driver made his way along the front of the long shed where the first teams of the day were being hitched to their green and yellow buses, ready for a six o'clock start.

Charlie nodded to the old groom working on the team nearest to his own under the corrugated iron shed roof. 'Mornin', Davey.'

'Mornin', Charlie boy.' Davey Feltscher was the senior groom in the White Horse Stables. He'd worked many years with Charlie's dad in the good old days and kept an eye on the young driver, so he nodded back and touched his cap with a forefinger, and then shifted position surreptitiously to watch this morning's performance. In the stables that ran at right angles to the bus shed the two older stable lads mucking out the long double row of stalls paused and found a vantage point, and another groom stopped brushing a horse being readied for the second bus and tiptoed to the nearest doorway. The stable staff were running a sweepstake on how long it would be before Charlie got his rag out with the horrible fifteen-year-old, and whoever won the pot, all of them were longing for it to happen.

Crawfurd lounged against a pitted cast iron pillar while Charlie inspected the strapping bay mare that would work on the nearside of his first pair of the day. All the bus companies had their own ideas about the best matches. Some insisted that geldings worked best together. The London General had always used only mares on their horse bus routes. Gilroy mixed and matched, putting together horses he felt would get along well together, regardless of gender, and he was almost always right. The mare was a three-year-old first year novice, but she was learning her job fast from the older horse, and Samson, of course, would have worked well with any partner.

'I fink you'll find everyfing in order, *Mister* Downs,' said Crawfurd.

Charlie ignored him. He stopped in front of each horse in turn and greeted them quietly so that they could recognise him in their narrow, blinkered field of vision, then he moved on round the mare first, hissing gently through his teeth so she could hear where he was, casting his eye over her harness and running his hand down her flank as he bent to feel the tension in the traces and check the drawbar was the right distance from the horses' hocks.

When he returned to their heads and moved across to Samson's side, Crawfurd took a couple of steps backwards out of his way, and then forwards again as Charlie resumed his inspection. Charlie ran his hand along Samson's gleaming neck and under his padded leather collar. 'Hullo, old lad,' he said gently, but loudly enough so the stable staff could hear him. 'What's the spotty little crow turd done to you today?'

He checked the collar and the traces that connected the collar to the bus, and he was still looking down at the big horse's hocks when he felt him flinch, and then he heard the slap of a hand hitting the horse hard and jumped away instantly as half a ton of muscle and bone jolted backwards against the bar, a steel-shod hoof stamping onto the cobbles where Charlie's foot had been just a split second before. There was another clatter of hooves and a bang as the badly startled mare jumped backwards into the bar too, rocking the whole bus against its brake.

Out of the corner of his eye Charlie saw Samson's head jerking upwards against the reins, and Crawfurd dropping his raised hand and retreating to the pillar. He guessed what had happened, but he moved quickly back into the big horse's view first, speaking to him again, and resting his hand on the soft nose so the horse relaxed and lowered his head. Davey had moved with the same quiet speed to the mare's head, and was calming her in the same way.

'What did you do to this horse just then, Crawfurd?' Charlie asked it quietly, but Gilroy's nephew shifted uneasily at the tone of his voice.

'I was just standing 'im straight. Bloody 'orse took a fright. Stupid bloody 'orse. He's a bloody danger.'

The stable lads watching nearby stiffened like pointers. Another of the grooms materialised in the stable doorway.

'You hit 'im across the 'ead, didn't you, you little shit?' Charlie's voice was low, but all the frustrations of his life were crystallising in a red blaze of loathing for the young groom, and Crawfurd knew he was in trouble.

'I never did!' he protested again. 'You should never of called me crow turd. I'll tell my uncle Ted you did that. Serves your bloody 'orse right.'

Davey shook his head and spat tobacco juice sideways in disgust. Hitting a horse across the head was a crime at any time. Hitting a blinkered horse that couldn't see it coming was a cardinal crime. Hitting a horse to get your own back on the driver was a one-way ticket to a monumental hiding, and Gilroy was in Romford.

In the dim light of the shed, Gilroy's nephew could not clearly see Charlie's face, but there was something unnervingly different in the driver's reaction this morning. Instead of the usual cursing, Charlie nodded his head in Samson's direction.

'Come 'ere and beg his pardon,' he said.

Tommy Crawfurd took a step towards Charlie and then stopped uncertainly. 'Wadya mean, beg 'is pardon?'

He looked round anxiously, but the stablemen had moved across the yard to block his escape route to the gates.

'Come 'ere and I'll fuckin' well show you,' said Charlie softly.

4

Rachel had to wait until the end of the day for the right opportunity to speak to her father, the moment when he emerged onto the front verandah in the evening lamplight, washed, brushed and ready for his hard-earned supper.

Jack Gallagher was fifty years old that year, a big man with grey in his thinning hair and his moustache, but still as strong as a feral bull, and as she came out onto the verandah from her own room, Rachel felt the rush of affection that always lifted in her whenever she saw his broad, reliable figure.

Her mother had died when she was two years old, and this tough, middle-aged man had been father and mother to her since then. She had also become aware as she grew older that he was one of the most respected station managers, stockmen and horse breeders in Queensland, and she admired him almost as much as she loved him.

But there were still some areas in which she thought her father could be improved, or at least updated, and she was not afraid to try.

Jack Gallagher adored his daughter without reservation and she knew it. He was putty in her hands when it came to almost any of her stronger views that did not involve the fundamental running of the station, and several that did. But on some matters he stood his ground, rocking on his heels, admittedly, and on most of those matters they usually agreed to disagree.

Rachel walked across the verandah to kiss her father. She was tall, but he lifted her effortlessly off her feet in a bear hug, whirled her in a half circle and set her down again against the verandah railing. 'Stop doing that!' she said with mock ferocity. 'Anyone would think I was twelve.'

'Well, you are to me, and always will be,' said her father, grinning at his serious, grown-up little girl. 'Sorry, but we've had a good day in the yards. You saw those youngsters in that first mob we yarded. Must be some of that Milbourne thoroughbred blood getting through the local brumbies. Anyway, there's nobody here but us.'

He did not include Rachel's old cattle dog, which had followed her out onto the verandah and had watched this greeting with a jaundiced eye. As soon as Jack let his daughter go, the bitch walked pointedly across to Rachel's side and lay down heavily as close as she could to her mistress's feet, panting in the evening heat.

The usual frantic swarm of insects was accumulating round the single kerosene lamp that hung from the verandah roof. Beyond the lamplight, countless cicadas were scraping their sandpapery love-songs among the trees, and above this pulsing static they could hear the white stationhands eating their dinner in the kitchen, waves of tall talk and raucous laughter washing across the gap between the buildings, and a squawk of outrage from Mella as one of the men tried to help himself as she served them up their steaks, two or three at a time, almost charcoaled, the way they liked them.

Lucy, the younger of the two women who worked with Mella in the kitchen, emerged in a sudden eruption of boisterous noise and carried their own supper across the gap between the buildings and around the homestead verandah to their table. In the presence of the manager the girl was almost paralysed with shyness, and Rachel moved to the table to help her lay the cutlery, serve the food, and pour a glass of rainwater each for her father and herself. 'Thank you, Lucy,' she said, 'that's lovely. You can finish now. I'll clear this away.'

Lucy attempted a jerky cross between a bow and a curtsy to Jack and murmured something so softly that not even the dog's ears twitched, then hurried away round the corner of the house, her bare feet slapping on the dark rosewood boards.

Many of the bigger, stuffier stations insisted on Aborigine house servants wearing shoes, but Rachel was happy to let the women on Warrigal work in the footwear that God, or Darwin, had given them.

They sat down to eat the same dinner that the stationhands had now finished. Rachel looked across at her father's plate, piled high with three large steaks, cooked rarer than the men's, two boiled potatoes and an onion. On a side plate next to his dinner a slab of damper bread soaked in beef dripping gave off enough heat to distort the air above it. 'Is that enough for you?' she asked. 'The veggie patch isn't doing too well just now, so there are no greens for another few days, I'm afraid, until you pick some up in Springvale.'

Jack smiled at his daughter and picked up his knife and fork. 'This is perfect,' he said. 'You know me. Day like today, I could eat a dead rat on dry toast.' He peered with mock suspicion at his food. 'This isn't rat again, is it?' Rachel looked at her father with mild surprise. 'Of course it is. Rat on Wednesday. Roo tomorrow. Goanna on Sunday. Same old menu.'

Jack laughed, and they ate without speaking for a minute. Other than the accustomed background drone of the cicada serenade and the occasional flare of laughter from the kitchen, the only other noticeable sound came from the old stump-tailed bitch, who was now sitting beside Rachel's chair with one hind leg cocked in the air, licking herself noisily.

Jack finished his first steak, then abruptly put down his knife and fork. 'She does this every time. She knows I damned well can't stand it.' He glared down at the dog, who stopped for a few seconds, looked up at Rachel, and then resumed her washing.

Rachel put her hand down onto the old dog's head. 'Give it a rest, Rosie. Good girl.' The dog gazed up at her, pushing her head harder into Rachel's hand, and then slumped down onto the verandah planking with a deep sigh. 'She's a dog, Dad. She's just keeping herself clean.'

Jack gave the reclining dog a look of loathing identical to the one she had given him earlier, and picked up his knife and fork again. 'It isn't civilised. You spoil that dog, and she spoils my dinner.' He cut a chunk off his second steak and rammed it defiantly into his mouth.

'Well,' said his daughter, in a surprisingly conciliatory tone. 'Let's not argue over that.' She paused. 'There's something else I wanted to talk to you about.'

Jack Gallagher stopped chewing and raised his head sharply like an emu at a waterhole sensing a dingo.

'Ah-hah,' he said warily, 'I thought you might have been cooking something up. Come on then.' As he spoke, the dog raised her head from the floor, and now she sat up again and stared at Jack intently, unblinking.

'Wait,' he said, putting his cutlery down again. 'This is something I'm not going to like, isn't it? Are we going to have an argument? Because if we are you can shut that thing in the kitchen first.' He gestured at the bitch with his thumb, and the old dog leaned forward towards him, her eyes locked on his face, her whole body tensing with the message that if he wanted a fight, she was ready to give him one.

'Look at her!' Jack laughed, but taking care not to antagonise the old dog. 'The last time you and I had a minor disagreement she did her best to bite me, and I won't be bitten on my own verandah. I'm not prepared to talk about anything controversial until she's somewhere she can't take a lump out of me. Besides, two against one isn't fair.'

'Exactly!' said Rachel emphatically. 'That's exactly what I want to talk to you about, and if you promise you'll agree with me, I'll take Rosie across and Mella can keep her in the kitchen, although the men won't like it.'

'Of course they won't like it,' said her father. 'They're petrified of her. She's bitten every male animal on the damn station at least once, and she's got a bite like a salty crocodile. You should chain her up with the others, but I know the answer to that.'

Rachel was on her feet, patting her thigh. 'Come on, Rosie, you're not wanted.' The old dog looked at Rachel miserably, then back at Jack, and stayed where she was.

'And I am not going to promise to agree with you until I've heard what you're going to say.'

This last proviso followed Rachel's progress along the verandah, dragging the reluctant cattle dog awkwardly towards the kitchen, her stump tail clamped down tight and her hunched back view a picture of thwarted truculence.

5

Halfway through his second route of the day, Charlie was sitting on the driving seat of the Number 4 bus, staring morosely over the heads of his two horses at the logjam of stationary vehicles blocking his route into the City.

He couldn't see the cause of the delay. It could be a pedestrian caught between two vehicles or kicked by a horse, a collision and a fight between two carters, a horse down or hopping lame, one of the effing motor buses broken down and stranded in the middle of the road, or just the sheer volume of traffic battling its way into the bottleneck at the heart of the city.

'Christ all bloody mighty,' he muttered bitterly. In every possible respect, his life seemed to be falling to pieces. His wife was heading for the nut-house, he was surely going to get an earful or worse when Ted Gilroy heard what he'd done to the crow turd that morning, and at this rate he was going to be late at every effing stop all the way round his effing route.

A long stoppage could throw the whole day out of kilter. He'd miss his place in the sequence of changes at the stables, the stable staff would have to scramble about to change the horses, his conductor would have to spend the morning apologising to angry passengers complaining about something that was not their effing fault, and worst of all, he might get clocked late by one of the effing bus inspectors and Ted Gilroy would be landed with another fine he couldn't afford.

Every day nowadays the jumbled procession of buses and trams, pantechnicons and drays, cabs, carts and commercial wagons snarled itself to a standstill somewhere in the city. It was mainly the motor buses that caused the problem, of course, as far as Charlie was concerned, barging around honking and backfiring, upsetting the horses, and then breaking down every ten minutes and bringing the whole overloaded system to a grinding halt.

A paperboy took the chance to skip off the pavement and weave his way through the traffic to the bus, using the spokes of the back wheel as a ladder to pass a copy of that morning's paper up to a passenger on the top deck and catching the coins in his cap. He winked at Charlie as he ran back along the bus to find more customers before the jam moved on.

The young driver hadn't the heart to warn him off. The paperboys would even try it when the traffic was moving and a slip could mean the loss of life or limb, just for the sale of a tuppenny newspaper. But when the traffic was jammed to a standstill like this most of the drivers turned a blind eye.

Charlie guessed he was about ten minutes behind schedule so far. He still had to negotiate the crowded warren of the financial district, weaving his way past the Bank of England into the bottleneck of Old Poultry, hurrying the horses to make time up along Cheapside and Newgate, onto the long, wide stretch of Holborn and then the plunge into the shopping maelstrom of Oxford Street.

Regardless of the delay, he had to stop every few hundred yards, too, dropping his cargo of complaining clerks and bleating book-keepers in twos and threes, and watching them scurrying away into the pitiless, stony canyons of the financial district.

Any longer stuck here and he wouldn't have time to water the horses at the municipal trough at his turnaround stop in Oxford Circus, or Regent's Circus as Ted Gilroy persisted in calling it. After six miles in this traffic on a warming day they'd need a decent drink.

Then he'd have to battle back the way he'd come at the height of the white collar eight o'clock rush, picking his way through the bigwigs heading to their offices with their buttonhole flowers and their gleaming top hats.

Chances were he'd still be running late by the time he swung into Gilroy's yard at the end of this run. He'd be bursting for a gypsy's kiss and Davey would be bellyaching about drivers not knowing their arses from their elbows and how it used to run like clockwork in the good old days, stumping about and making a song and dance about parking his bus in the right place to lead out the next route, unhitching the first two horses and backing the new pair up to the bus ready for the off again.

At least he wouldn't have to worry about the harnessing being done properly. Davey had been an ostler since he was twelve years old, so he'd been harnessing horses for nearly forty years and you could bet your life that every link would be hooked correctly, every buckle safely secured and every strap tidy in its keeper. Not like the crow turd. Gawd. What was Ted Gilroy going to do about that?

He might just have time for a smoke while his second team was led forward and the farrier gave their shoes a final check, then he would be back out again along White Horse Lane and out into the hustle and bustle on the Mile. And he would be ploughing his way through this traffic twice more today. And the same the next day. That was the London horse bus drivers' life. Four times a fuckin' day, six days a fuckin' week and twice on every other fuckin' Sunday... and no fuckin' swearing in front of the fuckin' passengers, as Arty Lockinge, Gilroy's senor driver, had told him emphatically on his first day on the job.

Charlie pushed his Bowler up and massaged his forehead. Above the red mark left by his hat, the skin showed dead white against the dark summer tan of his face. It was a coachman's tan, deeply weathered hands and face, boiled-egg white everywhere else. He'd been conscious of it even in the darkness when he first took his underclothes off in front of his new wife, but it was the mark of a man who worked long hours outside in all weathers and not some soft-fingered pen-pusher like these clerks, fidgeting behind him at the delay.

He pulled the hat down again and ran a forefinger along the edge of his moustache. It had thickened out nicely now after several years of self-conscious sparsity. He ran the finger under his nose to make sure there were no dewdrops forming to offend the travelling public. Or the stationary public in this case.

'G'day.' The voice was so close to his ear that he jumped on his seat and swung round to give this upstart passenger a bollocking.

The middle-aged man leaning over the rail at the front of the open top deck behind Charlie obviously wasn't a clerk complaining about the delay, or any of the other usual fares he carried into the City on a normal day. He sported a fashionable King Teddy torpedo beard, but in every other respect he was clearly out of the ordinary run of bus fares. He was wearing a well-cut, expensive tweed overcoat that looked brand new, and a wide-brimmed hat with a large dent in one side of the crown that had clearly seen a lot more service. But it was the drawling accent that confirmed the difference.

'G'day, son,' said the man again cheerfully. 'Sorry if I gave you a turn there. I've been watching you drive from Stepney and I thought I'd have a word with you.'

The man smiled cheerfully at Charlie and nodded at the crowded thoroughfare. 'Not getting along too well here, are we?' As a statement of the obvious it might have hit Charlie sharply on a nerve on this day of all days, but the man's gentle laugh was infectious, and Charlie found himself grinning. 'No, sir, we're not.'

The 'sir' came automatically and surprised him. Drivers should have nothing to do with passengers if they could help it. *'Passengers,'* his old dad had always told him, *'was mostly h'ignorant buggers what should sit tight on their arse'oles and keep their cake'oles shut.'*

Today's unusual passenger was regarding him as this thought crossed his mind, dark, deep-set eyes watching him with a friendly intensity from under the brim of his unusual hat. Normally it wasn't permitted for fares to talk to the driver, and normally Charlie would have told the man to return to his seat, but there was something about this stranger that made him hesitate.

'Hard on the horses,' said the man, 'all this stopping and starting.' He leaned forwards almost directly over Charlie's shoulder to make himself heard above the shattering din that had resumed as the vehicles in front of them began moving. After the relative quiet of the stationary traffic, the street was suddenly filled with a cacophony of noise as the logjam of traffic lurched forward, axles squeaking, trace chains jingling, wheels rumbling, and the clatter of hundreds of steel-shod hooves punctuated by the shrill cries of newspaper boys and street sellers and the mechanical coughing and horn-blaring of the motor buses.

Charlie had opened his mouth to reply at the precise moment the tangle of vehicles and people unravelled itself and began moving again. He took his foot off the brake and shook the reins to move the horses forward and join the flow. 'Getting worse every day.' He had to shout over his shoulder to make himself heard as they picked up speed again. Speed being a relative term. The bus was now moving at the same pace as the pedestrians walking the same way on the pavement beside them.

Fifty yards ahead of them they could see the vehicles nearest the pavement pulling out around an obstruction directly in front of them, and Charlie began edging his team away from the curb into the flow of traffic in the centre of the street. He tugged gently on the outside rein with a flex of his wrist, and Samson's offside ear flicked briefly in acknowledgement. That was another thing Charlie loved about him. He had a soft mouth and responded to the slightest pressure.

'On you go, Sammy,' Charlie called to him, tapping him gently with the long whip to urge his team into a trot. Samson recognised his voice above the noise and flickered an ear backwards towards him. Charlie could feel the power of the big bay leaning into his collar as the two tons of fully loaded bus picked up more speed.

As they drew closer to the obstruction, Charlie could see a horse lying at the side of the road, a huddle of chestnut coat and a white fetlock visible through a crowd of curious onlookers and urchins that always gathered round minor street-side dramas like this. It was a cab horse, still attached to a battered Hansom tipped sideways behind the shapeless body in the gutter, the upper wheel revolving slowly in the air, and at a glance Charlie could see that the dead horse was old and underfed, its coat in poor condition and the harness dull and dirty.

'Not so good,' said the voice close to his ear.

He shook his head and shouted over his shoulder. 'Pirate, most likely.'

'Pilot?' The noise coming from in front of them was growing steadily as the traffic moved on clear of the hold-up, and the passenger held a hand up behind his ear.

'Pirate,' shouted Charlie. 'No licence.'

'Jolly tinkers,' said the passenger. 'I reckon I know a thing or two about those.'

Strictly speaking it was unlicensed bus operators with their rickety old second-hand vehicles and cutthroat fares that legitimate busmen referred to as pirates, but pariahs like this were just as bad. The jobbing stables who leased out crocked old nags were worse still, buying up worn-out horses for knacker money at the dispersal sales and working them all hours until the poor sods dropped in their harness like this one. They'd scuttle away and leave the corpse to rot where it lay in the gutter, too, thought Charlie, if they could get away with it.

'Jolly bastards, more like,' he said out loud.

He realised his passenger was still close enough to hear him, and coughed apologetically, but when he glanced over his shoulder the man was looking down on the scene, not with the kind of pity or prim disgust that female passengers and fastidious clerks might display, if they took any notice at all, but with a knowledgeable curiosity.

The man turned back towards the street, caught Charlie's eye, and raised an eyebrow. 'Must happen a lot in a city this size with all this traffic?'

Charlie nodded. 'Regular. Not so bad now but the gaffer, Mr Gilroy that is, he says ten years ago something like fifty or sixty a week in London, maybe more.' It was another point of pride at the White Horse Stables that Gilroy's had lost just one horse in their last ten years of service from Stepney, and that had been through no fault of their own. He half turned his head again. 'Pick good 'orses and good men to look after 'em. That's what Mr Gilroy says.'

The passenger clapped a hand on Charlie's shoulder and leaned down again. 'Your gaffer is dead right, son. Top horses and top men. That's my philosophy entirely. You tell him I said so.'

Who said so, thought Charlie, should he know?

They began to pick up pace as they passed the body, and Charlie had the satisfaction of seeing the large blue form of a policeman with a formidable soup-strainer moustache pushing his way through the crowd towards the cabman, pulling a notebook out of his silver-buttoned breast pocket.

You can't be soft about working horses, his dad used to tell him, they have to pull their weight, but anyone with half a heart would agree they deserved a damn sight better than that, he thought. He lowered the tip of his long coachwhip and brushed it on Samson's shining back. Both ears flickered enquiringly at that and Charlie grinned.

'You like your work, son?' The stranger had been watching him.

It occurred to Charlie that this chap wouldn't miss much. He turned again to reply, keeping his eyes on the street ahead as the traffic thickened and slowed again, easing the reins towards his body with a gentle turn-in of the wrists. 'Used to like it when I started out in the country,' he called over his shoulder, shaking his head. 'Not so much now. Too much traffic. Too many motors taking over...'

'This your regular circuit?'

'Yes, sir. I've been driving this route for the last two years, almost,' shouted Charlie.

'How far is it?' asked the passenger. 'How long does it take you? How many times do you drive this every day?'

'It's about twelve, thirteen miles round the route,' Charlie shouted over his shoulder. 'We drive it four times a day except Sundays, which is twice. We got to do it in three hours to keep to the schedule, but it depends on the traffic, like this today.'

The passenger must have been leaning very close because he hardly needed to raise his own voice. 'Twelve miles on hard roads, four miles an hour average, all this stopping and starting. Must put a lot of strain on the horses. Do you change your horses every trip? How many buses do you run?'

Charlie was having a hard time keeping up with the questions and paying attention to his job, but this stranger was obviously knowledgeable and sympathetic, and Charlie was eager to oblige.

'Well, sir, we run a bus every quarter hour, twelve buses every route. Pardon me. Stop coming up.' Charlie guided the bus back towards the pavement and the small faded yellow square fixed to a telegraph pole that served as a Gilroy stop sign, matching the chipped yellow wheels of the dwindling Gilroy fleet.

'Saint Paul's,' he heard Sandy, his conductor, shouting over the din. 'Olborn and H'Oxford Circus.'

There was a busy knot of people crowding impatiently under the sign and he cast his eye over them to check for any sign of an inspector noting the delay, and for the pickpockets who would knife each other to work a jostling queue like this.

The top deck passengers disembarking at this stop were on their feet and making their way to the curved steps at the rear as his gentle pressure on the brake pedal and the reins eased the bus to a standstill. The man in the hat was evidently leaving here too, but before he moved away he patted Charlie on the shoulder, rummaged inside his overcoat, and held out a pasteboard calling card.

Charlie took it, and the man smiled and patted him on the shoulder again. 'I'm going to see a man about a dog in the country this weekend, but I'll be back here sometime next week. I like the way you handle your horses, son. I'll see you again.'

He disappeared down the steps and then Charlie saw the tall figure in its distinctive, dented hat join the throng hurrying north up Fenchurch Street, and wondered who it was that had made him feel so much better about his morning.

He looked down at the card while the new influx of passengers climbed the stairs and settled themselves in their seats, but it left him no wiser.

Sidney Kidman Esq
C/o Langham Hotel, Regent Street, London
(Eringa, Kapunda, South Australia)

6

Rachel shut the kitchen screen door firmly on her cattle dog and walked back across to the house verandah to tackle her father on a subject she knew would turn a companionable evening into an uncomfortable argument.

Behind her, the level of noise in the kitchen had fallen significantly, and she could picture Rosie sitting on the floor next to Mella in a corner of the kitchen, glowering at the men.

Jack Gallagher was also considerably more subdued than he had been previously, but he made a gesture of resigned encouragement with the damper he was holding as Rachel sat down at the table. 'Come on then, let's have it,' he said.

'It's about Mickey and Bluey, Dad,' said Rachel.

Jack stopped chewing. 'I reckoned that was it. Sweetheart, we've been over this one before. Don't open this old tin of beans again.' He made a joke of it, trying to deflect his daughter. 'Can of beans. Tin of worms. Whatever the damn thing is.'

Rachel leaned forward across the table. 'Dad, this is serious. Bluey and that little offsider of his beat the stuffing out of Mickey again this morning. Bluey's three years older and twice the size of Mickey. One of these days he's going to really hurt him. It's not right. You could do something about this. Stop it before Mickey gets seriously hurt.'

Jack dropped the remains of his damper on his sideplate and put his hands together, his elbows on the table on either side of his dinner plate. 'Rachel, you know as well as I do that Mickey's as much to blame here as Bluey or Spike, when he's here.'

Rachel shook her head, but her father went on. 'He is, you know. He winds them up until they have a swing at him, and he deserves what he gets if some of the things I've heard he says are true.'

'Like what?' Rachel had a sinking feeling she wasn't going to like what she heard.

'Like this morning,' said Jack, looking seriously at her. 'You know what he said to Bluey that started the fight this morning?' He raised his eyebrows at his daughter. 'I know what happened, and Ted told me what Mickey said to kick it off.'

Rachel said nothing.

'I admit that Bluey called Sally a...' Jack paused a moment. 'Well, he called her a whore, but then Mickey came right back at him and said she was only a whore because Bluey's dad had made her one. Then he kept stirring and said maybe he and Bluey were brothers. Or half-brothers, anyway.'

Rachel continued to look steadily at her father. There was not much room for delicate female sensibilities on an outback cattle station in the middle of Queensland. Sally had produced five children before Mickey and two more after him, and at least three of the eight had been fathered by white stockhands, Ted Turner certainly among them. It was unlikely that Mickey was right, but it wasn't a possibility that Bluey would welcome.

'Dad, that's not the point. I know Mickey backchats them but he's only standing up for himself, and what really starts these fights is that Bluey hates the fact that Mickey's already twice as good with the stock as he is, ten times as good with the horses, and a thousand times the rider that Bluey or Spike will ever be. So they keep kicking him away from the yards, telling him he doesn't belong, he's not wanted. But he sticks up for himself, so Bluey starts a fight and Mickey gets a beating every time. And if Bluey can't beat him on his own and Spike's here, he joins in and down he goes. It's not right.'

Jack listened, looking out over the verandah railing towards the yards, invisible now in the darkness, and shook his head again slightly. 'Sweetheart, I know all that. But Ted Turner is my head stockman and Bluey Turner is already on the books, and if it comes down to taking sides then I have to stand by my stockmen.'

Rachel leaned forward again, and her father caught an uncomfortable glimpse of his own defensive double image reflected in her eyes. 'You could stop those boys beating hell out of Mickey every time they get into an argument,' she said intently. 'Surely you could lay down the law, like you do for the men? You've always forbidden fighting on Warrigal. You don't even allow the men to get into a scrap at the pub. Surely the same applies to Bluey and Mickey?'

It was a sore point, and Jack Gallagher took a drink of water to give himself a breather before he replied. It was true, he didn't tolerate fighting or drinking on Warrigal, and any stockman who started a fight on the station or off it would be rolling his swag and looking for another job the moment he was fit to walk. 'It's different with the boys,' said Jack eventually. 'It's just boys sorting themselves out. Bluey's top dog and Mickey keeps yapping at him. He has to learn to keep his trap shut and stay out of Bluey's way.'

Rachel was shaking her head again emphatically. 'Bluey's nearly as big as you, Dad. He could do Mickey serious damage. God knows he tries to. The only reason he hasn't done it already is that Mickey's too quick and he's tougher than one of these steaks. But it's the same principle. You don't want the men fighting because of the injuries it causes. It's the same with Mickey.'

Jack leaned back in his chair and blew through his moustache. 'Strewth, Rachel.' He eased his shoulders and tried again. 'It isn't the same thing. They're boys. Mickey's what? Twelve? Bluey's fourteen.' He saw the contradiction coming and hurriedly corrected himself. 'Alright, he's turned fifteen. Neither of them works for me, yet. Mickey may never work here. It's not the same thing, and there are other things I have to take into account as well.'

'You mean because Mickey's an Aborigine?' Rachel said it as unemotionally as she could manage, but this was the real bone between them, and she refused to let it go. 'Or at least he's half an Aborigine, and the other half's white, because a white man took advantage of his mother for half a bag of sugar or the dregs of a bottle of rum. But as far as this issue is concerned, he's a blackfella, isn't he?'

Jack pushed his plate away and tapped his forefinger on the table. But he spoke quietly, too. 'I didn't want to argue with you on this again, Rachel, but you know there's a lot more to it than meets the eye, and when it comes to Mickey, yes, he's an Aborigine like his mother and his uncles and his grandfather. He spends more time walkabout in the bush with them these days than he does here at the station. It's in his blood and I wouldn't stop him even if I could.'

He looked hopefully at his daughter, but she said nothing.

'Come on, sweetheart. Be fair. I've always tried to treat the blackfellas properly on Warrigal, you know I have, and when Sid Kidman took a stake here after the dry that was one of the things he said he liked. They get good rations and we give the blackfellas stockwork if they want it and some of them are good hands, but you can't depend on them, no matter how good they are. You know how it is, Rachel. It's the white stockmen like Ted I rely on and I can't run this station without 'em. So yes, I have to put the whitefellas first and the blackfellas second.'

He paused for a moment, and his daughter looked down at her plate of food, growing cold on the table in front of her.

'It's the way it is in the bush, sweetheart, and we do better by the blackfellas here than most other stations I know. So I'm not going to interfere in something that's going to blow up into a big row, just because a boy with a high opinion of himself keeps cheeking his elders and...' he bit off the word he had been about to use, '...and getting walloped for it.'

He tilted his head to catch his daughter's eyes across the table, and tried to make amends. 'Come on, Rachel. In a better world things would be different. But it isn't a better world. It's getting worse. There are plenty of stations where the blackfellas are getting chased off. There are politicians sounding off now about '*The Aboriginal Problem*' and what to do about the blacks. They talk about them as though they were dingoes or rabbits. People like us are in a minority in this country, sweetheart, and I don't think it's going to be long before we start seeing things that make Mickey and Bluey scrapping look like a sandfly bite on a bull's backside.'

He drew breath. Rachel was looking at him across the table with the same expression of stubborn determination he could remember clearly on her mother's face, twenty years ago.

'We're already seeing bad things happening, Dad,' she said quietly, 'unacceptable things, right under our noses, but we're not doing anything about it. There are people in this area, people we know, who treat the blackfellas badly and now there's this horrible squatter on Berrie Berrie who's treating them like slaves or worse. You shouldn't be able to beat someone and rape them and kill them and take their land just because you're bigger and stronger. Or because you're white and you have a gun and they don't. Someone's got to stand up and do the right thing about the blackfellas. We should stand up for them. We should do the right thing here, at least.'

She got up and pushed her chair back. Jack stayed where he was and made a wry face at his daughter. 'I wish it was that simple,' he said wearily.

'It is that simple, Dad. You said you were going to talk to Sergeant Mack when we go into Springvale about that squatter duffing Warrigal cattle. You should report him for what he's doing to the blackfellas, too.'

Jack shook his head 'Mack won't be dealing with this, Rachel, you know that. Mack's handing over to the new man next week. He'll be coming up on the train when we're in Springvale and I want to find out about the fella first.'

'Well, whatever he's like, he's going to have to do his duty and enforce the law around here, including dealing with the squatter.' She pointed at his plate of food. 'Do you want me to heat your dinner up? It must be cold.'

Jack shook his head. 'No, sweetheart, I'm not hungry any more.'

His daughter made a face at him, half grimace, half smile, and turned away. 'I'll go and make you some tea, and I'll report him if you don't,' said Rachel, and walked away around the corner of the verandah towards the kitchen before Jack could reply, her long skirt brushing the white wooden railings as she swung away out of sight.

7

At ten o'clock in the morning, while the head porter listened for an answer to his discreet knock on the oak door of the Principal's first floor lodgings, William Saltwood adopted a look of bored nonchalance, leaned back against the balustrade and prepared for the worst.

He was more concerned than he hoped he looked. This was not the first time he had waited for the Principal of the college to pass judgment on his behaviour at Oxford, but this morning he knew that it would be the last.

Even the combination of his father's wealth and his mother's breeding would not be enough to ease him past the large hole he had made the previous night in the display window of Oxford High Street's biggest store. It wasn't the size of the hole that would send him down, but the fact that he had made it by knocking one of the local police constables through the window in a dispute about his capacity to walk back to the college under his own steam.

On the other side of the door, the Principal was sitting at his desk with his fingers steepled under his chin, bracing himself for a final interview with his most troublesome charge.

Tall, fastidiously dressed, bespectacled and stork-thin, the Principal had fallen in love with the college as an undergraduate fifty years previously and devoted his life to its interests ever since.

The only child of a provincial solicitor's clerk and a fiercely ambitious mother, Arthur George Joseph Thornleigh had made his way up the academic pyramid from Congratulatory First Class Honours to appointment as a College Tutor, election as a Fellow and then, ten years ago, the ultimate accolade of his installation in the Principal's lodgings.

Now, at the age of seventy, after a glass or two of Madeira he liked to trot out a creaky joke that so far he had spent more than five-sevenths of his life here, and hoped the Almighty would allow him to improve considerably upon that fraction by the time he passed hence to an even better place... if indeed there really could be a more exalted place than the Principal's lodgings in this ancient and beautiful Oxford college. *'Wheu, wheu, wheu.'* On the rare occasions that he laughed aloud, the Principal sounded exactly like someone blowing across the top of a very small bottle.

He wasn't laughing this morning. He took a final, baleful look out of the window at the hideous Victorian chapel rising behind the golden stone of the medieval quad, then sighed and turned his attention to the more immediate problem of the Honourable William Saltwood. He could console himself with the thought that this would be the last time he would have to deal with him, but for the sake of the college he wished it could be otherwise.

Adversus solem ne loquitor, he thought. No, one cannot argue against the sun.

He took a deep breath and exhaled slowly. 'Enter.'

When the head porter had ushered William through the door and withdrawn, the Principal gestured to the empty chair facing him across the desk. 'Please be seated,' he said. In the almost tangible quiet of the panelled room, the final, perfectly modulated consonant tapped in the air with the frigid precision of a hailstone hitting a windowpane.

Dr Thornleigh was aware that he was known by most of the undergraduates, and some of his colleagues, not as the Principal but as the Prick, but he rose above it. He had complete faith in the unassailable authority of his position, and he prided himself on being able to make himself heard across a lecture theatre full of noisy undergraduates without raising his voice, simply by enunciating his consonants with the utmost clarity.

On the other side of the door, the porter lowered himself ponderously onto one knee and glued his ear to the keyhole. From past experience he knew he would hear every syllable the Prick uttered, but he was anxious not to miss the Honourable William Saltwood's side of the interview. It might be worth a bob or two from his enterprising young contact at the Oxford Gazette. It might be colourful, or worse.

More importantly, he would be expected to report the interview accurately to Lord Saltwood's private secretary, who paid him a regular fee to keep his lordship informed of his younger son's activities, particularly those of an extracurricular nature. If seen earwigging, his excuse in this instance would be that he had been given to understand by the Principal that the interview would not be a pleasant one, and he needed to be fully alert to any possible requirement from the Principal for assistance.

The Principal's main concern was not for his own wellbeing but for the loss to his sacred college that would follow the sending down of such a wealthy and well-connected undergraduate. This morning there was no other course open to him, however, so he peered at William Saltwood over his round, tortoiseshell spectacles and shook his head gently.

'Dear me, William. Yes, indeed. How very unfortunate this is,' he said regretfully.

He leaned forward and studied a piece of paper placed precisely and squarely in front of him on the desk. 'I have here a report from a Police Inspector...' he peered more closely, '...Walby, concerning an incident in which I believe you were involved, on the High Street of the city, at approximately five minutes after midnight last night. Outside the college walls, therefore, after curfew?'

He looked up at William, who raised his eyebrows in a gesture of polite concurrence, but said nothing.

The Principal studied the paper for another minute in silence. The ticking of a grandfather clock standing against the wall beside the door was very loud. A muffled gust of voices and laughter carried up to them from the quad.

'Yes, indeed. This is very unfortunate,' said the Principal eventually. 'It appears that you were apprehended on the High Street in a state of... intoxication... by a Police Constable Silston, and that in...,' he looked down his nose at the report again, '...in an altercation resulting from your refusal to accompany the constable quietly back to the police station, you pushed Constable Silston through the window of a... shop.'

The Principal pronounced the word 'shop' as though he was not quite certain what it meant, and looked up once more at the figure sitting opposite him. He noted that young Saltwood was wearing cream-coloured tennis or boating flannels. Above the flannels an unusual blazer displayed an unrecognisable badge that he had a vague notion signified membership of one of those oafish Germanic dining clubs. There was no semblance of proper undergraduate academic dress, or any sign of sartorial respect for the Principal, the college or the situation.

Based on nearly fifty years of dealing with undergraduates, the Prick correctly interpreted this as a demonstration by the Honourable William Saltwood that he was above caring what anyone thought of him or his behaviour. The pause lengthened while the Principal reviewed a mental gallery of lofty young men he had known over the years who had advertised their uniqueness in an infinite variety of almost identical ways, and then he remembered himself and dragged his attention back to the police report.

'Where were we, William? Ah, yes. Upon the arrival of a second police constable and a university police Bulldog as I believe they are commonly called by the undergraduates, the Inspector states that you... enflamed the situation further by knocking the Bulldog's Bowler hat to the pavement and standing upon it. Dear me, William. Do you agree that this represents the facts?'

William considered this. 'I'd like to put it on the record that the Bulldog's hat actually fell off when he attempted to manhandle me. I trod on it accidentally. I did offer to pay for a new one, but apart from that I regret that those do appear to be the essentials.'

The Principal noticed that a gleam of something not entirely serious had appeared in William's eye, and frowned.

'It is indeed regrettable. Most regrettable.' He sat back in his wing chair and removed his spectacles. 'The Bulldog and his hat are very far from the issue here, of course, William. Very, very far from it. The involvement of the police constable takes this matter beyond my power or even the power of the university to control. We are very fortunate that Inspector Walby has allowed the university to act before he decides whether or not to press charges against you. Police Constable Silston has admitted that you did not strike him, but you resisted his attempt to detain you and in the ensuing struggle he was pushed through the shop window. Even without a blow, Inspector Walby points out that you are liable to charges both of resisting arrest and assaulting an officer of the law, an assault that might easily have caused injuries of a most serious nature.'

The Principal perched his spectacles on the end of his bony nose and peered at the paper again. '*Very* serious injuries, William. Broken glass! It is a miracle that you were not both cut to ribbons!'

He leaned back again and looked over his spectacles at the young man in front of him. 'I must tell you, William, that we must be seen to treat this with appropriate gravity if Inspector Silston is to refrain from pursuing the normal procedures. I assume that you would prefer not to appear before the magistrates... again?' He raised his own eyebrows interrogatively at William, who shook his head.

'We have tried very hard, William, to keep you within our fold here. Very hard indeed. But this, I fear, has made it impossible.' The Principal looked over his spectacles at the figure sitting opposite him. 'Your path with us has not been smooth, William. Indeed, very far from it. There have been many other infractions against the rules of the college and the university, and indeed the law of the land. There have been substantial fines and two occasions of rustication. I believe on the second occasion you received a formal warning that any further serious breaches of discipline would leave us with no other option but to send you down?'

William nodded again. He had been sent home for the remainder of a term twice before, and the second time his father had made him read the formal warning out loud. 'Yes, that was made clear.'

'How very unfortunate this is, then,' said the Principal. 'So unfortunate. Indeed it is.' He removed his spectacles again and wondered why William Saltwood had so persistently courted trouble during his two years in these hallowed groves of academe. He was not a stupid young man, and he did not seem to be absolutely degenerate. Rather the contrary, behind that blasé facade.

He was a great deal more intelligent than his rather bland older brother, who had been an undergraduate at the college five years before William, and a great deal more... attractive, thought the Principal. But he did suffer from the inconsiderate arrogance that seemed to infect the young sprigs of the aristocracy, and he also seemed to have cultivated a preference for dissipated company, inside and outside the college.

The Principal sighed again. 'The facts and the circumstances of this incident will have to be recorded by the Proctors, but unless you wish otherwise there will be no disciplinary hearing, and we will draw this matter to its unfortunate conclusion here and now. I am sorry to inform you that the university will not require you to attend any further lectures, and I would ask you to vacate your rooms here at your earliest convenience. I would suggest that you leave us quietly today, and Gissings will make the necessary arrangements to forward your belongings to you.'

William nodded again. He had realised that his time at Oxford was up from the moment the second constable and the Bulldog had come running in response to the first constable's whistle the previous evening. The scuffle with the university's policeman had been just another nail in the coffin. He had been frogmarched to the nearest police station, and it was a poor reflection on his reputation that both the constables and the Bulldog had known exactly who he was.

The Bulldog had told him with huge satisfaction that he was for the bloody high jump, despite the fact that they had only caught him because he had stayed to pull the first constable out of the shattered window display and onto his feet. Willam had been picking splinters of glass carefully off the constable's back when the two reinforcements arrived on the scene.

'Thank you for your patience and discretion,' he said to the Principal. 'I hope you will accept my apologies for any trouble I have caused you and the college. I will take myself off your hands as quickly as I can.'

The Principal was relieved by this polite acceptance of what to most undergraduates would have been a catastrophic fall from grace. The last undergraduate he had sent down, four years previously, had leaned menacingly across the desk and called him several extremely unpleasant names. The head porter had had to escort him out of the Principal's rooms. So this morning he rose from his chair and held out his hand to William across the desk. William stood up and shook it.

'Goodbye, William. I am sorry that your time with us should end like this, and I wish you well,' said the Principal, with genuine regret. His regret had very little to do with the fact that William would not complete his degree at the university, or the minimal effect he wrongly expected this would have on the young man's future. It had much more to do with the indication Lord Saltwood had given three years ago that he was prepared to make a very generous endowment if the college managed to steer his younger son safely through to graduation. The Prick took a personal pride in the enormous size of the college's endowments, but he was always greedy for more.

William Saltwood's thoughts at that moment were following surprisingly similar lines to the Principal's. He didn't give a damn for the loss of his degree. There were only a few aspects of Oxford he would miss. In most respects it had simply been a convenient base for his social life. His only serious concern, like the Principal's, was Lord Saltwood's reaction to this turn of events.

On the landing outside, Gissings reacted with a grimace of disappointment when he heard the interview's inevitable conclusion. The Honourable William Saltwood had been a regular source of extra income for the head porter during the past two years: generous tips for his help in certain social arrangements; even more generous tips to persuade him to turn a blind eye to entrances and exits into and out of the college after hours; occasional payments from the local reporter for inside information, and the regular fee from Lord Saltwood's secretary. With almost as much experience behind him as the Principal, however, Gissings was standing a discreet distance from the door, his face blank, well before it opened.

William emerged onto the landing and shut the door behind him. He walked slowly down the stairs and out into the quad, stopped and looked up at the sunlit stone of the rooms above the entrance archway on the opposite side of the courtyard, then turned to Gissings who was standing with his hands clasped behind his back a discreet pace behind.

The head porter and the young man looked at each other for a moment, then William grinned. 'Come on, Gissings,' he said. 'Don't pretend you didn't hear every word of that.' The head porter blew his cheeks out and gave William a brief but sincerely regretful smile. Not only was his income about to drop significantly, but college life was going to be considerably less interesting without this particular dishonourable ex-undergraduate. Hey ho, he thought. There'll be another one along in a term or two.

'How could you suggest such a thing, sir?' he said. 'I will send your scout up to help you pack.'

8

In the scullery of the Mile End public house, Tilly Downs stood hunched over the big, chipped pantry sink, weeping uncontrollably into the washing-up water.

She cried silently with her mouth open and her nose running, her tears dripping into the water with a syncopated pittering clearly audible above the buzzing of bloated flies butting against the filthy window. She was oblivious to the looming piles of last night's greasy plates and smudged glasses on the sideboard next to the sink. She didn't notice the stale smell of bitter beer and cheap gin in the big tin pail standing by her feet under the sink.

The slops and the heel ends of hard bread crusts and chop bones in the pail would be carried out after the midday lunch trade to the sty in the back yard where the Mile's landlord, Old Penny Holly, kept a couple of cheerfully alcoholic pigs.

It was said in Stepney you could get tipsy on half a dozen rashers of the Mile's best back bacon if you could afford Old Penny's prices, and Tilly used to love taking the slops out to the pigs before the baby was born, resting her growing bump on the sty wall and scratching the ginger-bristled pink backs as they guzzled the revolting cocktail ecstatically out of their wooden trough. They had never failed to make her laugh, but Tilly's tears had blotted out any memory of her affection for their slobbery companionship.

Weeping over the sink, she was oblivious to the little maid-of-all-works staggering under another load of dirty glasses on her way to the scullery. Little Aggie took one fearful look at Tilly's hunched back view, eased the tray wordlessly onto the end of the sideboard and fled from this awful spectacle of naked grief to tell one of the barmaids that Tilly was at it again.

It was more than six months since Tilly had lost the baby, but these sudden storm-waves of weeping could still overwhelm her without any warning, anywhere and at any time, and there was nothing she could do to control or hide them.

A hank of her thick auburn hair escaped the careless bun she had tied blindly that morning, and hung down unheeded over her right eye.

Charlie always joked it was a toss-up as to what had attracted him most when he first saw her two years earlier, her green eyes or the glorious confection of shining auburn hair piled on her head, gleaming in the glittering lamplight of the Mile End's enormous public bar.

It was the same hair, unwashed and uncared for now, that he had stroked helplessly at five o'clock that morning, trying desperately to find any word of comfort as she lay curled in a foetal ball in their bed.

He had known how to make her laugh at the drop of a hat before the baby died, but in the face of Tilly's inconsolable mourning there was nothing he could say that seemed to help, and he had hurried out of their lodgings into the chilly September dawn, baffled and ashamed of the resentment he felt at his wife's dull-eyed hopelessness.

A year ago Tilly's eyes had gleamed in the lamplight too, and they'd been worth a hundred quid a week in extra takings to the landlord of the Mile, so Charlie reckoned. Not that Old Penny Holly would ever admit to it and give her anything more than the barest minimum wage.

'It may be just a little old farden to you,' Old Penny would say lugubriously, retrieving a dirty copper farthing dropped in the hurly burly of a busy evening on the bar-room floor, 'but three more make a penny and them old pennies grow into pahnds'. He repeated the same caution to his bar staff at least once a day. 'Take care of them old pennies, and the pennies'll take care of the pahnds.'

It clearly worked. As well as the Mile End pub, Old Penny owned two shops on the high street and a string of tenement lodging houses in Stepney, including the two cramped rooms in Parfitt Court that Charlie and Tilly called home.

The Mile End was the biggest public house in the area, and Old Penny prided himself on employing the prettiest barmaids to run his big front bar. A year ago Tilly had been the pick of the bunch, the star of Stepney Green and an irresistible flame to the regular moths drawn to the Mile each evening on the chance of a word or a smile from the belle of the bar.

After the baby had died the light had gone out in her eyes, and in the six months since there had been not one flicker of a sign that it might rekindle. So Old Penny had moved her first into the small, dim

Ladies' bar at the back of the building, then into the scullery, cutting her hours and her wages both times, and he'd found another pretty young magnet to keep his casual trade from moving on to ogle brighter barmaids in other pubs.

Charlie had begun to dread opening the door to their pokey lodgings at the end of a long day on the bus. Before the baby was born Tilly would wrap her arms around his neck the moment they were safely across the threshold, full of the news of the day, most of it consisting of just when and how energetically the baby had kicked inside her. Now that she was home well before he was finished she barely looked up to greet him, and she remained as removed from him by her grief as if she had been widowed.

Behind her, Leonie, the oldest barmaid who had taught Tilly her trade in her first weeks at the Mile, including how to evade their employer's groping hands, appeared in the doorway. She checked that Old Penny wasn't within sight or earshot along the passageway and then leaned into the room.

'Tilly.' She leaned back and checked again, and she kept her voice low. 'Tilly, are you alright?'

Tilly shook her head without looking round.

'Come on, girl, you got to get on with it. That old bugger's on the lookout. Keep going girl. Dirty old slavedriver.'

She stopped and listened. 'Got to go, Tilly. Keep your chin up, girl.'

Old Penny's low rumble came down the passageway clearly. 'What you doing down there? Get yourself back here.'

The barmaid glanced briefly at Tilly's back view and disappeared towards the bar. 'Here I am, here I am. Call of nature, Mr Holly. A girl's got to do what a girl's got to do.'

'I'm paying you to serve customers in 'ere. You can take a piss in your own time.'

In the fly-humming scullery, Tilly pushed herself upright and wiped her nose on her forearm. She lifted the nearest column of smeared glasses into the lukewarm water and began washing them.

She was twenty-two years old. Charlie was twenty-six. They had been married less than eighteen months and they hadn't made love since a month before the baby was born.

9

It would have taken him half the time to drive straight from Oxford to his family's Chiddington Park estate in Berkshire, but in the afternoon of his final interview with the Principal, William Saltwood motored in the opposite direction up to his family's London house instead.

With the encouragement of a final backhander, Gissings arranged for a carrier to transport the contents of William's rooms to Chiddington, and William located the keys to the two-seater Napier that Polly Brockenden had left at the hotel where they had met for dinner the night before.

Polly had taken the train from Oxford in the morning heading for a mysterious and almost certainly illegal rendezvous in Brighton. He had left the Napier for William to drive to Chiddington for the weekend and then to return to Brockenden's house in London the following week.

Where, how or why the chronically impoverished Brockenden had acquired the Napier was a mystery from the dark side of Polly's life, but he was as besotted by motorcars as the toad in the book by that Bank of England chap everyone was talking about. William had promised to buy a share in the car, and having it in Oxford now made his banishment much easier to manage. The only drawback was that he was required to leave Oxford a day earlier than he had expected, and after giving it some thought he decided that a tactical diversion to London seemed a better option than heading straight into the lion's den at the Park, where he was due to join his father and mother the following day for a weekend house party his father had insisted that he must attend.

Sugden, the Saltwoods' London house butler, greeted William's unplanned arrival at the house in Grosvenor Square with only the faintest hint of a raised eyebrow, and confirmed that Lord and Lady Saltwood had indeed left town for the Park shortly after luncheon.

From past experience William knew that Lord Saltwood would be made aware of the latest *fracas* as soon as he reached the Park, and a growing realisation of just how dimly his father was going to regard this new development had taken a lot of the shine off the pleasure of driving the powerful Napier as fast as it would go up to town. But an overnight stay in London would give Lord Saltwood twenty-four hours to cool off, and might give his mother a chance to intercede on his behalf as she had so often in the past. He would have to take his medicine, he told himself as he swung off Park Lane and roared down Upper Brook Street into the square, and then lie low until the fuss had blown over.

What he would do in the longer term was another matter. There was the hunting season to occupy him through the winter, but after that? The only thing he thought he could be certain of was that Lord Saltwood would not make him take a position in his business empire. His father had made it plain that he did not want his younger son anywhere near his business interests until William could prove he had 'at least the barest understanding of the meaning of the word responsibility,' as Lord Saltwood had put it last time the subject of his son's future had come up.

As the shadows spread across the gardens in the centre of the square, William spent the last of the afternoon on the telephone in the library, trying unsuccessfully to find any of his cronies in London free to spend the evening with him. Brockenden was in Brighton, of course. Tom Ashbury was at his family's place in Scotland, shooting. Pascal de Vallain was otherwise engaged, and Bobby Bingleigh was in the south of France waiting for the dust to settle on his own latest scrape with the fifteen-year-old daughter of his father's coachman.

Two of the three other names in his pocketbook he might have called were still up at Oxford, and the third was more or less chained to an oar in a boat on the Cam, making a serious effort to win the bow seat in the Cambridge University rowing eight.

William tossed his pocketbook onto a side-table. He didn't feel like venturing out on his own, so at six o'clock he asked Sugden to see if the cook would very kindly rustle him up some dinner.

'Something simple please, Sugden,' he called as the butler stood with one white-gloved hand on the library doorhandle, 'in here.' The door froze for a fraction of a second as the butler registered the last part of William's request, and then closed without a sound. With no one other than the servants in residence, William decided he could eat where he liked and he wouldn't bother to dress for dinner, no matter what Sugden might think of this multiple breach of Lord Saltwood's house rules.

Ten minutes later another thought struck him, and he rang for the butler again. Could Sugden arrange for the Napier to be refuelled for his journey to Chiddington the following day? Sugden received this request impassively and withdrew once more.

William pushed one of the leather club armchairs closer to the library fire, put his feet up on the upholstered fender, and skimmed through the afternoon edition of *The Times* that one of the footmen had been sent out to buy for him. He skipped the news pages but read every word of an overblown eulogy by the paper's sporting correspondent to the glories of Great Britain's many successes in the summer's Olympic Games.

It was an embarrassing piece of jingoistic self-congratulation that William read with a series of groans. The correspondent trumpeted Great Britain's miraculous achievement not only in throwing up the brilliant, new White City Stadium in just a few short weeks, but also making a profit from the Games, which they had dominated in almost every sport worth winning. *'No other nation had come close to winning even half of Great Britain's gold medal haul,'* said the correspondent.

'No other country had half as many athletes,' William pointed out to the empty room. And there was more to come. The Games would resume in just three weeks' time, no doubt adding considerably to Britain's overwhelming gold medal superiority, particularly in the boxing ring. *'Why,'* the correspondent asked superciliously, *'had so few other nations put forth their pugilists to stand against Great Britain? Could it be that their courage failed them in the face of our giant heavyweight champion, Police Constable Oldman?'*

There was a lot more in the same vein, as heavy-handed as the heavyweight favourite. 'I'm damned glad it wasn't him trying to arrest me yesterday,' William murmured aloud again. 'Why don't you try fighting Albert Oldman, you pasty blowhard.' He glanced up at the bullet-headed first Lord Saltwood glaring out belligerently across the library from his portrait on the silk-covered chimneybreast. 'How long would he have stood up to you, Grandpapa? Ten seconds?'

He trawled half-heartedly through the society columns of the paper for references to his friends and acquaintances, and leafed back through the news where a small story on the third page caught his attention briefly. He recognised the name of the Australian who was to be a guest at Chiddington that weekend. Apparently the man was offering to employ London horse bus drivers on his cattle stations in Australia.

William knew that his mother had inherited the majority share of a large property in Australia two years earlier on the death of her uncle, Lord Teppermoor, along with twenty-eight thousand heavily mortgaged acres of midge-infested Scottish heather and the equally heavily mortgaged lease on the Grosvenor Square house. He imagined that this must be at least one of the reasons why his father had invited the Kidmans to Chiddington. There would, inevitably, be a business angle in this somewhere. Lord Saltwood did not entertain guests like this Australian fellow at Chiddington simply for amusement. But why his presence was required he had not the slightest idea.

'Why on earth is this chap offering jobs on cattle stations to bus drivers?' he murmured to his grandfather's portrait as he scanned the next page. 'How bizarre. Why do they call them stations? Even more bizarre.' Surely they weren't all connected by a railway, although that might help account for his father's interest in Mr Sidney Kidman.

His gaze moved idly down the crowded newsprint, and snagged briefly on a report of yet another murder of yet another prostitute in Whitechapel. There were the usual blood-curdling allusions to the ghost of Jack the Ripper, but to William the main interest in her fate was that she had been beaten to death in the alley behind a notorious criminal drinking den that he and Tom Ashbury had visited to win a bet, one hot, sultry evening only three months previously.

Sugden served dinner on a small table set in front of the library fire, his irritation under rigid control despite the casually inconsiderate demands being made on the staff. On Lord and Lady Saltwood's departure the household had been expecting a long weekend of light duties, but now they must run around after young Saltwood instead.

The butler's face registered nothing but smooth aloofness, but if Master Saltwood had tried this little charade in Lord Teppermoor's day, he told himself as he spooned white parsley sauce onto a perfectly cooked piece of halibut that he had been looking forward to eating himself, his feet wouldn't have touched any of the six marble steps on his way from the front door to the pavement. And good riddance to the arrogant little sod and his grasping, stone-faced father, thought the butler. What the hell was the world coming to?

To be fair, although Lord Teppermoor had referred to Lord Saltwood frequently and loudly as a jumped-up money-grubbing cold-hearted gutter-bred little shit, he had actually found his rake-hell great-nephew more of an acceptable chip off his own block. But this was taking unforgivable liberties.

He wished he'd served young Saltwood soup. He could have taken a leaf out of his old lordship's book of booby-traps for unwanted guests, and told the cook to lace it with her famously explosive homemade laxative.

'Can I bring you anything else, sir?' said Sugden. William gave it a moment's thought, glanced at his plate and the bottle of cold white Burgundy wrapped in a napkin within easy reach, and shook his head as he resumed reading the paper.

'No, thank you, Sugden. I'll ring when I've finished.'

10

On the Friday morning, Sid and Bel Kidman and their three daughters travelled down from London to Chiddington Park on the Great Western Railway.

Much to his delight, their nine-year-old son, Walter, stayed in London to be spoiled by the hotel pages and the governess they had hired to keep him up to scratch with his schooling. The rest of the Kidman family travelled first class on the Cheltenham Flyer, moving faster than they had ever moved anywhere in their lives, watching in wonder as the sun-dappled harvest countryside flashed past their compartment window.

The Flyer was reputedly the fastest train in the world, an express service to Bristol that normally roared straight through tiny Chiddington Halt at seventy miles an hour, shattering the rural calm in a deafening whirlwind of shocking industrial power, and leaving behind it a Satanic aftertaste of hot metal and a light shower of smuts falling like black snow gently to the ground.

Compared to the Flyer, the local trains bumbling daily in and out of his tiny station were of no consequence at all to the Chiddington Halt stationmaster. The milk train with its metal churns clanking and clonking London-wards before dawn. The Oxford train with its two or three shabby carriages shuffling to and fro at ten and four o'clock. Humdrum conveyances for country folk on their slow travels.

The Flyer he regarded with something close to religious awe. Whenever it passed through the Halt, he made sure he was present, standing formally on the platform with one hand behind his back and his other hand raised to his peaked pillbox hat, partly in salute and partly to prevent his precious hat from being blown off his head by the backdraft.

The holy Flyer stopped at Chiddington very rarely and only by special arrangement for the Saltwood family or their guests at the Park. Lord Saltwood owned the station, most of the village and all the land for a mile or more around it. Even more importantly from the stationmaster's point of view, he was a director of the Great Western Railway and so owned at least a share of the Cheltenham Flyer itself.

So on this red-letter day the stationmaster gave the GWR-engraved brass buttons on his black frock coat an extra polish when he had finished his mid-morning tea. He spent more than the usual amount of time in front of the mirror in the tiny hallway, setting his hat straight and jutting out his chin to check his beard for biscuit crumbs, before making his way at a stately pace onto the platform in plenty of time to greet the holy Express.

Arthur Wagstaff was a short, pear-shaped man, standing proudly on the lowest rung of the GWR stationmaster's pay scale, commanding one elderly porter he considered to be half a step away from an idiot and a half-share of a disrespectful platelayer who patrolled the line between Chiddington and the neighbouring stations up and down the line.

There had been a time when he had dreamed of taking another step up the ladder, but one official visit to the whirlwind of the GWR's hub at London's Paddington station had sent him scuttling thankfully back to the sanctuary of Chiddington. Here he could be the biggest fish in his own tiny pond. Here, he reminded his wife far too often, he had risen entirely on his own merits to the lofty heights of stationmaster in the GWR – *God's Wonderful Railway*. She should be proud and grateful to be married to a person of distinction, he lectured her, mindful of her responsibility to keep those below them on the social ladder firmly in their place, and to show every mark of deference due to the many more above them.

Heralded by a rising humming along the rails and a distant, whooping blast from its whistle, the enormous Brunswick-green Flyer and its train of GWR-liveried brown and cream carriages arrived dead on time at the Halt, easing gingerly alongside the small platform, snorting and hissing with the barely suppressed violence of the Chiddington Home Farm's famously bad-tempered Ayrshire bull.

When it had come to a complete standstill, the stationmaster hurried across the platform to open the compartment door of the first-class carriage that the driver had brought to rest precisely opposite the modest station building.

Five passengers descended. Three grown girls first, shepherded by a small, slightly portly woman, and then a tall man wearing an unusual broad-brimmed hat with a large dent in one side of the crown.

'I could tell at a glance, of course,' the stationmaster told his wife and anyone else who couldn't escape him many times during the following weeks, 'I could tell right away they were visitors from foreign parts. Oh, yes.'

Not exactly exotics like the Rajah from India in Jubilee year, with a carriage full of turbanned lackeys. The one that offered to buy Mrs Talbot, the Chiddington Park housekeeper. No, these were not the royal kind of colonials, but any guests of the Park were obviously Very Important Persons indeed as far as the stationmaster was concerned.

At the east end of the station platform, the Flyer's assistant guard helped the Chiddington porter to manhandle two steamer trunks, four large suitcases and three hatboxes out of the baggage car and onto his trolley.

As the baggage car's sliding door slammed shut, the stationmaster looked both ways to check that all was well with the Flyer's high priest in the driver's cab and his acolyte guard. Opportunities to minister to the sacred Flyer were rare and he was going to make the most of this one.

Acutely conscious of an audience of passengers watching him through the carriage windows, the stationmaster made a fussy show of checking that the compartment door was correctly fastened and that no one on the platform was too close to the train. Then he raised his green flag and the huge locomotive began to move again, gathering speed with great, deep exhalations as the shining pistons drove it forwards in a cloud of steam, accelerating westwards, leaving Chiddington Halt to settle back into the drowsy peace of a sunny autumn morning.

The Park party stood for a few moments watching the departing train. On a bench nearby, the station cat regarded them impassively over folded forepaws, then closed its eyes and returned to sleep. Birds stunned into silence by the thundering Express began to sing again, and the porter bustled along the platform towards the passengers, his trolley's metal wheels rattling and squeaking as he came.

Not sure where they were supposed to go, Sid, Bel and the girls stayed where they stood and watched the porter approaching. 'The male visitor... obviously the father of the family...' the stationmaster told his wife with that infuriating, worldly-wise nodding that made her want to stick a carving knife into the sloping expanse of his GWR-issue waistcoat, '...the man definitely had something about him if you know your Very Important Persons.' He had dark, deep-set eyes, and a sort of easy confidence that told the stationmaster that this was a person of considerable standing. 'Of course, I seen at once he was a gentleman of considerable standing,' the stationmaster told his wife, tapping his nose knowingly.

The VIP's deep-set eyes scrutinised the stationmaster as he moved forward to take charge of the visitors. The three young women remained close to their mother, and the gentleman nodded. 'Good morning, zurr,' said the stationmaster, his Berkshire burr making a soft bee's buzz of the last word.

The man nodded again. 'G'day,' he said. To the stationmaster and the porter, who now stood waiting with ill-disguised curiosity to see what the Flyer had brought in the way of novelty and possible remuneration, the accent was unfamiliar but it was encouraging to find that the language was more or less intelligible.

The stationmaster was not entirely sure what the colonial gentleman had said to him, but it sounded like a civil greeting. 'May I presume to h'ask if you are the guests for the Park, sir?' he asked, inclining his head more to the Park than to the visitors themselves.

'That's right,' said the tall passenger cheerfully. 'Lord Saltwood's place. I was told there would be someone here to meet us.'

'Yes h'indeed, sir,' said the stationmaster in his Sunday best official voice. In fact, the stationmaster's confidence in how to deal with the guests was beginning to waver. On every other similar occasion, someone authoritative from the Park had arrived well before the train to greet the visitors, and he merely bobbed and bowed in the background. Today he was on his own and he glanced anxiously at the gate that opened out of the station onto the dusty Chiddington road.

There was a pause and the stationmaster ploughed on hurriedly. 'The Park sent a message yesterday h'afternoon to h'inform myself there would be visitors arriving today, sir, as it were, this morning. I h'expect there should rightly be a carriage awaiting of you h'in the lane, sir.' The stationmaster made a deferential sweeping motion with his right hand, still holding his green flag, to usher the passengers towards the gate, but instead of moving, the tall man held out his own right hand.

'Kidman,' he said.

The stationmaster stared at the outstretched hand for a second or two, then hurriedly clamped the flag under his left armpit and shook the hand tentatively. 'Er... Wagstaff, sir. Stationmaster. How do you do, sir.'

This was even more disconcerting. Railway officials of his own lowly status and local farmers might offer to shake hands with the stationmaster of an insignificant country halt like Chiddington, but no visitor to the Park would normally dream of doing such a thing. The stationmaster looked doubtfully at this visitor, but met only a straight and friendly gaze from the deep-set eyes. The delighted porter filed every moment of the scene to be repeated in detail at the village inn that evening.

To the stationmaster's immense relief, at that moment one of the double gates opened in the hedge that separated the station from the lane beyond, and a tall young man in a tweed suit hurried towards the group, apologising as he came. 'Mr Kidman. Mrs Kidman. Misses Kidman. How do you do? Welcome to Chiddington. I am *so* sorry to have kept you waiting.' He smiled at the three young women and bowed slightly to Mrs Kidman. 'My name is Prior, sir. Lord Saltwood's private secretary. You won't remember me. We met briefly in London with Lord Saltwood last week. I do apologise for being late to meet you. We were detained by a flock of sheep in our way. I'm so sorry....'

The colonial visitor smiled at the young man and shook his hand too. 'Hello, Mr Prior. Of course I remember a smart young fella like you. Don't get yourself in a lather. Where I come from, running into a mob of sheep can hold you up for half a day. We've just arrived this minute.' He nodded towards the stationmaster. 'My friend Mr Wagstaff here has been looking after us.'

At least once a week for a year after he had discovered who the visitor was, the stationmaster managed to find a reason to repeat the story of how *the* Mr Sidney Kidman – 'Yes! the very one from the front page of *The Times* of London' – had called him his friend and shaken him by the hand. And his wife would mouth his words in silent mockery behind his back as she stirred his porridge or made his afternoon tea. It was her only recourse against his humourless pomposity in a dismal marriage that had hit rock bottom on the day of his promotion from deputy assistant stationmaster of the nearby market town seven years earlier. Standing in front of the range in their tiny cottage with his letter of appointment clutched reverentially to his chest, her husband had informed her solemnly that from then on she must refer to him at all times, even to close friends and relatives, as 'The Stationmaster'. If she had been holding even a breadknife at the time, she would have hacked him to pieces on the spot.

Arnold Wagstaff remained oblivious to his wife's murderous contempt on this sunny morning, and he marched importantly behind the visitors and ahead of the porter as they all followed Lord Saltwood's secretary out of the station.

When it became apparent that Lord Saltwood had sent his new, personal Rolls-Royce motorcar to meet them, the visitors rose several more notches in the stationmaster's estimation and he scuttled busily out into the lane to supervise the transfer of the luggage, beckoning the much taller porter officiously and unnecessarily to hurry along after them with his heavily loaded trolley.

Behind the Rolls-Royce stood a pair of horses harnessed to an open carriage painted in the same estate dark blue as the Rolls-Royce, a top-hatted coachman seated at attention on the driving seat and a groom standing by the horses' heads.

While the porter and the groom loaded the trunks and the cases into the carriage under the stationmaster's fussy direction, Prior ushered Bel Kidman and the three girls into the cavernous luxury of the Rolls-Royce's enclosed passenger compartment.

Sid Kidman turned reluctantly from his inspection of the horses and asked jokingly if they were sure the motor was really large enough for all his girls. The girls laughed with just enough nervous hilarity to make their mother frown slightly at their father.

'I'll ride in the front,' he said, unabashed. He opened the nearside door of the roofless driver's compartment before the secretary could protest, and slid onto the banquette seat beside the startled chauffeur. 'Thanks, Wagstaff,' he said as the stationmaster shut the door. 'I reckon you get a better look at the country from here, eh?'

The stationmaster stood watching the Rolls-Royce picking up speed along the road that ran parallel to the railway line, heading west to the main road and the main gates to the Park, while the coachman turned the carriage away and disappeared north between the high hedges that enclosed the narrow lane that led to the village.

Jem Waterson, the porter, stood behind the stationmaster gazing at the coin Kidman had dropped into his discreetly positioned open palm. Tips were rare and were shared two-to-one with the stationmaster, in the stationmaster's favour, of course.

'A whole bliddy sovereign! Damn his eyes if that little tub o'lard gets any'o thus'n,' he said as he showed it gleefully to the landlord of the Duke of Wellington public house in Chiddington that evening. 'And don't 'ee tell moi missus. Thus is just atween thee and oi.'

As the stationmaster began to turn towards him in the late morning sunlight, the porter stuffed the sovereign deep into his pocket, pulled out a tarnished sixpence in its place, and held it out on his open palm. He shook his head with weary disgust.

'Richer they be, meaner they be, eh stationmaster?'

When he came down to breakfast at Grosvenor Square late on Friday morning, William apologised to Sugden and admitted he should have found a garage to refuel the Napier on the way to Chiddington himself.

He also instructed the butler that if Polly Brockenden telephoned to ask where it was, he could be told that William would be back in London on the following Tuesday, if not before.

In the absence of both the Saltwood chauffeurs, Sugden had spent the best part of an hour of what should have been an evening off, arranging for a mechanic from the nearest motor garage to come and fill the Napier with petroleum and oil. But the butler digested this with exactly the same absence of expression he would display when accepting a five-pound tip.

He supervised William's departure, standing by the open front door as the young man adjusted his tweed cap and goggles, his driving dustcoat and his leather gauntlets.

'I hope you have a pleasant journey, sir.' Like all good butlers and sergeant-majors, he could pronounce the word 'sir' in many different ways, the variation so subtle that all but the most discerning employers remained completely unaware of the distinctions. This morning, his timing and intonation stripped the word completely of any possible hint of deference or respect.

To the footman standing in the hallway waiting to close the front door it was an insult as clear as a guttersnipe's catcall, and one corner of his mouth twitched. William was thinking about what he was going to say to his father and passed through the doorway into the sunshine unaware of Sugden's opinion of him.

As the door closed, the butler's face remained rigidly impassive.

'Never, ever let them see what you think, John.' His own uncle Alfred, old Teppermoor's previous butler, used to hammer the golden rule of service into the young Sugden when he had been first footman and then under-butler a dozen years ago, tapping his forefinger on his nephew's starched shirtfront to drum home every word.

During the twenty minutes it took the Rolls-Royce to travel from Chiddington Halt to the Park, the under-chauffeur told the second groom later, the tall Australian visitor never stopped looking around him, and he never stopped asking questions.

On the way, Sid Kidman discovered that the under-chauffeur's name was Harold Brightwell and he'd been working for Lord Saltwood for ten years, starting in the stables at the age of fourteen, but he preferred the motors any day. 'No kicking or sh... messing, begging your pardon, sir.'

Yes, there was a head chauffeur, Mr Carpenter, always in readiness in case Lord Saltwood needed him. Was his father in this line?

'No, sir, my father's a tenant farmer on the estate over by Lessed... Yes, sir, that's the village on the signpost back at the station. We call it Lessed round here but it's spelled Lesstead, opposite of Morestead further west...'

He came from at least ten generations of local farming stock but he'd been fascinated by machinery from the day he saw his first steam-powered threshing machine in the big farmyard at Lessed Manor. It was the shining mechanical future and he was hooked like a young trout.

'No, sir, my older brother Ted, Edward that is, sir, he would take over the farm, eventually...'

Sid discovered that the vehicle they were riding in was one of the first of the new thirty horsepower motors to be made at the new Rolls-Royce factory in Derby. Brightwell was delighted to tell him everything he knew about it.

'How far away is Derby? About, oh, more than a hundred miles north of here, as far as I know, sir...' The chassis and engine had been brought down by train from the manufacturers, and the bodywork made and fitted by Mulliner & Co the coachbuilders in Mayfair, London, to Lord Saltwood's own specifications with extended passenger accommodation so he could work while travelling. 'The best? Oh yes, sir, Lord Saltwood always has the best...'

His lordship travelled at all times with his private secretary and a stenographer who could take dictation on her knee even while sitting on a dicky seat travelling backwards at thirty miles an hour.

The finished motorcar had cost a whopping one thousand, nine hundred and twelve pounds sterling, and both the chauffeur, Mr Carpenter, and Brightwell had spent a week in London being trained in its driving and basic maintenance. 'Separate weeks, sir, always one of us on duty for his lordship...'

Yes sir, Brightwell agreed with feeling, that certainly was a bucketful of money, about twenty years' wages for an under-chauffeur at the going rate.

'The best kind of motor, sir?' Most people who knew what they were talking about told him the Rolls-Royce was the finest motorcar in the world, but other chauffeurs he had met in London swore by whatever marques they drove. The Germans also made a very good motorcar. Not as good as the Rolls, of course, but a lot better than those flashy French and Italian tin cans.

'Thornycroft? Yes, sir, I certainly have heard of the Thornycroft. Made down in Hampshire, not too far from here... Well I never, sir, Sir John Thornycroft is married to your wife's cousin? That is a coincidence and no mistake, sir. You certainly must have a Thornycroft then, sir. Very good car, the Thornycroft, sir.'

'Why do they call us chauffeurs? Well, I don't rightly know but Mr Carpenter said once it was French, sir... Yes, sir, makes more sense to call us drivers, you're right, sir. Good plain English, as you say, sir.'

'That big old building on the right, sir? That's just the old Hallam tithe barn.'

Sid Kidman arrived at the Park knowing that the tithe barn at Hallam Oak was seven hundred years old according to the previous vicar, who was himself so old he might have helped build it, said Brightwell. No sir, he was not pulling Mr Kidman's leg, just exaggerating about the old vicar, begging your pardon, who was actually reputed to be ninety-six years of age and still breathing, although deaf, blind and bedridden now. The old boy had been pushed into church in an invalid carriage to sit through Sunday morning service until about two years ago, when he had begun to call out 'Mildred?' plaintively

71

during the prayers, which was distracting, but also intriguing for the older parishioners who remembered that his long-dead wife had been called Agatha.

There were several buildings on the estate at least as old or older, including the church at Lessed Gabriel where Brightwell was baptised twenty-four years ago by the old vicar, already considered pretty ancient at the time.

Sid learned that the barn, the hamlet of Hallam Oak and all the land they could see along this road and over that wood on the right, 'Over that way, sir,' was part of the Chiddington estate, which stretched right the way over to Tritlington where the Thames turned north of west, and was altogether reputed to be in the region of nine thousand acres, give or take an acre or two, and therefore one of the biggest estates in the area.

'My dad's farm? Well, about a hundred and eighty acres, sir... Yes, sir, five of us to feed but that's a fair-sized tenant farm hereabouts, sir...'

How big were the paddocks? 'The paddocks at the Park stud, sir? Oh, the fields. I couldn't rightly say, sir. All different sizes, but the biggest field? Maybe as big as twenty acres, perhaps, if you don't count the deer park around the Park itself, sir...'

'Yes, sir, about a hundred head of deer in the park, at a guess, but you'd have to ask his lordship, sir...'

'No, sir, we don't eat the deer, although sometimes the old ones have to be culled... No, culled, sir... Well, yes, killed, as you say, it is the same thing... No, even then we don't eat them, sir. They're ornamental... I think they go to the hounds, sir.'

'Yes, perhaps it is a waste of good grazing, sir, come to think of it...'

'They water... they drink at the lake in the park, I think, sir...' No, he had never heard there had ever been any problems with water on the estate. Flooding along the river, occasionally, but not a lack of it, anyway.

As they turned off the Hallam lane and passed between the big stone gate-pillars that marked the entrance to the park, Kidman reached forwards to grip the top edge of the windscreen and pulled himself upright in the open compartment to get a better view. The Australian waved cheerfully to the astonished lodgekeeper standing next to the gates, and then clamped his free hand onto the top of his hat as the motorcar picked up speed again.

'Slow down a bit, son,' he called down to the under-chauffeur. 'I'd like to get a good look at these horses. My word. Are these Lord Saltwood's horses?' He leaned down to hear the chauffeur confirm that they were just some of Lord Saltwood's horses. 'These are the horses in work, sir, and some of the hunters. Over there, over beyond the chestnut tree, there, sir, you can just see some of the brood mares at the stud.'

'I'll tell you something, Brightwell,' Sid was leaning down towards the chauffeur again, and his eyes were gleaming. 'Any one of these would fetch top price at my sales at Kapunda by a country mile, any year. My word they would. Your boss has got a fine eye for a horse. I generally like a man who knows his horses.'

The young under-chauffeur almost laughed out loud at the notion that anyone would actually presume to like Lord Saltwood. Could anyone like Lord Saltwood? Nervous servants coming into contact with his lordship spoke briefly only when spoken to and avoided eye contact at all times. Maybe above stairs it was different. Maybe Lady Saltwood liked him. Not much in one respect, if the gossip in the servants' hall was anything to go by.

From the impression Lord Saltwood had made on Sid Kidman when they had first met at Lord Saltwood's offices in the City, it hadn't seemed to the Australian that his lordship was the sort of man he would want to share a billy of tea and a yarn with beside a drover's camp fire. Too jolly buttoned up. Too many small signs that however much land the Australian might own, to an English aristocrat he was still a colonial bush-wallah. But that was before he'd seen Lord Saltwood's horses. A man with horses like that was a man he could do business with. This chap had clout and more money than you could shake a stick at, but it was the horses that clinched it, as Sid Kidman wrote later to his business manager, Wally Will, back in Adelaide.

Kidman sat down as the Rolls-Royce rumbled out of an avenue of elm trees and Lord Saltwood's country house appeared in front of them.

The Kidmans had arrived wide-eyed in London in March of that year, and in the six months since they had grown used to the scale of the buildings in the imperial capital. Bel and the girls now breezed without a second thought into the palatial luxury of the Savoy Hotel for afternoon tea, or up the slightly alarming moving staircase in Mr Harrod's vast new emporium, or into the lobby of the Adelphi Theatre for one of the musical comedies they loved.

They had travelled round Britain extensively, too, and visited cathedrals and grand houses from Dundee and Durham to Canterbury and Cornwall. But the size of Chiddington Park, and the knowledge that it was a private residence for their host and his family, reduced them all to silence.

The chattering conversation the girls had struck up under the skilful prompting of Lord Saltwood's private secretary ebbed away, and Bel Kidman pursed her lips resolutely in her best effort to look as though arriving to stay at a colossal stately mansion was something she did every week at home.

'My word,' said Sid Kidman softly again, gazing up at the Doric columns of the portico, and along the rambling frontage of sunlit stone, marching away on either side. He glanced across at Brightwell and grinned at the chauffeur's obvious enjoyment of the impression his master's house had made on the visitors.

'You're sure this is all one place, son? We've got towns smaller than this back in Australia.'

The butler who greeted them on the steps, Bel Kidman told her friends in Kapunda later, was called Lightowler and was about seven feet tall and made you feel about eight years old despite calling you 'ma'am' every other word. But the housekeeper, Mrs Talbot, was charm personified, although she would have passed for a duchess in the swankiest house in the snobbiest part of Adelaide.

It was Mrs Talbot who led Bel and her three awestruck daughters across the echoing hall, up the sweeping stone stairway, and along the upper gallery to their bedrooms. You could have fitted our first house at Bald Hill into my bedroom, Bel recounted, and about ten times over into the great hall below.

Waiting in Mr and Mrs Kidman's bedroom was a maid Mrs Talbot introduced as Rydal, or Hannah as Bel discovered as soon as they were alone, and a footman called Blair, who would act as lady's maid to Mrs Kidman and valet to Mr Kidman respectively for the duration of their stay. And their luggage had somehow been spirited up secret

74

flights of back stairs to arrive in their rooms before them. How they had managed that was a mystery to Bel, mainly because she could not know that the carriage had taken the much shorter farm track across the estate from the village, but there they were, two of the trunks, two suitcases, and two of the hatboxes.

Rydal and Blair began quietly unpacking the Kidman's clothes as Mrs Talbot showed Bel the attached bathroom and the closed door hiding the discreet, separate water closet. Lord Saltwood had updated all the plumbing and installed electricity in the Park and the London house just last year, said the housekeeper. The principal bedrooms all had the very latest modern conveniences.

The girls were shepherded along a corridor that ran at right angles to the gallery into the depths of the house by the assistant housekeeper, a much more motherly body who took the girls under her wing when they asked anxiously how they would ever be able to find their way back to their parents' quarters. 'My dears, you'll get to know the place like the back of your hand in a trice. Anyway, if you ever find yourself puzzled just ring for one of the servants and ask for me. If there is anything you need or any questions you have while you are here with us at the Park, you just ask for Mrs Percival. That's me.'

Lord Saltwood's private secretary detached Kidman discreetly from his
family almost as soon as they set foot in the Park's echoing great hall.

As Mrs Talbot led Bel and the girls upstairs to their rooms to
'refresh themselves' before meeting Lady Saltwood, Prior ushered Sid
the other way along a gallery that led to Lord Saltwood's offices at the
west end of the house.

'I hope you don't mind, Mr Kidman, but Lord Saltwood suggests
that it might enable you and Mrs Kidman to enjoy your stay at the Park
more completely if we discuss business matters immediately.'

Sid Kidman was more or less the same height and lean build as
Prior but he had to extend his stride to keep up with the younger man
along the stone-flagged gallery. Prior gave no sign of hurrying, but he
was moving fast nevertheless.

'I don't mind at all,' said Kidman. 'His lordship doesn't let any
grass grow under his feet, eh?' Prior smiled. 'No sir. *Carpe diem* is
very much our motto. Lord Saltwood believes in seizing the day.'

At the end of the gallery, Prior opened an arched, iron-studded oak
door that the Australian estimated must have weighed a good half-ton,
and stood aside for Kidman to enter another large and lofty room. Did
they have any small rooms here, Sid thought. What kind of money did
it cost to run a place like this?

On initial impressions he couldn't decide what this room might be
called. Library? Study? Office? The entire wall to the right of the door
was lined with bookcases. There were more mahogany bookcases with
ranks of leather-bound volumes on either side of the magnificent stone
fireplace on the left-hand wall, a fire burning despite the warm
September weather. Above the fireplace was a large oil painting of a
racehorse, standing foursquare in profile, bridled but not saddled.

There was a trestle map-stand in front of the bookcase nearest the
window, beyond the fireplace, and Kidman noted with amusement
that the map on display was of Australia. In front of the stone-
mullioned bay window and facing the door stood a massive walnut

kneehole desk with a green, Moroccan leather inlaid top. Except for two buff card folders, a pen, a new-fangled candlestick telephone and a bell-button, the expanse of immaculate desktop was bare.

At right-angles to the big desk and close to the side wall of bookshelves on the right-hand side of the room stood another, smaller but still impressive desk, comprehensively covered with neatly squared folders, a sheaf of papers, another upright telephone speaker and handset, a large leather-bound diary, three huge ledgers and the assorted paraphernalia of a private secretary to one of Britain's wealthiest businessmen.

On the oriental carpet that covered almost the entire expanse of parquet floor, half-turned towards each other in front of the bigger of the two desks, stood two large leather armchairs and an occasional table carrying a silver cigar box, that morning's edition of *The Times* newspaper and a large crystal ashtray. Prior gestured to one of the chairs. 'If you would care to be seated, Mr Kidman, I will tell Lord Saltwood that you are here. He will be with you immediately.'

Prior walked across to the middle of the far wall, pulled open a door set deep in the shelving, and disappeared into what was clearly a busy working office. Sid Kidman caught a glimpse of the back of another tweed-suited male figure standing next to a baize-covered table where two young women were typing at an extraordinary speed on gleaming, black, metal-framed Underwood typewriters, the latest word in office technology.

The Australian heard the murmuring of Prior's voice in the next room against the background clatter of the busy typewriters. He had time to take a look around the room, and he stood up to admire the oil painting above the fireplace just as Lord Saltwood emerged through the doorway. Prior followed, pushing the door closed and seating himself unobtrusively behind the smaller desk. The metallic rattle of the typewriters dropped to a muffled thumping, punctuated by the pinging of their carriage return bells.

Lord Saltwood strode across the room towards his guest with his hand outstretched and a smile that looked, thought Sid, more like a bull terrier eyeing a lame cat than a host welcoming a guest. Lord Saltwood was in fact making a conscious effort to look as pleasant as possible, but it did not come naturally to a man who very rarely found it useful or necessary in his business dealings to smile at people.

'Mr Kidman. How do you do? I am very glad to see you again. Welcome to Chiddington. And Mrs Kidman and your daughters are with you? Good. Good. Your son remains in London, I think? I am sorry not to meet him.'

Lord Saltwood was at least three inches shorter than his Australian visitor, but stockier and somehow more condensed. He gave off a sense of barely contained energy very like the Cheltenham Flyer, and he shook hands with three precise piston strokes that left Kidman's hand tingling with the static electricity of power.

Lord Saltwood had inventoried his guest thoroughly in the few seconds between entering the room and shaking hands, and noted his interest in the painting. 'Crecy,' said Lord Saltwood. 'He should have won the Derby for me in 'eighty-eight. Boxed in on the rails a furlong out and beaten a short head making ground on the outside. The jockey never rode for me again. Or anyone else for that matter. You know your horses, I believe.'

'I like to think I know a good horse when I see one,' said Sid, with sincere admiration. 'But that's a long way out of my league.' He smiled at his host. 'Mind you, you could get round your cattle pretty quick on a horse like that.'

Lord Saltwood made an abrupt barking noise that his startled guest realised a moment or two later passed for a laugh on his host's part. 'You could indeed,' he said, 'and the remarkable thing about him is that he would have let you. He was an exceptional racehorse and he sired the winners of one hundred and seventy-four races for me in twenty years at stud here. He died of the colic last spring, and we buried him in the park just beyond those oaks.' He gestured towards the window, and about fifty yards away from the house in a direct line with the room they were standing in, Sid could see a carved headstone enclosed in black iron railings, framed by two ancient oak trees and the view of the park beyond them.

'I'm sorry you lost him,' said the Australian, 'although that makes him a good sort of an age. Twenty-three, if he ran as a three-year-old in 'eighty-eight.'

'Just so.' Lord Saltwood looked appraisingly at the Australian. 'He was a very special horse in every respect. Exceptional turn of foot and

78

as kind as a lamb, which is not generally the case with thoroughbred stallions.'

'Not much beats a good horse, I reckon,' said Kidman, 'and the good ones are the ones that do their best for you, don't you think? I've had a few over the years that I miss to this day.' He was still gazing at the Derby runner-up, but in his mind's eye he was remembering the bony, one-eyed screw that had carried him across half of South Australia when he had run away from home looking for work. Not much in common with the shining creature in the ornate gilded frame, but it was the first horse he had ever bought and owned himself and he'd been ludicrously proud of it.

What had he been? Thirteen or fourteen? About half the age of the horse, anyway. They'd laughed at him when he walked into the Burra leading the poor old bag of bones, but he'd traded him to a drunken bushman for ten shillings and the bushman's new boots, and walked on north into the beginnings of his new life. Those blokes wouldn't be laughing if they could see him now, if any of them were still alive and kicking.

He suddenly became conscious that Lord Saltwood had been watching him while this train of thought rattled through his mind, and he knew that he was dealing with a man who would miss absolutely no sign that might be of advantage to him.

Lord Saltwood smiled his uncomfortable smile again. 'Forgive me Mr Kidman. Why don't we sit down? I thought it might help to go over some of the issues we discussed in London straight away, give you the opportunity to consider a proposal and raise any questions you might like to ask while you're here. Then later I would like to show you the park and the stud if you are interested. Perhaps the stud tomorrow,' he added as an afterthought.

'I am entirely in your hands, Lord Saltwood. You fire away.'

Sid sat down in the leather chair Lord Saltwood had indicated and crossed his legs.

Lord Saltwood seated himself in the other chair opposite Kidman and placed his hands with careful symmetry flat on the arms. He looked across at his guest.

'When we met in London we spoke at some length about your views on the future of the pastoral industry in Australia, and I asked you to come here to Chiddington to pursue the possibility that I may be interested in making an investment in your enterprise. To be more accurate, I invest in people, not enterprises, people with vision and the determination to carry them through. Some people in the world can see beyond the normal horizons, Mr Kidman, and you are certainly one of them.' Sid smiled and tilted his head.

'I hope I can count myself with you on that score,' went on Lord Saltwood, 'particularly in choosing the right people to invest in.'

Sid smiled again and nodded his agreement. His agent in London had put together a file on the Saltwood empire very like the two he had noticed on Lord Saltwood's desk when he entered the office, the upper of them showing his name clearly, and presumably on purpose, on the front cover. On the other file, half hidden by his own, he could make out only the letters *W.M...*, which meant nothing to him.

His agent had also briefed him personally on Lord Saltwood at the Australasia Club and warned him that he was dealing with a businessman widely regarded as a 'ruthless so-and-so' even by those who admired him.

The file with his name on it was close to half an inch thick, so Lord Saltwood or his minions had clearly been doing their homework too. 'Knowledge is as good as money in the bank, Sid,' his older brother Sackville used to say, and he never spoke a truer word, God rest him.

For a few seconds the two men sat in silence, evaluating each other, and then Lord Saltwood spoke again. 'I think I understand your views on the development of the outback, and I agree with them completely. It is a big country, and it demands a big vision.'

Kidman nodded and smiled.

'I have been considering making a significant investment in the cattle industry in Australia for some time prior to your visit,' said Lord Saltwood. 'Your visit to London has stimulated a great deal of similar interest among investors, but I don't believe they are looking in the right direction.' He paused, and Kidman waited. Lord Saltwood rose from his chair and waved a hand at the map. 'I am not interested in the north west, but I am very interested indeed in what you are doing in the east.'

He gestured again at the map. 'Please correct me if I am wrong, but as I understand it your vision is to establish a chain of properties north to south right up the spine of the eastern side of the country. You already have your network, here, in the southern area.' He pointed to the thirty or more stations that Kidman already owned, part-owned or leased, marked on the map with red circles, clustered mainly in South Australia and the interior of New South Wales. 'And now you need to extend your network north.' He pointed to the scattered circles petering out in the great empty spaces of Queensland and the Northern Territory.

Lord Saltwood went on to demonstrate how clearly he understood how Kidman's vision depended on filling in those wide gaps with more properties, to take advantage of the river drainage system that carried the semi-tropical rainfall of the north into the parched heart of a vast, island continent. His grasp of the detail was comprehensive, and he cited property values and stocking levels and Australian cattle market prices with pin-point accuracy, and without a single prompt from his secretary.

When Lord Saltwood finally paused again, Kidman nodded yet again and leaned forwards. 'That's about it,' he said. 'I couldn't have put it better myself, Lord Saltwood.'

His host glanced at Prior and waited a few moments for Sid to add to this, but then continued himself. 'I think I am right in suggesting that your current landholdings give you access to, what? Fifty thousand square miles? That is a great deal of land, but how much more could you achieve if you could double that immediately? By that I mean, extend your network fully throughout Queensland and the Northern Territory within the next two or three years? I'd like you to consider the possibilities if the capital could be made available to achieve your vision, Mr Kidman. Now.'

Kidman had learnt to say little and listen hard in London. Doing business in the capital of global finance had proved to be much more complicated than he was used to, but he loved the wheeling and dealing and he had learned fast. Lord Saltwood was not the first to offer to invest in the Kidman vision. There were two other business syndicates close to buying large chunks of two of his properties even as he sat watching his host across the quiet room. But those were opportunistic sales of shares in individual properties at profits he couldn't resist. One of those deals was potentially the biggest private land deal ever struck, but Lord Saltwood was hinting at something much, much bigger.

As if he had read his guest's mind, Lord Saltwood leaned forward slightly. 'I am not joining Brassey and Wittenoom in the Bovril consortium bid for Victoria River Downs. I have met John Doherty and considered the Connor, Doherty and Durack proposition in the north west, but I do not think you would be selling so much of your holding in Victoria River Downs if you believed there was a serious future in the Kimberleys. Not until someone invests in proper shipping facilities up there in the gulf. But I believe that at least some of their enthusiasm is due to their very vague knowledge of my interest in your wider enterprise.'

Kidman digested the many implications behind Lord Saltwood's remark about the record-breaking Bovril land deal, but he tried to give no sign that he was in any way impressed or disconcerted by his host's inside knowledge.

The financial world in London had proved to be a bushwackers' paradise of insider dealing, secret alliances, mutual backscratching and poisonous feuds, and he knew that Lord Saltwood was one of the most powerful players in this murky game. So he sat in silence and waited for his host to put his money where his mouth had been for the past quarter of an hour. He knew he had not been invited to his lordship's country house for his social graces or his small talk, but he had no idea how much or how little Lord Saltwood was prepared to invest.

Lord Saltwood returned to his seat and his hands returned to their places on the arms with a soft smack. 'This is a sensitive matter, Mr Kidman, but I believe I must trust in your discretion. Political knowledge, let us say, plays a very large part in shaping a successful business strategy, as you of course know.'

Sid noticed that his lordship's hands tightened on the arms of his chair, and then relaxed again as he continued.

'Anticipating, or perhaps more accurately being in a position to... ah... influence which way the wind is going to blow through Westminster can create a significant advantage in investing in the right markets early. In this case, I have a premonition, shall we say, that certain changes are in the wind concerning the allocation of land in the Northern Territory. I believe there will be an opportunity within the next few years to secure control or even ownership of very large tracts of land in the Territory and northern Queensland. Precisely those areas that you have earmarked for your expansion, as I understand it, and as I indicated to you in London, the bank I control is prepared to invest the capital to speed your plans along faster than you presently find possible.'

Sid's intelligence on Lord Saltwood had included a clear pointer to the extent and value of his political influence, and his reference to changes in the Northern Territory's status was riveting. The Australian was keenly aware of the agitation within political circles at home to attract settlement and investment in the whole of the undeveloped 'Top End' of his country, but Lord Saltwood clearly had the inside track on something a lot more effective than agitation.

What was even more interesting, however, was just what scale of investment his lordship had in mind, and as if he had read Kidman's thoughts again, which Sid was trying hard to prevent him from doing, Lord Saltwood answered his question.

'My bank is prepared to provide up to twenty million sterling over the next five years. We will match you pound for pound in the purchase of any property you think is suitable in the Northern Territory and Queensland. We will share the costs, the ownership and the profit with you equally, and we can also provide favourable access to shipping and an important degree of ...' he paused for a moment, weighing the appropriate word, '...political preference in access to the markets here in England.'

Kidman managed to keep a straight face, but his heart had jumped in his chest like a shot wallaby at the figure Saltwood had just put forward. Twenty million pounds? He could hardly prevent himself from leaping out of his chair and thumping his lordship on the shoulder.

'That's a great deal of capital,' he said equably, as if they were discussing the loan of a pound or two. With twenty million pounds on the table the Australian minded not at all that Lord Saltwood was dominating their discussion so completely. The market access was an interesting angle he must look into, but the capital to buy so many more acres was another billy of tea altogether. It was a flash flood of money, enough to double his landholdings virtually overnight.

It was also obvious that Lord Saltwood would want a powerful say in this joint venture. What would his lordship be looking for in return? This was a negotiating process, and the Australian reminded himself that no matter the size of his lordship's wallet, or his desk or his country pile, in this deal the Englishman was doing the courting, and he gave no sign of the elation that flooded through him at the mention of that magical figure.

In any case, this was just a preliminary position. Dazzling bait hiding all sorts of potential hooks. Lord Saltwood could change his mind. If he did, Kidman could find the money he needed somewhere else. It would take much longer but he'd raise the money one way or another. Among the many, many things he had learned in England, it turned out there were plenty of potential investors mesmerised by the sheer scale of the outback, the acreage in its tens of millions, the cattle and sheep and horses in their hundreds of thousands. This was a humdinger, but there were many other powerful men in England inviting him into their panelled city boardrooms and waving chequebooks in his face.

The extent of this land-hunger had surprised him and it gave him a huge boost in confidence in his dealings with British businessmen like Lord Saltwood. Without any false modesty, Sid believed that he himself was probably the only man who had the knowledge and the head start to exploit the immense resources of the Australian outback to the full. He could do it without Lord Saltwood, but even a wolf like Saltwood wouldn't stand a lamb's chance among a pack of starving dingoes in the outback without Sid Kidman's help, knowledge and experience. And Lord Saltwood clearly knew it, or he would not be proposing this deal.

Besides all that, Sid told himself sternly, in his offer Lord Saltwood had used the words 'up to' which his previous dealings with men of finance had taught him included the figure zero. The twenty million could turn out to be substantially less than that, so there were no chickens to count until this deal was signed and sealed. There was going to be a big mob of spidery terms to negotiate, too, thought Kidman, scanning Lord Saltwood's equally inscrutable face across the desk. There was a lot more behind this proposition than met the eye, and clearly a businessman like Lord Saltwood was not going to commit twenty million pounds of investment capital without gaining as much advantage for himself as possible.

Lord Saltwood returned Sid Kidman's gaze with a similar lack of any emotion. He was, however, irritated to find that in this meeting he felt that he was, perhaps for the first time in a deal of this size, not entirely in command, and he didn't like it. He was not accustomed to discussing business deals in which he did not hold an overwhelming whip hand. Or in which he would need to ask a favour.

Lord Saltwood advanced further into uncharted territory. 'As you know, I own... ah, Lady Saltwood owns a substantial property in Queensland. Milbourne Downs. We discussed it briefly in London. It borders a property you have taken an interest in quite recently, and it is one of the reasons for my interest in you. If you will manage it, we will include Milbourne in your chain while you secure other properties in the area. So as well as capital I can bring some land and livestock to the table. I believe that might fit well into your plans.'

14

Lady Saltwood was waiting to meet Bel and the girls when Mrs Talbot led them back downstairs into the great hall.

Although Bel's Scottish roots and Australian outlook gave her a wary determination not to kowtow to English aristocracy, she had thought long and hard about how she was going to get along with Lady Saltwood, and she was feeling more apprehensive about their meeting than she would like to admit as they approached each other across the acres of black and white marble floor.

Lady Saltwood was tall, elegant and smiling, and she greeted Bel and the girls with a quiet warmth that melted Bel's concerns away in the instant their eyes met.

'Mrs Kidman, I am so happy to see you here. Thank you all for coming.' She smiled at the housekeeper. 'Thank you Mrs Talbot, we'll be in the blue drawing room, and I expect Mrs Kidman and the girls would like something to drink after their journey.' She turned back to Bel. 'Would you like tea, Mrs Kidman? Or coffee?' She smiled at the girls. 'Or lemonade? I know you are Gertrude and Elma and Edna, but you must tell me immediately which of you is which.'

Bel introduced them one by one. 'This is Gertrude, my eldest. This is Elma, and this is Edna.'

Lady Saltwood took their hands in turn as they were introduced and repeated their names. 'How lovely. I do hope Chiddington won't be too quiet for you after all the excitement of London.' She smiled at them all again. 'Now, what can I offer you? Tea? Coffee? Lemonade?'

Bel would have tea, thank you. Gertrude and Elma had acquired a sophisticated taste for coffee in London. Edna, the youngest, chose lemonade.

Lady Saltwood turned to the butler, who had been standing a few paces away with his hands behind his back. 'Mr Lightowler, would you please send us tea for two, coffee for two and a jug of lemonade with glasses for all of us.' She smiled at the girls. 'I think you might like to try the lemonade. We make it from lemons we grow ourselves here in the hothouse and chill it in the dairy, and it really is delicious on a warm day.'

The butler beckoned to a footman standing at the foot of the stairs and repeated the order to him. The footman disappeared through the left-hand side of a pair of wide, green baize doors set in a large stone archway at the back of the hall, and the butler moved the other way across the marble space, past the glass-panelled double inner front doors, to open another door for Lady Saltwood and her guests.

'Shall we go through?' said Lady Saltwood. 'I always feel as though I'm in a church here in the hall.' She moved towards the doorway and Bel and the girls followed her through and into the blue drawing room.

It was another huge room, beautifully decorated and furnished, but with a feminine touch and an elegance that Bel was certain must have come from their hostess. She loved everything about this room, from the white coffered plasterwork of the ceiling to the Chinese silk carpet and the soft, grey-blue, hand-painted *chinoiserie* silk wallpaper that separated them. She liked the low oak panelling and the pale, delicate satin-sheened walnut furniture and the Chinese vase lamps that stood sentry on walnut pedestals behind the grouping of upholstered chairs and chaise longues that surrounded the enormous Georgian fireplace.

Bel had overseen the decoration of the house Sid had built her in Kapunda, and then rebuilt following the fire, and she had seen what was available in wallpaper and furnishing in London's leading stores. So she knew how much these things cost, and she had been ushered into enough overblown, overstuffed society salons to know that any amount of money spent without restraint and good taste did not buy you this effect, or the sense of welcome that she and her girls all felt in Lady Saltwood's drawing room.

Reminding herself that first impressions could be deceptive, Bel thought that she was probably going to like Lady Saltwood very much.

15

Sid had been expecting Lady Saltwood's property to be included in any proposal Lord Saltwood made to him, and he gave no indication of being impressed by this thousand-square-mile bonus, with its very handy proximity to the east coast meatworks and shipping facilities.

He also suspected that it might be a sweetener for something less palatable that accounted for his host's sudden awkwardness, and as the thought crossed his mind, Lord Saltwood cleared his throat.

'Ah... I wanted to outline this proposal now to give you the opportunity to consider it during your stay here at Chiddington, and I hope you won't hesitate to raise any questions that might occur to you at any time. If it is of interest to you we shall meet again at my bank in London next week with our business people to go into more detail.'

Lord Saltwood looked over the cigar box at his guest, who nodded again slightly. 'There is one more element I would like you to consider while you are here with us,' he continued, 'in relation to Milbourne. This is a matter that has, ah... come up only very recently and it is by no means conditional to our business, but I would be obliged if you would give it some thought.'

The Australian raised his eyebrows and smiled again. 'I'll be glad to help if I can.'

Lord Saltwood leaned backwards a little, as if relaxing, but Sid noticed his fingers had again taken a tighter grip on the ends of the leather armrests.

'If we can come to an agreement on my proposal, I would like to send my younger son William out to Australia with you, Mr Kidman. I would be very glad if you would help him learn how to manage Milbourne Downs and perhaps take a wider part in our enterprise at some point in the future.'

Sid shifted slightly in his seat and his expression must have changed because Lord Saltwood raised a hand. 'Let me assure you that this has nothing to do with our investment proposal. I wanted you to meet William here anyway because I had been planning to send him out to

Australia when he completed hs studies at the university next summer, but circumstances have changed rather suddenly and he is... ah... this is an appropriate time for him to go with you when you return home. I would like him to be involved in the restoration of Milbourne. It would be an excellent opportunity for him to make himself useful in a sphere that... ah... offers fewer distractions than his present way of life. I think it is something of a tradition for young men to go out to Australia to find their feet.'

Lord Saltwood finished this with another smile that Sid Kidman noticed did not reach any further north than his moustache, and he also noticed that the regular sound of Prior's pen taking notes at the desk behind him had stopped.

The Australian looked at his host for a moment of two. Even if it had no bearing on their deal, the request carried some potentially troublesome implications. There was indeed a tradition of the British packing people who were surplus to their requirements off to Australia. A hundred years ago it was British judges dumping their unwanted crooks in Botany Bay, thought Kidman, and now the upper classes are exiling their unruly younger sons as far away from home as the Empire allowed. He would bet his hat the younger Saltwood was a troublemaker or a waster, or both.

Sid leaned forward in his chair again and rested his elbows on his knees as though he was holding his hands out to a campfire. It was his turn to blow a bit of smoke.

'Well, Lord Saltwood, first things first. I appreciate your confidence in me and my plans. You are quite right. I don't believe the Kimberleys have the best future in the pastoral industry. Not for the eastern markets like Sydney and Melbourne or the British market here. Not until they can sort out a meatworks somewhere handy on the north west coast. So as you said, I'm concentrating on the eastern and northern areas of the central belt, what we call the river country, and with the kind of investment you're talking about we could jump ten or twenty years ahead and fill in the top of the chain in Queensland and the Territory pretty quick. As you quite rightly said, that's where the water mostly comes from, and that's our insurance against the drought.'

Kidman raised his hands, palm outwards. 'But you have to know raising stock in the outback is like climbing onto a wild horse without a saddle. You've got to reckon on taking a buster somewhere along the ride.'

Sid looked up under his eyebrows at his host. 'I lost over a hundred thousand head of cattle and half a million sheep in the big dry five years ago. That's over a million pounds worth of stock in just one drought. And about ten thousand horses and the same in donkeys and mules, come to think of it. Maybe a million and a half pounds worth all told. That's a big buster to take in one year, and I have to warn you it's the kind of risk you have to be prepared for in the outback.'

Not a flicker of emotion crossed Lord Saltwood's face.

'In a long drought you could lose everything,' Kidman continued, 'but with access to the water in the north and a string of stations down the river country carrying good feed you could shift your stock and beat old man drought when he comes again, which he will, no doubt about it. In the good years we can stage cattle down from the north and get the best fat stock prices for 'em at market in Adelaide, and Melbourne and Sydney too for that matter. And we can ship meat to England from the east coast and Adelaide at a cost that will land it here at a competitive price. That's the picture exactly as you sketched it out just now, and your investment would make it happen a jolly sight quicker than I had expected.'

Lord Saltwood nodded brusquely and looked as though he intended to speak, but Kidman beat him to it and carried on.

'As for Milbourne Downs, well, it's a good-sized property with big potential but there's been nobody on the place for years and it's pretty run down, you know. She needs new fencing, new yards, tanks, maybe boreholes and the like. The termites have pretty much chewed the homestead down to the stumps and you'll find the big drought and the duffers between 'em have pretty much wiped out your breeding cattle too, so it needs restocking. They reckon the Milbourne horses were some of the best in Australia twenty-five years ago and maybe they will be again, but what's left has gone feral and there's hardly a horse on the place right now you wouldn't shoot if you could get close enough to it. But as you say, I've already got a share in a place nearby to the north of yours, and there's a top man running it. I reckon Jack Gallagher would take it on and knock Milbourne into shape in two or three years.'

Kidman sat back in his chair, but once again he continued before Lord Saltwood could speak.

'Now, your boy coming out... Well, I'd be the first to recommend the bush as a perfect place for a young fellow to grow up and learn a thing or two. It worked for me, but I have to be honest with you. Back home we call them pommie jackaroos, young fellows like your son coming out from England, and the stationhands are not what you might call tenderhearted and welcoming when a pommie jackaroo comes strolling down the track. Especially a jackaroo whose father is a lord and owns the station these men are working on. They don't take kindly to it. I would advise you against it, Lord Saltwood, but I thank you again for your proposal, and I will certainly consider it very carefully indeed.'

He placed his own hands on the arms of his chair and sat quietly to let Lord Saltwood pick the bones out of what he had said.

'Thank you, Mr Kidman,' said Lord Saltwood after a moment. 'You are very clear about the risks and I appreciate that, but I believe I understand them and I also believe that your approach means that the odds of success are very much in your favour. Or in our favour, because I hope that our interests in Australia may soon run hand in hand.' He smiled again but remained seated.

Sid Kidman took his cue from his host and also confined himself to a smile and nod. A business proposition this size back home would have been celebrated with a flurry of hand-shaking, back-clapping and possibly even hat-slapping, but Kidman had to be content with a mental picture of the reaction this was going to cause in Kapunda if he and Lord Saltwood agreed terms. Wally Will was going to have a flying fit at all the paperwork he would have to organise back in their Adelaide office. Jack Gallagher might not exactly dance a jig of delight on the Warrigal verandah, either.

'As far as my son is concerned,' Lord Saltwood went on, 'I appreciate your words of caution and I understand your reservations. But I would like you to take him out with you, Mr Kidman. March, I understand, you are planning to return? I believe it is time to see what he is made of.'

Young Saltwood would certainly be coming to the right place to see what he was made of, thought Kidman, if he did come, but he smiled back at Lord Saltwood again. 'That's right, Lord Saltwood, we're due to sail in March.'

His eye caught the painting over the fireplace. Perhaps with the Saltwoods involved in the station a racehorse like that might be bred again at Milbourne Downs one day. Maybe he and Jack Gallagher would breed one on Warrigal. That would be an achievement to be proud of in itself.

Kidman looked back at the financier. If the son was anything like his father he would be a double handful even for Jack Gallagher.

'I'll tell you what,' he said eventually, 'let me meet your boy and take a good look at him over the next couple of days, and then I'll tell you if I think he's got it in him. If he has, we'll take him to Queensland and see how he gets on. I can't say fairer than that. Is he here now?'

Lord Saltwood glanced at the clock and shook his head. 'He will be here in about an hour's time. I would prefer it if he does not know about this conversation until I discuss it with him myself, but in the meantime I hope you will be able to form an opinion of him, and we might talk about this again tomorrow.'

Behind Sid Kidman, Prior coughed discreetly, and Lord Saltwood glanced at his secretary over the Australian's shoulder.

'Ah yes. We must join the ladies for luncheon. I believe Lady Saltwood has ordered lunch to be served in the summerhouse as the weather is so good. I hope that will suit you, Mister Kidman.'

An image of lunch in the bush flashed through Sid's eye, dusty stockmen boiling a blackened billy over a small fire, and he almost laughed. He doubted whether lunch on the lawn at this great country house would bear much resemblance to that.

'Well, Lord Saltwood, I eat outside quite often back home, so I'd like that very much.'

16

William Saltwood drove the Napier as unobtrusively as he could around the big house into the stableyard and left it with the chauffeurs, using the servants' entrance in the hope that it would postpone the inevitable interview with his father.

With its bright green body and yellow wheels, and the huge, brass pot headlights mounted on the front, the Napier was hardly inconspicuous, but he had timed his arrival just after lunch hoping that this was a moment when it was least likely he would be noticed. He almost tiptoed into the house, past the green baize doors that led through into the hall and the front of the house, and ran down the broad stairs to the kitchens to see what leftovers he could cajole out of the cook.

From the moment he was tall enough and strong enough to push his way through them, the baize doors had been an escape route into another, easier world for William. They were a magical gateway that separated the stiff formal family life in the big house dominated by his father from a foreign realm governed by the housekeeper, Mrs Talbot, Mr Lightowler the head butler, and Mrs Courteney the cook.

Lord Saltwood had only ever been through these doors once and would have been lost below stairs within seconds in its maze of corridors and pantries and storerooms. Lady Saltwood ventured here only to deal with a very rare and exceptional crisis, and only at the housekeeper's request.

But William had spent as much time in this domain during his boyhood as he had in the nursery wing and the grand family rooms above the below-stairs warren.

For a small boy, life was infinitely more mysterious and entertaining on the forbidden side of the baize doors, and he had been fascinated by the beehive hum of servants hard at work, bustling about the complex business of running the huge house.

In this shadow-world, a ten-year-old son of the house could beg a glass of milk or the unbelievable luxury of bread and dripping, ambush the maids and marvel at the silver store. He could explore the cellars by stolen candlelight, and he could pick up a salty new vernacular peppered with words that made the vicar's wife spill her tea and earned him a day confined to his own room the first and only time he tried them out in public upstairs.

More than bread and dripping and the glee of jumping out of a dark corner to make the laundry maid shriek and chase him down the drab, bare corridors, William loved the casual relationships and the banter below stairs.

Above stairs the family and the guests that came and went behaved at all times according to the strictest rules and schedules. They lived their lives as though they were on stage, always conscious that every word they spoke or wrote, every look they gave each other, every move they made, every tear they shed and every stain they left came under the scrutiny of their servants. They were on show every second of their waking lives, trussed up and stifled by the privileges of their social position.

Below stairs, there were social hierarchies and rules as rigid as their reflections upstairs, but there was far more freedom, too. The men-servants showed off to him and the maids made a fuss of him. He was Master William but the servants learned that he would not tell tales, and when he could escape into this underworld he could be part of a way of life that loosened off the whalebone corsets of propriety when it thought no one was looking.

In the servants' hall he saw the footman who stood stiffly and silently in the great hall pat a kitchen maid's bottom behind cook's back. He heard visiting ladies' maids and gentlemen's valets swopping intimate secrets about their masters and mistresses, and discovered things about his own family that they would have been horrified to know he knew.

And when he was twelve he tracked a noise he didn't recognise to the stillroom and surprised one of the grooms helping a laundry maid with her chores so energetically that she was agreeing with him regularly and increasingly loudly in a way that made the hair on the back of his neck and another part of his anatomy stand up as though he had plugged a finger into one of the Park's new electric light sockets.

He soon learned who was who in the pecking order in the servants' hall and which of them he needed on his side. He became aware that the housekeeper and the butler guarded their own spheres of power like jealous gods, and that they could be played off against each other to his own advantage. He discovered very quickly that neither of them would dare encroach into the cook's kitchen kingdom by so much as half an inch, and Mrs Courteney was easily the most important target for his earliest conscious attempts at a charm offensive.

He also discovered that there was a web of family ties below stairs that dwarfed his own small family network. The head housemaid was the daughter of the stud groom, and the second groom was his son and so her brother. John the second footman was the cook's nephew and two of the kitchen maids were his cousins. The under-butler and the head groom were related, and the third footman was cousin to a scullery maid and one of the stillroom maids. Many of the servants who didn't owe their places to family ties with other staff in the Park itself came from the estate. As William grew older he learned very clearly that pretty maids on your own patch, even if they were lined up all in a row, were strictly off limits. It was John the second footman who taught him that one. 'Don't shit in your own nest, Master William,' he had advised him with a wink, passing on the benefit of his own personal experience.

Family ties bound many of the staff together in loyalty to one another and to the Park. As a small boy William was puzzled at first to hear the servants referring proudly to the wonder of 'our new bathrooms' or the superiority of 'our hothouse peaches' as though they owned the place themselves.

But he soon understood that this gave him common ground with the staff. He was family, but so were they, even if they reserved their affection for his mother, a proper toff of the old school and a cracker at that, he heard one of the footmen say, oblivious to his presence. 'She may be nigh on fifty but I'd give her lovely ladyship a good seeing to...What? Is he? Bloody hell...' He didn't understand then what 'a good seeing to' meant exactly but he did realise that it wasn't something he could ask his mother to explain when she told him one afternoon that he must be careful not to overstay his welcome in the kitchen and the servants' hall or trespass on their goodwill and privacy.

Like all female big-house senior servants, Mrs Courteney was given the courtesy title of a married woman but was married only to her position. William knew that behind the defences of her brisk severity she had grown very fond of him, watching him grow and come and go since the day he was born and she was an under-cook, learning the culinary arts from the chef Lord Saltwood had brought from London when the family first moved into the Park, just before William's older brother, George, was born.

But on this day there was no sanctuary for him even in the kitchen. Mrs Courteney was delighted to see him, but she warned him immediately that Lord Saltwood had given orders to the household that he wished to see his younger son as soon as he arrived.

This was not a good sign. William hurriedly ate the cold beef and the apple tart Mrs Courteney pretended to reluctantly spare him, kissed her on the cheek and asked her to wish him luck, and then hurried back upstairs. He stood for a moment with his hand ready to push open the swing doors, reminding himself of the possible outcomes that he had listed mentally the previous day in Grosvenor Square. Then he braced himself and strolled into the great hall to discover from Lightowler, the butler, where he might find his father.

Lord Saltwood's instructions were that William should be directed to his lordship's business quarters.

After the same long and echoing walk that Sid Kidman had taken along the stone-flagged colonnade earlier in the day, William stood in front of the oak door outside his father's offices for a few seconds, ran a hand over his hair, took a deep breath and knocked. There was a pause, and then the door was opened by Prior, who smiled sympathetically, which was another bad sign, and stood to one side to allow William to walk into his father's lair.

Lord Saltwood was seated at his desk near the window, striking sharp lines through the document in front of him. Prior moved quietly past the big desk without a word and disappeared through the bookcase into the inner office, shutting the door softly behind him. Worse and worse. There was no chair positioned close enough for William to sit down, and in any case he knew better than to sit before his father invited him to do so.

The resolve William had been nurturing up to this point was now congealing coldly in the pit of his stomach into an unpleasant sense of foreboding.

Lord Saltwood continued to annotate the document, but even though William knew this was deliberately belittling on his father's part, he also knew better than to speak. Then at exactly the moment when William reached the point where he felt he would have to speak or explode, his father stopped writing, replaced the cap on his fountain pen, closed the file, pushed it to one side of his desk and placed the pen precisely on top of it. He pulled a much bulkier file across the desk until it was in front of him and stood up. Lord Saltwood was three inches shorter than his son, but to a young man who could remember his father towering over him both physically and metaphorically for the first dozen years of his life, he would always cast a giant and unnerving shadow.

'I gather you stayed at Grosvenor Square last night?' Lord Saltwood spoke matter of factly, but the look in his eye was chilling. William agreed that he had indeed stayed at Grosvenor Square.

'You should have been up at Oxford, of course. But the university has informed me that your presence there is no longer welcome. You have been sent down. Dismissed. Permanently.'

'Yes, sir,' said William. 'I am afraid I have.' The last of William's *sangfroid* evaporated. His forecast of a storm that would blow over easily or quickly was clearly very wrong.

'And instead of coming here as soon as you discovered we had left London, and telling me this in person, you made a damned nuisance of yourself in Grosvenor Square and put the household to a great deal of unnecessary trouble.'

Lord Saltwood regarded his son as though he was one of the under-gardeners caught fornicating with a scullery maid, and William looked down at the file on his father's desk. With devastating impersonality, he saw the typewritten label on the front of the file contained only four initials, upside down, but unmistakeably his own: W.M.R. S.

'So now I would like to know what you are planning to do next,' said Lord Saltwood. 'I would like to know how you intend to support yourself. I would like to know where and how you are going to live.'

William's mouth opened, but he was still grappling with the implications of what his father had just said, and he closed it again without a word. Lord Saltwood continued to stare at him in the ensuing silence, then he looked down at the desk, flicked open the buff file, picked up the top sheet of paper inside it and dropped it onto his son's side of the desk. 'This was delivered to me yesterday afternoon.' William tilted his head enough to recognise the police report the Principal had read to him the previous morning.

Lord Saltwood picked up the next sheet of headed paper from the pile and dropped it onto the police report. 'I understand that this incident followed a dinner you attended in the town.' He did not explain how he had come to know that, or how he had received a copy of the police report and the hotel bill so quickly. William did not ask. He simply nodded.

Lord Saltwood gestured at the second sheet of paper. 'I understand that the Granton Hotel where you shared this dinner holds you responsible for this bill for the dinner and a room.' William reluctantly agreed that this was his understanding, too. 'I would like to know how you intend to pay that account,' said Lord Saltwood. 'It comes to four pounds, six shillings and eight pence. I would also like to know how you intend to pay twenty-eight pounds for the replacement of a plate-glass shop window.'

Lord Saltwood dropped a third sheet on top of the first two, and then more in rapid succession. 'I would be interested to know how you intend to pay this outstanding tailor's account for one hundred and forty-two guineas, and this wine merchant's account for eighty-six guineas. And this for repairs to a motorcar you drove through a wall near Didcot last term. Presumably not the same motorcar that you arrived in here today, which I assume is not your property.'

A vivid image of the Napier in the Park stableyard released a sudden flash of adrenaline into William's system. He had planned to pay Polly Brockenden for the half share from his allowance in January. Fortunately his father was looking down at the bills and did not see the spasm of guilty alarm on his son's face.

'And then there is a dinner for twelve people at the Red Rose at Hoppley, still unpaid. And how will you pay the balance of your account at the college? How do you intend to pay these debts? Why do they remain unpaid?'

William's first thought was that he was certainly going to have to trespass again on his mother's love and generosity, but Lord Saltwood cut that one off at the pass immediately. He picked up half a dozen more sheets from the file and dropped them onto the desk. 'How will you pay these debts now that I have stopped your allowance and forbidden your mother to advance you any more money?' Lord Saltwood was looking down at the bills on his desk as he said this.

William raised both his hands in a placatory gesture. 'Sir, I can explain...'

Lord Saltwood cut him short simply by lifting his head and fixing him with a look of chilly indifference that could reduce an entire City boardroom to shuffling silence.

'No, you cannot,' he said. 'This is a copy of a bill from the Lion and Unicorn at Littledean for nearly fifty pounds in damages incurred during the course of a private dinner you hosted in May Week. A copy of the bill for the dinner is also attached. Neither of these bills has yet been paid. In May, you had already overdrawn your account by over one thousand pounds, and had been made aware of that fact by my secretary.'

'Sir!' protested William, 'I...' His voice petered out into the wasteland of Lord Saltwood's implacable gaze.

'These bills and accounts have been submitted to me because you have failed to deal with them. I do not believe you have the faintest notion how much money you now owe your creditors, so I will tell you. Including the bills I have here, your debts currently amount to one thousand, six hundred and seventy-six pounds. I allow you one hundred pounds a month; one thousand, two hundred pounds each year. In case you had forgotten, your next half-yearly remittance does not fall due for payment for another two months.'

Lord Saltwood had been looking down at the file while he spoke. He looked up at William again. 'The only reason you have not been arrested for debt is that you are my son and your creditors expect me to settle your accounts. Again. You make a mockery of me,' he said icily. 'You make a mockery of your name and your position. You have done it yet again despite my warnings and you appear to do it without any regard for the distress it causes your mother or the embarrassment it causes me.'

'But sir!' William took another half step forwards.

Lord Saltwood said nothing and simply stared at William until he stepped backwards again. 'I have dealt with matters like these repeatedly for the past three years or more. I have paid your bills and protected you from the law. I have cleaned up the mess you leave behind like a nursemaid chasing after a spoiled and thoughtless brat. You have repaid me with more bills, more failures and more embarrassment. You have twice been rusticated and now you have been sent down from the university. You will not complete your degree. You are twenty-one years of age, so you are legally a man in your own right but you have no means whatsoever of paying your debts now or supporting yourself in the future.'

Lord Saltwood's tone remained businesslike, but the anger behind his next words was like another blow. 'You have been given every advantage and every opportunity at every turn, and you have persistently abused them. You defy me deliberately and constantly and I will tolerate it no longer.'

Lord Saltwood looked away from his son for a few moments, but his face was still tight and his eyes when they returned to William's were iron hard. 'I do not expect you to live like a monk. But I will not have you flaunting your spendthrift stupidity in my face.' A slow tide of colour rose to William's own face above his white collar, but in his eyes there was also a glimmer of anger, and Lord Saltwood noticed it. He leaned further forward over the desk. 'Was my warning to you last time not clear enough? Did you not believe me?'

William's face was now flushed, and he spoke with a heat that made Lord Saltwood's eyes narrow into an expression that under other circumstances would have warned his son to shut his mouth again. 'I know my finances are in arrears, sir, but as you say yourself I have a position to keep up. Chaps like Tom Bingleigh have two thousand a year of their own and I have only one! Even Polly Brockenden seems to have more than I do.'

The moment he mentioned the name he knew he had made a mistake.

'Brockenden?' Lord Saltwood's voice dropped another ten degrees and a muscle twitched in his jaw. 'Brockenden. Yes. You continue to associate with Brockenden, despite my repeated warnings that you should avoid him.'

He lifted the pile of bills, then dropped them again on the desk. 'If Brockenden had any money of his own at all I would send these to him to settle. How much of this expenditure have you incurred at his instigation or on his behalf, apart from the cost of the dinner and the room in Oxford on Thursday evening?' Lord Saltwood stared hard at William for several moments. William declined to answer.

'Brockenden is mortgaged to the last penny and at his present rate will be bankrupt within twelve months.' Lord Saltwood glanced down again at the bills on his desk.

'He certainly does not have the resources to throw away thirty-eight guineas on three dozen bottles of vintage Champagne for his disgusting little cronies to guzzle at a May Week dinner, and I'm damned if I will pay for you to do it for him. Your allowance comes from the money I make, whether you like it or not, and I will not have you throwing it away on the worthless company you keep.' Lord Saltwood picked up another bill. 'Neither will I pay Maxwells twenty-two guineas for a new pair of top-boots. You will not be needing new top-boots since I will not be keeping your hunters or paying your subscription this winter.'

Lord Saltwood turned to the window and looked out at the sweep of beautifully kept lawns and the park beyond, dotted with mature trees, dappled with the pale, almost invisible forms of fallow deer grazing slowly westwards in the afternoon sunshine.

William took a deep breath and waited for the worst.

'I have taken steps to ensure that you will inherit none of this or my business,' said Lord Saltwood flatly.

He turned back to face his son. 'So I have no concerns that you might ever be in a position to squander it. Nevertheless, until now it has always been my intention to provide you with a suitable income that would allow you to live like a gentleman, even if you cannot behave like one. It is clear that you have failed completely to manage your own financial responsibilities, and now you must learn the consequences.' He paused. 'As of today, payment of your allowance will be suspended indefinitely. You can find your own way to satisfy your creditors, because I will not and neither will your mother. I doubt very much indeed if any of the cretinous wastrels you call your friends will have the means or the inclination to help you, but that is for you to find out for yourself. And you will find somewhere else to live. I will

101

not have bailiffs calling for their money on my doorstep, here or in London.'

William Saltwood had endured his father's severe disapproval many times in his life before, but when he closed the oak door behind him after this interview, his hand was sweating.

Before dismissing him, Lord Saltwood had told his younger son that he would speak to him again on this matter on the following Monday. So there was more to come, and William knew his father well enough to realise that he must have something else up his sleeve. He had no idea what it might be, except that he was unlikely to like it, but at least it suggested that he was not to be simply kicked out onto the Chiddington road to fend for himself.

His father had also told him that he would be expected to help entertain the guests now staying at the Park as arranged, to meet them at tea with Lady Saltwood, and to attend dinner, properly dressed.

Standing safely on the outside of the huge oak door, William Saltwood wiped his damp hands on his handkerchief. He took a deep breath and set off again along the gallery with more purpose. He needed to talk to his mother.

17

Tommy Crawfurd's mother, Gilroy's half-sister, was waiting for Charlie when he turned into the White Horse Stables at the end of his third run of the day. She was standing foursquare in the middle of the cobbled yard, wearing her best dress and her best hat, her umbrella gripped in her hand like an oiled silk cudgel.

Mrs Hilda Crawfurd was built broadly on the same lines as her half-brother but she was nearly fifteen years younger than Ted Gilroy and a lot quicker on her feet. By the time Charlie drew up alongside the bus shed, she had crossed the yard and was stationed on the spot where he would normally step down from the driver's seat. As the grooms took charge of his horses and began unharnessing them, Charlie looked down at Mrs Crawfurd's large, set face and decided to stay where he was. It was not very dignified, but he guessed that climbing down to a violent reception was likely to be worse.

A few long seconds of silent stand-off was broken by the movement of the horses being led away, leaving Charlie ridiculously exposed on the driving seat of a now horseless vehicle.

'Come down here, you... you...!' Mrs Crawfurd's jowls quivered with the violence of her feelings. 'How dare you lay hands on my boy. Come down here and I'll teach you a lesson you'll not forget, you... you...' Short of the right word to describe him, she lashed out and smacked her umbrella loudly against the footboard, a foretaste of the kind of education she was planning to offer Charlie.

Charlie stayed put and glanced towards the stables in the hope that one of the staff might intervene. Davey, the senior groom, was standing in the stable doorway watching the show. Charlie jerked his head in Mrs Crawfurd's direction. Davey grinned at him and touched his cap.

'Come down here this minute, you... you bully.' Twenty years of verbally flaying her late husband had given Hilda Crawfurd a voice with the cutting power of a steam-driven bandsaw and complete confidence in her capabilities when it came to conflicts with men, vocal or physical. She whacked the bus again with her umbrella, and raised her right foot to the edge of the step the drivers used to mount up to their high seat.

Fortunately for Charlie, the step was only just within reach for a stout middle-aged matron wearing six yards of pleated silk and all the undergarments needed to support her bulky figure. The dress was older than Tommy Crawfurd, and had grown tighter over the years since he had been born. Now it was protesting under the strain.

Mrs Crawfurd glared at Charlie, and took her foot off the step.

'Don't you think you can sit up there like a... like a cock sparra,' she screeched. 'I'll have you off there. I'll teach you. And Gilroy'll have you out of here on your ear when he hears what you've done to his little nevvy.' The crow turd's mother actually used the old-fashioned word with deadly seriousness, and saw no irony in calling her son 'little'. Tommy Crawfurd took after his mother's side of the family, and not his much scrawnier father's. Charlie could see him standing next to the door into the driver's snug, washed and wearing clean, dry clothes, enjoying the spectacle of his mother fighting his battles for him.

The sight of Crawfurd's smirking face galvanised Charlie. He was damned if he would sit marooned up on the bus and let Mrs Crawfurd make an organ-grinder's monkey of him. He swung his legs round to the offside of the bus, the side opposite the angry widow, and was down on the ground and several yards clear before she had bustled furiously more than halfway round the back of the vehicle.

Charlie chose his ground in the middle of the yard and braced himself for the onslaught.

Mrs Crawfurd set sail straight at him like a ship of the line and it was as much as Charlie could do to stop himself beating a tactical retreat. He put a brave face on it and received a shower of spittle as the crow turd's mother let fly at close quarters.

'You dirty great bully,' she spat, so close to him that Charlie could clearly see a wire of ginger hair sprouting at one corner of her mouth. 'You lay your filthy hands on my Tommy and see what you get. I know what you did, you trumped up.... poppingday.'

This was delivered at the top of her voice, and greeted with a gale of laughter from the watching stable staff.

She rounded on the men. 'You'll be sorry, too, you useless layabouts. You'll be sorry, all of you, you wait and see. You'll be out on the street like this one.' She pointed her umbrella at the small crowd of grooms and stable boys. 'You'll be laughing on the other side of your stupid faces soon enough, you see if you don't. You're finished at Gilroy's, all of you.'

The men stopped laughing, and Mrs Crawfurd took a step towards them, nodding her head so hard her hat rocked to and fro on its anchorage of long pins. 'Oh yes! You lot won't be laughing soon. You wait and see. You don't know nothing, you don't, but I do.'

She whirled back round at Charlie, who had folded his arms in self-defence, and this goaded her into another furious outburst. 'Don't you defy me, you... pipsqueak!' The umbrella whistled through the air with a noise like a loose sail in a hurricane and landed with a crack on Charlie's shoulder as he ducked away from a direct hit to his head.

For a second or two the blow seemed to take some of the wind out of her momentum. It may also have vented some of her lust for revenge, but then the ring that held the umbrella's split cane spokes slipped off. The umbrella fell partially open, and it was clear that at least one of the spokes was broken.

Hilda Crawfurd stared at her umbrella, and then at Charlie.

'Look what you've made me do! You've broke my ma's h'umberella!' She was trembling with outrage, the colour draining from her face, staring from the umbrella to Charlie and back again with horrified disbelief as though he had snapped a piece of the true cross. Her eyes narrowed and she raised her arm to point straight at the young driver. 'You'll go to hell, Charlie Downs,' she hissed at him, 'raving drunk in a wheelbarra like your pisspot father did before you.'

There was a dead silence in the yard for a few moments as the men absorbed this curse, and then the Number 5 bus came clattering and creaking loudly round the corner off White Horse Lane and rumbled deafeningly under the archway.

Arty Lockinge was the only man working for Ted Gilroy with a louder voice and worse temper than the boss's half-sister, and he made good use of them both to galvanise the staff. 'Mind your fuckin' backs, there, clear the way you lazy bastards,' he bellowed, and the tableau broke up instantly, the grooms and stablemen scattering back to their work and even Mrs Crawfurd hurrying to the safe side of the yard next to her son as the Number 5 team clattered to a halt behind Charlie's Number 4 bus.

Arty was not especially big and in his early fifties he was old for a driver, but he was the senior driver in the company, a proper horseman to his marrow, and the man Gilroy left in charge when he himself was absent, now that Ellie Gilroy was gone. The rheumatics that plagued all older drivers made him limp when he walked and wince when he released the reins for the last time at the end of the day, and his aches and pains made him short-tempered with people, so the staff kept well out of range of his long whip when he rolled into the yard. Without leaving his seat, Lockinge could flick a running stable lad on the backside with the tip of the lash and leave a red welt that lasted a week.

Today he badly needed a leak, so he climbed stiffly down from his seat and limped towards the muckheap, unbuttoning his flies and calling over his shoulder. 'You shouldn't be in this yard, woman, causing bloody trouble. Get out. And you get on with your bloody work, you idle windsuckers.' He relieved himself with a long, ecstatic groan and farted loudly.

His appearance in the nick of time was a relief to all the staff, and several of the men cheered his performance ironically. One of the stable lads thumped his left hand into the crook of his right elbow and jerked his forearm skywards in an uppercut at Mrs Crawfurd, who ignored the insult. She had done what she had come for, and now she gathered up her bag and lopsided umbrella, patted Tommy on the cheek, and marched out of the yard with her head up. She stopped, though, in the middle of the arch, for a parting shot. 'You're finished, the lot of you. You mark my words.'

She turned on her heel and strode off up White Horse Lane towards the Mile End Road to catch the tram home to Bow.

Lockinge was limping back across to his bus as Charlie stepped up to his seat and prepared to drive his new team out onto the Mile for his fourth route of the day.

'What the 'ell was all that about? What did that ugly bitch want 'ere?' asked the older driver, generally.

Charlie left the grooms to tell him. He slapped the reins on his horses' backs and walked them across the yard and out under the flaking archway, with a sinking feeling spreading in the pit of his stomach.

18

William found it impossible to talk to his mother privately at any time during the remainder of the day. When he asked Lightowler immediately after his interview with Lord Saltwood if Lady Saltwood might be free to see him, he was told that she was not, but that she was expecting him to join her for tea later in the blue drawing room she normally used when entertaining guests.

He whiled away the rest of the afternoon out in the stable yard, looking at the horses, explaining his predicament to the head groom, Daniels, and then reluctantly showing Brightwell the mechanical glories gleaming under the Napier's grass-green bonnet. Brightwell knew far more about the car than William, and was still explaining how many records the sixty-horsepower engine had broken when the church clock struck four o'clock and William had to make a dash for the back entrance.

The guests were there before him, and the complicated mechanics of formal afternoon tea were purring smoothly under the watchful supervision of Simmonds, the under-butler. William took in the unfamiliar group of two adults and three young women as he crossed the room and then looked into his mother's eyes as he bent to kiss her cheek, and saw in that brief connection that she was fully aware of his situation and completely powerless to mitigate it.

He patted her small, woolly dog, which squirmed onto its back, wagging its tail frantically and grinning at him from a cushioned basket next to her ladyship's chair, and turned to be introduced to Mr and Mrs Sidney Kidman.

The three Kidman daughters were presented formally in order of age by their father: Gertrude, Elma, Edna. They smiled and said 'How do you do' with a recognisably colonial accent. The two older girls were confident and self-possessed, but there was something more open and less guarded about the way they carried themselves than he would expect to encounter in society from English girls of their age.

When he was introduced to Mrs Kidman, he also noticed that

there was none of the subtle *frisson* of heightened alertness that he was beginning to expect when he met marriageable young women with their mothers these days. Until his engagement six months ago it was his older brother, George, who had attracted this invisible vibration of matrimonial hope, generated by husband-hungry mothers who homed in on wealthy, aristocratic potential sons-in-law with the needle-taloned accuracy of owls hunting mice on a moonless night.

The Kidman girls' mother in this case was polite but beady-eyed. In ten minutes of unpacking, Bel Kidman had extracted a great deal of below-stairs detail about the Saltwoods out of her temporary maid, and she would be keeping her eye on the younger son's dealings with her daughters.

Their father was under no such constraints. He raised his eyebrows at William and grinned when he noticed him making himself agreeable to the girls. 'They're good girls, William,' he said, 'but they're costing me a fortune ramping round London buying up dresses and frilly what-nots, I can tell you. The sooner we get them back to Kapunda the better, don't you think Bel?'

The girls pretended to be mildly scandalised by their father, but it was treated as a family joke, and Lady Saltwood joined the laughter. 'Your girls are a great credit to both of you, Mr Kidman. You must be very proud of them, and I suspect that any blame for indulging them lies entirely with you!'

Under normal circumstances, with guests unused to the scale and grandeur of Chiddington, and coping with juggling porcelain cups and saucers and plates and silver spoons and knives and tiny, crustless sandwiches and five kinds of cake, William would have expected a certain slightly flustered tension in the drawing room, a best-behaviour stiffness that even Lady Saltwood's kindness and consideration usually took some time to thaw.

With the Australian family, there was none of that nervousness at all. The two younger girls were chatting to Lady Saltwood about shopping expeditions and theatre performances as though she was an honorary aunt they had known all their lives, and looking up under their eyelashes at the best-looking of the footmen as he offered them the cake stand.

Gertrude, the eldest, chatted easily with William, too, but with enough reserve to let him know that she was not going to be impressed simply by his father's enormous house and fortune. They were wise to the ways of his world, and they were not easy pickings for some titled English boy to trifle with. Not like those poor sacrificial American heiresses they had met in London.

At eighteen, Edna was the youngest of the Kidman girls and still young enough to drop her eyes when William smiled at her. But Gertie and Elma in their sophisticated twenties had higher benchmarks to measure him against. He was handsome enough, Gertie told her mother casually when the girls gathered later in their parents' room prior to dinner, but not as handsome as Charlie Blewitt back home, and not as manly as Sidney Reid either.

'I thought he was very charming,' said Edna hesitantly.

Her mother glanced at her in the dressing table mirror. Charm was not a quality Bel Kidman valued highly. Charm was the product of practice, and she did not want to imagine the sort of practice William Saltwood had been putting in to acquire his easy confidence. She would light a fire under him if he tried it on with her girls.

Bel had also observed that the charm froze immediately when Lord Saltwood appeared briefly and belatedly in the drawing-room at tea-time. He apologised to his wife and his guests for his absence, but hoped they would understand that he was a slave to the unexpected demands of business, and asked the girls if they had done proper justice to the cook's famous chocolate cream cake?

From Lord Saltwood the question felt more like a test than a hospitable enquiry, and the girls mumbled a response between them of which an incongruous 'delicious' and 'lordship' were the only two words that anybody could hear clearly. The cake was wonderful, said their mother. Might Lady Saltwood be able to persuade her cook to allow them to take the recipe back to Australia?

'I will ask, of course,' said Lady Saltwood, but she couldn't be at all sure that Mrs Courteney would be prepared to share this secret, and she would not be able to press her.

Tomorrow, said Lord Saltwood emphatically, he would be entirely at his guest's disposal for the entire weekend, with the exception of the first part of Saturday morning, 'but William could show Mr Kidman some of the estate tomorrow morning,' suggested Lord Saltwood pointedly. 'You might care to ride, Mr Kidman?'

Sid nodded enthusiastically. 'My word, yes. I would like that. I reckon you can see twice as much in half the time when you're up on a horse.'

Lord Saltwood agreed. 'Of course. The hunt will be out tomorrow, cubbing, so we must check that they're meeting at a safe distance. You must check the card with Daniels, William.' William nodded. 'In a couple of hours on one of my hunters,' Lord Saltwood went on, 'you should see a good deal of the estate, Mr Kidman, but you must remember that we are not one of your outback stations. It won't take you a week to ride across Chiddington.'

As Lord Saltwood excused himself to his guests and to his wife and turned to leave, William noticed a curious, silent exchange of signals between the Kidman girls and their mother. They were looking imploringly at her, and she then glanced at their father, who shook his head very slightly with an apologetic smile.

19

Even though they would be dining only with the Saltwoods that evening, the Kidmans were still expected to dress in regulation evening wear, although for this family dinner Sid at least was let off with a dinner jacket instead of the formal tails.

So when the girls had left their parents' bedroom to change into their second best finery, Sid sat at the foot of the bed and told Bel the details of Lord Saltwood's proposition.

His wife watched him in her dressing table mirror. She had bathed and her hair had been dressed expertly by Hannah, and even Sid noticed that she was looking exceptionally well in her recently acquired London evening gown, even if the fashionably low neckline did make the beginnings of a double chin rather more obvious when she frowned and tucked her original chin into her neck in disapproval.

'So what do you think, Bel? Twenty million over five years! Nowhere near signed and sealed yet, but you can't ride past that without looking twice!'

Bel Kidman waited a moment and then shook her head slightly. 'That's a lot of money, Sidney, but will it really come through, and what will Lord Saltwood want in return? Do you think you can trust him? Do you really think he's a man you want to go into partnership with?'

Sid nodded. 'Yes, Bel, his lordship likes the sound of his own voice even more than I do, that's a fact, and he's used to getting it all his own way, I know that, but I think I can make this work in my favour. He's a hard man, but he's a businessman and he knows which side his bread is buttered and he doesn't make many mistakes, you know. He knows what he's doing, not like a lot of these London city boys chucking their money into any old patch of country the speculators wave in front of them. He's investing in me, Bel, and he'll be on my territory, and he believes I can make this work for both of us.'

He caught Bel's sceptical eye in the mirror and laughed. 'Now, Bel, you know I listen to what you say, and I always tell you fair and square what's in my mind before I try and jump over a crocodile, so I'll tell you the rest right now so you know the whole story.'

He described the Queensland property that Lord Saltwood, or rather Lady Saltwood, was putting on the table. And then he told her about Lord Saltwood's request that they should take William Saltwood back with them to Australia. Bel's eyes opened and she shook her head as vehemently as she dared without jeopardising her elaborate hair arrangement.

'William Saltwood coming home with us? As a remittance man? Sidney, you cannot seriously consider it. That young man is a ne'er-do-well if ever I've seen one. You know he was sacked from Oxford University, just two days ago, and that's just the tip of the iceberg. The servants take his side but Hannah tells me he's been in and out of all sorts of trouble since he was a boy, and he fights with his father all the time. Do you really want to take responsibility for him?'

Bel Kidman came from good Scottish protestant stock who had taken their religion and plain-speaking lowland morality with them when they had emigrated from Alloa to the far side of the world and settled in Kapunda when Bel was eight years old. Bel had grown up to become a Sunday School teacher and a leading light in her church, and she had come back to the old country not just as the wife of the world's biggest landowner but as the appointed official delegate to the International Congregational Council in Edinburgh, representing the Congregational Church Union of South Australia.

She and Sid had spent time that summer flapping away the midges and digging up her mother's family roots around Broughty Ferry, and Bel took her Scottish ancestry, her religion and her Church Union role very seriously. So in her book an aristocratic Church of England youth like William Saltwood was already a long way down the broad and slippery path to damnation, with precious little hope of regaining his footing on the penitential stairway to salvation.

'And never mind the son,' she went on. 'What about his father? I'm sorry to say it here in his own house, but I wouldn't trust him an inch, and I'd be watching him every single moment I could keep my eye on him. Lady Saltwood is a different thing altogether, I think she's a far nicer person, but he's a tyrant and a bully, Sidney, and it seems to me you should steer clear of him entirely.'

Sid grinned at his wife in the mirror. Whereas his own hair and beard were already grey, Bel's thick, dark brown hair showed no sign of her forty-six years. There was a little more to her than there had been when she first caught his eye, especially around the chin and the waist, perhaps, but she had borne him six children and put up with his long absences without one word of complaint, and what he saw in the mirror looking back at him sternly was the slim young Sunday School teacher he had fallen for in Kapunda a quarter of a century ago.

'D'you remember that trip to Queensland you took with me, Bel, when I bought Carandotta. Four years ago, wasn't it?'

'I will never forget it as long as I live,' said Bel.

'Well, you were a game one, Bel, and I know it was tough on you, and I'm very sorry about your bedspread, but the point is that it was a prime property in the middle of the river country, right where I want to expand my chain, and you saw how good that country was, Bel, didn't you, when you weren't knitting that thing?'

It was the first and only, never-to-be-repeated long-haul trip that Bel had taken with Sid. They had travelled in almost unbreathable heat to see the station Sid had bought on the Queensland-Northern Territory border, nearly a thousand miles in a buggy filled with luggage, the enormous lace bedspread she crocheted during the trip, and various animals her husband rescued en route. At one point this had included three orphaned calves that patterned her white bedspread with virulent yellow stains she never managed to completely eradicate afterwards.

Every mile of the way, Sid had pointed out the quality of the feed, the cattle, the watercourses and the possibilities of adding more of this unbeatable cattle country to his chain.

'I did see it, of course I did, and you know I understand your plan. I agree with it...'

'Well, there you go, Bel,' Sid interrupted gently. 'And you know how lucky I was buying Carandotta at that time. It was a gamble... another gamble, like most of the stations I've bought and I needed luck on my side to sell the wool off it here at London prices, and those bullocks we sent to Sydney. We took a gamble then, and you backed me and we won.'

Bel sighed. She had backed him, knowing her husband had rarely had the capital to pay anything close to the full price outright for any of his stations. He had been £20,000 short of the £60,000 asking price for Carandotta's four thousand square miles.

'My dear, I trusted you because you know the country you're buying better than anybody, and you know the value of the stock on it better than anybody too. So I know you're not relying on luck. But Lord Saltwood is an unknown quantity...'

'Yes, Bel, you're right about that, and he's out for himself, of course he is. But he's picked me because he's seen my plans can work. He knows I'm on the right track and he's offering me the capital to finish off the chain through Queensland and the Territory. That's all he's doing, putting up the money, so I won't have to scrape it together myself or pay a fortune to borrow it from those jolly thieves at the bank.'

Sid jumped to his feet and put his hands gently on his wife's shoulders. 'He's investing in me, Bel, so I'm in charge of the drafting gate here, and I think I can handle him. If I can't, well, we can part company, and that goes for young William, too. I've told Lord Saltwood I need to have a good long look at the boy before I decide whether we take him or not, and I want you to do the same. Give him a day or two and see what you think, hey?' He grinned at her in the mirror. 'Maybe find out a bit more about him from Lady Saltwood?'

Bel raised her eyebrows. 'Sidney Kidman, we are guests here and I will not spy on our hosts for you any more than I would jump up and dance on the dinner table. But I know we've been invited here for you to talk business with Lord Saltwood and I will help you as much as I can to make the right decision about this.'

Sid squeezed her shoulders. 'Thank you, Bel. I won't be hasty, I promise you, but I have to admit I like the idea of restoring that property. It was a top place once, you know, and it's almost next door to Warrigal, so Jack Gallagher can keep an eye on the boy and the station. It couldn't be a better fit.'

Bel smiled in the mirror. 'I'm sure Mr Gallagher would be delighted to have that dropped in his lap. You always see the best side of every deal, Sidney. Anyway, we should reserve judgment until we know them all better, but I still think you shouldn't touch Lord Saltwood or his money with a barge-pole. Or at least if you're going to sup with the devil you had better use a very long spoon.'

She glanced at the carriage clock ticking quietly on the mantelpiece. 'Which reminds me, we need to be downstairs for dinner with the girls in less than thirty minutes and you haven't tied your bow tie yet. You know it takes you at least three tries to get it half right and then I have to finish it off for you.'

20

When Charlie drove his last team of the day into the gaslit yard at the White Horse Stables on Friday evening, he found Tommy Crawfurd waiting eagerly to tell him that his Uncle Ted was back and wanted to see the young driver in his office.

Crawfurd stayed carefully out of Charlie's reach, but with his uncle on the premises he was brave enough to gloat. 'You're for the sack now, you'll see. Serves you right. See how you like that, *mister* fuckin' Downs.'

Charlie ignored him. Last day at Gilroy's or not, he always spent ten minutes checking over his horses at the end of the day, and he would see his duty out today. This pair was the fourth team he'd driven since six o'clock that morning, and Gilroy had taught him to give all his teams the once-over when he'd finished his last run. It wasn't that he didn't trust the stablemen, Crawfurd excepted, and like any good driver he would be mortified if he hadn't noticed a horse losing a shoe or over-reaching the moment it happened. But he liked to see them settled in their stalls, rubbed down and eating up their evening feed in the low gaslight of the stables, and he finished each day with a pat and a quiet word for Samson.

This evening he ran a hand down each horse's legs as he always did, feeling for lumps and bumps or the tell-tale warning of unusual heat. Eight horses. Thirty-two legs. There was nothing tonight that hadn't been there before, and Ringer Bell the farrier would be there the next morning before daylight, checking every horse's shoes carefully before the teams went out on the road. Charlie patted each horse and spoke to them quietly as he inspected them, and then he patted Samson gently on his offside quarter one last time and turned towards the office. 'See you tomorrow. I hope.'

Crawfurd was loitering in the shadows near the door into the drivers' sanctuary. He was still walking gingerly, and for all his gloating he followed Charlie at a safe distance into the room and between the odd-job lot of worn seats, to the doorway that led into Ted Gilroy's office. Two steps before he reached the door, Charlie stopped and turned abruptly. Tommy Crawfurd retreated smartly backwards and collided with an old wooden armchair. Charlie sneered at him. 'Whatever happens, crow turd, it was worth it, you little berk.'

Ted Gilroy's voice cut off any reply his nephew might have managed to dredge up as Charlie turned back towards the door. 'Charlie? Is that you? Come on in here.'

Charlie pushed open the door and stood for a moment looking into Gilroy's office. The drivers joked that since Ellie Gilroy had died at the best of times it looked like the morning after a Saturday night catfight in a pawnbroker's shop, but this evening it seemed somehow even more decrepit and uncared for. A broken bus wheel slumped against stacks of old newspapers; rats' nests of bills for feedstuffs and harness and carriagework repairs littered the table that served as Gilroy's desk; pieces of broken harness and fittings were overflowing onto the floor from an old wooden packing case, and a fine grey compound of feed and coal dust settled on every surface.

It was driving old Ned Waterhouse, who had taken over the bookkeeping, into an early grave.

Ted Gilroy was sitting in his ancient wheelback chair, his arms resting on the desk, and he looked terrible, thought Charlie, forgetting his own predicament. The old man looked ten years older than he had three days ago when Charlie had seen him leaving for the farm near Romford. Battered. Defeated.

Gilroy nodded Charlie towards the plain wooden chair standing opposite his desk, but before Charlie could move to it Tommy Crawfurd pushed his head round the door. 'D'you want me to tell you what he did again, Uncle Ted? I didn't do nothin' and he just had a go at me... for nothin'...'

Ted Gilroy screwed up his eyes as though in pain and raised a hand in the air, palm forwards. He waited for his nephew's aggrieved complaints to trail away, and then opened his eyes and pointed a knotted, arthritic forefinger at the door. 'You got your tram fare, Tommy. Go on home.'

The youth opened his eyes and his mouth wide simultaneously. 'But Uncle Ted you got to...' Gilroy waved his hand at the door again and interrupted firmly. 'You get away home, Tommy. Off you go.'

His nephew opened his mouth to protest again, but before any sound could emerge Gilroy propelled his bulk out of the chair and leaned over the desk. 'Get out of here and clear off home,' he shouted. 'And don't come back tomorrow, d'you hear me? You been nothing but trouble ever since you came here. Get out of my bloody sight.'

Tommy Crawfurd retreated a couple of steps as though his uncle had physically pushed him backwards through the doorway, his mouth a perfect O of shock and disbelief.

'Shut the door, Charlie,' said Ted Gilroy, slumping back into his chair. 'If I hear another word I'll kill the little bugger myself.'

Charlie pushed the office door shut in Crawfurd's face, catching his eye for one exultant moment just before the old green door slammed to. But when he turned back to Gilroy, his surge of triumph blew into tatters like the cobwebs in the door's sudden draft. After his outburst, the old man looked grey and shrunken. Charlie would have sworn that his long grey sidewhiskers had turned whiter since he saw him last.

'Christ. Fambly.' Gilroy slumped back in his chair and rubbed a gnarled hand across his face.

'Ted, I'm sorry about what happened,' said Charlie. 'I'll understand if you have to sack me.'

Gilroy shook his head wearily. 'No, Charlie, I wouldn't sack you for him or anything. You're more proper fambly to me than that maggot, you know that. Maybe that's why his mother takes against you like she does.' His voice trailed away to silence and he shook his head again. 'What a bloody pair. Hell's teeth.'

Again he stopped speaking, and in the silence Charlie heard another bus come rumbling into the yard and the call of the driver to the grooms waiting to attend to the horses.

'I heard she was here and she had plenty to say.' Gilroy sighed. 'She always does. Talking out of turn, as usual. Bloody woman.'

Charlie looked across the desk and said nothing, and the old man rubbed his hand across his face again. 'It's no good, Charlie, there ain't an easy way to say it. I shall have to tell it clean out.'

Ted Gilroy looked up at the younger man under his hedgerow eyebrows. 'You know the London General's made me an offer for the business, like I told you. Well, I'm taking it, Charlie.' He rubbed his hand over his eyes again. 'No. I've taken it. Signed the papers.'

Charlie stared at the old man. He hadn't really believed that Gilroy would take his nephew's part and dismiss him, but now the bullet had been fired from a different direction altogether. His stomach turned over and Hilda Crawfurd's words that lunchtime came back to him with a vengeance. No wonder she was so full of herself. The crow turd's mother, crowing.

'Sell up to the General? It can't be that bad can it, Ted?'

Gilroy winced and shook his head. 'It is, Charlie. I'm sorry my boy, but it is. We're knackered. Can't go on like this any longer.'

The business had been losing money for over two years before Ellie died, he said, and his savings had been leaking away into a black hole that would swallow him entirely if he didn't sell up now. 'Maybe Ellie would have sorted it, Charlie, but she's not here and I can't do it.'

Elspeth Gilroy had been the old man's wife and business partner, office manager and anchor. They had not been blessed with any children in their long marriage, and when Ellie went down with pneumonia in the winter of 1906, gone in a week, a large part of Gilroy's life force and almost all his business acumen had gone to the grave with her in Romford. The unattended paperwork had begun to pile up, and the dust had settled thickly where it would never have been tolerated before.

'I don't have the heart for it, Charlie.' He flicked a hand at the pile of bills. All this bloody stuff here. Juggling the blasted books or whatever they call it. Turning good men away. Selling horses. Cutting routes. It's nearly killed me, Charlie. I just hoped we could go on like before but we can't. Nothing left to cut now. It's the end of the line for Gilroy's, my boy.' The old man looked up from the desk.

Charlie leaned forwards urgently. 'Couldn't we make it work, Ted? We could find some more money and give it a go.' Even as he spoke he was struggling to think of anyone who could lend him more than a shilling or two, let alone hundreds of pounds to prop up a limping horse bus company.

Gilroy shook his head. 'You're a good lad, Charlie, but it won't wash. Your old man talked about buying a share in the business, years ago, but he never managed it, and there wasn't any money when he died. But I wouldn't have brought you in anyway, Charlie. It wouldn't have been fair and it wouldn't have worked, the way things are going.'

It couldn't go on, even if there had been the money to add **& Downs** to the archway sign. The company had become too small to be profitable, they were down to just the Romford circuit and one route here in London, and the days of the horse buses in London were numbered anyway. If Gilroy did not sell up now, there would be nothing left to sell at all.

Another of the remaining buses came clattering into the yard outside. Four more would come home to the White Horse Stables over the next hour, as they did every evening at the end of their final route of the day.

Gilroy shook his head again wearily. 'It's a new world, Charlie. When I was your age we still thought steam was a one-day wonder. Then along came the electric, trams, telephones and what have you, and now these bloody motors. Everything's happening too fast. Few more years there won't be any horses left on the streets of London at all. I should have done this sooner, but I couldn't.'

Gilroy stared past Charlie for several moments, unseeing, into the deep shadows in the corner of his office, but then his eyes focused suddenly on the young driver sitting in front of him. 'I should have told you sooner, too. I'm sorry, my boy. We'll have to find you another way to make a living. Maybe you should learn to drive one of these motorbuses. Lots of drivers at the LGOC and London Tramcar are doing it.'

Charlie shook his head. 'I'm a horseman, Ted. Always will be. I don't want nothing to do with motors.'

The old man sighed. 'Well, we'll find you something with horses or die trying. Got to support that lovely little wife of yours. How is Tilly? Any better?'

Charlie shook his head again and pinched his trousers loose at the knees. He didn't want to imagine the effect this news would have on Tilly in her present state of mind. He could hardly comprehend it himself. Gilroy's and the White Horse Stables had become the only solid cornerstone in his life since the baby had died, and now it was suddenly melting away. He looked at Gilroy with a sudden surge of hope. 'They might keep us on for a while, Ted, mightn't they? The General? They'll need drivers, won't they?'

Gilroy looked back at him and the lines in his face seemed to

120

deepen. 'Not horse bus drivers, Charlie,' he said quietly. 'They're not buying the horses or the buses. The General's offered for the route and the premises here. Taylors have offered for the Romford route and the horses and buses out there. The General's going to run all motorbuses from Stepney and Bow, Charlie. I might be able to sell the buses upcountry, maybe, but most of 'em are getting past it. The horses'll go to the sales. I'm sorry, my boy. It's a bad go, but there's nothing else I can do.'

Charlie looked across the littered desk at the old man who had been God on earth to him when he was a boy, and saw his world dissolving before his eyes like a sandcastle sinking into the oncoming tide. We had a warning this was coming, he thought, but now it was happening and he wasn't prepared at all for the sense of dread that enveloped him like a London fog.

He had seen Gilroy's as his future since he had been old enough to start work in the old man's stables at Romford more than half his lifetime ago. There had been hints that he might go into the business when he started as a driver. His life with Tilly was built on his job and a vague daydream of running the business one day, and now suddenly the whole foundation of his future was crumbling under his feet.

Ted Gilroy was watching him and he nodded sadly. 'It's a bugger, Charlie, I know it. I'm glad your old man isn't here to see this. But you're just a yearling, Charlie. Something will turn up, you mark my words. We'll find something for you.'

He leaned forwards. 'You take some time off to look about, my boy. As much time as you like. Paid time, of course.' The old man leaned back in his chair and rubbed his face again. 'Have to tell the other men tomorrow. Most of them'll need to find other work as well. Christ, what's Arty going to say?'

Charlie looked at the crumpled figure sitting opposite and nodded with a resolution he didn't feel. There were plenty of horses working in London still. He suddenly thought of the big brewery, just a stone's throw away across the Mile End Road. But his heart sank as quickly as it had lifted. Jobs for dray drivers there were like heirlooms, passed down from father to son for generations. He could be a cabbie, he thought, but that would be a comedown and a one-way fare into another dead end.

The two men sat in silence for several seconds, and Charlie realised with some surprise that somewhere in the turmoil of panic where his stomach used to be, there was a faint sense of guilty relief, too, and in the circumstances he could admit it. It might make the old man feel slightly better.

'Tell you the truth, Ted, it hasn't been everything I thought it was cracked up to be, driving in London.'

Gilroy's eyes focused more clearly again.

'Not what I was expecting, you know,' Charlie went on. The old man nodded slightly. 'When my dad was driving for you I used to dream about it. I was on top of the world when you gave me a start on the Romford route. But you know how things are in the city.' He looked up apologetically at Gilroy. 'All the traffic getting worse and worse... pushing and shoving... delays and all that, and more and more bloody motor buses...'

It had been the only thing he had wanted to do since he was old enough to listen to the stories his dad and Ted Gilroy used to tell each other about the good old glory days. 'D'you remember telling me about little lads running to the roadside to watch your dad or my grandad go by? Running alongside the Brighton Mail shouting, 'That's Jim Gilroy driving!' and suchlike.'

Gilroy nodded and his shoulders straightened for a moment. 'I remember. They were the kings of the road in those days and no mistake. People used to buy pictures of them. Engravings, you know. Famous, they were. The toffs used to pay a fortune to sit up with them and drive. Corinthians, they called 'em.'

'That's what I used to think it would be like for me, Ted, me driving a four-horse express through the city,' went on Charlie, 'and boys standing on the pavement watching me go past and saying, 'That's Charlie Downs driving the Express...' Gawd.' He grimaced. 'When you started me on the Romford run, folk out there still thought the bus was something special. Riding on a bus was a treat. You were someone when you were driving a bus out there. But in the city boys don't watch a two-horse bus go plodding by. They watch a pissy little two-seater motor dodge round us, and that's what they dream about.'

They both listened to another bus arriving home. The reassuring sound of hooves clopping and clonking as the two tired horses were led into the stables. The creaking rumble of the bus being manhandled into the sheds. Voices of men finishing their long day, eager to be home themselves now.

The old man swivelled on his chair and rummaged in a drawer under a heap of files and folders on the sideboard. Several sheets of creased, yellowing paper slid from the open folders onto the floor. Gilroy ignored them. He retrieved a bottle a quarter full of pale brown liquid that the label claimed was YE FINEST OLDE FRENCHE BRANDYE, rummaged again and produced a dirty glass and a chipped china teacup missing its handle. He ran his forefinger round the inside of the teacup and blew the dust and two dead flies out of it.

'We better have a medical.' He splashed half the liquid into the glass, and the other half into the cup. 'You'll be alright. You're a good driver and a damned good horseman. Something'll turn up.' He pushed the teacup across the desk towards Charlie.

'Hey ho, my boy,' said Gilroy, 'it's all change in the old world and all for the worse.' He sat up and squared his shoulders properly. 'You're a young man and we'll find something for you, I swear it. I'll put a word out in a few ears. Come on, here's to the future. You and Tilly.' He raised his glass across the desk, and Charlie raised the old teacup and clinked it against Gilroy's filthy glass. They both took a deep swallow and tears sprang suddenly into Charlie's eyes. He couldn't speak.

Ted Gilroy looked at him again with concern and leaned forwards. 'I know it's a bugger for you, Charlie, but it ain't going to be a picnic for me neither you know. I'm going to have that maggot and his mother living with me on the farm. That's the worst of it. Almost.'

He tipped his glass and swallowed the rest of his mislabelled brandy. It was a poisonous concoction whose main ingredient was raw alcohol, made in a Limehouse ship's chandlery behind the docks, and the second dose robbed Gilroy of the power of speech for a while, too. He thumped his big hand on his chest twice and caught his breath. 'God bless us, every one,' he said in a strangled wheeze. 'That'll do us a power of good.' He frowned at Charlie. 'I wish you hadn't of done that to Tommy, Charlie.'

The old man started coughing, his face turning from weathered red to dark purple. 'Not when I wasn't here to see it.'

The nightwatchman making his way into the yard outside stopped dead in his tracks, startled by the sudden outburst from the office. It took him several seconds to realise the noise was Ted Gilroy laughing. It was a rusty sound no one had heard here since Ellie Gilroy had died and there was more pain in it than amusement.

The long lines of horses in their narrow wooden stalls heard it and some of them lifted their heads, their ears cocked towards the office. Then they lowered their heads again to their hay in the warm darkness, unaware of the deal that would see the old stables empty and cleared for demolition in less than six months' time.

21

In the five-acre holding yard at Warrigal, the big mob of moving stockhorses looked deceptively small, circling and ducking away as the men waved their arms to push them into the funnel that channelled them to the drafting yard.

This was the second muster of Warrigal stockhorses they'd run into the yards during the past two days, the younger horses whirling round the outside of the mob, and the mares with foals at foot closed ranks in the middle of the mob, snapping at the young males that galloped too close.

This was the breeding herd, so none of the young horses was older than two, and all the males over the age of half a year had been gelded and branded in previous musters. But the oldest of them arched their necks and showed off like stallions to the mares, and the mares laid their ears flat and bared their teeth in contemptuous reply.

'*Steady.* Steady there,' Ted Turner shouted from the drafting yard gate. He was mostly hidden behind the gate that opened into the hexagonal yard, but he was managing this delicate operation this morning, and the last thing he wanted was a stampede that could easily hurt men and horses in this small enclosure.

'Let 'em settle,' he shouted at the advancing stockmen. 'Give 'em a bit of space for Christ's sake.' As usual it was the younger white stockmen who were pressing the horses too hard, and his own son taking his cue from the two new twenty-year-old hands Jack Gallagher had taken on for the dry season stock-work.

They weren't stockmen born and bred like Ted or the older men who had learnt how to keep stock alive through three droughts and an end-of-the-world flood during the past twenty years or more. They were just hired hands, bored by the routine, boasting and showboating to young Bluey, daydreaming about the day they'd hightail it into town when Jack paid them off in just a few weeks' time.

Ted watched the horses slow down as the men gave them time and space. He spat in the dust and wished for the umpteenth time the young buggers would take a lesson from their older peers, Jimmy Tim and the black stockmen, Plato and Shoe, who were hunkered down now, motionless under the shade of their hats, waiting for the horses to settle. But good, bush-bred young stockmen were hard to find these days, and these two cocky know-alls would hardly be told anything even by a tough foreman like Ted, never mind by shy Jimmy or the wary blackfellas. They'd be off to the coast to blue their cheques at the end of October, and they'd stay there if they could find a clean job with better money, up in Townsville or south in the bright lights of Brisbane. Let 'em go, the foreman thought sourly. If there's any justice they'd end up with the clap, being eaten alive by the mozzies in a canecutting gang. Good riddance.

Nolly Nolan was an exception, but he must be thirty now, and he was away now with the boss to see his girl on Strathspey, taking young Spike with him.

And then there was Bluey, shaping up to take after the ignorant young ringers, showing no evidence of having inherited his father's love of the bush or his feel for handling cattle and horses. Ted looked across the yard to where his son was standing by the fence next to the two young ringers, face tilted up to the lanky Lorcan O'Donnell, sniggering at some stupid remark, probably a snide crack at one of the older men. Maybe he should send Bluey away to learn a different trade, because it didn't look as though he was going to be much good at this one.

Turner raised a hand to his men and called out, 'Bring 'em on now boys. *Gently* now...'

As the stockhorses moved more steadily up the yard on Warrigal, Jack and Rachel Gallagher were three hours down the track that would take them to Springvale.

They had started well before first light to travel as much as possible in the cooler parts of the day, and they were making good time in the lightweight, American wagonette that Westy Westfield had built in Springvale years back to Jack's specification. Nolly Nolan rode with them as far as Strathspey, and young Spike, Jimbo Thompson's 'little mistake', not so little now aged twelve, rode an old retired stockhorse beside him. Amy Shelford had arrived in the area eighteen months previously to act as governess to the Leyton's three feral girls, and to

126

universal astonishment had found the spare energy and determination to choose Nolly Nolan as a prospectve husband three weeks after she first met him at the Springvale races.

So now whenever Jack and Rachel made their way to Springvale, Nolly travelled with them to visit his betrothed and spend a day or two watching her shyly from a distance and wondering what on earth he had done to deserve this utterly unexpected and slightly frightening stroke of luck.

Spike Thompson, the equally unexpected son of their stockman Jimbo and the long-time object of his quarterly affections in Bowen, now spent most of his time on Strathspey under the governess's all-embracing care. To everybody's relief, including the boy's, he was returning to this much more normal life after a brief visit with his baffled father.

When Rachel was younger, Jack Gallagher had split the Springvale journey into two easy stages, staying overnight with the Leytons at Strathspey, but as Rachel had grown and Ash Leyton's first wife, Honour, had joined Rachel's mother in the Springvale cemetery, leaving her husband and three sons to revert to an old-fashioned outback batchelor existence, the Gallaghers had taken to camping a night beside the Burdekin instead. Rachel had loved those two-day journeys with her father, a hundred and twenty miles through the unfenced bush, and the nights cooking damper bread in a campfire under the stars of a black velvet southern sky, listening to the dingoes singing to the firelight in the pure, unbroken darkness all around her.

They would remain among her most vivid and treasured memories of childhood in the outback, but in her late teens when the railway arrived at Springvale and the world began to shrink, she suggested to Jack that they should save time and do the journey in a day as he always had as a young man, starting before dawn with the pick of the Warrigal horses in harness and a spare tied behind, sharing the driving, stopping under shade at midday to rest and water the horses, and pressing on as the day cooled to arrive in town late in the evening.

When they reached the Strathspey track, Nolly waved and he and Spike turned away as Jack turned the horses southwest on the dirt road that joined Springvale to the coast at Bowen.

22

In the sparkling days of their marriage before the baby died, it had never taken Charlie more than ten minutes to walk the few short streets from the White Horse Stables to the Mile pub where Tilly held court each evening.

If he took off his hat and ran part of the way, which he did more often than not, he could be there at the bar in five minutes flat, smiling into Tilly's eyes just after the brewery clock struck ten.

Those had been magical evenings when he would hurry to the pub and Tilly would be waiting for him with a kiss behind Old Penny's back and a tankard of Charrington's best bitter that the landlord never failed to dock from Tilly's wages. He also docked the three or four other tankards that a thirsty bus driver needed to wash down the dust and dirt of a London day, and a shilling for a supper of mutton chops and potatoes or beef and kidney pie and greens.

Because Tilly worked seven evenings a week, Old Penny clawed back a hefty proportion of her wages in Charlie's beer and suppers, but to the newly-weds it was a small price to pay for their evenings together.

For Charlie those evenings had been the best of his life, and the luck of life was running in his favour. The most beautiful barmaid in London was his wife and he was the envy of every other man who saw her smiling for him and him alone.

When Tilly put on her coat at the end of a hectic Saturday evening's trade, he held the engraved glass door open for her and escorted her out of the packed public bar into the gaslight of the Mile End Road as though she was the queen of the night, and as she emerged onto the street she seemed to bring with her a cocoon of brighter light and warmth that enveloped them both.

They would walk with his arm around Tilly's shoulders up the Mile, pushing their way through the raucous crowds milling around the whelk and eel stalls outside the Paragon Variety Hall, fending away the pie and chestnut sellers and the drunks, wrapped entirely in each other, past the sprawling brewery and then left at the carbolic bulk of the Scottish Laundry, away from the Mile along the narrow alleyway of Lime Street and into their creaking, squeaking bed in the two-up in Parfitt Court.

Even as Tilly's bump grew they slept very little and laughed a lot. To Charlie, being allowed to have sex with a more than willing Tilly almost every night was a miracle, barring those few days every month when she was dealing with the unmentionable mystery that afflicted the female of the species, humans and horses, in a similar fashion.

Life was uncomplicated and the future would take care of itself. Charlie was up and off to work at half past five every morning. Tilly would tidy the lodgings, whisk through their few domestic chores, do up her hair, dab on a lick of rouge and walk down to the Mile at midday for her twelve-hour shift. The sun always seemed to be shining, even when it wasn't, and the world lay at their feet.

Less than a year later, the world was a barely recognisable place to Charlie. He no longer set the dogs barking, pounding down the pavements towards the Mile after work. Tilly's demotion to scullery maid meant that she finished work an hour or more before he did, and Charlie had taken to spinning out the short journey home, putting off the moment when he would shut the door of their lodgings behind him and try to find something cheerful to say to his wife.

This evening, the news that Ted Gilroy had given him lay as uneasily on his stomach as the old man's so-called brandy. In the warmth of the office, sharing a drink and the unexpected release of the old man's laughter, the revelation that he was about to lose his job and his livelihood had seemed much less immediate and threatening. Something would turn up for him, as Gilroy kept saying. Gilroy would see him right.

In the dark back streets the shadows reached out across the cobbles and anxiety clenched like a fist under his heart. Tilly was earning less than half the wage she had commanded before, and where was he going to find another job in London? Gilroy's was just the latest in the long line of small bus companies that had disappeared into the LGOC's red maw, and hundreds of other displaced horse bus drivers were already quartering the city for a sniff of a vacant position.

In the good days before the baby was born, Charlie would take the shortest possible route from the stables, striding along the substantial frontages of Eastbury Terrace towards the Conservative Club, and then whisking round the corner onto Beaumont Street and out onto the broad Mile End Road. He would trot across the road, dodging the dwindling traffic and the last tram rattling north up the middle of the road towards Bow, the clapping of his boots echoing off the pale brick facade of the brewery offices as he accelerated towards the lights and the voices spilling out of the glowing frontage of the Mile End pub.

On this evening he stood for a moment in the archway of the stable yard and then walked slowly across White Horse Lane and straight on along Eastbury Terrace, parallel with the Mile, away from home.

There were lights shining in some of the houses whose curtains had not been closed, and glimpses of comfortable lives being lived behind the parlour windows. Two of the houses carried the signs of genteel trade and prosperity. Miss Batt, Dressmaker, said one polished brass plate. Walter Airie, Pianoforte Tuner, announced the other.

By the time he reached the corner of Beaumont Square his imagination had already led him and Tilly to the workhouse door, and instead of turning right towards the Mile and Parfitt Court, he turned left. Huddled into his old driver's coat, he walked down the long side of Beaumont Square, looking into the front windows of the houses as he passed. Many an evening a year ago he had promised himself he would bring Tilly to live in a house like this, one day when he was running **Gilroy & Downs**. Now these smart brick frontages seemed to mock his ignorant ambition, and the tree-lined lawns and flowerbeds of the square mocked his longing to leave the fields of Essex for the glory of driving a horse bus in the big city. Look where that had landed him now. No job, no prospects, no money, not much of a marriage and a dark, unknown space where his future used to be.

Tilly would be waiting from him in their dismal lodgings, keeping his supper warm for him. It would probably be sausages again. She had never learnt to cook, and now that she was no longer working late in the Mile the quality of his evening meals had taken a sharp turn for the worse.

As that thought crossed his mind someone began to play the piano in the house he was passing, and a woman laughed. It felt as though she was laughing at him, and he stepped off the pavement and hurried across the corner of the square, eyes down on the cobbles, into the dark obscurity of the cut that led past the Jewish School to Stepney Green.

He emerged into a pool of gaslight and turned right under the trees lining the long, narrow green that gave this street its name. It was a busy commercial thoroughfare and there were lights still burning in many of the shops and office windows that faced the road on either side. People were shopping on their way home, and a woman holding a basket smiled and bade him goodnight as she approached him. He tried to smile back but it must have been a lopsided effort, and the woman hurried passed with a look of awkward concern that made him feel like a leper.

Early in Tilly's pregnancy, Gilroy had given Charlie a sunny Sunday off work, and he and Tilly had walked the length of Stepney Green for the first time, right down to the High Street and past Saint Dunstan's famous Church of the Sea to the public gardens. They had strolled down the Green like millionaires, window-shopping and reading out loud to each other the signs with the funniest names. Abraham Winkel, Engraver, he remembered had made Tilly giggle, but when they stopped outside a double-fronted, four-storey house overlooking the wide green space surrounding Saint Dunstan's, Tilly had simply doubled over speechlessly, one hand clutching her bump and the other flapping at the wording on the painted sign. East London Diocesan Deaconesses Home, read the large gilt lettering in a golden arc across the top half of the black signboard. And then underneath in straight-faced, smaller text: Deaconess – Miss Mary Cock.

She had laughed so hard she couldn't breathe, and Charlie had helped her to a bench, alarmed for the baby and embarrassed at the attention they were attracting from the many families also enjoying an outing in the peaceful sunshine of this ancient, holy place.

When a severely dressed young woman had turned in at the Deaconesses Home and glared disapprovingly at them, Tilly doubled over again in peals of laughter. Charlie had tried to apologise to the outraged lady, but she was standing stiffly next to the sign in a position that left the words Deaconess and Cock separated neatly by the crown of her hat, and he had started laughing too.

Eventually he had bundled Tilly across the High Street to King's Eel Pie Shop & Café, where he watched in amazement as in slightly less than six minutes his slip of a wife put away a whole eel pie, two rounds of toasted bread and butter, a piece of seed cake and a pot and a half of tea. 'Eating for two,' she explained radiantly in a shower of cake crumbs when he asked how on earth she had managed that. Her joy was so infectious that even the morose older couple sitting next to them had smiled as they brushed her crumbs off their own table.

It was a different Charlie altogether who made his way back up Stepney Green now, reading the signs that he could dimly make out in the gaslight in the shadow of the trees that lined the Green. People were running businesses and making a living doing an infinite variety of things he knew nothing about: Swadling's Dairy. Alfred Arnold Boots & Shoes. Mrs Maytum's School for Girls, with coloured decorations in the windows to advertise her credentials in the art department. Beyond Mrs Maytum's school was a shop advertising the specialist services of a Shirt & Collar Dresser. What the hell did a shirt and collar dresser do? He walked on past Patrick Mahoney Haberdasher with his heart sinking lower with every step, past the cheerful windows of the Angel and Trumpet public house and more soberingly, right next door, Chilvers Pawnbrokers.

Many of the shops were still bright and busy with light, but between the baker's and the grocer's shops the tall, darkened lancet windows on either side of the Methodist Chapel doors gave it a look of haughty disapproval. And then Charlie could smell horses.

He was approaching a set of gates that led into the stable yard of Ford & Amor, Carmen. Commodities. Furniture. House Removals. Goods All Kinds Transported, read their sign.

As he read it he heard men's voices in the yard behind the half-closed gate, and with a twinge of guilt he remembered Gilroy's words. The old man had given him a head start on the other drivers in the search for a new job, and he couldn't afford to look any gift horse in the mouth.

He took two steps towards the gate, and then realised that the voices and two sets of footsteps were approaching from the other side. The gate swung another quarter open. Charlie could see the stabling around the far side of the yard and then the view was blocked by two men who stared at him curiously. 'What's up then, matey?' asked one of them as the other fastened a large padlock on the yard gate.

Charlie opened his mouth, and discovered that he had no idea what to say. The older, middle-aged man shook his head. 'You alright? One too many?' Charlie pulled himself together. 'No, I'm alright. I was goin' to look in and see if there was any work for a driver here, that's all.'

The other man had finished locking up and he laughed, not unkindly. 'Nothing here, mate.' He looked Charlie up and down. 'Bus driver, right?' Charlie nodded. The men looked at each other and one of them tutted sceptically. 'Best get yourself over to the London General. You never know. Learn to drive a motor, chum.'

Both men nodded to him again and moved away down the Green. Charlie watched them go until one of them looked back over his shoulder, and both men stopped and turned. Charlie walked on quickly, the cold, hard knot of anxiety growing in his stomach.

Ted Gilroy had tried to tell him that he would find plenty of chances when he went looking for them. There were thousands of horse vehicle drivers still making a living in London. But Charlie knew his way around London well enough now to recognise that his chances of getting another job driving were so slender they were practically invisible.

The carmen's reaction confirmed what he already knew. He was a horse bus driver, and horse buses in London were on their way out.

He was not a carter or a carman or even a cabbie. The carters and the draymen and the coal merchants were as distinct as hostile tribes, all of them with their own loyalties, their own sons and nephews lined up to step into any boots that fell vacant. He was a bus driver and he had no family in the city, no connections or inside knowledge.

Two years ago he had been a Romford lad, driving Gilroy's rural routes, and he had as much chance of finding a job in these closed-shop cliques here in London as he had of being taken on by Miss Batt the dressmaker.

23

Unseen by Ted Turner or any of the other ignorant whitefellas, Mickey watched the drafting of the horses from the shadows under the flame trees that shaded the far side of the yards.

The men pushed small batches of horses along the funnel into the drafting yard, no more than five or six at a time, and Jimmy Timburoo followed them into the hexagonal enclosure to help his foreman separate the horses through the two exit gates on the far side.

The young horses dashed into the yard and circled it, but the older mares had experienced this before, and most of them trotted quite calmly into the middle of the space, with their wide-eyed foals tight against their mothers' flanks.

Jimmy Tim eased round the yard to the drafting gates, and Ted Turner shepherded the spookier young horses along the same side so the older man could pull the gate open into the yard and steer them through into the holding yard beyond. Sometimes the yearlings and two-year-olds ran through the gate together, making Jimmy jump back in case they crashed against the gate and pinned him. Sometimes a younger mare would try and run with them, and the gate would be closed until she and her foal had separated from the young adults. Then when the young horses had bolted along the rails and through the first gate, that would be closed and Jimmy would move to open the second gate to allow the mares and foals out into their own holding yard.

Even in the early morning heat it was swelteringly hot and dirty work. The horses gleamed with sweat from the heat and stress, and the two men doing the drafting were choked and caked in the pungent dust that clung to the sweat on their faces and shirts.

After an hour, Mickey reckoned half the horses had been drafted, and Ted Turner called for a break to take a drink and to give Jimmy Tim relief on the drafting gates.

Egged on by his two heroes, Bluey Turner walked across to where his father was rinsing his mouth with water from the trough, and asked if he could have a turn on the drafting gate. His father shook his head. 'Come off it, Bluey,' he said quietly, so no one else could hear. 'You're not half ready for that and you should bloody well know it.'

It wasn't just a dangerous job, but a mistake in drafting that let even one animal into the wrong yard could mean half an hour of extra work to retrieve it, and drafting was only ever entrusted to the older stockmen. Ted raised an arm and beckoned Plato to come and take Jimmy Tim's place.

Bluey scowled and slouched away, and as Plato approached he kicked a cloud of dust in the old blackfella's direction.

His father sighed and blew his cheeks out in lieu of apology to the older man. He didn't know how to deal with his adolescent boy-man son, and not for the first time he cursed the bad luck that had taken the boy's mother from them when Bluey was just a crawler.

24

There were two shops with lights blazing in the next short stretch of terrace, and the grocer's apprentice lounging in the doorway next to the post office hefted a brown-blotched cauliflower and hailed Charlie cheerfully.

'Here you are, gaffer. Take your missus home a flower. Bargain cauliflower. Only a penny. Just for you. Cheer you up.' He looked as though he might have slipped down the street to the Angel and Trumpet a little earlier when his employer wasn't looking.

Charlie shook his head.

'Come on, gaffer. Your missus not worth it?' Or perhaps Charlie looked vulnerable enough for a weedy apprentice in a soiled apron to cheek him like that. He reminded Charlie of Tommy Crawfurd's now irrelevant insolence.

'Fuck off,' Charlie snarled at him, and kept walking with the lad's voice rubbing salt into the wound. 'Fuck off yourself. Silly bugger.'

Twenty-four hours earlier it would have been inconceivable for him to walk away from an insult from an apprentice. Twenty-four hours previously no apprentice, except the crow turd, would have been stupid or cocky enough to have said anything like it to a confident twenty-six-year-old bus driver. Tonight Charlie felt as though his insides had unravelled. He felt hollow and he was sure the apprentice, along with all the other passers-by, could see right through him.

There had been two things in his life that had made him feel like a proper man. His job as a horse bus driver, and his marriage to Tilly. Now Tilly was a tearful shadow of the ravenous, beautiful consumer of eel pies, and his marriage was an empty shell. And now he was going to lose his job too, and with it would go the last remaining shred of his self-respect.

Charlie put his head down and walked the final stretch to the Mile End Road without looking up. He jogged across the road and bolted into the narrow alley that led to the backyard courts. Eastbury Terrace? They would be looking for something cheaper even than Parfitt Court in a few weeks, he thought bitterly. Common lodgings, if he couldn't find a job and earn the rent.

At the foot of the rickety stairs that led up to the two rooms that he and Tilly had thought were such a love-nest when they first tumbled into the old bed, Charlie took a deep breath and pulled himself together. He'd married Tilly for better, for worse; for richer, for poorer. He'd said so, more or less, in St Dunstan's and it was his responsibility to make sure it was better and richer rather than poorer and worse. He remembered the old joke that he was one down and fifteen marriages to go: four better, four worse, four richer, four poorer. But it didn't make him feel any better, and he started up the stairs like a man going to the gallows.

Tilly had cooked him sausages for supper, again, on their small fire, overcooked sausages, and boiled potatoes that had dried by the fire and grown a second skin as he lingered on the way home. He sat at the rickety table on one of their two chairs, sawing at his supper with a blunt table knife, and Tilly sat on the other, her hands clasped in her lap, on the opposite side of the small coal fire.

The gaslight that had seemed romantic a year ago deepened the shadows under her eyes tonight and made their lodgings seem even emptier and seedier than in daylight, another crushing judgment on his failure to provide. For a fleeting moment he felt a surge of anger. It wasn't his fault the baby had died. It wasn't his fault that Tilly couldn't cope and had slipped out of Old Penny's favour. It wasn't his fault that Gilroy's was going down and taking his job too. He looked up to find Tilly staring at him, resigned to bad news, already guessing that life was about to pile more misery onto her already overloaded plate.

'What is it, Charlie?' she asked him tonelessly. He shook his head, trying to swallow a piece of cheap sausage that had the taste and texture of cooked sawdust.

In a rare moment of communication a few weeks previously, Tilly had tried to explain to him what she was feeling. 'Like being at the bottom of a well,' she had said. 'Like being trapped in the dark. There's no way out. When I call for help nobody hears me.'

'I'm here,' he had said. 'I can hear you.' Tilly had shaken her head. 'Nothing comes out. I call out but there's no sound. No voice. Nothing. Just the dark.' At the time it had baffled and irritated him.

Surely she could pull her stockings up and get on with it, he had said, bracingly. Chin up, best foot forward, be brave, quick march. She had looked at him as though he had spoken in a foreign language, and then taken herself to bed without another word.

Tonight Charlie did begin to understand. He felt as though he was sliding into the same dark hole with her. The only significant difference was that he felt they were in it together, but that only increased his sense of responsibility for getting them both back out into the daylight again. But it was difficult to think straight, and much harder to be optimistic.

'Put the kettle on, Till,' he said when he had managed to swallow. 'Make us a cuppa tea.' Tilly waited for him to say more, but he pushed another forkful of sausage and potato into his mouth, and she turned sideways on her chair and lifted the kettle onto the hook above the fire. The flower-patterned teapot Ted Gilroy had given them as a wedding present was already waiting on the hearth, with its two matching cups and saucers next to it, and she opened the tin tea caddy and spooned in two small heaps of tea leaves.

In the rooms beneath them they could hear the scrape of old Mrs Hoddle's chair, and even the rustle of her dress as she moved slowly across the cluttered shrine to the late Queen Empress that the old lady referred to as her 'best parlour'.

Outside in the narrow court, a man's voice rose in argument against a woman's as loudly as though they were in the room downstairs, and a second, even louder man's voice urged them both to give over and put a fuckin' cork in it. They could hear the sound of children's voices too, the tough, scoffing calls of street urchins still loose among the tenements, hunting for anything they could steal and sell for a penny or two to buy tobacco or booze.

Charlie put every shred of his remaining energy into convincing Tilly that things were not as bad as they seemed. Gilroy had not sacked him, but had finally kicked the horrible little crow turd out of the stables for good. The bad news was that the business was to be sold and would probably close down, 'but the General might keep us on,' he lied, with a reassuring confidence that sounded false even in his own ears. 'You never know what might happen. There are plenty of horses and driving jobs in London. Or maybe we could go further out, back to Romford or out that way. The horse buses are still running there.'

Tilly had remained motionless while he spoke, a look of weary hopelessness on her face that tightened the knot of cold anxiety again. She had drawn in a sharp breath when Charlie told her that Gilroy had sold up, but she shook her head emphatically at his suggestion that they could try their luck back in Romford. 'Come on, girl,' said Charlie urgently, 'we could give it a go. Annie might be able to get you work in the Bull.'

He had a sister married to a baker in Romford who had given him a home grudgingly and briefly when their father died, and another sister, Annie, married to the gloomy landlord of a small, rundown pub in the village of Chadwell Heath, first stop from Romford on the London road. Pubs, Romford and a lack of parents were important things he and Tilly had had in common when they first met.

As he spoke he could see it happening. Maybe Taylors might give him his old job back driving buses on the Romford service. And surely his brother-in-law would recognise the value of a barmaid like Tilly. Even a nappy, useless bugger like his brother-in-law would see the benefit, if Tilly could buck up and pull herself together? Lodgings would be half the price in Romford and they could start again.

She was shaking her head as he built this ramshackle castle in the air, and his heart sank again. 'No,' she said flatly. 'We're staying here.' She didn't want to go back and live in Romford or anywhere near the home for girls in Barkingside. Anyway, if there were any jobs going with Taylors, Tinker Taylor and his son Tiddler would get them, wouldn't they? They were family. He'd find a job. Gilroy was right. There were plenty of horses in London and plenty of employers who'd be lucky to get a driver as good as Charlie. She could look for another job herself, she said, a second job. Maybe try shift work at the Scottish Laundry.

She stopped. In her present state Tilly was hanging on to her job as a scullery maid in the Mile End by the skin of her teeth, never mind take on another menial job for a few shillings a week, and they both knew the idea was absurd. They both also knew the real reason for her refusal to consider the possibility of leaving London. It hung in the air between them like a glimpse of a ghost.

25

It was a good advertisement for the quality of the Warrigal horses that the dray bowled past the Springvale sign looking as though it had travelled twenty miles that day, rather than a hundred and twenty.

They were Walers, bred to carry a stockman from dawn until dusk and beyond it, but in the deep darkness of a semi-tropical evening, nobody in Springvale saw or appreciated their remarkable powers of endurance other than Licky, the young blackfella who vaulted up into the tray behind the seat when they stopped at Westfield's livery yard on the outskirts of town. Westfield himself came to the door of his workshop and waved in the lamplight. 'G'day, Jack. Hello there, Rachel. See you tomorrow.'

They called greetings back and Jack clicked the horses forward onto the main street, past the lights in the Commercial Hotel and the darkened display window of Plashey's General Store. Although there was nobody else on the wide street, Jack let the horses walk the rest of the way, past the post and telegraph office and the imposing stone frontage of the Queensland National Bank to the Leichhardt Hotel. He pulled them gently to a standstill alongside the steps up to the hotel's wide verandah, and Licky carried their bags up the steps, one small holdall for Jack and a much larger leather case for Rachel's ongoing journey to Brisbane.

The Leichhardt was the second largest building in Springvale, with three lamplit windows glowing on either side of the double front doors on the ground floor, and four of the seven guest bedroom windows showing lamplight on the first floor, and it looked even more welcoming to the tired and dusty travellers when the front doors were pulled open suddenly and Herbert Heinemann came bustling out to greet them.

The young black boy skipped back down the steps and hopped up onto the seat, gathering the reins to drive the patient horses back to the livery yard.

'Thanks, Licky,' Jack said to him. 'I'll be there to check they're good tomorrow before I go to church. Mind you don't sleep in now.' The boy's teeth gleamed in the low light. 'G'night, Mr Gallagher. G'night, Miss Rachel. I'll take care of 'em.'

'I know you will,' said Jack. 'Good night, Licky.' He slapped the side of the tray gently as the wagonette moved off, turning in the wide street, and then turned himself and trotted up the steps behind Rachel to greet their host.

'Jack! Rachel! Come in. Come in. How very good to see you.' In the hall of the hotel Herbert Heinemann shook Jack's hand with both of his own, and then took Rachel's hand and bowed over it as though he was going to kiss it. But instead he clicked his heels in a parody of his father's old Viennese gallantry, laughed, hugged her and kissed her on both cheeks in much the same way he had every time he had seen her since she first stayed at the Leichhardt with Jack at the age of two.

'Lovely as ever, my dear Rachel. Maureen is longing to see you, but she is supervising the schnitzel. That's the good news. Schnitzel and strüdel, made by my wife's own fairy hand, as Papa used to put it.' He made a pained face. 'The bad news for me is that the Simpson-Parkers have sent in a message that they'll be here next Saturday, but never mind. We can enjoy a civilised evening or two together and then I'll have to brace myself for the royal visit.' He turned to call for help with their bags and nearly fell over a boy who was the spitting image of him, minus the moustache, standing shyly right behind his father.

The hotelier clapped a hand over his heart. 'SSShhh...ugar and salt, Wolfgang, don't do that to me will you!' He put a hand on the boy's shoulder and propelled him forward a step or two. 'Say good evening to Mr Gallagher and Miss Rachel.'

The boy mumbled good evening and kept his eyes fixed firmly on the polished hardwood floor until Jack put his hand out to shake. 'Hello, Wolfie. You on duty tonight, are you? Good for you. You can show us up to our rooms.' The boy gave Jack and Rachel an enormous smile, looked at his father and nodded proudly.

Heinemann laughed and ruffled his son's hair. 'He needs to get out from under his mother's apron and join his brothers at school, don't you, Wolfgang?'

The boy's smile disappeared and he shook his head silently. Rachel extended her own hand. 'Come on, Wolfie, never mind these old

141

dads. You show me the way. Are we in our usual rooms?' He perked up considerably, took her hand and they set off for the stairs.

Jack and the hotelier looked at each other ruefully and Jack grinned. 'What do we know, eh Herb? Oh yes, you know how to run the best hotel in Queensland and I know how to run a cattle station, but that's not much as far as they're concerned.'

He hefted both cases easily. 'And I can just about manage these, I reckon. No need to disturb old Lenny. Long as the water's hot and we can make ourselves respectable, we'll be down in half an hour. Why don't you go and pull a couple of corks and tell Maureen I've been dreaming about her cooking for a couple of months now. I'm just about ready to eat the carpet.'

26

On Saturday morning, William came down to breakfast at half past eight, dressed to ride. The horses would be brought round to the front of the house at half past nine for William and the Australian, but of Kidman there was no sign.

There was no one else in the breakfast room, except a footman stationed next to the sideboard and a maid standing with her hands folded in front of her, waiting by the tea and coffee pots.

Unusually for Lord Saltwood, Chiddington Park did not insist on a precise timetable for breakfast except on Sundays. On other days family and guests could help themselves from the long row of silver warming dishes on the sideboard until the breakfast room was cleared at ten o'clock.

'Morning, Mary. Morning, Joe.' William greeted the footman and the maid. 'Good morning, Master William,' they replied together. William helped himself to a large plate of kedgeree and was sitting down at the table when his father and mother followed him into the breakfast room. He rose to his feet again. 'Good morning,' said his father. William returned the greeting. 'Good morning, sir. Good morning, Mother.' Lady Saltwod smiled at him as she sat down, the footman discreetly guiding her chair in behind her. 'Thank you, Joe, and good morning.' The footman bowed his head. 'Good morning, your ladyship,' he said.

William waited until his mother was seated and then moved around the table and picked up the cup of tea the maid had poured. 'Thank you,' he said. 'Let me take it.' He carried the cup to his mother's place and delivered it, then bent and kissed his mother's cheek. 'Thank you, William,' she said. Lord Saltwood was helping his wife to a small plate of kedgeree, which he handed to the footman to deliver to her, and helped himself to a larger plate of bacon, scrambled eggs and devilled kidneys. He took his plate to his own place at the head of the breakfast table and sat down, looking at William as he spread his napkin on his lap. The maid carefully placed a large cup and saucer on the table beside his right hand. 'Thank you,' he said briefly, continuing to look at his son. 'Have you seen Mr Kidman this morning, William?'

The footman had resumed his place by the door, and he cleared his throat quietly. 'Beg pardon, your lordship. Mr Kidman has had his breakfast and left a message that he has gone to the stables. He said he hoped you would not mind if he had a ...'a bit of a poke around...,' sir.' The footman delivered Kidman's message deadpan, with very clear quotation marks, staring at the wall between the windows where the sunshine was streaming into the room.

Lord Saltwood looked at his wife, and then at William. 'I see.' He picked up his cup and gestured with it in his son's direction. 'Then you had better make haste and follow him, William.'

William did make haste, and nearly collided with Mrs Kidman and the three Kidman girls as they followed the third footman into the breakfast room. There was a brief confusion of apologies and good mornings before he could extricate himself, explaining that he was in hot pursuit of Mr Kidman, and then he escaped into the echoing great hall, turning left towards the back of the house, through the double doors that led into the servants' area.

Tracking Sid Kidman through the baize doors, William skirted the head of the stairs that led down to the main service quarters and the kitchens. The door at the rear of the Park was open to the day, and he paused on the top step to look around the great courtyard. He knew that life for the upper and lower classes was usually defined as being upstairs for the privileged and downstairs for their servants, but at Chiddington and other big houses he knew, the class division seemed to him much more a case of front and back.

The yard was a space in keeping with the size of the house, enclosed on three sides by two-storey buildings detailed in the same dressed stone as the house, interrupted on the north side opposite the back door by a taller gatehouse and clock tower. William's father had more than doubled the scale of the yard and its buildings when he had been given Chiddington Park by old Lord Saltwood as a wedding present, nearly thirty years previously.

Since then, until just a few years ago, the wide, high arches to the right of the gatehouse had housed three carriages and the stable stalls next to them had been filled with carriage horses. This morning, the open doors under two of the arches showed that the carriages had made way for his lordship's Rolls-Royces, and Brightwell, the under-chauffeur, was running a cloth over the Napier in the third bay.

But all the stabling to the left of the gatehouse and along the west side that joined the house was still the preserve of the Park's hunters and riding horses. This was the fiefdom of the head groom, and it was where William had always felt most at home. Across the paved and cobbled courtyard he could see two of the stable staff moving about their business, one of them wheeling a barrow through the doorway that led into the main stable building.

On the far side of the courtyard, half sitting on one of the stone-stepped mounting blocks, he could see a tall figure in a wide-brimmed hat, listening intently to the head groom himself, who was clearly explaining something to the Australian with a sweep of his arm that took in half the courtyard and the back of the Park in one expansive gesture.

Both men looked up towards the servants' door as the head groom's gesture finished pointing straight across the courtyard at William, and Kidman raised a hand in greeting and beckoned him. 'G'day, William,' he called. 'Come on over here and tell me if Mr Daniels here's pulling my leg.'

'Good morning, Master William,' said the head groom as William approached them across the yard. 'I have just been telling Mr Kidman how we ran the stables when we were hunting three days a week.'

Kidman levered himself upright. Apart from his hat, he was dressed very much as the head groom was in good quality twill breeches, brown ankle boots and gaiters, a tweed jacket, waistcoat and tie. William was similarly dressed, only his highly polished riding boots marking any difference between him and the other two men.

Like the head groom and all the other stable staff in the courtyard, William was wearing a soft tweed flat cap with an exaggeratedly wide top.

The Australian was well aware by now that the rules governing what you wore on your head in England were as complicated as any other aspect of the Byzantine prescriptions covering the correct clothing for different occasions, many of them dependent on your station in life.

A Duke would wear a silk top hat to a formal social gathering, or to Ascot, or out hunting. The Duke's coachman or a footman on outside service might also wear a tall silk topper, but theirs would be shorter in the crown and have a livery cockade on the hatband.

Bowlers were for bus drivers and tradesmen, but Sid had also seen toffs wearing them when hacking their horses along Rotten Row in Hyde Park. Sid had tried a Bowler on at the royal hatters, Lock's of St James, the oldest hat shop in the world, he had been told, but he hadn't liked the rigid structure even when the fitter assured him they could steam and shape it to fit him so perfectly he wouldn't even know it was there.

Soft flat caps in a wide variety of styles and shapes were worn by everyone from the coalman to the king himself, but the extra wide flat hats seemed to be a sort of informal badge of horsemanship that bridged the gulf between masters and servants, worn by grooms and rich boys alike as a sign of equal membership in the timeless, classless brotherhood of the horse.

The deerstalker Sid had also tried on at Lock's had made him laugh so he had bought it to take back to show his friends, but he stuck to his own broad-brimmed felt hat at all times and for almost all except formal occasions. He liked the fact that it had become his trademark in England. The press mentioned it regularly, and the Cattle King's distinctive hat was becoming something of a badge that drew crowds of gawkers on the busy streets of London.

Apart from the hat, he seemed to be getting the hang of the English dress code. Everyone in the courtyard that morning, including young Saltwood, appeared to be dressed in a uniform that more or less matched his own outfit. The younger staff wore their shirts collarless and open at the throat, and in the warmth of the morning sunshine the youngest groom pushing the mucking out barrow had dispensed with his waistcoat too. But the caps remained on every head.

What had that urchin in Whitechapel called it? His titfer? Tit for tat. Cockney rhyming slang for hat. Getting to grips with the dress code was manageable, but slang and argot was often beyond him. On many occasions in England, Sid had struggled to understand what was being said to him when it was spoken in a strong local dialect. Up in Scotland he had tried questioning an Edinburgh cabbie about his horse and been completely baffled by a five-minute stream of gibberish that might as well have been Swahili.

Back in Australia, no one followed any sartorial rules when they were working with horses. Everybody, including his own daughters, tended to wear a wide-brimmed felt hat of one shape or another in defence against the southern sun. Otherwise you wore what you liked. Sid did sometimes put on breeches and boots, and the girls wore the Indian jodhpurs that were becoming popular, but Bel had given up admonishing her husband for drafting horses down at the Kapunda yards in a three-piece suit he had put on for a meeting at the bank early the same day. She had grown used to seeing Sid's suit trousers stiff with dust and dried horse sweat, and she knew only too well that when he was out in the bush the Cattle King reverted to the same motley mismatched combinations of old suit jackets and flannel trousers held up with a stirrup-leather belt that most of his station hands, managers and drovers wore.

At the first country house party they had been invited to in England, back in May, he had suggested to his host that he was quite happy to ride in a new tweed suit made for him in London just a fortnight earlier. The following Monday he had been steered firmly to the tailors and bootmakers by Bel to acquire the regulation breeches, boots and stiff, buckled gaiters he was sporting at the Park this morning.

Sid himself couldn't have cared less, but having the right kit did avoid embarrassing Bel and the girls, and he was doing his best to avoid embarrassing his wife and daughters more often than he could help it on their visit to the heart of the Empire.

'Good morning, Mr Kidman,' said William to his guest. 'Good morning, Mr Daniels,' he said to the head groom. 'Morning, Jim.' He nodded to a groom of about his own age who had materialised behind Daniels and was standing awaiting orders at a respectful distance. The young groom grinned back at the young master. 'Morning, Master William,' he said cheerfully. 'Lovely morning again.'

The Australian noticed that the head groom had called the young man 'Master' and touched the peak of his hat to William as he approached them, but there was little sense of a master-servant relationship between Daniels and his boss's younger son, who smiled at the older man and then at Kidman.

'I hope Mr Daniels hasn't been giving you the full chapter and verse on the Good Old Days, Mr Kidman. We won't get away until it's too dark to ride if we get started on the Good Old Days.'

Daniels looked at William and shook his head. 'Only explaining why there's so much stabling. Anyway,' he said to Kidman, 'Master William can sit in the tackroom and chew the hind leg off a donkey along with the best of us when it comes to talking horses and hunting, you mark my words.'

'I would guess that Mr Daniels has been telling you that in the good old days there were forty hunters stabled here at the beginning of a season. Am I right?'

Kidman laughed. 'Well, yes, I reckon that was about it.' He looked around the courtyard. 'But they wouldn't all have been just for hunting, surely?'

Daniels and the groom standing behind him both nodded at the Australian. 'Yes sir, this time of year, all hunters fit and ready for the season,' said the head groom emphatically. 'Six in for his lordship, six for her ladyship, three each for Master George and Master William, and...' The head groom stopped with a look of embarrassment and glanced at William. 'Well, then there were the ponies, and youngsters and spares for guests and such-like.'

'That reminds me,' said William. 'Mr Lavery said last night the hounds were meeting at Plough Lane End for Woodcock Wood. They won't be coming this way, will they?'

Daniels shook his head. 'They're drawing Woodcock Wood first and then over to Lazy Mary and the Three Wise Men. Didn't your uncle say that was the draw, Jim?' He and William turned to the young groom. 'Yessir. Uncle Alfred said last night they're going to hold up Woodcock again today. Two big litters in there and another one in Lazy Mary, so they could be in there all morning. But you know Mr Lavery, Master William. He might let 'em hunt one away, but not over this way, and there won't likely be a lot of scent on a morning like this.'

William looked at Kidman. 'I apologise for all this gobbledegook, Mr Kidman. Jim's uncle is the huntsman to the Woolton hounds and they'll be cubbing this morning not too far from here, so I want to be sure we don't bump into them.'

'I wouldn't mind if we did,' said Kidman enthusiastically. William looked at him for a second and then shook his head regretfully. 'I'm afraid the Master... Mr Lavery would, though. You meet the hounds at the appointed time and place, or you stay well clear. And dressed correctly, of course, must remember that. The Master doesn't mince his words, does he Mr Daniels? We would get our ears pinned back, I'm afraid.'

The young groom spoke up again. 'Excuse me, sir. Horses are tacked up and ready, and you know the filly don't like standing still. Can we bring them out?' Daniels nodded. 'Aye, Jim.' But then as the groom turned away he stopped him again. 'Hold hard there a minute.' He looked at William. 'Let us put her in a double bridle for you, Master William. She's been lunged every day but she hasn't been ridden since you took her out three weeks ago.'

William smiled at Daniels and then at Kidman. 'She's just a four-year-old, Mr Kidman, and just a bit full of herself, but I like a young horse to have a bit of spirit. Makes a better horse in the end.' He shook his head. 'Let's stick to the snaffle, Mr Daniels.' The head groom ducked his head in reluctant agreement, but he didn't argue and nodded to the young groom. 'Off you go then, Jim.' The young groom touched his hat and turned away again, and Kidman caught the conspiratorial wink that he gave William behind the head groom's back.

'These youngsters, Mr Kidman!' Daniels looked at William with a mixture of resignation and pride. 'Master William's the only one who can ride one side of her in a snaffle, or anything else come to that, but I wouldn't want it to go to his head. He might be landing on that in a minute.'

William laughed. 'Everything I know about riding young horses I learned from you, Mr Daniels, so if we part company it's your fault for not teaching me properly.'

Sid Kidman watched this exchange acutely conscious of Lord Saltwood's request the previous day, and his own promise to see what the boy was made of. So far, so interesting, he thought.

'I'd like to have a look at your stables sometime, if you'd show me?' he said to Daniels.

The sun was shining directly on this western side of the courtyard, and Kidman could see that the stabling inside was no longer the

149

traditional stalls, but a series of high-sided enclosures or pens, which intrigued him. But then they heard the sound of a horse's hooves inside the building and one of the grooms emerged, leading a big chestnut horse out into the sunshine.

'This is your horse now, sir,' said Daniels. 'We can show you the stables when you return, perhaps?'

Kidman was now inspecting the chestnut horse and nodded vigorously. 'My word, this is some horse. Are you sure this is for me?'

Daniels had been told that the guest was a man who knew his horses, at least as far as horses went down there in Australia. So the head groom accepted the compliment. If push had ever come to shove, he would have wagered his own life that this was one of the best hunters in England. Several very distinguished hunting guests including the legendary Lordy Lonsdale had told him so. But he was the latest of five generations of grooms and the poker-faced conventions of the stables were bred into his bones, so he simply nodded slightly.

He waved the groom to lead the horse closer, and then bent forward and brushed an imaginary speck from the gleaming chestnut coat. The horse's skin flickered slightly at his touch, and he patted it gently. 'This is Trafalgar,' he said, 'Lord Saltwood's favourite hunter. Home bred, of course. Getting on a tad now, but he'll carry you very nicely, sir.'

The chestnut horse had turned its head towards Daniels' voice, and Kidman noted a kind and intelligent eye, with that hint of amusement that marked a confident and relaxed horse. The Australian took his cue from the head groom and put on his best deadpan, horse-dealing expression, but this really was a horse he would have bid through the roof for. Long, sloping shoulder. Tremendous bone. He measured him mentally at the wither. He reckoned the chestnut was sixteen hands and an inch or possibly a fraction more, although a deep chest like that could be deceptive.

'Sixteen two,' said the head groom, as though Kidman had been speaking out loud. 'He'll carry his lordship up front all day and still clear a five-foot hedge at four o'clock as if it wasn't there.'

Daniels also said this in a flat, matter-of-fact tone, but he ran his hand behind the saddle and gave Trafalgar a soft clap on his backside that might have been construed as affectionate, or at least approving.

At the same time, another set of hooves could be heard making their way towards the door inside the stable building. These were not the calm, measured steps of Lord Saltwood's favourite hunter. They were the syncopated staccato of a horse on its toes, with a regular accompaniment of, 'Steady, steeaaddy,' from Jim, rising to an urgent, 'Steady there,' as the second horse cannoned through the doorway into the sunny courtyard.

The groom leading Trafalgar had taken the precaution of moving him well away from the vicinity of the stable doorway, and the older horse had swung his quarters round so that he was half facing the newcomer, watching her calmly as she spun excitedly around her own groom.

The head groom, William and Sid Kidman also retreated a few more yards to a safe distance, and then the whole group waited silently for a moment while the filly stood stock still but quivering with energy and excitement, only her head turning suddenly and her ears flicking towards a distant sound. Then she tossed her head against the hold of the groom and danced another few steps, stopped and listened again, shivering, raring for any excuse to be off.

'You sure you don't want something stronger, Master William?' asked Daniels.

William smiled and shook his head. 'She's just a bit skittish, Mr Daniels. She'll be fine, won't you girl?'

The head groom's eyebrows disappeared under his hat. 'Skittish?' he muttered under his breath. 'God help us.'

William took a couple more steps away as she sidled towards him, and he laughed out loud. 'Behave yourself, will you!' He grinned at the head groom. 'You'll give Mr Daniels a seizure if you don't mind your manners. And we have a visitor.'

As if that had simply encouraged her, the filly barged sideways and then threw her head up, pulling her groom off balance. 'Beg your pardon, sir,' the young groom said to William. 'She's been on the lunge for half an hour, both ways. I thought she'd blown off enough steam. Could be coming into season. Maybe best to keep her on the move, sir.'

'Absolutely. Yes.' William moved quickly away down the courtyard towards the gatehouse archway. 'Leg me up, Jim, and then you can give me a lead out just until we're clear of the arch.'

Daniels nodded to the other groom holding Trafalgar, and he and Sid followed the chestnut horse to a long, stone mounting-block in the middle of the yard. At fifty-one, Sid Kidman was perfectly capable of swinging into the saddle from the ground the bush way, but this wasn't Kapunda and the magnificent chestnut was no dusty stockhorse, so he climbed the stone steps, put his left foot into the stirrup and swung a leg sedately over his lordship's favourite from the mounting block the English way, like an old woman. He gave silent thanks that Charlie Coles and The Colonel couldn't see this. He'd never hear the last of it.

As this thought occurred to him, he watched William slip quickly and smoothly into the saddle as the groom legged him up on the move, like a jockey.

Lord Saltwood's chestnut stood like a statue at the mounting block, gazing ahead as the filly sidled and skittered sideways through the archway, the young groom with a hand on the nearside rein as William settled his full weight gradually into the saddle.

Kidman settled himself into the unfamiliar English saddle, and realised that the stable staff had calculated the length of the stirrup leathers to suit him perfectly. He gathered his own reins and squeezed Trafalgar's sides gently with his legs. The chestnut followed on as stately as the Lord Mayor's parade, but even in those first few strides Kidman could feel the power under him, and he grinned at the head groom, who was doing his best to keep at least one eye on both of the horses as they left the courtyard.

'Thank you Mr Daniels. I'm not going to forget this horse in a hurry. I'll tell his lordship it's an honour and I'll take care of him.' He shook his head. 'Or more likely he'll take care of me, I reckon.'

The head groom touched a finger to the peak of his hat and nodded. 'Thank you, sir. Yes he will, sir. But I'd be grateful if you'd give that madam a wide berth until she's settled down.'

27

In the middle of the night on the day that Jack and Rachel Gallagher left Warrigal, Mickey raised a corner of the canvas sacking that served as a door to the wurley he shared with his mother and three of his younger siblings, and slid out as soundlessly as a wreath of smoke.

He crouched, motionless, invisible against the dark dome of the wurley, and listened. It was a clear night and the station was sleeping in half-moonlight. Old King Harry was snoring gently in the big wurley next to his mother's, but Mickey could hear nothing to indicate that anyone else was moving outside. He rose upright gradually, checking in every direction, and then stood for several minutes making certain there was no one in the dunnies, the nearest of the whitefellas' buildings to the blackfellas' camp.

Ten minutes after emerging from the wurley, he moved silently westwards towards the yards. He was almost naked and the night air was cool, but he stopped and listened without moving a muscle every few seconds until he reached the deep shadows cast by the yards.

There were twenty or more young stockhorses under the poinsettia trees in the small holding yard, and they turned their heads to watch him as he approached. They all moved towards him simultaneously, their hoofprints soft in the deep dust, and he stopped by the rails and waited until they were still again.

In a small drafting ring off the holding yard another horse stood on its own. The moonlight picked out pale lines of dried sweat-salts on its back, along its sides and flanks, and Mickey could clearly see the raised welts left by whips and sticks. The horse was trembling slightly and favouring a hind leg with exhaustion, but the look it gave him out of the corner of its eye was ferocious and unbowed.

The horse couldn't turn its head to look at him properly because the rope headcollar it was wearing had been fastened tight to the yard rails, and its tail was lashed just as tightly by another rope to the nearest ironbark post behind it. Even from outside the yard, Mickey could see that the headcollar had made raw friction burns on the horse's head and down the cheekbone nearest him, and rope burns had left more bare patches around her fetlocks and shins, some of them caked in blood and dust, where she had been hobbled and thrown to the ground earlier that day.

Mickey had watched the breaking, or the failed breaking in this case, from his hiding place behind the poinsettia trees, barely able to contain himself. Breaking horses in the outback was rarely a gentle process, but this was unforgivably brutal, and if the Gallaghers had been on the station the boy knew that nothing like this would have been allowed.

The two younger hands had offered to take on this hard case in the afternoon while Ted and the other men broke the more subservient young horses, and Bluey Turner had joined them, keeping well out of the horse's way until it was tied down, and then gleefully wading in to kick it and even piss on it in the way that roughriders recommended a recalcitrant young horse's spirit should be broken.

Jimmy Tim and Plato had watched this from the far side of the yard for a minute or two without speaking, then Plato had looked across to Mickey's hiding place, shaken his head almost imperceptibly, and both older men had turned away. If Mickey had tried to intervene, Natty Ferguson and Lork O'Donnell would have been within their rights to half kill him, and Bluey would have taken his turn.

The horse was a young female, big and strong for a two-year-old but with a thoroughbred head and almost certainly a brumby from one of the many wild herds that bred in the safety of the bush. And the worse they treated her, the more furiously she fought them, screaming with rage and lashing out wildly until the spider's web of noosed ropes entangled her and she crashed on her side in the shit and dust.

They had abandoned her eventually, spitting at her as they went, claiming they'd showed her, the fuckin' bitch, and telling each other she'd think again after a night tied to the rails without water. And if she died, serve her fuckin' right, said Bluey as they climbed out through the rails. That'd fuckin' show her who's boss.

Mickey ducked through the lower yard rails and moved very slowly towards the mare, keeping his eyes down as Plato had taught him but conscious of her fierce one-eyed glare every step of the way.

When he was close enough to feel the heat of her body, he began whispering to her very softly and calmly in a mixture of Gudjal and the whitefellas' clumsy language, and then gently extended his hand and rested it on her shoulder. Her skin shuddered violently when he first touched her, but he kept his hand where it was, talking to her under his breath and scratching gently with his fingertips. 'I'm not going to hurt you, eh, *gudhana yarraman.* We're mates, eh. Don't bite me, sister. *Gudhana yarraman.* We're mates.' He told her very softly she was the best horse ever. She was his top horse, his gun horse. She could run quicker than any silly *gundulu* and jump higher than a big grey *yunggura.* 'We're mates, eh, *gudhana yarraman.*'

After a few minutes he felt the filly relax and she stopped shivering. He continued whispering almost inaudibly, and gradually moved his hand higher across her shoulder and up to her wither. Her skin flickered again and she laid her ears back in warning so he stopped moving. 'Hey, sister. Hey, *gudhana.* I got to get these ropes off you. Be nice, eh?'

When she settled again he moved on, sliding his hand along her back, and then cautiously over her flank. Again she laid her ears back and again he stopped and waited, murmuring to her, very slowly easing the stump of an old knife he had brought out of the old leather strap fastened round his waist.

It took him nearly ten patient minutes to move around her to the rails, holding his breath and waiting for the savage kick that could take his head off the split second he came within range, and then he sawed as gently as he could through the rope until it parted, and the mare immediately swung her hind quarters away from the rails, staggering and almost going down, and for a few seconds she fought instinctively again against the rope that held her head.

'SSShhhh. Hey, sister, don't wake 'em up now, eh?'

Mickey slid through the rails and moved fast towards her head. He could see the moonlight reflected in her eye, and a wide crescent of white as she watched him approach again. He raised a hand slowly and rested it through the rails on this other shoulder, and then as quickly as he dared he sawed through the stiff headrope. She had pulled against the slipknot with so much force it was as solid as the ironbark post, and she was still pulling away so hard as he cut that when the rope parted, this time she did go down with a muffled thump in the dust.

He held his breath until he was certain no one had woken, then he slipped between the lower rails again and walked slowly with his eyes down out into the middle of the yard in front of the mare. She had regained her feet, shakily, and watched intently with her ears locked onto him, not moving as he came up alongside her and reached up to remove the remains of the headcollar. The rope that had been cutting into the top of her head as she pulled away was bloody, and he hissed softly as he eased it away from her head, but she allowed him, even dropping her head to make it easier for him. She shook her head when it was gone, and closed her eyes.

'Let's go, *gudhana yarraman.* Don't go to sleep on me, eh? Nice and quiet now. Sssshhhh.' Mickey moved away, listening to her soft footfall as she followed him to the yard gate. He opened it enough for the mare to follow him out into the big holding yard, and he walked in front of her all the way to the next, open gateway that led out into the creek paddock.

The mare must have been desperate to drink, but she continued to follow close behind the boy as they moved further away from the yards and the homestead, until he turned slightly towards the big billabong and then at last she couldn't help herself but trotted round him and down to the waterside, splashing in up to her knees and burying her muzzle in the darkened water.

Mickey waited for several minutes while she drank, and then after she had raised her head to listen to the night sounds, he moved closer to the billabong, between the homestead and the horse, and spoke to her again. 'Go on then, sister. Off you go.'

The mare turned her head and cocked her ears at him, a coil of water running like mercury out of her mouth, splashing loudly into the rippled billabong, until he raised his hand and took a step towards her. 'Go on.' He said it louder, urging her to break away and head out south and west into the bush, and after a moment more she moved, walking at first, and then trotting as the water flowed through her body. Standing in the creek had washed her lower legs and hooves clean, and he could see the regular glint of the moonlight on her wet hooves as she trotted, even when the night shadows had absorbed the rest of her and then as she reached the trees she was off, cantering away out of reach of the whitefellas and their ropes and whips.

That's where Mickey knew that he must go too. There would be blazing hell to pay when dawn showed the yard empty. So he followed the mare's tracks southwest, walking quickly through the first, scattered trees. He was one more moon-shadow among theirs and he broke into a steady loping trot, picking his way through the turkey bush until he came to another stretch of the creek. There was a clear reflection of moon and starlight on the still surface of the water, and it caught his paler skin as he moved between the trees.

Then ahead of him a tall, thin silhouette moved into his path from behind a ghost gum, holding a sheaf of weapons in both hands.

Mickey walked up to the figure and the man held out the weapons in his left hand. Mickey helped himself to a spear, a throwing stick and a boomerang, and the two turned westwards and disappeared into the night.

28

Lord Saltwood excused himself and left the breakfast room as soon as he had finished his second cup of tea, heading inevitably to his business quarters where Prior would be waiting for him with his morning report.

Prior had disappeared along the colonnade an hour before the family came down, and had already finished the first of the three silver pots of coffee that would be brought to his lordship's offices during the morning's work.

Bel and the girls finished their breakfast in a much more relaxed atmosphere with Lady Saltwood, discussing their plans for the day. Later in the morning, they would all walk across the Park to the village, where Lady Saltwood would call on two elderly, retired servants with gifts of fruit and vegetables from the Park gardens, and eggs, cheese and butter from the home farm.

After lunch they might walk in the gardens, or the girls could play shuttlecock before tea, when Lady Saltwood's sister, Lady Whiteley, and her husband, Sir Francis, were expected to arrive.

Lady Saltwood would visit the vegetable garden now to agree the choice of vegetables and fruit they would take to the village, and would Mrs Kidman like to see the kitchen gardens, too, and perhaps the girls as well? The girls politely declined, but growing vegetables back in her own garden at Kapunda was one of Bel's passions, and she was sure from her experience of viewing other great country house gardens that Chiddington's would be well worth a visit, thank you.

It was clearly part of the order of things among those with large country houses, gardens and estates. In the autumn and winter, high-society ladies might hunt but their main function was to play hostess to shooting house-parties or attend other people's house-parties, and make admiring or sympathetic noises about how many pheasants their menfolk could blow out of the sky. In the spring and summer the women were required to parade the latest fashions and say the right things at the big showcase events of The Season, but at home in the country they put on their straw hats and their old skirts and they gardened. Or they supervised their gardeners. It seemed to be one of the few areas of life where upper-class ladies could escape the strictures of society, loosen their stays and get their hands dirty. Not that Lady Saltwood's figure looked as though she needed much help from whalebone stays, thought Bel, with a twinge of envy.

'I would be delighted if you really would like to come and see the vegetable gardens, Mrs Kidman,' said Lady Saltwood. She turned to the footman. 'Joe, would you please tell Mr Franks that Mrs Kidman and I will be with him in about ten minutes? Thank you.'

The girls were rising from the breakfast table. 'Shall we gather in the hall at eleven o'clock?' Lady Saltwood glanced at Bel. 'That will give us nearly an hour to visit the garden now and then make ready for our expedition. It is no more than a twenty-minute walk to the village, so that will give us plenty of time to spend a quarter of an hour or so each with Miss Pearson and Mrs Meades, and be back in time to change for lunch at one.'

Lady Saltwood guided Bel westwards through the house, preceded by her dog.

Bel had not been able to decipher what breed of dog it was. There was so much woolly coat that it wasn't easy to see which end was which when it was lying down. But now it was moving like a small rag rug in front of its mistress, presumably head first, claws clicking as busily as knitting needles on the stone-flagged floor of a garden room with glazed double doors that opened onto a formal garden still filled with flowers even this late in the season. It was bounded by high brick walls covered with climbing roses to the north and the east, but to the south Bel could see lawns and topiary and beyond that the parkland, and in the centre of the flowerbeds was an immaculate circle of manicured grass.

Bel and Lady Saltwood turned back from admiring the view just in time to see the woolly dog trotting across an equally immaculate gravel pathway and squatting on the grass. 'Oh No! No, Muffin! Oh dear.' Lady Saltwood sighed. 'Mr Franks will be furious with you again. I do apologise, Mrs Kidman, she is such a nuisance. The gardeners do hate it when she does this on their beautiful grass.'

She moved to stand beside the spot where the dog had relieved itself and called out, 'Mr Franks, are you there?'

'Yes I am, your leddyship,' came a disembodied reply from the far side of the west wall.

Lady Saltwood made anxious face at Bel. 'I'm so sorry Mr Franks but could you come through here, and perhaps bring a watering can with you? For Muffin...'

There was a moment's silence, then she and Bel smiled when they heard the barely muffled chuntering clearly audible over the wall. 'Glory be, that little dog... markin' the grass... oi dunno... seed it all agin oi 'spect...' Then louder, 'Right, your leddyship. Billy, come on boy, get that can filled quick sharp now. *Sharp* mind, boy.'

They heard boots on gravel, and then the scraping of a doorlatch lifting in an archway in the wall. The door was opened by an older man doing his best to mask his concern at the desecration of *his* lawn. He already held his brown Bowler hat in one hand and he knuckled his forehead to Lady Saltwood with the other. 'Good morning, your leddyship.' He knuckled again to Bel. ' Morning, ma'am.'

He moved aside to let an under-gardener through the doorway.

'Good morning, Mr Franks. Thank you so much, Billy.' Lady Saltwood pointed down at her feet and moved a couple of steps away as the younger man tugged the peak of his hat at his chatelaine and her guest and hurried awkwardly across with the watering can to dilute the concentration of caustic urine on the offending spot.

'Better safe than sorry, your leddyship, arter this dry spell.' Franks replaced his hat and moved across to peer at the patch of grass being watered. 'Terrible thing for killing the grass...' He coughed.

'It is, Mr Franks, I know,' said Lady Saltwood. 'I'm so sorry she's done it again. I do try to persuade her to choose the gravel, I really do.' The woolly dog was greeting the gardeners with tail-lashing contortions and her ingratiating grin, and when she rolled onto her back the older man bent down and rubbed her stomach gently with the back of a forefinger that had the colour and texture of a rosebush root. 'You'm a naughty little old dog, you are, but we'll let you off this once more, shall we.' He stood up and beamed at Lady Saltwood. 'No harm done, I daresay, your leddyship.'

'Thank you, Mr Franks, you are very kind, and thank you, Billy. I am sorry we've put you both to this trouble.'

She turned to Bel. 'I have tried so hard to train her not to. I'm afraid she just doesn't listen so I have to hope that Mr Franks will keep forgiving her.'

In less than twenty-four hours at Chiddington, Bel had seen enough to know that every one of the senior staff would have laid down and died for Lady Saltwood if they thought she wanted them to. She smiled at the head gardener.

'I'm sure he will, Lady Saltwood,' she said, 'I have something like the same problem with my old dog at home. He follows me around my vegetable garden when we're watering, and then he rolls in the lettuces to cool off in the heat. It drives my gardener demented, but he puts up with it very patiently.'

They moved through the door into a vegetable garden whose size, precision and fecundity brought Bel to a standstill on the brick paved path between the first two immaculate beds. The sun was high enough now to bathe the enormous, warm-walled space in light and to dazzle them with reflections from the white-framed glasshouses ranged along the whole of the south-facing northern wall. But it was the sheer variety of greenery growing in their regimented ranks that really took Bel's breath away.

'Well,' she said after a few moments taking it all in, 'what an absolutely wonderful garden, Lady Saltwood. I do love flowers, but if I had to choose between them it's the vegetables that come first for me, and this is just... well, wonderful!'

Bel Kidman was an unsentimental, down-to-earth woman not easily impressed with the works of man, and she doled out praise with Presbyterian thrift, so her sincere admiration for the Chiddington vegetable garden was obviously heartfelt. It brought another beaming smile to the head gardener's face, stretching almost as widely ear-to-ear as his chinstrap beard.

Lady Saltwood touched her guest's sleeve. 'I am so pleased you like it, but all the credit goes to Mr Franks and his men. He is very courteous and pretends to consult me, but everything that grows in our garden here grows because of him, and because he grows things so beautifully we can supply the best fruit and vegetables to everyone here on the estate, the London house and most of the village. He is a green-fingered miracle worker, summer and winter.'

By the time she had finished, the head gardener's weathered face had turned scarlet under his leathery tan and he was looking at his boots, muttering self-deprecating remarks about hardy new strains and the good weather and the quality of the manure they were fortunate to get from the stables and the stud. It consolidated Bel Kidman's early impression that Lady Saltwood was by a long stretch the best-bred woman she had met in her six months in England.

Among other things, she liked the respect that Lady Saltwood showed for her servants. She invariably addressed all the senior servants as either Mr or Mrs, and all the junior servants by their first names. Most employers of servants Bel had come across in England used the servant's last name only, and employers like Lord Saltwood used the servant's job description rather than any name at all.

Coincidentally, this subject cropped up just five minutes later as they strolled around the garden together, while another of the under-gardeners gathered a large basket of county show-quality carrots, onions, beans and some of the more exotic vegetables grown under glass for the village visit.

They had stopped to admire an intricate trellis of canes supporting rows of runner bean plants. It was a work of art in itself, and Bel was trying to fix the pattern in her mind to take home to Kapunda.

Lady Saltwood looked at her guest. 'I wonder if I could prevail on you to call me Eleanor?' She smiled rather uncertainly. 'I should be very grateful if you would. I always feel these wretched titles are horribly stiff and unfriendly...'

Bel didn't tell her hostess that behind her own pragmatic exterior she harboured a secret little daydream that one day Sid would perhaps become Sir Sidney Kidman, and she would be his Lady. Here in the Chiddington vegetable garden she felt it was a privilege to be asked to use Lady Saltwood's Christian name.

'Well, thank you, I would be honoured, and I hope you will call me Bel. It's Isobel, of course, but the only person who ever called me Isobel was my mother when she was scolding me, so Bel is much more reassuring.'

Lady Saltwood laughed. 'My mother refused to allow our names to be shortened, so I never knew when I was being told off. Hardly ever by my mother but my father was rather a stickler for following the rules and regulations. My sisters and I were expected to behave as the daughters of an earl at all times, and he insisted we were addressed accordingly. That means we were 'Ladies' in our own right, so I was 'Lady Eleanor', ever since I can remember.'

She smiled and shook her head. 'All very complicated and formal, and very silly.' The head gardener and Billy were out of earshot, and Lady Saltwood leaned towards Bel. 'Holes in the roof but appearances must be kept up. Quite ridiculous, all of it.' She looked up at the stable clock tower over the greenhouse wall. 'We must come back again when we have more time, but shall we just make a quick tour now and then we must bolt for the house. Mr Franks will have the basket taken to the stableyard. He is such a very good man. I would like you to see the Jerusalem artichokes. They are simply astonishing.'

Bel was more than happy to inspect the vegetables for another few minutes, and they moved together along the path. The woolly dog trotted in front of them, and then stopped suddenly to sniff, one back leg suspended in mid step.

It made them both smile. 'Hope springs eternal,' said Lady Saltwood. 'One day she's convinced she's going to find an old rabbit hiding in here slow enough or deaf enough for her to catch. But I don't think it will ever happen. Rats, though, that's another matter altogether. You're quite the ratter, aren't you, Rags?'

'Rags?' said Bel. 'I misheard you. I thought you called her Muffin.'

'Oh, I did. We called her Ragamuffin when she first arrived, and she answers to both Rags and Muffin, if she feels like it. Usually, I'm afraid she answers to neither.' Lady Saltwood looked at Bel. 'I'm very weak with her, I'm afraid. She was given to me by William at a very... difficult time. He found her abandoned in Windsor when he was starting school there, and he brought her home to me. Nearly ten years ago.'

She turned her head away and cleared her throat, and then turned back to Bel with a bright smile. 'We have no idea what breed she is. Several terriers and perhaps some French poodle somewhere in her family tree. What do you think? One of nature's lucky accidents. It was such a lovely thought of William's to bring her to me.'

They heard the church clock strike three quarters in the distance beyond the house.

'My goodness, that is a quarter to eleven already. I am making us late! The girls will be wondering where we are. We must hurry.'

Both women hitched up the fronts of their long skirts out of the way of their side-buttoned boots, and set off at a brisk pace back to the house.

29

Just a matter of yards away from the vegetable garden, Sid Kidman was keeping Lord Saltwood's chestnut hunter well out of kicking distance behind William's filly, not that they were in any danger while she jogged impatiently out of the yard and onto the drive leading away from the back of the house.

William thanked the groom as they passed under the arch, and the groom let go of the rein and stepped back as the filly attempted to break straight into a canter along the grass strip that ran between the curving gravel wheel-tracks.

Kidman saw William sitting apparently quite still on the young horse, but the filly moved steadily over onto the grass next to the tracks, and as she moved forwards her head came down, accepting the bit, and the Australian knew she was moving under the pressure of her rider's legs, collected between that pressure and the gentle restraint of the bit in her mouth. Kidman could see that she was playing with the bit, not fighting it, and within a few more strides she was accepting her rider's invisible control, trotting and then slowing to a walk, her neck arched, her quarters swinging in a long stride.

William appeared to be as relaxed as if he was sitting on a seaside donkey, but Kidman noticed he was watching her head and her ears in particular, catching a glimpse of her eye as her head swung slightly in the athletic rhythm of her walk.

'I'm sorry to be so unsociable,' said William, without turning his head. 'Give me another hundred yards' grace and I'll be with you. We'll go left onto the home farm lane up there ahead.'

Well before they had travelled a hundred yards they came to a point where the track forked, the main branch curving sharply to the right in an arc that would have taken the two men round to the front of the main house, the other in a shallow bend towards the stone buildings of the stud. William kept the filly moving on the verge alongside the left fork that led to the stud. For another twenty yards or more they rode in the lee of an enormous brick wall, fifteen feet high, that formed the northern boundary of the kitchen gardens, and then when they reached the corner of the wall William turned left onto a half-grassed lane that took them due west away from the stud and the church.

As he followed, Kidman could see the rectory to his right, and glimpses of the church through the churchyard trees further to the right still. To the left of the rectory he could see a row of cottages, and another hundred yards beyond them the broad spread of the stud, surrounded by its network of high-railed paddocks. He could see mares and foals in the paddocks nearest the stud buildings, and the figure of a groom standing watching them in the archway that led into the stud courtyard, a considerably grander version of the stabling behind the house. The Australian raised a hand, and after a momentary pause the groom touched a finger to his cap, puzzled by the sight of a stranger in an even stranger hat, but riding what was clearly his lordship's favourite hunter and following on behind young Master William on that wicked bitch of a bay filly.

The stud groom watched them on their way along the track, and he saw the guest in the hat break into a dignified trot that took Trafalgar carefully up alongside the filly. William had moved across onto the far side of the track to give Kidman room to ride beside him, but still keep a couple of yards of space between the chestnut and his unpredictable young mare.

'I reckon you've got her eating out of your hand there, William,' said the Australian, 'but I'll keep my distance and we'll steer clear if she gets back up on her toes.'

The young man looked across at his guest and nodded. 'Much obliged to you. She's bred to be a lady but she gets a touch of the circus in her sometimes. But if we can jolly her along in the right direction, she'll make a really high-quality hunter or maybe even a point-to-pointer. Loads of stamina, racing speed and she jumps like a stag.' Now that she had settled, the future high-quality hunter appeared to be taking a leaf out of the chestnut's book of impeccable behaviour.

'If she turns out anything like this fella, she'll be a good'un, that's for sure.' Kidman patted his horse's neck.

William nodded. 'He's about as confidential as you could get, old Trafalgar. A bit too good for me. I like 'em with a wicked streak, just to 'keep it interesting, and you don't get that in geldings very often.'

'You're right there. You can't beat a really good mare for spirit, you know. Bel and I went to the Derby with Lord Brassey and saw that mare win in the summer. Now that was something special.'

William looked at his guest more keenly. 'It was, wasn't it? Signorinetta. Italian bred. A hundred to one against, I think. I was there. Biggest upset ever. Not a single cheer for her that day except from me, but they cheered when she won the Oaks two days later. I don't think the crowd liked her beating the boys.'

Sid mentally filed that away and they rode on side by side along the straight track that led westwards to the Home Farm. On their right the lane was bordered by a beech hedge almost as high as the garden wall. 'Those are the stallion paddocks,' said William, nodding at the hedge. 'We're currently standing Agincourt, son of Crecy. My father names his racehorses after land battles and his hunters after sea battles. Preferably the names of victories over the French or Spanish. I'm not sure what comes after Agincourt, but before Trafalgar his favourite hunter was called Armada.'

On their left, for the first three hundred yards, the brick wall of the kitchen gardens and the hothouses kept pace with them. Along the final stretch where the hothouses ranged on the south side of the wall, it was punctuated every ten yards by small fireplaces whose heat would keep exotic fruit growing for the Park dining room throughout the winter. On this September morning the Indian summer was holding and the air was warm, and Kidman undid two of his three coat buttons.

When the wall ended in a right angle and turned away from the track, they could see the park stretching away south on their left over the railed fence. In the English landscape of tiny fields and frequent woodland that Sid had grown used to over the previous six months, the landscaped park at Chiddington was one of the biggest open spaces of pastureland that they had seen since leaving Adelaide. The moors of Yorkshire and Scotland that he and Bel had visited on their travels didn't count, but the English aristocracy competed with each other over the size of their parks, he'd discovered. One lord he'd met in London had apparently wiped two of his farms off the map on his estate in Cumberland – farmhouses, barns, walls, the lot – to make his park bigger than the park belonging to another lord he didn't like.

In the sunshine this morning, Lord Saltwood's park reminded him of a few places on his own stations in Victoria and New South Wales, green after rain. There was a herd of old English White Park cattle grazing in the distance, beyond the lake. The air was so clear he could distinctly make out their black noses. He wouldn't mind taking a few of those back to Australia with him.

'This is the Home Farm,' said William, and Kidman turned back to his companion. The younger man tipped his head towards the farm buildings on their right as they approached them. A short stretch of gravel and turf track led up to a big farmhouse, a row of cottages and a quadrangle of double-storey barns, all in golden stone, all immaculately tidy, the farmhouse garden picture-perfect in the autumn sun.

As they passed, Kidman could see fields behind the farmstead, beautifully hedged and railed, thick with sleek brown and white cows. 'Now these must be milkers, I suspect, William?'

William nodded again. 'Yes, this is our dairy herd,' he said after a moment. 'Ayrshires. I remember the first bull and a dozen heifers arriving from Scotland when I was just a little chap, and now we have the highest dairy yields in Oxfordshire. All our milk and butter comes from these cows.'

The cows grazing in the field nearest the lane lifted their heads and stared at the two horsemen. 'They had better keep eating,' said William. 'Lord Saltwood doesn't like it when production drops. My father runs the estate on the latest scientific principles and he likes the figures to prove he's right. We also have the highest yields of barley, oats and wool, and we're the second biggest producer of beef per acre. Tom Lavery specialises in beef cattle at Woolton and he has the edge on us there.'

They rode on for what Kidman judged was the best part of half a mile, the park on their left, and the perfect fields rising slightly upwards on their right, until they came to a wide gate in a hedge with woodland beyond it. As they approached, Kidman asked William if he should get off and open it. William shook his head. 'No, thank you. All part of the education. Perhaps you could hold hard there for a moment.'

As the Australian eased the chestnut horse to a standstill, William nudged the bay filly ahead of them and across the track. He brought her to a halt just to the left of the catch that held the gate closed, leaned forward and dislodged the catch, eased the gate ajar with his right hand and then pushed it open. It was done so quickly and smoothly that the filly had only a few seconds to stand still, and William patted her on the neck as she moved through the gateway. He walked her a few yards along the ride between the trees and turned her to face the gateway.

'If you would come on through and stand your horse just beyond us, I'll close it again. Could be a little trickier.'

Kidman walked his horse through the gate and past the filly, as William had asked, and then turned Trafalgar to watch the younger man negotiate the next part of the manoeuvre. It was indeed trickier. The filly objected to being asked to retrace her steps even those few feet, tossing her head and snatching at the bit until William insisted, and she moved reluctantly up alongside the gate with a petulant whisk of her tail. William sat still on her for a few moments, waiting for her to settle. Then he reached down with his left hand to push the gate closed and the filly immediately jumped away, swinging her backside round at right angles to the gate.

William sat still again and then turned her head gently, easing her with his leg back alongside the gate. Once again he sat still, this time for longer, and then again he leaned deliberately down and put his left hand on the top of the gate. 'That's a girl,' he said quietly as she stood this time. He pushed the gate closed, the catch bar locking into the sneck with a soft metallic clank.

William turned the filly towards Kidman and patted her on the neck again, congratulating her for being so clever. He apologised to his guest for the delay. 'She can do it perfectly well, but she's feeling her oats rather this morning. This may not last.'

Kidman shook his head. 'Looks to me as though you're making a fine job of her.' As horses so often do, the filly made a liar of him as she turned away from the gate, sidling and snatching at the bit, and William asked Kidman if he would keep Trafalgar clear of her again for a moment or two. 'We'll be out onto old grass at the top of the ride and we can stretch their legs up there, but she may just need to get this out of her system before we get there.'

As if it had been waiting for the cue, the moment he finished speaking a cock pheasant clattered loudly out of the trees a dozen yards ahead of them and the filly sprang violently sideways across the ride as though she had been peppered with shot. The moment her toes hit the ground she lunged forwards, and then in the next stride her head went down between her knees and she travelled the next twenty yards in a series of bucks so explosive Kidman swore afterwards all four hooves lifted three feet off the ground each time.

The Australian had ridden some talented bucking horses in his time, and he had watched many a stockman sailing through the air after a demonstration half as energetic as this, so he was impressed to see that William Saltwood appeared to regard the young horse's antics as a matter of relatively minor high spirits.

He must have been gripping like a leech with his legs, Kidman told the head groom later, but he didn't seem to be making any undue effort, and he gathered up the reins when they landed the third time and collected the filly as though she had simply stumbled, rather than done her best to fire him into the sky.

Lord Saltwood's hunter stood like a rock with his ears locked on the filly, unmoved by her spectacular performance.

'You big baby,' William said affectionately, and then apologetically to Kidman, 'Sorry about that. I think that should be the end of it. If you could come alongside I'm sure we'll get along without the firework display from now on.'

Sid Kidman's academic education had been patchy at the best of times and had come to a full stop the night he climbed out of his bedroom window and ran away into the bush at the age of thirteen. Even though Bel had taught her husband to read and write during their long, intermittent courtship, Sid had regarded reading as a necessary chore best left to others. But it was a line from a bush poem that sprang to mind as he watched young Saltwood riding the bay filly: '*The man from Snowy River never shifted in his seat; It was grand to see that mountain horseman ride.*'

As far as Sid was concerned, the Bard of the Bush knocked the Swan of Avon sideways, and *The Man From Snowy River* was self-evidently the greatest work of literature ever committed to paper, so he couldn't have thought of a higher compliment to pay William's horsemanship.

'You did well to sit that,' he said as Trafalgar came up alongside the filly. 'Well done.'

'Oh, I knew it was coming and she always keeps straight, so it isn't as bad as it looks.' The young man said it with a straight face but then caught Kidman's eye, and both of them laughed.

'That was plenty bad enough,' said the Australian. 'You could win a bob or two at the rodeo, my word you could.'

More importantly, he thought, if you can ride like that you might get along on a Queensland cattle station after all.

They continued along the woodland track with the mid-morning sunshine now slanting steeply through the trees on their left. The track bore to the right and began to rise, taking them to another gate beyond which they could see pasture and clear blue sky. This time Kidman asked if he could try the gate, and without being asked Trafalgar moved into the right position to allow his rider to undo the catch.

'This horse could do the whole thing on his own,' said Kidman ruefully. 'I bet he can let himself out of his paddock any time he likes.'

William laughed. 'Actually, you're right. We tie up the gate when he's out, just in case. He's a clever one but he hasn't quite worked out the knots yet, but he will.'

The hiatus in the wood had sparked a small, shrill cacophony of blackbird alarms, and two more pheasants had followed the first, cockling hysterically as they rocketed skywards. But the two men rode clear of the wood without further incident and on up to the top of the rise, and drew their horses to a standstill in almost perfect silence.

30

Two of the Kidman girls walked ahead of the pony and trap, with its two big, wicker baskets of produce from the gardens and the dairy. Lady Saltwood and Bel Kidman walked together some yards behind it along the raised track that led across the park to the village.

The three young Australians had fussed over the grey pony and begged to be allowed to drive the trap, so honours had been divided and the middle Kidman girl, Elma, was sitting very upright beside the young groom, driving sedately to the village. Gertie as the eldest would be allowed the responsiblity of guiding the pony through the village, and eighteen-year-old Edna would take the reins on the way home.

The pony and trap trundled along the track at walking pace. Gertie and Edna were pretending to chase the dog, which was racing around them, her eyes and nose shining like wet blackcurrants as her woolly coat blew away from her face.

'I'm afraid driving Pegotty won't be very exciting for them,' said Lady Saltwood, glancing at Bel. 'She must be very nearly thirty years old now and she could do this blindfold without any human help. They wanted to ride with William and Mr Kidman, I know. I'm so sorry we really don't have anything suitable for them to ride at Chiddngton now.'

'This will do them no harm at all,' said Bel. 'They do love riding at home, but they've had plenty of opportunities while we've been in England.' Bel had never quite lost the accent she took with her to Australia as a serious eight-year-old girl, and for some reason the word 'opportunities' sounded particularly Scottish. 'They've been taken riding in Hyde Park a number of times, the last time just a fortnight ago, so they're quite spoiled and they need to learn how to behave like young ladies.' She smiled at Lady Saltwood. 'I keep telling them that nice men don't want to marry tomboys in jodhpurs smelling of horses.'

Lady Saltwood laughed. 'I'm not sure that will be true of William. I think a girl who likes horses may catch his attention quicker than a demure girl with ladylike manners.'

She stopped and looked ahead. 'Dear me, that sounds a little as though I am match-making... of course I am not, but I do very much want to tell you that he really is a much nicer boy than you might think on first impressions. A nice young man, I mean.' Then she looked at Bel again, and Bel was surprised to see a look of entreaty on her hostess's face. 'I would like to plead his case to you, Bel, if you would let me. So you understand him a little better and see him in a true light. I am sure you know of the plan my husband has put to Mr Kidman, to take William out to Australia with you and help him restore the property we own...' She tailed off.

Bel hesitated a moment, remembering what she had said to Sid the previous evening. She felt slightly flushed and trod carefully. 'Yes I do. Sidney told me something about it. He told me it was Lord Saltwood who suggested it. I gathered it was quite a new idea?' She hoped Lady Saltwood might take the opportunity to give her views on this enterprise.

'Oh yes,' replied Lady Saltwood immediately. 'Or, rather, no. I mean, the idea that William should go out and restore Milbourne Downs is not new. Lord Saltwood has been thinking for some time of sending him out when he finished his studies at Oxford, but the idea that he should go to Australia with you now, or when you return, that has come about very recently. Within the last day or two.' They had been walking on side by side across the park so that the others did not get too far ahead, but Lady Saltwood stopped again and turned towards Bel.

'It has all come about in a rush, because William has been sent down from Oxford, and my husband believes it would be best for him to go away and do something useful as soon as possible, and of course I agree... wholeheartedly...' She tailed off again and they walked on.

To Bel it wasn't at all clear that Lady Saltwood was wholeheartedly behind this plan, and she was certain it would make no difference whatsoever to Lord Saltwood whether his wife agreed or not.

'My husband says this is too good a coincidence to miss, although we wish the circumstances were different, of course, and now I have met you and Mr Kidman I hope you won't mind if I tell you how relieved I would be to know that he was in your care. He would have the best chance of making a success of things, with your help.'

Again she stopped and turned towards her guest. 'I mean to say, under your eye. I don't mean to burden you. I know William may sometimes give the wrong impression, but he has a very good heart and I am certain he would make a success of himself under Mr Kidman's guidance.'

They were approaching the far side of the park, and the roofs of the village of Chiddington were coming into view behind the great oak trees that stood sentinel along the park's high stone wall. The track led to a pillared gateway whose wrought iron gates were closed, and as the pony and trap came to a halt the young groom jumped down and ran to pull them open.

'Here we are,' said Lady Saltwood as they caught up with the girls. 'Thank you, John,' to the groom, who was standing by the grey pony's head, pushing her nose surreptitiously away from the piece of carrot hidden in his pocket. 'Well done, Elma. Beautifully done. Now I think it is Gertrude's turn to drive through the village. We're going right up to the far end first, and then you will need to turn Pegotty round and we'll come back to call on Mrs Meades, over there in the cottage next to the post office on the other side.'

She turned to Bel again. 'We'll visit Miss Pearson first. She was the second housekeeper at the house when Lord Saltwood and I came here nearly thirty years ago, and she must be eighty now, and very hard of hearing, so that will take longer than Mrs Meades. I like to make sure she doesn't feel I'm hurrying, but on the other hand we don't want to tire her.'

The three sisters walked to the village green and sat under the chestnut tree that stood in the centre, while Bel went into the tiny cottage with Lady Saltwood up at the top end of the village street.

The old housekeeper was as near stone deaf as made no difference, and conversation was carried out mostly by lip-reading on the old lady's part, with several repetitions and corrections, while the next-door neighbour, who looked after the old lady, squeezed her bulk with a lot of apologetic huffing and puffing past the two visitors into the small, single downstairs room that clearly served as Miss Pearson's living room and bedroom, to boil the kettle on the range for the obligatory cup of tea.

Lady Saltwood went across to the old lady, who had struggled to her feet when they entered, took her hand and helped her lower herself back into her wing-back chair. Then she introduced Bel, with the old servant watching her lips carefully and nodding.

'Mrs Edmond? How do you do. Please forgive me for not standing to welcome you.' Although her dentures interfered somewhat with her pronunciation, her voice was surprisingly unaffected by age, and her eyes were still clear.

'Mrs *Kidman*,' Lady Saltwood enunciated slowly. 'Mrs Kidman is from Australia.'

Miss Pearson lip-read Austria but understood the second time and was suitably impressed, and then the conversation slipped by more easily as they moved on to familiar ground. She was well, thank you, excepting the obvious ailments and failings of old age, although she was finding sleep difficult in this warm weather.

That wasn't surprising. The day was hot enough as it was, but the fire in the range made the room unbearably stuffy and the front door and the window looking out onto the green had been firmly shut.

Bel noticed that Mrs Porteous, the neighbour, was surreptitiously wiping beads of perspiration from her face with a drying cloth as she made the tea, but she couldn't wipe when she reached the final stage of pouring from the brown teapot, one hand on the handle and the other holding the lid in place, and several drops of sweat escaped from the end of her nose and landed with audible *plips* in the teacups.

Lady Saltwood had also noticed, and asked the neighbour if she would be very kind and pop out to check that all was well with the girls and the groom, and perhaps leave the door open if Miss Pearson didn't mind.

Mrs Porteous didn't wait to find out if Miss Pearson minded or not. She shot the visitors a look of intense relief and gratitude and squeezed herself out as fast as she could.

'This is very kind of you, Miss Pearson. This is just what I need after our walk across the park, thank you.' Lady Saltwood sat perched on one wheelback chair and sipped her slightly salty tea as though it was nectar, and Bel perched on the other, smiling whenever Miss Pearson looked at her and summoning the resolution to drink hers.

Fortunately, the old lady's cup of tea had been placed on a side table next to her chair, because two minutes after the large, hot neighbour's exit had lowered the temperature in the front room just enough to stop the ladies melting, Lady Saltwood's woolly dog scuttled into the house, weaved through the crowded room and hurled itself into the old lady's lap.

Miss Pearson was delighted to see the dog, and laughed as her hands and face were licked thoroughly, and then the dog rolled onto her back and invited the old lady to stroke her stomach.

Miss Pearson stroked the stomach and crooned endearments to the dog, and then she looked up at Lady Saltwood and smiled and said, 'It does my heart good to see her, your ladyship. Dear little Rags. Dear soul. So sad. So sad.'

Five minutes later they took their leave from the old lady and walked out into the sunshine. Mrs Porteous was waiting anxiously at the gate that separated the tiny front garden from the unpaved street, with her big, rough hands clasped anxiously in front of her. The girls and Philippa waved from the chestnut tree and stood up.

'Thank you so much, Mrs Porteous, you are looking after Miss Pearson so kindly, and she looks so well.'

The woman's broad, red face split into an enormous smile, and she bobbed her head. 'Thank'ee y'leddyship. She'm gettin' along pretty well fer that age, and she does live for yer visits, y'leddyship.'

'Well, you are making her life very comfortable and I'm very grateful to you for your care. John will bring in the basket now for you to unpack. You must tell me if there is anything else you need, and if you have enough money... There is some cheese and butter for you and Mr Porteous from the dairy. How is he, and the children?'

Mrs Porteous bobbed again and assured Lady Saltwood that they were all blooming, except for her husband's rheumatics in his hands and knees, all her eight grown children doing well and many of them breeding grandchildren. It had been a grand autumn, so far.

They stood aside as the groom hefted the big provisions basket past them and into the cottage, and Lady Saltwood smiled. 'There. We mustn't keep you, Mrs Porteous, and I will look forward to seeing you and Miss Pearson in a fortnight's time, if that's convenient?'

Of course it was a regular red letter day in Miss Pearson's calendar, so the neighbourly Mrs Porteous bobbed one more time and excused herself, and Lady Saltwood and Bel were free to move away.

Lady Saltwood fanned herself with her hand and glanced behind her to make sure they were out of earshot. 'Thank you for bearing with that. The heat... and the tea...' She closed her eyes. 'Oh dear, the tea, did you notice poor Mrs Porteous...?'

'I'm afraid I did,' replied Bel, 'but I wasn't as strong as you and I only pretended to drink mine.'

Lady Saltwood leaned closer and put her hand on Bel's arm. 'So did I! Isn't that awful! I generally manage to drink some of it, but today...' They both giggled. 'They are so kind, but if I drank all the tea I am given I would drown, and one has to be so careful how much tea one drinks out and about anyway.'

Bel knew exactly what Lady Saltwood was referring to. The dreadful plight of an Edwardian lady needing to powder her nose in a house with only an outside lavatory, or worse still, no lavatory at all.

The girls were approaching across the village green. 'What are you laughing at, Mama?' asked Gertrude.

Bel pulled herself together and avoided looking in Lady Saltwood's direction. 'Nothing, my dear. Lady Saltwood and I were just talking about some of the many things that women have to plan for in this world that men don't. Anyway, we must go or we shall be late. Hurry along and turn the trap round, Gertie. Look, the dear old pony hasn't moved a muscle.'

All attention shifted to the grey pony, who was standing motionless where the groom had left it, unattended, its head low, dozing in the sun.

'Would you bring her down to the trough, Gertie?' asked Lady Saltwood. 'Let's see if she would like a drink too. They do drink more as they grow older, don't they? There look, next to the pump at the corner of the green.'

The groom had emerged from Miss Pearson's cottage with the empty basket, and after he had deposited it next to the second, full basket in the back of the trap, Gertie clicked the pony forward a couple of steps and then turned it easily in the broad street. 'Good girl,' she told her, and then steered her back along the side of the green to the pump and trough.

The pony did want a drink and while she buried her nose in the trough and noisily sucked up a good half gallon of Berkshire spring water, Lady Saltwood and Bel walked to the memorial stone that stood in a niche cut into the foot of the green, just a few yards from the trough.

Like everything in the village, it struck Bel that the memorial was not very old, and she saw that it must have been erected only within the past few years because the plaque fixed to the face of the stone obelisk commemorated the local men who had died in what Bel regarded as the disgraceful wars Great Britain had waged against the Boer farmers in South Africa.

To The Greater Glory Of God
And In Honour Of Those
Who Laid Down Their
Lives For Their Country
In Two South African Wars
Far From Their Homes
1880-1881
1899-1902

There had been some difficulty in choosing the right wording for the memorial, said Lady Saltwood. 'It caused the most awful ructions because the old Queen had died in the middle of the second war with the Boers, so they couldn't say, '*...laid down their lives for their queen and country...*' because those who died in the last year of the second war had actually laid down their lives for their king and country. There was a very heated debate.'

The Parish council had spent weeks arguing over the best way of covering this and had eventually put forward what they thought was a dignified and even poetic solution that the seven men from the parish had, '*...given their lives for their Queen, their King and their Country'*.

As Lord Saltwood had accepted his seigneural duty to make up half of the public subscription to pay for the memorial, he assumed the right to have the final say, and his lordship had decided the monarchy should be left out altogether.

'I'm afraid my husband has very little respect or affection for either the old queen or the present king,' said Lady Saltwood. 'He thinks it isn't the kings and queens who have made us great and built the

Empire. It is men like him and Mr Kidman who have the enterprise to conquer the world with trade and commerce, and the generals and admirals win battles to maintain our trading supremacy.' She sighed. 'It is a rather prosaic view and he's right, of course, but I wish we didn't have to fight so many wars.'

Edward Colleyer, aged 22, and Thomas Brightwell, aged 24, had given their lives as Yeomanry troopers in the first Boer War. Lady Saltwood pointed to their names at the top of the memorial. 'They went away to the war in the year I was married, so I hardly knew them at all, but they were a part of the estate family. Thomas was uncle to Harold Brightwell, our under-chauffeur, who drove you to the house from the Halt yesterday. A lovely young man, full of promise, and Edward Colleyer was a cousin of his, just like him. He was whipper-in to the Woolton hounds. Edward worked on the estate, and Edward's mother was a milkmaid with Mary Porteous and her husband Dick was the cowman, and they were also just married when Lord Saltwood and I first came to Chiddington.'

She sighed. 'Such a terrible waste, isn't it? I count myself very fortunate that the boys were too young to fight in Africa, and I pray we won't see another war in our lifetimes.' Bel imagined what her own small boy might be doing that moment up in London and agreed wholeheartedly. Walter was just nine, as good-natured and enthusiastic as his father. In nine more years he would be old enough to be a soldier.

Of the five other names of men killed in the more recent, second Boer War, four were from families who still worked in the house or on the estate, said Lady Saltwood. They had joined the local Yeomanry and died in the fly-infested veldt thousands of miles from this green and pleasant land.

The final name was an older man from the village who had run away down to Portsmouth and joined the navy between the two wars to avoid marrying the girl he had made pregnant. Like four of the seven men, he had died of disease rather then enemy action, but in his case the past had caught up with him with a vengeance, and he had died from a septic mosquito bite inflicted on his genitals in a Cape Town brothel.

Lady Saltwood was not aware of those sordid details, so she and

Bel silently and separately said a brief prayer for all the fallen, and moved on down the village to visit Mrs Meades.

On the way, they were passed by another pony and trap heading in the other direction and driven, Lady Saltwood told Bel as his back view dwindled up the street, by the Methodist preacher whose chapel stood just outside the village on the lane to the Halt. He had acknowledged the two women with a nod but no smile. 'Mr Shaw is very fierce and he does not approve of the 'decadent aristocracy' any more than he approves of strong drink or loose women. What a ludicrous expression that is, don't you think? He makes very good furniture. I have tried to talk to him, but he avoids me. Here we are.'

Without any bidding, the grey pony had come to a halt outside another small cottage in a terrace on the shaded north side of the street. 'Would you like to come in and meet Mrs Meades?' Lady Saltwood asked Bel as they walked towards it. 'Or would you prefer to avoid the tea? We won't be here for quite as long.'

Bel was very happy to support her hostess, and they stopped in front of three small girls in smocks who had been standing shyly outside the front door waiting for the visitors from the big house to visit their grandmother. They all curtsied with varying degrees of success to Lady Saltwood, and she bent down to greet them each by name in order of size and seniority. 'Hello Liza. Hello Charley. Hello Jo. How nice you are all looking. Are you all well and being good?'

They all nodded emphatically, and the smallest girl, a stocky body of about three, produced something from the pocket of her smock and offered it up on a grubby palm for Lady Saltwood to look at.

It was a shapeless piece of cooked pastry with a smear of something that might be jam on it. The little girl wiped her nose on the other sleeve of her smock and squinted up at Lady Saltwood.

'I made it.' The two other girls looked horrified and the middle one tried to snatch the pastry object out of her little sister's hand.

'No, no, please don't spoil it, Charley. That's very nice, Jo. Why don't we go in and show it to your grandmother.'

Just over ten minutes later the expected questions had been asked and answered, the basket delivered, the tea sipped and they were back on the main street and the entourage moved off again towards the park gates, past the post office and the Duke of Wellington public house, whose landlord came to the door to salute the big-house party, and on past the bakery.

More people were visible on the street than had been when they had arrived, standing outside their homes to pay respects to Lady Saltwood, and she greeted them all by name and hoped they and their families were very well. A growing scrum of children followed them to the gates. As they waited for them to be opened, Lady Saltwood produced a shilling, and there was a murmur as she held the coin out to the tallest child.

'Here you are, Liza. That should be enough for an iced bun for everyone.'

There was a ragged chorus of thank'ees and leddyships and then the children turned and raced back to the bakery.

Lady Saltwood looked at Bel and smiled. 'I'm afraid it probably all seems very feudal, but I do hope we're doing a little bit of good. We have so much and they have so little... Now, are we all ready?' She looked around her. 'Oh dear. Where is that dog? Does anyone know where that wretched dog has got to?'

31

Foley back-handed the young black girl so hard she dropped to the hard earthen floor of the bark hut, half stunned. The big whitefella swallowed the remains of the rum in his tin cup and placed it carefully on the arm of his squatter's chair.

The girl moaned as he pulled her to her feet and he tutted at her feeble effort to fend him off. 'You've only yourself to blame. Behave yourself now.'

Then she wrenched herself free of his grip and he lunged after her clumsily as she scrambled sideways along the hut wall. She was over his truckle bed and out of reach, and before he could catch hold of her again she pulled open the flimsy door and disappeared into the dark.

The big white man was breathing heavily and sweating profusely in the humid Queensland night, so he stopped to pick up his half-full bottle of rum and sucked down a quarter of it before he followed the girl outside.

There was a deadly stillness among the wurleys, and the two old men hunkered just within the firelight shrank away, averting their eyes.

Foley could hear the girl crying in one of the nearer wurleys, and he weaved round the fire towards it. As he passed the oldest of the men, he stopped and made a gesture to him to get up, and then when the grey-haired elder rose warily to his feet the big whitefella grabbed a handful of the old man's beard and jerked him up onto his toes.

'I'd bet you want her yourself, don't you? Well now, I'm going to have her, Grandad, and you can listen but there's nothin' you can do to stop me, is there? You miserable old sinner.'

The big whitefella's voice was educated and soft, almost womanly.

Foley threw the old man backwards into the dark dust and wiped his hand on his own filthy trousers. He took another few steps, heavy and deliberate, and stopped in front of the wurley where he knew the girl was hiding. 'Come on. Out you come. I'm not going to hurt you.' He kicked the bent bough that framed the wurley's entrance.

There was a wail from inside the wurley, hushed by another voice, and Foley tutted again. He took another swig from the bottle he was holding in his left hand, and bent down slowly to rap his knuckles on the frame.

'Oh, come on out, little flower of Jessie.' He half sang the words in a parody of plain chant. He waggled the bottle. 'Come and see what your uncle Foley's got for you.' When the girl failed to appear he fumbled for the sacking that covered the doorway and ripped it away. 'Get your lovely little black arse out here, little girl,' he chanted, 'or I'll come in and you'll be sorry, so you will, and your mother too, God help you, which he won't.'

The girl's mother emerged first, bent double in the low doorway. Her face was slobbered with tears and she rubbed the hem of her tattered dress across her face as she stood upright, and tried to smile. She pleaded with Foley to take her instead, as he had many times since he had arrived on the deserted Berrie Berrie outstation almost a year before, but the white devil-man just swept her sideways without looking at her, staring instead at the young girl, who crawled out of the wurley on all fours, her eyes fixed in terror on her mother.

'Give us this day...' said Foley. 'Come here and be good, Jessie.' He took another long pull at the bottle, and then held out his free hand. 'Come on here. I'll teach you a few tricks and you'll be grand.'

The girl crouched motionless, out of reach, still staring imploringly at her mother, who moved forward again, begging the whitefella to leave her daughter alone.

'She not a woman, boss. She no good.' She clasped Foley's free hand in both of hers.

Foley stared down at her until she let go and shrank back. 'There now, let's be civilised, shall we? Get up, girl.'

The girl hesitated but when her mother remained silent, weeping again, she stood upright. She took a step towards her mother and Foley caught her by the wrist and tucked under his arm as easily as if she was a new-born poddy calf.

He walked slowly back to the bark hut and pushed the door closed behind them with his big backside. He stood the girl on her feet and tore her threadbare dress off with one hand.

'Glory be...' The big whitefella cocked his head, listening, and they both heard the high keening outside.

32

From their vantage point, Sid and William could see for miles across the countryside, a panorama of rural England laid out at their feet in perfect early autumn late morning sunlight.

Pasture fields patterned with white sheep and dark cattle, cornfields pale gold with crops ready for harvest or paler where the reapers had already taken the wheat. An English idyll chequered with neat hedges, dotted with pale cream stone farm buildings, and the dark green of woodland everywhere touched with the first hints of autumn red and gold.

It was so still they could hear the voice of an unseen farmer calling his dog somewhere in the far distance, the sound floating to the edge of their hearing so tiny and remote it might have come from another country.

The movement of a well-grown lamb running to its mother three fields away caught their attention before they heard its high-pitched bleat, and the mother's low, gurgling reply.

Kidman realised that William was concentrating on something in the middle distance in front of them, and both the horses had stiffened suddenly and cocked their ears. The young man half turned to the Australian and grinned. 'Did you hear that?'

'I heard a fella calling a while ago?'

'No, not that.' William held up a forefinger. 'There it is.'

Sid listened intently for a couple of seconds, and then he heard it. 'Geese?'

'Geese?' William stared at him blankly for a moment and then laughed and shook his head. 'I see what you mean but no, that's hounds speaking. They've found.'

Both horses were riveted to a point in the distance, and the filly started shivering with excitement. 'I hoped we might get a look at them. Not too close, but you can see a lot of country from up here.'

He pointed his whip. 'Do you see the covert... the wood... there, with the three big fir trees sticking out of it? Norfolk pines.'

Kidman followed the direction of the whip. 'Yes!' he said. 'I've got them.'

'That's the Three Sisters. They must be drawing that now. I'm sorry, that won't mean anything to you. I mean that's one of the places they're cubhunting this morning.'

This didn't mean much to the Australian either, but explanations would have to wait. 'Look,' said William urgently. 'They're away.' He pointed his whip between the filly's pricked ears, where a flickering of pale shapes showed against the dark background of the wood.

As Sid's eyes adjusted, the shapes moved out of the shadow into sunlight and became a stream of hounds, cream and tan and black, flowing over the corner of the wood's boundary wall and running east along a hedgeline.

A horseman followed the hounds over the wall out of the wood, conspicuous in a red coat, cantering wide of the hounds, half a field behind them. As they watched, they saw him raise a hand to his face and a moment later heard the sound of a horn.

'That's the huntsman, Joe Wroxall,' said William before Kidman could ask. 'He's blowing *Gone Away*, so Lavery must have told him to let hounds hunt this one.'

Having stood rigidly for at least two long minutes while this scene unfurled in front of them, the filly boiled over with excitement at this point, snatching at her bit, doing her damnedest to escape William's restraint and join the action she could see below them.

William collected her and soothed her and she froze again, her ears and eyes locking onto a second red-coated figure on a grey horse that appeared from behind the wood, galloping in pursuit of the hounds and the huntsman, and then some moments later a scattering of mounted followers, with one more red coat among black and tweed.

Even at that distance in the clear morning air the two watchers could hear the faint drumming of hooves, and see three of the field were women riding sidesaddle. 'The grey horse is the Master, Tom Lavery,' said William. 'You'll meet him this evening.'

The hounds had disappeared over or through the next hedge, and Kidman was intrigued to see the huntsman gallop towards it and sail effortlessly over and into the field beyond it.

The sheep that had been spread across this pasture field, grazing in the morning sunshine, raced in a tight, panic-stricken mob in the opposite direction. The Australian turned back and watched Lavery clear the hedge just as easily on his grey horse, and then the followers approaching, the leaders spreading out to tackle the obstacle in a line of four horses, one of them a side-saddle rider, and the remainder slowing, jumping more carefully or awkwardly, several more ladies riding side-saddle, and one horse veering away down the hedgeline towards an open gate.

Although William had his hands full controlling the sweating filly, he snorted derisively. 'That's Colonel Farrowby. Never take a fence alongside the Colonel. He looks as though he's going to jump right up to the last stride and then he'll carry you out and damn your eyes while he does it.'

Sid counted forty-three horses as they disappeared over the next hedge, the Colonel finally fading into the landscape, cutting diagonally across the field at a ponderous canter.

The hounds had long since passed out of sight and hearing, so the dwindling drumming of the Colonel's hooves was the last the watchers heard of the Chiddington Vale Hunt that morning. William sat on the filly for two or three minutes more, watching the empty landscape in case the fox circled home again. If it was a cub it might, he explained to his guest, but it may have been a travelling dog fox and he would head for the horizon.

'Well, that was a sight,' said Kidman. 'It looks like a lot of fun. I like the idea of jumping these hedges.'

William turned back towards his guest. 'You must come hunting with us. If Lord Saltwood would put you up on Trafalgar you could jump as many hedges as you like, I guarantee it. It's the best test of horse and rider in the world, Mr Kidman, on a good scenting day.'

Sid Kidman had been in England long enough to understand that die-hard foxhunters were as deeply single-minded about their sport as religious fanatics, and just as dogmatic.

No doubt the foxes took it pretty seriously, too, he thought.

He would like to know more about how it worked, but before he could ask his usual stream of questions, William turned away towards the countryside spreading away north and east and west from their vantage point. 'Well, there we are then, we've seen the hunt in action, but I'm supposed to be showing you the estate, so we must give you a proper guided tour.'

William pointed over the filly's ears at a church spire rising above a considerable village about a mile to the east of the Three Sisters wood, almost directly in front of them. 'That's Somersby Magna. We stop just this side of the village.' He swung the whip in an arc towards the northwest and pointed to the crenellations of another, smaller church tower in the centre of a cluster of roofs. 'And that's Somersby Parva. Everything between here and those two points is part of the estate. The rest of it lies on the other side, east of the Park.'

Sid gazed across the landscape, picking out the curving glint of a river to the right of the spire, and a body of silver water away in the distance. 'Nine thousand acres? If I remember rightly, that's what Brightwell told me yesterday. Is that about right?'

William looked across at him. 'Yes, just over nine thousand. It's a very large estate for this part of the world but I daresay it seems rather on the small side compared to your stations. I've been meaning to ask you, why do you call them stations?'

Kidman had been absorbed in the view, but he looked across at the younger man sitting on his bay filly. The sweat on her neck was drying, leaving a faint line of salt. He raised his eyebrows and blew through his moustache. 'Well, that's a very good question. I don't reckon I've ever considered it. It's the homesteads they used to call stations a while back, maybe because they were the only places on the tracks between them, but we just call the whole property a station now. I can't say more than that. I'll have to ask Wally Will. He'll know. That's Bel's... my wife's brother-in-law back in Adelaide. He runs the business side of things for me.'

'Are they all enormous?' asked William.

'Not all of them, no. They vary a lot depending on how much grazing and water they have. But out in the dry where you need a lot of room there are plenty of stations that run to more than a million acres and quite a few a sight more than that. I reckon the biggest station I have an interest in runs to about fifteen thousand square miles. That's about ten million acres or thereabouts.'

William whistled softly. 'Good lord. So you could fit Chiddington Park into that one about a thousand times over?'

'Yes, but on most of my places you'd need a thousand acres of grazing to match one acre of this.' Sid waved a hand in front of him and turned in his saddle to look more directly at the younger man.

'I've been to a few famous spreads in England, but this is as good as it gets. I reckon you won first prize growing up here, William.' He remembered Lord Saltwood's request the day before. 'Mind you, Lady Saltwood's got a pretty nice spread there in Queensland too. Milbourne Downs is a good size. Nigh on a thousand square miles there, well over half a million acres. Could be a top property too, with a bit of proper management.'

William turned the mare slightly. 'I thought it was abandoned?'

'Well, it isn't what you'd call in top condition just now,' said Sid carefully. 'But nothing a bit of effort and investment couldn't put right in a couple of years.'

William's attention had turned to the horses. 'I think we should move on, if you don't mind. Don't want the horses getting cold.'

Sid turned parallel to William's filly, and the two began to move along the gentle ridge, the vale on their right and the sun filtering through the woods over their left shoulders.

The Australian glanced sideways. 'I think you might like it,' he said casually. 'Some of the best horses in Queensland used to come from Milbourne Downs, twenty or thirty years ago. Thoroughbreds. Some of the best racehorses in Australia were bred at Milbourne.' He smiled at William. 'You should come and have a look.'

William raised his eyebrows. 'One of these days perhaps, but I don't think Australia is for me just now.'

It occurred to Sid that he would like to be a fly on the wall when William discovered what his father was planning for his younger son, but he tried another tack that might help the young man to take a more positive view.

'Well, Australia's a great country and a great place for a man to find his own way and make something of himself, you know. It might be in your blood too, William. Follow in your grandfather's footsteps. It's a wonderful place to make yourself a life and maybe a fortune. Stand on your own two feet.'

He was looking ahead as he spoke, so he didn't see the change in William Saltwood's expression.

When he did look across at the young man riding beside him, for a second he saw on his face the same barely concealed contempt that he had encountered a hundred times before during the six months he had been in England.

Normally it was a patronising expression of cast-iron aristocratic superiority, but in this instance there was anger and something else even hotter in young Saltwood's eyes. Then his host recovered his manners and the look was gone, but so was the growing openness that Sid had felt was developing between them.

'This is a good place to open up,' said William politely.

'Shall we canter on?'

33

As the village party cast their search wider for the missing dog, they heard a high-pitched yell and looked back towards the village to see a boy trotting back from the bakery with it struggling in his arms.

'Oh thank you, Gilbert, that's so helpful. She does love being with you children, doesn't she?'

The boy put the dog down and pushed it towards Lady Saltwood, then grinned, revealing a wide gap where his front teeth should be. 'He came in the bakery'm. He wantph one o' vey bunve.' He was backing away as he spoke, and then he turned and sped away again to the bakery to claim his own bun, his hobnailed boots crunching up the stony street.

Lady Saltwood called the dog, who rushed towards her, swerved past and shot into the park in pursuit of the girls.

'She must be at least ten now,' said Lady Saltwood, 'but she doesn't seem to have slowed down for a moment. I do find the country way of ignoring gender quite mystifying. Every animal seems to be a 'he'. Cows, ewes, mares, Pegotty, Rags, they're all 'he' to the village children. But ships and machines and motorcars are all 'she'. Do they do that in Australia?'

'I don't think I've come across that at home,' said Bel. 'They all seem to like her very much, though.'

They walked on behind the pony and trap, now driven by Edna, the youngest, who was chatting to the hitherto speechless young groom. The dog was still dashing to and fro, turning on a sixpence to smell something fascinating, rushing on, making the girls laugh.

'Everyone loves her and spoils her and she adores young people especially,' said Lady Saltwood. 'I find it very moving that she trusts people so completely, despite the horrible beginning she had. When William found her she was skin and bone, and she had a piece of knotted twine embedded in her back leg. She was only very young, but we think she had managed to chew through the twine and escape. It was near the end of William's first year at Eton, and he left school to bring her to Chiddington for me. He got into awful trouble for it.'

Lady Saltwood lifted a hand as the church clock struck a quarter hour after twelve. 'The tyranny of the all-powerful clock. We march to a strict timetable at Chiddington, I'm afraid. I do hope Mr Kidman and William have enjoyed their ride, but William must be sure they will be back in time.'

'I hope he is,' said Bel. 'My husband loses all sense of time when he's on a horse.'

Lady Saltwood smiled at Bel again. 'William knows how important punctuality is to Lord Saltwood.' Her smile disappeared. 'Although he doesn't always behave as his father would like. He has a tendency to rebel against... well, against what he regards as unfair authority, so I'm afraid he locks horns with his father rather too often, and I know he had a turbulent time at school.'

The midday sun had finally got the better of the dog and the girls. The dog sprawled in a clump of grass, tongue lolling, its back legs splayed out behind it. The girls were fanning themselves with their hands.

'Poor boy. I think it went rather badly for him after he ran away to bring me Rags, but Lord Saltwood insisted he must go back and stay the course. It was not very long after his sister... after my daughter died,' said Lady Saltwood quietly. 'He adored her, and he thought having Rags to look after would help me. And he was right.'

Bel was lost for words for a moment, but then as she realised the implications of what Lady Saltwood had just told her she felt an immense wave of sympathy for her hostess. 'I'm so sorry. That must have been very hard for you.'

Lady Saltwood laughed rather shakily. 'I do beg your pardon. It was ten years ago and one must not talk about these things. So many other mothers lost children to consumption at that time, here in the village and on the estate. But life goes onwards and so must we.'

Bel shook her head. 'We cannot ever forget them, though, can we? I lost my first boy in ninety-five and my fourth girl ten years ago. Norman was fifteen months and Edie was three years old.'

Lady Saltwood stopped and turned to her guest. 'Oh! How terrible for you. Eighteen ninety-eight. The same year... But you lost two... How truly terrible. I am so sorry I mentioned this. It is the mother's lot, isn't it?' Her eyes filled with tears. 'Almost unbearable.'

The two women stood in silence and looked at each other for a few moments, understanding completely the pain of love and loss across all the many differences that divided them, and then Lady Saltwood summoned up her reserves of self-control and convention. 'My dear Bel, we must catch up with the girls.'

She put her hand on Bel's forearm. 'We are so lucky we have them to live for. Your girls and your son. My two boys. Lord Saltwood says we must never look backwards, but you are right. I think of Marianna every hour of every day and I will always have her with me...' she patted the pale cream lace over her heart, '...and I am sure Norman and Edie will be with you wherever you are, all your days.'

She gave Bel a rather lopsided smile and they both turned back towards the big house, following the pony and trap and the two young women now strolling companionably behind it with the woolly dog.

34

When Charlie drove into the White Horse stable yard at the end of his final route on the Saturday evening, Ted Gilroy was standing framed in the office doorway, clutching a copy of the *Daily Mail*.

He waved the paper at Charlie as the empty bus rumbled to a standstill on the cobbles, and as soon as the young driver climbed down from his seat, Gilroy called across the yard to him. 'Come in here and see this, Charlie boy, soon as you're ready.'

Sandy Wallis, Charlie's conductor, followed Gilroy into the building to check his satchel of takings and his ticket dispenser into the big cast-iron safe, and then called good night as he strode away across the yard on his hurried way home.

Before he jumped down from the bus, Charlie stowed his oilskin apron under the driving seat and dropped his whip onto the upper deck floor so it wouldn't catch on the shed roof. He checked all his day's horses, asked Davey to mark a couple of loose shoes for the farrier to tighten in the morning, patted Samson on the backside, and made his own way across the yard to the drivers' room.

Even though the fire was dying, the old man was standing with his back to it and his coattails raised to warm a large expanse of well-worn corduroy breeches. He waved the *Mail* at Charlie again, and then thrust it and a large, chipped magnifying glass into his hands as soon as the young driver was close enough.

'Take a gander at this.' Gilroy tapped a thick forefinger on the front page. 'I told you something would turn up, and blow me if Frosty didn't show me this when he came in this afternoon.'

Charlie took hold of the paper and read the headline, making it out slowly to himself first and then aloud. '*Cattle King Offers Omnibus Drivers New Life In Australia.*' He started reading the story, following the dense black type haltingly with his own forefinger, and then stopped abruptly and pulled out the calling card that had been sitting forgotten in his greatcoat pocket.

'Sidney Kidman! Bloody hell, Ted, I think that was the gent on my bus this last Thursday! He gave me this card. Look here.' He offered it to Gilroy, who held it as far away from his face as he could stretch and peered at the name. Charlie handed back the magnifying glass and Gilroy's hedgerow eyebrows rose an inch as he read it. 'Well I'll be damned,' he said. 'You already met him? That's fate, my boy.'

'He climbed up behind me at the Aldgate stop and started asking questions,' said Charlie. 'Big, friendly cove with a funny way of talking. South Australia, look, on the card. Christ. This is a turn-up.'

Charlie read the rest of the story and looked up at Gilroy, who was nodding gleefully like an old magician who had just rediscovered the knack of pulling a rabbit out of a hat.

'There you go my boy,' he said. 'Just the ticket for you and Tilly. Look...' Gilroy grabbed the edge of the paper and pulled it towards him, stabbing it emphatically with the now crumpled calling card. 'Biggest landowner in the world, it says. Thirty of these damn great cattle and sheep places, Charlie. Horses, coaching business, horse sales, the lot.'

According to the report, Sidney Kidman Esq of Kapunda, South Australia, the self-made largest private landowner in the world, currently visiting England with his wife and family, was offering the horse bus drivers of London jobs on his properties in Australia. Any horse bus driver that wanted a job was guaranteed it, with their passage paid.

Mr Kidman was quoted as saying that he had travelled all over London on the omnibuses, and he greatly admired the way the drivers handled their horses in such difficult circumstances. There was a great need in Australia for British-born men of their character and quality, said the Cattle King, and he would be glad to offer any and all of them a new life working for him.

'That's what he said to me when he got off the bus on Tuesday, Ted, at least the bit about the horses.' Charlie tried an approximation of the Australian's accent, not so very different from his own. 'I like the way you handle your horses, son. That's what he said.'

He pulled the paper back towards him and angled it to the light of the fire. It was Ellie Gilroy who had made him learn how to read properly when he was dodging off school to work in the Gilroy stables at Romford years ago, but it wasn't a skill he practised much.

'Jobs for any driver what wants one,' he read aloud again, hesitantly, picking out the Australian's quoted words. 'It says here he sells two thousand horses a year from his own places, Ted. Bloody hell. Two thousand horses! *'Always in need of good horsemen for breaking and bringing on young horses... Stock work... Wagon drivers... Good hands always welcome. A grand life in the...'* I can't make it out if you keep smacking the paper like that, Ted... *'A grand life in the outback. A land of opportunity for young men,'* it says. Good wages. Hell of a lot better than England.'

He stopped reading aloud, embarrassed at Kidman's reported astonishment at the hours the London bus drivers were expected to work for their meagre pay. He glanced up at his boss. Gilroy was still nodding.

'You've been bloody good to me, Ted,' Charlie said awkwardly. 'You gave me a start driving before any other firm would have. Time off with pay when Tilly's been bad. Nobody else would have done that. But this bloke's offering half as much again Ted, and a house and the chance to earn more. Maybe there'd be work for Tilly.'

The thought of Tilly's reaction to the idea of moving half way round the world hit him like a bucketful of cold water, and he shook his head.

'She won't have it, Ted. Never in a month of bloody Sundays. Pie in the sky and no mistake.' Charlie dropped the newspaper onto the nearest chair, but the old man scooped it up again and pushed it back into his hands.

'Take it home, Charlie. Read it to her. Tell her about the sunshine and the free house, Charlie. Hundreds of folk go out to Australia every year voluntary, you know, so there must be something in it.'

Charlie nodded dubiously. 'I'll try, Ted, but I can't get nothing out of her now. She might listen, maybe, but I don't think she will.' He smoothed the rumpled paper carefully and folded it small enough to fit into his greatcoat pocket with Sidney Kidman's calling card.

'Good boy, Charlie. That's the spirit.' Ted Gilroy patted Charlie tentatively on the shoulder.

Charlie looked at the old man miserably. 'One of the blokes told me I should give her a belting. Wake her up.'

'Christ no, Charlie, who the hell said that?'

'Can't tell tales, Ted. I wouldn't lift a hand to her, you know that.'

Gilroy nodded. 'It was Nobby, wasn't it?'

'Well, yes,' said Charlie. 'He said I should give her a belting. Kick her down the stairs. Bloody hell, Ted, I nearly belted him instead.'

Gilroy shook his head wearily. 'Nobby's old school. Knocked his missus about all the time. *A wife, a carpet and a walnut tree, the more you beat 'em the better they be.* He thinks that's right. Poor little woman, there wasn't a Saturday night she didn't get a black eye or worse. Ellie always said I should have got rid of him, but he's a good driver and he wasn't breaking the law, and I always reckoned if he lost his job it would be worse for her. Ellie used to try and help her out, you know, stood up for her, but it didn't do her any good and she lay down and died a month or two after Ellie went.'

They stood and listened to the thunderous arrival of another bus in the yard, and when the noise died down Gilroy sighed deeply and scratched among his sidewhiskers.

'You have to give her time, Charlie. Takes a bit of getting over, you know, losing a baby.' He waved his big hands helplessly. 'Ellie wanted a pile of nippers, but she lost the first one and she couldn't have no more. I would've liked a nipper or two myself, but women feel these things keener, you know.'

The pair of them looked down awkwardly at the floor. 'Maybe it's a bit like losing a foal,' said Gilroy with a sudden gleam of inspiration. 'Maybe that's something like, you know, so you get an idea. I always felt that badly, myself. Like a kick in the guts.'

Charlie looked at the old man hopefully. 'D'you think that might help if I told Tilly that?'

Gilroy considered it for a moment and then shook his head. 'Maybe not, Charlie. I wouldn't mention that if I were you. Kid gloves, you know. Quiet and steady. Slowly does it. Tell her about this Australian chap. That's the ticket.'

'You're right, Ted. Tilly doesn't feel the same way about horses we do. This is what we need.' Charlie slapped the paper in his coat pocket. 'New life in a new country. New start an' all.'

He looked at the old man again. 'We've got to do something different, Ted. I don't know how much more of this I can take.'

35

A family dinner the previous evening was hardly a true test, so the Chiddington staff were interested to see how the Australian guests would step up to the more complex formalities of dining in high society. But if they were hoping for any entertaining colonial lapses they were disappointed, to begin with anyway.

Bel Kidman and her daughters descended the stairs for dinner dressed in the latest fashions, and Sid followed them impeccably turned out in white tie and tails that even His Majesty The King, the royal dictator of the correct dress code, could not have criticised.

Six months in London had lifted the Kidmans' sartorial standards to a level the dressmakers and tailors of Adelaide couldn't begin to compete with, and a regular succession of invitations to dinner with the great and the rich had given them enough practice in the intricacies of social etiquette to steer them through an occasion like this with few qualms. Sid was almost becoming comfortable in the constrictions of his white tie outfit, with its stiff collar and starched white waistcoat and its infuriating, fiddly stud fastenings.

They met Lady Saltwood's other dinner guests at a quarter to eight, standing beside one of the two fireplaces in the great hall and making the usual small talk until the butler announced that dinner was served, and then all present assembled with their correct partners as Lady Saltwood offered Sid Kidman her arm and led the way into the dining room.

Even eighteen-year-old Edna took it for granted that her chair would be eased magically under her by a footman as she sat down, and as the courses followed each other up from the kitchens below their feet, and the staff moved behind and around the guests in their silent minuet of service, the five Kidmans worked their way without any hesitation through the ranks of shining cutlery and dazzling glassware that surrounded their places.

By the Park's standards it was not a full-blown or frighteningly grand dinner party, consisting of the three Saltwoods, the Kidmans, the

Saltwoods' nearest neighbour, Mr Thomas Lavery and his son Freddy, and Lady Saltwood's younger sister, Lady Amelia Whiteley, who had managed to cajole her husband Sir Francis south from his estate in Northumberland to visit her sister in Berkshire.

There was no sign of a Mrs Thomas Lavery or any mention of one. Bel Kidman had discovered from her maid while dressing for dinner that a Mrs Lavery did in fact exist but no one referred to her in public and certainly not in her husband's hearing. The story below stairs, said Hannah, was that Lavery's wife had managed to tolerate her boorish husband until four years ago, but when her son started to grow whiskers and behave exactly like his father she had had enough, and fled to Italy with a society portrait painter and several valuable pieces of Lavery family jewellery that she and local opinion felt she had more than earned.

Because this was a relatively small dinner party, Lady Saltwood had included Prior and his very pretty new young bride Phillipa, who was a distant relative of Lady Saltwood's and had come down from London on the afternoon train to be with a husband who spent a great deal more of his time with his employer than he did with his wife.

Lady Amelia was seated opposite Bel Kidman on either side of Lord Saltwood at one end of the table, and Sir Francis was seated opposite Sid at the other end, on either side of their hostess. It was a seating plan dictated by convention but it worked extremely well, at least at Lady Saltwood's end of the table. Sir Francis was a tall, angular, courteous example of the English aristocracy at its least obnoxious, and his wife was blonde, charming and knew a great many of the people the Kidmans had met in the more salubrious parts of London.

The old rural aristocracy, Bel had discovered during their stay in England, had more than its fair share of dullards, bigots and buffoons, but on the whole they tended to be much more relaxed and ready to talk to you without looking down their noses than the newly enobled.

Hannah, her temporary maid, had discreetly explained as she helped Bel dress her hair that Lady Saltwood's sister was also the daughter of an earl, of course, so was addressed as Lady Amelia rather than as Lady Whiteley, as her own title took precedence over her husband's baronetcy. Despite that, Bel quickly discovered that they had more in common than she might have expected, just as she had with Lady Saltwood. Just like the Kidmans, the Whiteleys had three grown daughters and a late-arriving tail-end son, and the two women shared a mutual understanding of the secret relief of safely producing a son and heir after a succession of daughters.

Mr Lavery, on the other hand, was everything Bel Kidman had been warned by her friends to expect in the English upper classes. He was a commoner by his own admission and proud of it, but that was completely misleading. He was the twenty-second Lavery to occupy the rambling, moated warren of Woolton Court, the latest representative of a family that prided itself equally on the scale and longevity of its unbroken landownership, and the inverted snobbery of having turned down any sort of title during the eight centuries that they had held their lands in Oxfordshire and Berkshire, despite having been offered high honours at the going rate by a succession of money-hungry monarchs and prime ministers.

Behind his thick, dark eyebrows, Lavery's brain was considerably sharper than a stranger would have guessed from his behaviour. As a land-owning neighbour he was a regular guest at the Park, but he was also a shareholder in some of Lord Saltwood's business interests, and the two shared a competitive passion for agricultural improvement.

But as far as the other dinner guests were aware that evening, the only topic of conversation that seemed to interest him at all was foxhunting. He talked foxhunting almost exclusively to Lord Saltwood, William and Lady Whiteley for the first two courses, until the conversation was adroitly deflected by their hostess towards different topics that the other guests could share.

At that point Lavery's attention turned more or less entirely to his food and the wine, punctuated by an occasional snort when something was said that he considered particularly trivial.

Gertie, Elma and Edna Kidman were so disconcerted by the snorting that their own contributions to the conversation dwindled away to silence. In other circumstances, their mother would have been quite capable of squaring up the black-browed bully sitting on her left-hand side. But Bel minded her manners and managed to hold up her end of a rather awkward and stilted conversation with Lord Saltwood about the South Australian banking system and the state of her country's roads and railways.

Lady Whiteley, sitting on her host's other side, talked to William.

Sid Kidman, seated next to his youngest daughter on Lady Saltwood's left side at the other end of the table, caught Edna's anxious eye as a footman lifted away her plate after the fish course, and winked.

For Sid and Lady Saltwood, the soup and fish courses passed largely unnoticed, Lady Saltwood listening intently as the Australian described the outback in general, and the cattle station she had inherited from her uncle in particular, as far as he knew it.

Sid had ridden across a corner of Milbourne Downs just two years before when he was inspecting Warrigal, and he described for her every detail of the country he had memorised.

He had seen only a very small fraction of the property, he said apologetically, but it had been in decline for many years, that much he knew from the manager at Warrigal, the station that touched the southwestern tip of Milbourne Downs.

'You describe it so vividly, Mr Kidman,' said Lady Saltwood, 'but it is difficult for me to imagine what it must be like. It seems so unreal to think we own it, and the scale is inconceivable to us here in England. To me it seems impossibly large, but in your terms is Milbourne a large property, Mr Kidman?'

Sid nodded his head towards the other end of the table. 'Well, I was telling William this morning, properties vary a lot, you know. I have several properties much smaller than Milbourne Downs, and some much bigger. I have a stake in one station I've been told is bigger than Yorkshire. Milbourne is about a tenth of that, around a thousand square miles, so that's about medium-sized, I would say. Around half a million acres.'

Lady Saltwood's eyes widened. 'Half a *million* acres! Five hundred thousand acres! Of course, I knew it was huge by our standards here in England, but I simply cannot begin to imagine a single property being that size.'

Her eyes strayed briefly up the table towards her husband and then back to her guest. 'I do hope that it will be possible to restore it. I have a painting of the Milbourne Downs homestead that my uncle Teppermoor left in the house we use now in London. You must see it and tell me if this is how it really is. One day I would very much like to see it for myself. It looks very beautiful but...' she paused for a moment, searching for the right words, '...it looks very lonely in all that wild space. The never-never. Isn't that what you call it?'

Kidman smiled back at her and shook his head. He could hear Prior entertaining his youngest daughter with a promise of the fun she would have at the pantomime if the Kidmans stayed in London for Christmas. 'Such a hoot.'

He also heard a sudden loud snort from Mr Lavery that utterly dried up poor Philippa Prior's attempts to find a subject, any subject at all, that might spark a glimmer of a response from Freddy Lavery, who dealt with a bad stammer by drinking as much as he could in the shortest possible time and not saying anything at all if he could help it. He was sitting silently on her right with his head down, ploughing through his dinner in faithful imitation of his father.

Sid glanced up the table and saw that both his older daughters had also been gathered up safely into Prior's orbit, and Bel was doing what she did so well, confounding a bull-headed autocrat with her calm, school-teacherly patience and determination.

He knew that expression on Bel's face, as she politely pressed Tom Lavery to give his opinion on a remark Lord Saltwood had made, and it nearly made him laugh out loud, knowing how surprised that jolly fellow would be if he ever made the mistake of locking horns with Mrs Kidman, never mind that she was not much more than half his size.

He looked back at Lady Saltwood, and wagged his head. 'Well, Milbourne Downs is a long way the right side of what we call the never-never, Lady Saltwood. It's only just what you might call the outback. We don't call it the never-never until you're right out in the back of beyond, heading out into dry country. There's plenty of water and feed on Milbourne, except in a really bad drought. There's a couple of creeks and a river that run most of the year round there, and she's far enough north to get floodwater when there's good rain in the Gulf and down through the river country. Good water. Good grass. Good cattle country. It could be a tip top property if it was managed properly.'

And then he remembered William Saltwood, and hurriedly added another advantage that was of no interest to him whatsoever, but might appeal to the boy's mother in the circumstances. 'It's only three or four hundred miles or so from the coast, anyway, and pretty close to a good-sized town too, so you're not much more than a day's ride from

Springvale if that's what you want. Maybe quicker than that in one of these motorcars, if it survived the track.'

Philippa Prior had given up trying to engage Freddy Lavery in small-talk and had been listening to Sid Kidman as avidly as Lady Saltwood.

'My goodness me! A whole day from the nearest shops! How do people manage?' She realised that she had intruded unbidden into their conversation, and blushed. 'Oh, Lady Saltwood, I am so sorry, please forgive me...'

The secretary's young wife had been talking across Sir Francis as she spoke, but both he and Lady Saltwood hastened to reassure her, and Sir Francis admitted that he too had been listening and it had indeed been fascinating. He turned to his hostess.

'This is your Australian property Mr Kidman is referring to, Eleanor?' he asked.

'Yes, Uncle Teppermoor's Milbourne Downs.' She turned to Sid again. 'Lord Teppermoor was my mother's older brother, rather a wild character as a young man, and apparently he won the property in a game of cards during his travels in Australia. I think he lived there for some years but we knew very little about it at all until he left it to me when he died two years ago. It was an ill-gotten gain, and it has gone to wrack and ruin in my uncle's old age, but perhaps Mr Kidman will help revive it.'

'And am I right in thinking Milbourne is in Queensland?' asked the baronet.

'Slap in the middle of Queensland, Sir Francis,' confirmed Sid.

'Well then,' said Sir Francis, 'I think we may have a connection with you there even in Northumberland, where I live.' He smiled at Lady Saltwood, Kidman, Philippa Prior and Edna Kidman, who had caught the sound of a name from home, and leaned closer to her father as Sir Francis opened his mouth again.

'Oh dear,' said Amelia Whiteley before he could speak. 'You're going to tell your cattle dog story again, aren't you, Francis?'

Sir Francis laughed. 'I am, my dear. I have never had a better opportunity.'

By now everyone at the table was listening to him.

'May I ask you, Mr Kidman, do you use cattle dogs in your work?'

Sid looked at Sir Francis with some surprise. 'Yes, we do, on the stations, and the drovers couldn't do without their dogs. One good dog is worth ten good men, they say, and I reckon I've had a few dogs that prove it.' He tilted slightly towards Lady Saltwood. 'First dog I had when I was just fourteen or thereabouts, we worked together herding sheep for a squatter. I loved that dog, Lady Saltwood, and I don't mind telling you I shed a tear or two when he died.'

Lady Saltwood's and Philippa Prior's eyes misted slightly. Very few British men would have admitted to that kind of emotional weakness.

Sir Francis coughed discreetly and continued. 'Your dog wasn't by any chance a blue heeler?'

Sid agreed that it had been.

'Was it a stump-tailed blue heeler, by any chance?'

Kidman, intrigued, agreed that it had been.

'Well,' Sir Francis went, 'this is a perfect connection. We have a tenant on one of our farms in Northumberland who breeds cattle and sheep dogs famous all over the north of England and Scotland, and he has told me, many, many times over and in great detail, that the famous Queensland blue heeler cattle dogs originated from the dogs his family bred up along Hadrian's Wall.'

The baronet leaned forwards as far as his starched shirtfront and white waistcoat allowed. 'According to the older Mr Hall... that's his name, the farmer I am talking about... although his son farms now... according to Mr Hall one of his father's cousins emigrated to Australia and became a cattleman many years ago, but he couldn't find a breed of dog that was hardy enough to help him drive his stock hundreds of miles to market, as you do, I think, in Australia...' He looked at Sid, who agreed that this was the case. 'So the Australian Mr Hall wrote home to Northumberland and his family here despatched two dogs and two bitches... I beg your pardon, Eleanor... they sent these four breeding dogs all the way around the world. They were an ancient breed of cattle dog with almost no tail to speak of, and that is how your Queensland stump-tailed heelers began.'

He smiled at Lady Saltwood. 'George Hall. Very good tenant but he does tell the same stories over and over again whenever I see him. I don't know how much truth there is in this one.'

Lady Whiteley was about to say that George Hall wasn't the only one to repeat the same stories over and over again, when Sid Kidman startled everybody into silence by slapping the table. Philippa Prior jumped an inch out of her seat.

'George Hall! My word! I've heard this story back home and I knew a fella by the same name!' Kidman said delightedly. 'I always thought that was just a yarn, you know. I met an old cattleman with that same name, George Hall, when I was a young fella just starting in South Australia. He always claimed he crossed a tame dingo with a stump-tailed blue cattle dog from England and started the heelers, and now you say they came from your place! Maybe old George Hall was the man, after all. I'll be...'

They didn't find out what he would be because at that moment Sid caught his wife's eye and laughed. 'Did you hear that, Bel?'

Bel Kidman was used to her husband's sudden noisy enthusiasms. Sitting diagonally opposite him, she had to crane her head to see him around the elaborate confections of exotic fruit and hothouse flowers that decorated the middle of the vast mahogany table. 'I think they probably heard you in the village, Sidney. But it shouldn't be very surprising, should it? After all, most of us Australians started over here too, and we've been bringing all sorts of animals with us ever since we arrived.'

She was right, of course, and the conversation took on the aspect of a parlour game for some minutes as everyone around the table in turn volunteered another species that had made the long journey from the British Isles to Australia. Cattle, sheep, pigs, horses, chickens, dogs, goats. They were easy. Donkeys? Yes, said Kidman, plenty of those. Rabbits, of course, and rats, prompting a small squeak of disgust from Philippa Prior. Cats? Yes. Perhaps the cats would catch the rats and rabbits, suggested Lady Saltwood. You'd need a lot of cats to catch the plagues of rats and rabbits that appeared from nowhere in the outback from time to time, said Kidman. Tens of millions of them. Hundreds of acres covered in grey fur. Another squeak from Philippa Prior.

Camels, volunteered Sid as the others ran out of suggestions. Not from Britain, of course, he went on amidst laughter, although the Kidmans had watched a camel pulling a lawnmowing machine in Regent's Park Zoo only a fortnight before, but from up in northern India. Really? Yes, he confirmed, thousands of them and their Afghan drivers, the 'Ghans'. They were brought in to haul supplies across the desert areas of the interior, especially in the never-never, he said, with a smile to Lady Saltwood.

The Laverys had both failed to volunteer any suggestions, but the father looked up from his plate when Gertie Kidman, who had been sitting sandwiched between the two Lavery men and had been too demoralised to speak for at least twenty minutes, offered the suggestion that foxes were another wild animal the British had brought out to Australia. Absolutely, confirmed Sid. It gave Gertie the courage to add that she thought dingoes looked something like the English fox, but with longer legs. Maybe they had interbred?

'Well, I don't know about that,' said her father. 'But if foxes here are the same kind of nuisance the dingoes are at home, I'm surprised you haven't shot them all by now.'

Lavery was raising his wineglass as Kidman spoke, but he put it down again and stared across the table at the Australian. The servants stiffened. This was more like it.

Lady Saltwood intervened in a diplomatic whisper. 'Oh dear, Mr Kidman, I'm afraid you have blasphemed! We mustn't even mention the words 'fox' and 'shoot' in the same sentence.'

She leaned towards him. 'To hunting men in England the fox is a sacred animal, and a huntsman,' she glanced anxiously at Tom Lavery, 'as the famous Mr Jorrocks said, loves the fox only marginally less than he loves his hounds.'

William Saltwood smiled across the table at Gertie Kidman. '*It hain't that I 'ates the fox, it's just that I loves the 'ounds more!*' I think that's how Mr Jorrocks put it. Is there any hunting in Australia?'

Gertie was baffled by the quotation and by William's attempt at a Cockney accent, but the question had thrown her a conversational lifeline and she gave him a dazzling smile in return. 'Oh yes, I think there is in some parts,' she said in a rush, 'not that we go hunting ourselves, but we all ride whenever we can at home. Not Mother, but Elma and Edna and me, we've been riding since we could walk. Father has taken us with him to the stations sometimes and we've been mustering. It's terribly exciting...' She ran out of steam, conscious that everyone was looking at her.

'You must come back and have a day's hunting with us here while you are in England,' said William. 'I think you might find it even more exciting than your mustering.'

Sid Kidman saw Lord Saltwood frown slightly at that, although he missed the momentary look of deep distress on his hostess's face, and then Tom Lavery switched his gaze finally away from the Australian and stared at William across the table as though he had suggested something indecent.

William raised his eyebrows at Lavery across the table. 'Don't you think they would enjoy a day's hunting with us, Master?'

'No,' said Lavery, and drained his glass.

36

Charlie had woefully underestimated his wife's reaction to the idea of moving away from Stepney, let alone emigrating to the far side of the world.

Tilly stared at him blankly as he tried to show her the article in the paper and struggled to paint a picture of the wonderful new life they could build together in a new country.

'Australia?' she said incredulously when he finally stuttered to a halt. Her horrified astonishment was even more demoralising than Charlie had expected, and it changed quickly to something worse. She lunged suddenly for the newspaper he was holding, ripped it from his hands and crumpled it furiously into a ball. 'Australia?' Her voice rose to a wail. 'We're not going to bloody *Australia.*'

She hurled the paper as hard as she could towards the fire in the small grate that was their sole source of heat, and Charlie stepped quickly across the hearth to retrieve it, their future, tossed onto the unswept floor before she had given him half a chance to explain it to her properly.

Tilly sank onto the hard chair on the other side of the hearth, her face in her hands, sobbing uncontrollably, and Charlie dropped to his knees in front of her and tried again. 'Just hear me out, Till. Just listen a minute.'

She shook her head vehemently, sobbing louder. But in the few minutes it had taken Charlie to walk from the White Horse Stables back to their lodgings, the offer in the newspaper had taken on a golden, redemptive glow. The miraculous possibility of cutting free from the uncertainties of their future in London and the helpless frustration of Tilly's torment seemed to Charlie like a shaft of brilliant sunshine breaking through the sulpherous peasouper that seemed to be enveloping their lives. Charlie raised his voice and spoke fast.

'Tilly, listen to me. You got to listen to this. There's nothing for me in London. In another ten years there won't be a single horse working on the streets of London, that's what they say, girl. But it's different in

Australia. I've *met* this bloke, Till.' He rustled the newspaper. 'He said to me *personal* what it says in the paper, right on my bus, close to me as you are, Till. He wants men like me to work for him in Australia. It's a chance to start a new life. Start again. We could have our own house. It says that in the paper, Till. Our own proper house, and better money, and a good life. We could have more kids and give them a decent life, Till. It's the chance of a lifetime.'

She had stopped sobbing as he spoke, and that stirred a glimmer of hope.

'Honest, sweetheart, this Kidman is famous. He owns more land and horses than anyone else in the world. He's rich, Till. He'll pay our way to Australia and set us up. It's all here in the paper, look.' He tried to smooth out the crumpled newspaper and offered it to her again, the incontestable truth set in dense black print.

But when Tilly looked up at him, her face was chalk white and the deep, dark smudges under her eyes made her look deranged.

'How can you talk like that?' she asked him, shaking with ferocious intensity. 'How can you talk about moving to Australia? You think I can go to Australia?' Her voice was rising again, and spots of colour showed in her cheeks. 'My little girl is lying in her grave not a mile from here, and you're talking about going to fuckin' Australia?'

She stood up, and Charlie hurriedly got to his feet and stepped backwards away from her.

'You don't bloody well understand nothing, do you?' Her fists were clenched by her sides as she spoke, but then she shot out a hand and grabbed for the newspaper again. 'Gimme that nonsense.'

Charlie pulled the paper out of her reach, but Tilly hurled herself at him screaming, 'Give it to me. Give it to me,' until he gave it to her. She tore it apart as if her life depended on its utter destruction, stamping on the shreds of newsprint that fell at her feet, and then she crammed the remains of the paper into the fire, pushing it deeper into the back of the grate and holding it there even as the flames caught and the ball of paper flared alight with a muffled thump in the updraft, singeing the edges of her sleeves.

Charlie stepped forwards again quickly and pulled her arm out of the fire, but she turned on him like a Wapping fishwife, shrieking and spitting, a demonic caricature of the girl he had courted in the Mile less than two years before, flailing at him with her fists and swearing at him, the casual curses he used every day hitting him with shocking force like sharp stones.

'Fuck Australia. You can fuckin' well go to Australia if you want. *Fuck* you, Charlie...' She was gasping for breath between words as though someone had hit her in the solar plexus. 'I got... to stay... with my... baby.'

It was first time he had heard Tilly utter any swear words at all since he had met her, and somehow this was even more appalling than her rejection of the idea itself.

Tilly started shaking and her face crumpled. She wrapped her arms around her own body and began sobbing again, her voice so full of pain that Charlie flinched as though she had struck him again. 'I lost my baby. I lost my little girl.' She bent forward as though a gigantic hand was folding her in two, and her voice died to a moan. 'I... lost... my... baby... girl.'

Charlie crossed the hearth in two quick strides and put his hands around his wife's thin shoulders. He eased her upright and she collapsed against him, and he held her to his chest and spoke to her instinctively in the same way he would speak to a frightened horse. 'Easy Till. Eeeasy. Easy girl.' He held her tightly, and felt her hands clenching in the rough material of his coat, but she was clinging to him, and he felt a surge of immense relief at this gesture of need. He buried his face in her hair and kissed the top of her head, and felt her hands tighten again.

Until five minutes ago, he had thought that Tilly's misery could not possibly sink any deeper. For the six months after the death of their baby she had shut him out, locking herself into her own private world of maternal grief. He had grieved for their baby, too, but not like Tilly. He had understood how much harder the loss had been for her, but he had had no idea how to deal with Tilly's grief, and the longer it had gone on the more frustrated he had been both by his own incapacity and her inability to cope. Everything he had tried to say or do had met with the same blank, impenetrable misery.

Then this attempt to offer her a glimpse of a better future had turned his beautiful girl into a terrifying harpy even less recognisable than the cold, withdrawn ghost he had been struggling to understand before. And now, seconds later, there was more of the old Tilly back in his arms than he had seen for half a year.

Charlie had not one inkling how or why this shattering sequence of emotional explosions had brought them suddenly to a better place, but he recognised that the door that might lead them back to some sort of normality together was at least ajar.

He had no idea how long he and Tilly stood together as the ashes of the newspaper settled in the grate, but all too soon the intimacy of the moment was dispelled by a knock on the real door of their rooms, and the voice of their downstairs neighbour enquiring through the thin, worm-eaten panelling if everything was all right.

Mrs Hoddle lived in the ground floor lodgings directly beneath them, and she could hear anything above a whisper through floorboards almost as thin and worm-eaten as the door. The young couple had grown used to the fact that they could hear the old lady moving about below them. The knowledge had frequently reduced Tilly to stifled squeaks of suppressed laughter in the days when they were discovering what the curate who had married them had meant when he intoned disbelievingly that their union was intended by God for their mutual joy and the procreation of children.

Living alone on her late husband's small savings and an even smaller allowance from her three sons, Mrs Hoddle had the spare time to take a well-meaning interest in the young couple.

Fortunately, she had also turned out to be deaf or discreet enough to ignore any conjugal noises she might have heard coming from the room above her, and Charlie had to admit that her presence had been a God-send since the baby had died. She had sat with Tilly in the evenings, waiting for Charlie to come home from work, sighing occasionally, and patting Tilly's hand whenever Tilly left it close enough for the old widow to capture.

'Shall I come in, my ducks?' Mrs Hoddle had already lifted the latch and opened the door slightly as she spoke. It was part of the ritual of familiarity they had developed over the months when Tilly's bouts of weeping had drawn the old lady up the stairs to offer her kindly but fatalistic brand of comfort. 'Ours not to reason why, my ducks, as the good Lord said.' Somewhere in Mrs Hoddle's mind the words of Alfred Lord Tennyson had taken on an authority he would never have claimed for himself, and she would have sworn the words came from an even higher Lord than the poet laureate.

Charlie disengaged himself hurriedly from Tilly as the old lady pushed their lodgings door closed behind her, and helped his wife to sit down on the chair nearest the fire. Tilly glanced up at him, and her almost imperceptible, watery smile sent another detonation of love and elation through his entire being.

Mrs Hoddle was a small, square old body with only half a dozen mainly back teeth in her head, who appeared to exist on a diet of tea-soaked Huntley & Palmer assorted biscuits. In every conversation she had with anyone, familiar or stranger, she managed to mention that she was seventy-nine, the last remaining relic of the last of the Spitalfields Huguenot silk weaver families, Jean Hottel... 'but he changed his name to be more English when we got married... 1850, it was... we were married the year the old Queen got that Cohen diamond, you know, from India and that hippopotamuse came to the zoo... that was from India too I remember... John took me to see it... I'm seventy-nine years old, you know, did I tell you, twenty-one when I was married, nearly eighty now...' She said she knew her time must be drawing near, but her three daughters-in-law agreed bitterly she was as tough as a Limehouse docker and would probably outlive them all.

This evening, the stays under her bombazine Victorian mourning dress creaked loudly as she ploughed obliviously like a small black tugboat through the storm-tides of emotion washing around the room.

Charlie retreated as Mrs Hoddle took over the care of his wife, who sat slumped in the chair next to the fire. The old lady stroked Tilly's hair for some time, murmuring, 'There, there my duck, you get it off your chest.' Then she turned to the remains of the fire and picked up the tongs. She dropped a few lumps of coal carefully onto the embers that glowed among the grey flakes of newspaper ash and lifted the small, blackened kettle from its stand.

'We'll have a nice cuppa of tea, shall we?' The old lady shook the kettle gently to check there was enough water in it, and then hung it on the hook over the smoking coals. 'Put us all to rights, my ducks. Nice cuppa tea.'

37

When the ladies had followed their hostess out of the dining room to take tea in Lady Saltwood's withdrawing room at Chiddington Park, the gentlemen gathered at Lord Saltwood's end of the long table.

The last evidence of dinner was discreetly cleared away. Port glasses were set for each of the seven men and the butler poured from the first of two crystal decanters, setting it when every glass was filled at Lord Saltwood's left elbow.

Cigars were offered. Only William declined. As one footman cut and presented the cigars to each of the other men, another followed with a lighted taper, and each man drew the flame into an eight-inch cigar that had cost more than half of a footman's weekly wage.

When all the cigars were drawing properly and his guests were comfortable, Lord Saltwood raised his glass to Kidman, who was sitting to his right. 'I give you the king, gentlemen, but tonight I mean the Cattle King.'

The other men raised their glasses in unison. Both the Laverys drained theirs. Kidman raised his own glass. 'To you Lord Saltwood, and thank you.'

The after-dinner rituals of port and cigars were certainly grander but essentially not much different here than in South Australia, and although he rarely drank alcohol at home he had developed a partiality for port in England, especially when it was of this quality.

Lord Saltwood had not reduced the level in his glass noticeably with the toast to his guest, but he topped it up and moved the decanter to his left, where Sir Francis also topped up his own glass politely and passed the decanter on to Lavery. The butler and the remaining staff withdrew from the dining room, leaving just one footman standing by the door, almost invisible in the shadow beyond the glow of the candlelight.

In his six months in England, Kidman had been astonished by the amount of food and drink that British gentlemen in high society could put away at a three-hour, twelve-course sitting, and he was no longer surprised if an evening of colossal over-indulgence ended with at least one male guest being bundled into his motorcar or carriage by a couple of burly footmen. High society women ate and drank like mice in public, but many of their menfolk made up for it with a lack of inhibition that a parched boundary rider would have had trouble matching in an outback grogshop.

Sid was not a teetotaller but he was careful, and he had noticed that most of the other men around the Park dining table had also paced themselves through the succession of wines offered by the footmen with each passing course. Sir Francis was speaking with the same quiet courtesy to guests and servants alike. William appeared to be completely in control of himself as the port was poured, and Prior was as sober as you would expect a man to be, dining with an employer like Lord Saltwood. Only Lavery had evidently absorbed his full share of alcohol during the evening, and his son was gazing down at the table with the bleary preoccupation of a man trying to work out whether it would be worse form to be sick on top of it or slide underneath it.

Lord Saltwood had drunk enough to relax his tight smile fractionally and he directed it at Kidman. 'We have had a king with us at the Park before now, but never an Australian king, or a Cattle King,' he said. 'Although of course our King Emperor...' Saltwood nodded his head slightly as he said this, and Lavery did likewise but with heavy irony... 'our King Emperor is also the King of Australia and all the dominions.'

Sir Francis raised his glass. 'If I may, I give you our own king, with my apologies to Mr Kidman for usurping his royal authority.' The other five men dutifully raised their glasses. 'The King,' they said, and drank again.

The real king, short, fat, frog-eyed and looking in his old age exactly like a bearded version of his late mother, had acknowledged the same toast in person at this table on one strained occasion since he had inherited the throne, despite the fact that Lord Saltwood had always despised and avoided the playboy Prince of Wales and his expensive friends. Playing host to the king had been worth the irritation and the cost to impress foreign business connections.

It was another view he shared with his neighbour. Both men particularly disliked the Prince's assumption that he was entitled to pay court to other men's wives as his fancy took him. A younger, slimmer Prince Edward had never disguised his admiration for Lady Eleanor Baylesley, ever since she had been presented at court twenty-eight years before, and there had been rumours that he had been keen to console Mrs Lavery in the early days of her unhappy marriage. Like Lady Saltwood she had been a noted beauty, but her husband had made it very clear he was not inclined to join the queue of cuckolds prepared to stand aside and look the other way while the royal playboy dallied away his afternoons with their wives.

'He seems a decent sort of a fellow,' said Sid reasonably as the men sat down after the toast, and Lavery grunted loudly. 'You liked our royal master, did you? Where'd you meet him?'

Sid explained that he and Bel had been presented to the King and Queen at the Franco-British Exhibition in June, and again a month later at the Olympic opening ceremony at the White City Stadium. 'Of course you can't really tell,' said the Australian, 'but he was very pleasant at the time and he asked some sensible questions about Australia and my cattle business.'

Lavery grunted again. 'That's his job, being civil to colonial visitors. You'd see a different side to the royal presence if your...,' he stopped. Lord Saltwood blew cigar smoke into the awkward pause that followed this, and William caught Prior's look of warning. They both knew enough of Lavery to realise that he had been about to tell Kidman that the King would have taken more of an interest in him if his wife had been younger and more glamorous.

Even Lavery seemed to realise that he had very nearly gone too far, and abruptly changed tack. 'You'd see him differently if you got between him and his shooting. Or his food, eh Saltwood?' The King's libido appeared to have dwindled as he grew older and fatter, but on his visit to Chiddington his appetite for the ladies had been replaced by another.

Lord Saltwood nodded at his guest. 'There is a long tradition in England of royalty ruining their hosts when they invite themselves to stay, Mr Kidman,' he said. 'There are men in England today living on the charity of their friends because they beggared themselves to entertain the Prince of Wales. Isn't that so, Lavery?'

Lavery nodded. 'What was the name of that idiot who set fire to his own house rather than have to invite Bertie to shoot again?'

'Suffield,' said Lord Saltwood. 'Gunton Park. Norfolk.' He glanced at William again very briefly. 'Perfect example, Mr Kidman. Lord Suffield was a great toady of the Prince of Wales and more or less bled a perfectly good estate dry entertaining his Royal Highness and all his cronies. Shooting parties and weekends when the prince could meet his current mistress out of range of the society gossips, that sort of thing. But eventually the money ran out, and when Bertie buttonholed Suffield in London and told him he wanted to come shooting again, Suffield contacted his butler at Gunton and told him to set fire to the Prince's bedroom, to give him an excuse to put him off. Unfortunately for Suffield the fire ran out of control and his estate fire engine didn't have hoses long enough to reach the house from the lake. Half the house burned down and Suffield can't afford to rebuild it. The prince went elsewhere to shoot and hasn't been anywhere near Suffield since.'

'I can sympathise with the poor fella,' said Sid. 'My house burned down four years ago.' Lavery's expression at this suggested that he wasn't surprised, but Prior made the necessary sympathetic noises.

Sid laughed. 'The whole town turned out to help us but we couldn't stop it. Bel wanted the same again so we rebuilt the whole house from the ground up. Still smells a bit of smoke, mind you.'

There was a short pause. Lavery stared at the Australian.

Lord Saltwood topped up his glass and passed the decanter, and then returned to what he had been saying. 'Anyway, nowadays our king is less likely to ruin your bank account and more likely to ruin your bedclothes with food.' The other men laughed. 'These days when our king invites himself to shoot someone's pheasants,' he went on, 'he demands a cold roast chicken on his bedside table in case he should wake up feeling peckish in the middle of the night. A whole cold roast chicken. I have it as a fact.'

Prior turned to Sid. 'Can you tell us where your title originated, Mr Kidman? Has it been conferred on you by our press here, or are you the Cattle King at home in Australia as well?'

Kidman smiled and raised his hands. 'Oh, that's just a bit of an old joke. I reckon it's been around in the newspapers back home for a while. They call a few of the big pastoralists cattle kings or sheep kings and your newspaper fellas have cottoned on to it and keep printing nonsense about my empire and suchlike. Mind you, it's not as good as what the blackfellas call me back home.'

Lavery had been revolving his port glass on the table with his finger and thumb, but he stopped and looked across the table at Kidman. 'The blacks? I damned well hope the niggers call you *sir* at all times, even in a penal colony.'

William was sitting to Kidman's right, half turned towards the Australian, and he saw him frown slightly in response to Lavery's words, or perhaps to the offensive tone of his voice.

'Well,' said the Australian. He looked across the table under his eyebrows at the dark, belligerent figure opposite him, and then laughed gently and looked around at the other men. 'I'll tell you what they call me, but you have to remember that in Australia we promote all the tribal chiefs to kings to keep 'em sweet. All the chiefs who stay on the right side of the government, anyhow. They get a bit of a pension and a big brass medal on a chain with King George or King Alfred on it, or whatever name they like.'

Prior glanced at Lord Saltwood and leaned forwards in his chair. 'Is there much trouble with the blacks? I was under the impression they were under proper control.'

Sid shook his head. 'Not what you would call trouble like there used to be, no. There are some isolated dust-ups here and there from time to time, but most places now there aren't that many blackfellas left, and mostly it happens in the towns when they get hold of drink, or on the stations where they don't give the blackfellas a fair go. There are still a few places out in the bush where you'd want to mind your step.'

He looked at his host. 'Up in the top end and in the Kimberleys they might chuck a spear at you if you took a line through their territory without asking, or if a whitefella takes one of their women. One of Patsy Durack's boys was killed up there not long ago, on the Doherty and Durack properties, you know.' Lord Saltwood and Prior both nodded. 'They spear cattle, too, and stir them up, which runs the beef off them and makes 'em hard to muster. But I get along with the blackfellas pretty well and we don't have trouble on my stations.'

Lavery had finished his third glass of port and had been looking increasingly sceptical as the Australian had been speaking. 'Giving niggers medals doesn't work and never has in two hundred years of

Empire. The more you pander to them the more trouble they cause, and the only answer to native trouble is artillery or the Maxim gun. We learnt that in India, we learnt it in Africa, we learnt it in Egypt, and I'm damned sure it isn't any different in Australia, medals or no medals.'

Sid Kidman was well aware that Lavery had taken against him, presumably because of his remark about shooting foxes, and he refused to rise. He leaned back in his seat and stretched his legs out under the table. 'Oh, the blackfellas learned that lesson alright,' he said mildly. 'Forty, fifty years back they learned their place, the ones that survived, and we got pretty much everything we wanted so we can get along without killing each other now. There are some who say we can't but in all my years working with blackfellas I've found the bargain has mostly worked out in my favour. They've taught me everything I know about how to get along in the outback, and I reckon I've had pretty good value out of the bits and pieces they've asked for in return. Tins of jam, mostly. They can't get enough jam.'

Lord Saltwood barked his short, hard laugh. 'Ha! Jam? There you are Lavery, next time your men ask you for higher wages, you must offer them jam.'

Lavery scowled across the table. 'Jam be damned. When you show weakness you encourage them to ask for more, and then where are you? It's a damned bad example. Same with the Chartists and the unions, and these damned stupid women screaming and shouting for the vote. You give them an inch today and tomorrow they want the whole damned mile.'

There was another short, awkward pause while cigar smoke drifted and coiled in the air around the men's heads, and then William turned to the Australian. 'You haven't told us what the Aboriginals call you, Mr Kidman.'

The Australian looked at him and grinned. 'Yes, well, it's just a bit of blackfella nonsense, but the old blacks who know me in the bush call me Bigfella Kidman King of all Adelaide.'

Kidman was the first to laugh at himself, but Lavery stared at him across the table again. 'For a colony full of Fenians and republicans, you seem to have a lot of kings down there.'

The discourtesy was so blatant even Prior was at a loss to say anything to defuse the sudden tension that charged the dining room, and it was only Lord Saltwood who had the authority to metaphorically step between his two guests. 'Don't mind Lavery, Mr Kidman.' He shot a somewhat sour look at his neighbour.

It had been his idea to invite the Laverys to meet the Kidmans, against Lady Saltwood's advice. He had suggested that a spell in Australia might be good for the useless, stuttering Freddy Lavery, too, but his neighbour's contrariness had backfired on him. Lord Saltwood could not imagine why he had taken against the Australian in this fashion, but he did know that once Lavery had decided he didn't like someone, he would take no trouble to hide it.

Lady Saltwood could have told him that Lavery's rudeness was indeed partly due to Sid's *faux pas* about the foxes, but he had only reacted to that so disproportionately because he had already taken umbrage at being invited to dine with colonial guests he thought beneath him.

She might also have reminded her husband that a large part of the Lavery fortune had been secured by marrying into the West Indies sugar trade five generations earlier, and the present squire of Woolton still bitterly despised any hint of the wishy-washy liberal attitude to the rights of the black races that had led to the abolition of slavery.

But while the men were rather uncomfortably covering up Lavery's breach of good manners in the dining room, Lady Saltwood was discussing the raising of children and vegetables with her sister and Bel Kidman in her drawing room, while Philippa Prior taught the girls a card game that involved a great deal of luck and laughter and not much science.

In the dining room, Lord Saltwood mended fences in the only way he knew, which was to force the conversation back into a channel that he could dominate. 'I'm sure you have felt the appreciation in the City for your success during your stay, Mr Kidman. We know the contribution Australia is making to the Empire, and I am certain she will play a greater part before very long.'

'Particularly on the cricket field,' interjected Sir Francis helpfully. Lord Saltwood was not going to allow the talk to wander off his chosen course again, especially not onto the subject of cricket. For one thing, this was an opportunity to take a sounding of the Australian's political views, and for another, he detested cricket. Anything as trivial as a game that could distract the working man from his responsibilities for up to five days at a time was a canker in the economic if not moral fibre of the nation.

'There's a good deal of truth in Lavery's view, you know,' he went on. 'The world is changing. Everybody wants their say these days, including the women, and when it comes to politics and business, most of them don't know what they're talking about. They want the vote, but they don't know the first thing about how to use it in the interests of the country as a whole. And the workers are the same. They want more power and more pay, and damn the consequences. It's a threat to our way of government, to business and the economy.'

Lavery was nodding grimly as Lord Saltwood said this, and Kidman judged it best not to tell them what he thought. He had watched a demonstration of the unemployed in Trafalgar Square that summer from the top deck of a horse bus, and he had been only a few yards from the gaunt, unshaven men holding the banner closest to him. *Starving To Death In a Land of Plenty,* said the hand-painted lettering on the old sheet, and the worn, hollow-eyed faces suggested it wasn't very far from the truth.

'No,' went on Lord Saltwood emphatically, 'we need order to function properly.'

'Hear, hear,' said Lavery.

'Not just law and order, but social order, governed by the people who know how to govern, and managed by the people who know how to manage. If that natural order breaks down, the whole country breaks down. Look at the English Republic, or the French revolution, or the Americans. Civil war. Chaos. Disaster. It doesn't work. Don't you think, Mr Kidman?'

The sudden question put Sid in something of a quandary. In other circumstances he would have said plainly what he really thought and argued his corner. He had always thought everyone should be given a fair go and a decent wage, and he had been appalled by some of the working and living conditions he had seen right at the core of the biggest and richest empire the world had ever known.

He took a sip of port to buy a few seconds while he struggled to find a way to be honest without offending his host or coming to blows with Lavery, who was watching him across the table, and then Sir

Francis took his chance to steer the subject back onto his own favourite ground, partly to rescue the Australian guest and partly to twist his brother-in-law's tail.

'Speaking of Americans and kings,' he said, 'did you see in the papers who is top of the bowling averages in England this season?'

Lord Saltwood was caught on the back foot by his brother-in-law's neat piece of conversational fielding, but William nodded.

'Isn't it Bart King? The American bowler? Yes. I saw him play at Oxford in June.' His father frowned, and William stopped.

'It's rather embarrassing,' continued Sir Francis, smiling at Kidman. 'We seem to have exported our national games across the Empire rather too successfully. First you took the Ashes back from us in February down there, didn't you, very easily I'm ashamed to say, and now this American chap Bart King has been skittling out our best batsmen like ninepins all summer. Very embarrassing indeed. Not part of the Empire, of course, America that is, not now, but they still play cricket, and rather well too in his case.'

Lord Saltwood took a savage pull on his cigar that made the tip glow suddenly a vivid red.

'No wonder old W. G. has retired,' Sir Francis continued. He leaned across the table and lowered his voice in reverence, 'Dr W. G. Grace, you know, our greatest living Englishman, since Wellington died. Probably the greatest batsman the game will ever see.'

'Oh come on, Uncle Francis, surely not?' said William. 'When you took me and Hughie to see him in that exhibition match at the Oval, he was bowled first ball and then refused to leave the crease.' He leaned towards Sid. 'Do you know what he said when the bowler complained?' Sid shook his head. 'It was in all the papers the next day: "These people have come to see me bat, not to see you bowl". Hardly cricket, was it?'

Any further argument about the greatness or otherwise of England's greatest living cricketer was sidelined by the resurrection of Freddy Lavery, who had begun to recover after his cigar had gone out, and suddenly sat upright and said, 'S-s-s-seven for forty-seven. MC-C-C-C. B-b-b-bart King. 'Merican. D-d-d-damn good b-b-b-bowler...' He looked round at the others with a look of pleased astonishment at his one and only contribution to the conversation, until he caught his father's eye, and he reached hurriedly for his glass again.

'You're absolutely right,' replied Sir Francis kindly. 'He took seven wickets for forty-seven against the M.C.C. Remarkable bowling.' Sir Francis paused for a moment and Lord Saltwood drew a breath. 'But he was a very fine batsman too, you know,' went on Sir Francis. 'That is, he still is a very fine batsman, present tense...'

'The port is with you, Francis.' Lord Saltwood had had enough and swotted the subject decisively into the long grass. Not even a cricket fanatic could ignore the dictates of the port decanter. Sir Francis poured a teaspoonful into his glass and passed the decanter on.

He leaned conspiratorially towards the Australian. 'I think my brother-in-law agrees with the French mother at the Eton-Harrow game who said the tea was excellent but why on earth did we ruin such a lovely afternoon playing such a dreadful, silly game.'

Sir Francis raised his glass ironically to Lord Saltwood, and the talk swung away like Bart King's famous and unplayable 'angler' into the common interests of imperial trade, the dangerous posturing of the bumptious little German Kaiser, the state of agriculture across the Empire he envied so acutely, and the fascinating topic of the weather on both sides of the world and its effects on the previous subjects.

38

Although she adamantly refused to attend Mass, Rachel did walk with her father to the church on Sunday morning to visit her mother's grave, carrying flowers that Maureen Heinemann ordered for her from Rockhampton and kept fresh in the Leichhardt cold store.

Jack Gallagher kept a respectable suit at the Leichhardt for his visits, and he was already regretting the waistcoat by the time they reached the paling fence that protected the cemetery from dogs, stray cattle and the occasional hungry dingo.

He took off his hat and fanned himself as he and Rachel stood beside the last resting place of the only woman he had ever loved. Rachel had been just short of her second birthday when her mother had been bitten by the big Brown Snake, and the only memory she retained was the sense of fear and bewilderment that pervaded the homestead on the day her mother died.

Jack could remember every detail of that terrible day, and every mile of his journey through that night to bring his wife's body to Springvale, wrapped in their bedding, for immediate burial here at the church of Our Lady of the Immaculate Heart.

They were twenty minutes early for mass but Father Paul must have seen them because he came hurrying out of the priest's house, already fully dressed in his vestments, and limped towards them between the tilted wooden crosses to Florence Gallagher's marble headstone.

'Rachel, my dear. Jack. Jack. Rachel. God bless you both, are you well and are you coming to celebrate Holy Mass with us, Rachel?' He was puffing and beads of sweat were forming along the edge of his biretta. He dabbed at them with the end of a stained and faded stole, and put his other hand out to steady himself on the gravestone.

'G'day, Father Paul,' said Jack. 'You look as though you're going a bit lame there? Is your gout bad?'

'Bless you again, Jack, it is, it is. These things are sent to try us and I thank God for teaching me to suffer with a cheerful heart.' He eased himself upright and winced. 'Holy Mary, it's a hard lesson, it is indeed it is. But here you are and Rachel, you're growing lovelier every day, even if you don't come to church with us any more. Think how radiant you'd be if you came to Mass. We'd be blinded by it, wouldn't we, Jack. Will you come this once to make an old man even happier than I have any right to be on this beautiful sabbath morning?'

He was no thing of beauty to look at himself, this rumpled country priest with his sunburned, fair-skinned Irish face and broken-veined nose. Dandruff was snowing onto the black collar of his soutane, and there was enough of last night's whisky on his breath to blister paint. But Rachel loved Father Paul second only to her father and her uncle Daniel, and she shook her head gently and with genuine regret when she declined the invitation. He had baptised her, buried her mother, stood in as an image of God when she was small, and tried very hard to answer all her questions when puberty propelled her into rebellion and a convent education ushered her all the way to disbelief.

'Well now, you'll be going to see Charity May, of course you will...' he looked downcast for a moment... and you must tell her I'm praying for her even though she doesn't want me to, and I will come and see her before you go off down to the great metropolis... Heavens, it is a sad thing, indeed it is, a terrible shame...' They all noticed at the same time that a knot of worshippers was watching them from the front of the church, and Father Paul gave them a wave. 'We must be away to serve the flock, Jack, look, the multitude is gathering...' He made the sign of the cross in Rachel's direction and again over her mother's grave. 'God's mercy on you dear girl, and on dear Charity, and your dear mother, God keep her. You're the image of her, you are my dear, she was a lovely girl... Give me an arm here, Jack, will you...'

Rachel watched her father supporting the hobbling priest slowly across the cemetery, and then she waited until the last of the churchgoers had disappeared into the cool relief of the stone interior. It was easier not to run the gauntlet of their reproachful pity for her betrayal of the faith.

When she heard the first faint notes of the Mass beginning, she set off back into Springvale, avoiding the clapboard Baptist church but not the dirge they were singing. She could hear the pastor bellowing *'We shall overcome'* at the top of his voice and picture him conducting his exhausted wife on the tiny harmonium and the choir of his own seven children. Pastor Braithwaite paraded his hail-fellow holy calling loudly and sweatily around the district but two years previously before the annual race meeting dinner in the Leichhardt he had pressed himself suggestively against Rachel in the crowded bar, and the look in his protuberant blue eyes made it very clear that gathering her into his flock was not uppermost in his mind.

The memory of that moment made her quicken her step past the solid, staid stonework of the bank, and she was glad to turn off the main street beside the building and see the manager's house close behind it. In a modest country town like Springvale, the manager of the Queensland National Bank was at the top of the civic pecking order, and the house reflected his position in its size and its gleaming state of repair. Rachel knew it very well. Lucas Barrymore had been appointed manager when she was only five years old, and he and his wife, Marjorie, had brought a daughter of exactly the same age to Springvale who had become Rachel's schoolmate in Brisbane and her soulmate in the district.

They had also become atheists, republicans and suffragists together, so on this Sunday morning Rachel knew that Lucas and Marjorie Barrymore would be attending Mass, and Charity May would be waiting impatiently in the house for her visit. When she reached the steps up to the Barrymore's verandah she could see her friend's wheelchair inside the entrance, so she called out, 'Hello, Barry. It's me,' and a breezy reply came immediately from inside the house: 'You're *late,* Gally. Hurry on in here *quick, quick, quick...*'

Rachel was already in the house and standing in the door of the sitting room as May Barrymore finished speaking, and she moved swiftly across the room to the chaise longue where her friend was lying, propped up against a pile of cushions. Rachel stooped down and they hugged each other, and Rachel stood up again and cocked her head.

'Hello, Barry. How are you bearing up today? Not in the chair this morning, I see.'

'Bearing up bravely,' said the other girl, 'but paying the price for overdoing it yesterday, as my dear mama puts it.' She brightened up suddenly. 'Oh but Rachel, Daddy got Westy to bring the chariot along to show me yesterday and it's going to be *wonderful.* Really, just perfect. I'm going to be independent again!' She had been sitting up straighter in her excitement, but winced with pain and slumped back on the pillows.

She held up a hand as Rachel started forward. 'It's nothing. Just a twinge. Bother it.' She smiled brightly. 'Patience is a virtue, they tell me, but I've been *longing* to see you and I think Patience must be a feeble-minded fool.' She patted the chair next to her. 'Come on, take the weight off your wooden leg and talk to me.'

Rachel bent down again and kissed her friend on the forehead. 'You're such a tough nut, Barry. I have come specifically to talk long and hard about anything you want to talk about, but mostly about the expedition. Let her buck, boys.'

May pushed herself up higher against her cushions. 'God, Gally, you have no idea how much I have been *longing* for Monday. Stuck here day after day with no one but Mum to talk to, in this heat...' She fanned herself and Rachel with an Aborigine paddle fan. 'But I must not complain. Doctor Stefan comes as often as he can, and Father Paul won't give up on me, bless him. Remind me I must not complain Gally. I sometimes forget.'

Rachel leaned across and squeezed her friend's hand. 'You're doing well, Barry. Amazingly well. I don't know how you do it, and I will do every last thing I can to help you fight this horrible thing. It will get better, you know. The doctors can do wonders nowadays, you'll see. Aunt Tina has mustered up the best specialists in Brisbane and they'll be able to make this easier for you...'

May tilted her head back and blinked back tears. 'Of course they will. I hope they will. But I remember what it was like before, Gally, all those things I took for granted, and sometimes it gets me down, knowing I'll never be like that again. Oh hell.' She wiped a hand impatiently across her eyes and laughed shakily. 'What is it old Jamie says? She'll be right. My very word...'

Rachel looked down at her own hands and summoned up her own resolve to be bright and cheerful, and not howl with rage and grief at the shocking damage polio had arbitrarily inflicted on her friend. They had both swum in the same public seawater bathing pool near their Brisbane boarding school, but Rachel and all the other girls who had swum with them had been unaffected. May Barrymore had felt unwell the following day, then slipped with terrifying speed into fever, pain, weakness and finally into the shattering realisation that she would never walk or run or ride again.

Rachel had stayed by her friend's bedside for as long as she was allowed, learning everything she could about May's condition and fighting off the doctors' gloomy caution. It could be much worse, they told her. It could have paralysed more than her legs. It could have destroyed her capacity to breathe, and suffocated her slowly.

'Worse!' Rachel had almost shouted at the senior consultant physician, who had brought his students to see his latest case, and patted her patronisingly on the back of her hand. 'What about better? What are you going to do to make her *better*?'

She had been hushed away by the scandalised Matron and given a cup of tea by a sympathetic trainee nurse, which she couldn't even pick up, never mind drink, her hands were shaking so badly. But the consultant had made amends, sitting with Rachel in the visitors' waiting room and explaining the different forms the disease took, and the treatments he would recommend to help make May as comfortable and pain free as possible. Most of all, he said, May would need her friends and family to be strong and positive, to help her adjust to the reality of her disability and find different opportunities and consolations in a much-restricted new life.

'You mustn't waste your energy and spirit crying over spilt milk, Miss Gallagher,' he had said as he stood up to leave her. 'It is a terrible thing to have happened, but be brave and Miss Barrymore will be brave, and life will go on.'

Life had gone on, but not as they had known it. May had left school and returned to a tiny life in Springvale, gritting her teeth through endless hand-wringing sick-calls from well-meaning townspeople, and buoyed by the visits Rachel paid whenever she could. In the two years since the polio had robbed her of her legs and such a large part of her life, they had organised three expeditions to see the specialists in Brisbane, and Lucas Barrymore had pulled every string he could think of to persuade his employers to find him a new position in a larger, coastal town, preferably in Brisbane itself. The bank had reluctantly agreed to try, but the wheels of change at the Queensland National Bank turned exceedingly slowly.

Rachel looked up at May and May made a wry face. 'Cheer up, old chook,' she said. 'I'm looking forward so much to this trip.' She reached over and grabbed Rachel's hand. 'My new chair! I'm going to get the latest, fastest, shiniest chair this time. You can run me along the main street like a racing machine and I can wave to the admiring crowds as we scoot by. Talking of admiring crowds,' she nodded towards the window behind Rachel, 'look who's come to say hello.'

Rachel turned and met the dog-like, haughty stare of the town kangaroo, looking down his long nose through the window at the two young women. He had been brought from the bush as an orphan joey by Jamie Jamieson, the district's dingo trapper, to his corrugated-iron shack behind Westfield's livery, and back then he had been a loveable pet, all legs and feet and tail and large, soft ears. Now he was a spoiled, man-sized menace with a kick that could disembowel a horse, and he spent his days patrolling the streets, eyeing up the town dogs, lounging in the shade of a handy verandah, or browsing through the best veggie patches just as he pleased.

'Hello there, Joey,' said Rachel. 'How are roo today?' May groaned but laughed, and the big grey kangaroo looked from one to the other and then turned away disdainfully and hopped with effortless power over the Barrymores' garden fence.

39

It was a walk of not more than four hundred yards from the big house to the church, but under Lady Saltwood's gentle prompting the dozen people preparing to make the pilgrimage on Sunday morning began to gather well before the church bell began to toll for the ten o'clock morning service.

Lady Saltwood's timing was based on long experience. It took the small party a long time to assemble in the vast hall with a full complement of bibles and prayer books, hats, gloves, handkerchieves and peppermints. After three minutes of watching Lord Saltwood's very limited patience evaporate while Philippa Prior tried to make up her mind whether or not she should take a parasol, Lady Saltwood tactfully suggested that the gentlemen should set off with Lord Saltwood, and the ladies would follow.

Lord Saltwood accepted this offer instantly, instructed Prior to escort the ladies, and strode out of the front door and down the wide steps onto the broad expanse of gravel that fronted the house.

Sir Francis looked enquiringly at Lady Saltwood, then at his wife, and back at Lady Saltwood again. His hostess smiled and urged him not to keep her husband waiting any longer, and the baronet hurried after Sid Kidman and William, who were already halfway down the steps. They turned left along the gravel drive that skirted the east end of the house, and Lord Saltwood stopped for a moment to allow the others to catch up with him.

Sid Kidman stood gazing across the parkland spreading away south and west, and put a hand up to shade his eyes against the dazzling glitter of the lake. There was just enough of a breeze to ruffle the surface into a million shards of glittering light, and stir the leaves of the primaeval oak tree that stood just beyond the ha-ha.

'I believe the weather will turn this afternoon,' said Lord Saltwood authoritatively. All four men looked up unanimously at the sky. It was a cloudless, deep blue above them, but to the west there was a streak of white on the horizon that confirmed the forecast Prior had reported to his employer before breakfast, as he did every day as part of his early morning briefing.

Sid nodded. 'It feels as though it might be going to change.'

'We mustn't tell Philippa,' said William to Sir Francis. 'She won't know whether to bring her parasol or an umbrella.' Sir Francis smiled, but Kidman noticed that Lord Saltwood reacted with an impatient frown, and he ushered his guests onwards along the drive with William bringing up the rear.

The gravel drive they were walking on was designed to allow carriages and cars to move from the front of the house around to the rear and into the courtyard. At the apex of its curve it joined the main driveway for a few yards, and at that point another path turned at right angles towards the churchyard lychgate a hundred yards away.

Lord Saltwood stopped at the end of this path and nodded towards the old stone church, whose roof and tower were all they could see above the dark greenery of the yews that lined the churchyard wall. 'The Church of Saint Barnaby, Mr Kidman. Early thirteenth century. Still as much in use today as it was when it was built.'

Sid looked dutifully at the grey-green, lichen-mottled castellations at the top of the tower. 'Castles and churches, those are the things that stand the test of time in this old country,' said Sir Francis. 'And land, of course. I wonder how many factories and ship-building yards will still be standing a hundred years from now?'

The Australian realised that William had been watching him as they looked at the church. 'I can't say I know much about churches, myself, but Bel's a pillar of the church at home and she always says plenty of prayers for the pair of us. I hope she does, anyway.'

Lord Saltwood was moving away towards the church again, but Kidman delayed so that he and William were walking side by side. 'Just between you and me,' he said to the young man, 'I reckon the Lord likes a man to get along on his own two feet and not bother him too often. What do you think?'

William was startled. Even on a walk to church on a Sunday morning, one's religious beliefs were not normally regarded as a suitable topic of casual conversation. 'I really don't know,' he said guardedly. 'I like our old church. But this?' William hefted his bible and prayerbook in his right hand. 'I think your theology may well be closer to the mark, Mr Kidman.' He glanced up the drive at his father, walking with Sir Francis. 'In this world the good Lord does seem to help those who help themselves. Or those who own the banks. Or the cattle stations.'

They walked a few more paces towards the lychgate. 'This was the village church when the village was still here,' said William. 'Then about two hundred years ago the people who owned the Park had enough spare cash to move the entire village a mile and a half away and rebuild it where it is now.'

Kidman stopped. 'You don't say! They moved the whole village? What for?' William smiled and shrugged. 'To improve the view, probably. It happened on many large estates when they landscaped their parks. I would think they preferred not to have the ugly unwashed with all their dangerous diseases right on their doorsteps, reminding them of their duty to take care of the poor. Not exactly Christian of them.'

The Australian looked hard at William to make sure he wasn't having his leg pulled. William's remarks revealed a surprising point of view from a son of the big house, but then he was discovering that the Saltwoods in general, and this younger son in particular, were more complicated than he had expected.

As was his own role in what he had anticipated would be a straight-forward matter of business. He felt uneasy about the secret vetting that Lord Saltwood had asked him to carry out on William, and he knew after their ride together the previous day that William was not going to take kindly at all to the plans his father was making for his future.

Getting ready for dinner in their bedroom the previous evening, Bel had told him everything that Lady Saltwood had told her about her daughter and her son. It had softened Bel's view about taking the young man back to Australia, but it hadn't shifted her distrust of Lord Saltwood. Sid and Bel now knew that William had been sent down from the university, which must be one good cause of Lord Saltwood's irritation with him, but there was clearly something more deeply out of joint in the relationship between father and son. Living in this glorious place, with all the privileges of their enormous wealth, the Saltwoods, thought Sid, were a surprisingly troubled family.

On the face of it, however, they appeared in church just as the congregation expected, the last to enter, walking past the rows filled with their servants, tenants and dependants up to the Saltwood pews at the front of the nave, just as the lord and lady of the estate had done for centuries.

The servants were required to make their way to church from the back of the house in plenty of time to be seated before his lordship emerged from the front door, and woe betide any who crossed his path in a late scurry to the lychgate.

The single bell rang one more time to signal that the service was about to begin, and as the clock struck eleven times in the tower above them the Park party settled itself in formal order, Lord Saltwood closest to the aisle, Lady Saltwood next to him, the Whiteleys and William making up the front row on the north side of the aisle, the Kidmans and the Priors filling the front pew on the south side.

The Park party was the first to leave the church, too, when the service was over an hour and a half later, walking down the aisle between house staff on the north and estate workers on the south, Lord Saltwood nodding curtly and Lady Saltwood smiling left and right.

Lord Saltwood planted himself in the middle of the paved pathway outside the church porch, blocking the way so that the other members of the congregation were forced to walk respectfully round him on the grass between the old stone gravestones. Philippa Prior, inevitably, had left her prayerbook in the church, and her husband hurried back inside to fetch it. Lady Saltwood had enquired after the head groom's elderly mother, and was listening sympathetically to an all-to detailed description of the old lady's latest troubles.

Bel and the girls and Lady Amelia had stopped to exchange courtesies with the vicar at the edge of the porch, so Sid moved a yard or two along the path, following William and Sir Francis, and he couldn't help overhearing their conversation.

'How did you like the sermon, William?'

William gave a small cough. 'I must admit I lost the scent after the first five minutes, Uncle Francis, but at least I kept my eyes open.'

Sir Francis smiled at William with a warmth that Kidman suspected he never received from Lord Saltwood. 'I was thinking deeply about the vicar's words on the prodigal son. I daresay you were, too. I wonder if your father ordered that particular topic today. Your mother told me about Oxford. I'm sorry, William. What a rotten thing to happen.'

William looked down at the path for a moment, and then shrugged. 'Well, worse things happen at sea, but it certainly has put me in rather a bind. Or to be more honest, I've put myself in a bind.'

'What will you do now, d'you think?' asked the baronet. 'You must let me know if I can help.' He leaned slightly closer to his nephew. 'Your father has already warned me off giving you any direct financial assistance, but *in extremis*, you know, you must...' William's eyes had strayed warningly over his uncle's shoulder, and Sir Francis stopped speaking as Lord Saltwood advanced towards them. 'Thank you, Uncle Francis, I will,' said William quietly, and then more loudly, 'I think we're moving off.'

The party made its slow way back out of the churchyard under the covered lychgate, and headed back along the path towards the house and lunch. The wind was strengthening, and as they passed the entrance to the rectory they saw the vicar leaving the churchyard by a side gate, his white surplice billowing out and more or less completely obscuring his wife.

40

Since she had been put on scullery duties at the Mile, Tilly had taken to visiting the baby's grave at the municipal cemetery in Tower Hamlets most days during the midday hours between her shifts. On Sundays she went without fail, and as this was his Sunday off, Charlie went with her.

It was a bright day, made all the better by the shy, hesitant smile Tilly had given him when he woke up. Still a long way from the double row of pearly whites she used to greet him with, but a big step forward after last night's emotional explosion.

Several huge steps forward, it seemed, as Tilly took his arm for the first time in months and they walked the whole way together along Bridge Street and over the Regent's Canal on the Gunmakers' Arms Bridge. They crossed South Grove next to the forbidding old Union Workhouse, which gave Charlie a minor flip of anxiety, and then up to the lodge gates that guarded the entrance to the huge expanse of the cemetery.

When they stopped to buy a tuppenny bunch of violets from the women who kept the stall outside the cemetery gates, Tilly suddenly reached her face up and kissed Charlie on the cheek.

She knocked her black straw hat sideways doing it, and Charlie raised a hand to help her set it straight again. Tilly grabbed his hand with both of hers and held it tight.

'You're a good man, Charlie,' she said, and tears welled up in her eyes. 'I'm sorry. I'm not much good to you like this, am I?'

Charlie's heart felt as though it had turned a somersault in his chest, and he couldn't do anything but stare at his wife for a few moments. He felt that they were emerging miraculously from the darkness of the past few months, but he knew they were on the thinnest ice and he was terrified he would make a wrong move or say a wrong word.

He had the intuitive good sense to make light of it. 'Get on, Till. You're the best thing that ever happened to me, you are. Always will be 'til the day I die. *Till* the day I die, eh, Till?! Problem is, I'm not much use to *you* now, eh? Neither use nor ornament.' He pulled her hand through the crook of his arm again. 'Come on, Till, we'll get through it, you'll see.'

They were standing in front of the stall, blocking new customers and one of the black-shawled flower women chivvied them along, not unkindly, 'Make a space there, missis. Give us a bit of room.'

Tilly took a deep breath and they walked into the cemetery, heading towards the children's corner beyond the Church of England Mortuary Chapel where the baby's brief funeral service had been intoned to Charlie and Tilly and four other grieving families. Tilly's grip on his arm tightened as they approached the cramped rows of tiny graves, and Charlie patted her hand. 'On we go, my girl.'

As always on a Sunday after morning services had ended, there were dozens of groups of people scattered across the cemetery, which was so big those at the far side looked like marionettes. There were at least two funerals in progress, too, not surprisingly considering that this was one of the few local burial grounds with room for the hundreds dying every day in the seething back-to-back streets of Bow, Stepney and Tower Hamlets.

As they drew closer to the children's corner, Charlie and Tilly could see that a burial was finishing close to their baby's grave. A weeping woman, a mother presumably, was being led away by a man, both dressed like Charlie and Tilly in their shabby Sunday best, followed by an elderly couple and a single younger woman, all in as much black clothing as they could muster, all looking as unconsoled as Charlie and Tilly had been by the clergyman's promise that their young one had been gathered into the arms of Jesus.

As the clergyman came closer Charlie realised it was the same curate who had married them in Saint Dunstan's church and then buried their own baby less than eleven months later, and Charlie could clearly remember his sing-song, meaningless delivery of the liturgy in both short services.

The clergyman was one of the three curates who served under the vicar of Saint Dunstan's, a bitterly disappointed, over-worked, middle-aged man who had once been confident that he might rise to the heights of a wealthy parish or, God willing, maybe even a deanery in a rich and powerful establishment church. But newly ordained and determined to make his mark, he had instead made the catastrophic mistake early in his first appointment of arguing an obscure point of theology with his bishop, and his efforts to achieve even a moderate vicarage of his own had been blocked ever since the vindictive old tyrant had marked his card with a red-inked commandment that this would-be highflyer should spend his days learning the blessings of humility for the good of his eternal soul.

This Sunday, long after he felt he should have been sitting down to roast beef in a comfortable rectory somewhere in Barchestershire, here he was conducting burial services in an East End municipal cemetery for the offspring of the poor, who died like flies without any consideration for the day of the week or his own dwindling reserves of Christian charity. Dwindling? Empty. Bone dry.

He was making his way back as quickly as he decently could to the mortuary chapel to shed his cassock, surplice and stole, followed by his fiercely loyal but deeply stupid wife, who insisted on supporting her husband at every service he took, and in all his many duties to the people of the parish, including burials.

They were moving along the path between the children's corner and the chapel, in the opposite direction to Charlie and Tilly, and as they approached, Charlie stood to one side, took off his hat and said, 'Good afternoon, sir.' He expected the clergyman to remember them, but the curate only nodded and wished them an unsmiling good afternoon as he made to pass.

Charlie glanced at Tilly. She had been halfway back to her lively old self on the walk here. Now she was staring at the curate and her face was white and pinched again.

He held out a hand as though to touch the curate's white surplice. 'Excuse me, sir, do you remember us? My wife and me? You married us and you buried our baby a few months back? Just over there.'

The curate turned back towards them and brushed a hand irritably down the sleeve of his surplice. 'I'm afraid I don't. I cannot be expected to remember every marriage and every burial service I conduct. I have another this afternoon before evensong and I must go. Good afternoon to you.' He was about to turn away again when he clearly remembered his clerical manners. 'I am sorry for your loss. God bless you both.' He made the sign of the cross in the air.

Charlie took a step forward. 'Thank you sir, but could you say something for my wife? She's taken it badly, sir. It's very hard for her...'

A flush of colour crept up from under the curate's dog-collar and the lines on either side of his mouth seemed to pull it down even further. He took a deep breath. 'You must take comfort in the knowledge that your child is with God. The Lord giveth and the Lord taketh away.' He motioned to his own wife to move away again, but they were both stopped in their tracks by the anguish in Tilly's voice.

'Why did God take my baby? What did He want with *my* baby?' Tilly let go of Charlie's arm and her fists were clenched by her sides.

The curate was a tall, stooped man who suffered badly from piles, and he stared down at this impertinent woman, losing what little patience he had left. 'Why? My good woman, we do not question God's will! You must be thankful your baby was baptised in Christ, otherwise it could not have been buried in this sanctified ground and taken up to heaven. So you must give thanks to our saviour for his redemption and thank God for all his mercies.'

'She,' said Tilly. 'My baby was a little girl. Just a few days old she was. What good was she to God? Why'd he have to take her? You tell me where's the mercy in that?'

The curate's wife was goggling at Tilly from behind her husband. 'How dare you say such things to the reverend gentleman?' she hissed. She pulled at the curate's arm. 'Come along, Everard. She is not in her right senses. People are looking.'

A few of those nearest them in the cemetery were indeed looking curiously at the little tableaux, but Tilly remained staring intently at the curate, and his wife moved defensively around him and glared at this upstart, demented troublemaker.

'Do you come to church? I don't remember seeing you in Saint Dunstan's. Do you support your church and its ministers, working so hard to save your souls? No, you don't, do you? How dare you blaspheme at the curate? You should look to your own sins and repent and then you'll see why God took your child...'

The curate and his wife had lost one of their own children many years earlier, and the misery in Tilly's face touched a man who had long since lost any real faith in the version of God embodied in the church he represented. He frowned at his wife and hushed her, and then he sighed and looked down at Tilly with as much human kindness as he could find in his scarred and shrunken heart.

'My dear woman, His works are a mystery even to those of us who serve Him.' He gestured at the cramped checkerboard of children's graves. 'Suffer the little children to come unto me, said the Lord. He takes them from this world of misery and sin, and we must bear our loss and be thankful that they are in a better place. Go to church and pray for your child, and I will pray for it... for her at evensong. Now I must go. Come along, my dear.'

The curate and his wife turned and hurried away along the path. She was leaning into him, gobbling with outrage and casting fearful, triumphant glances back at Tilly as though she had just survived being ambushed by the devil.

Tilly stood rigidly looking after them, shaking just as she had done the evening before. When Charlie tried to take her hand she snatched it away from him, and he noticed she had crushed the flowers he had bought to a mud-coloured pulp.

He could barely suppress the urge to run after the clergyman and punch his wife, but then he wondered if perhaps it was his own fault for asking the clergyman to comfort Tilly.

He realised that Tilly was walking stiff-legged down the path towards the baby's grave and he hurried after her. The children's graves were laid out in rows, dozens upon dozens, separated by thin strips of grass, all recent in the area where their own baby had been buried, all with almost identical miniature headstones carved with the simplest inscriptions at minimal cost.

Before he could reach her, Tilly had sunk to her knees and he could see her whole body heaving. He leaned over and put his hand on Tilly's shoulder. His eyes were no more than a couple of feet from the inscription carved into the baby's small headstone.

Eliza Downs
Gone to God
5ᵗʰ April 1908

'Excuse me. Can I help?'

Charlie stood upright and turned to see a slight young woman holding a much younger boy by the hand. She came closer and then dropped to one knee beside Tilly, heedless of her good coat, and put her arm round Tilly's shoulders. 'You poor thing. I'm sorry to intrude but I heard that. It was horrible.'

She tilted her head to look into Tilly's face. 'Don't I know you? Did you used to work for the Kennedys? I think I've seen you in my dad's shop, the fruit and sweet shop on the five roads corner. Burdett Road? Cappuccio's?' The stranger was speaking quietly and calmly, stroking Tilly's back, just as he would to calm a nervous horse, thought Charlie, and Tilly stopped sobbing.

'Take your time. Plenty of time.' She looked up at Charlie. 'I beg your pardon for intruding like this. I hope you don't mind?'

Charlie shook his head and then nodded in case she misunderstood. 'No, no, Miss, not at all, thank you very much, Miss.' He made a helpless gesture and shrugged. 'We was doing alright but that's put us back to square one...' He gestured towards the chapel and the direction the curate had taken.

The young woman nodded and looked back at Tilly, who was fumbling in her coat pocket for a handkerchief. 'Here you are. It's clean, I promise.' She held out her own folded white handkerchief. Tilly took it and blew her nose without looking up, and then she took a deep breath and pulled her shoulders back a little.

'I'll wash it for you, Miss. I'll get it back to your shop tomorrow. Thank you very much. I'm sorry to be such a nuisance...'

'Don't worry about the hanky,' said the young woman. 'Just you take your time and get your breath back.' She rubbed Tilly's back again and Charlie could see the tension in her shoulders relaxing.

'Why don't you come and sit down? There's a bench just there. Come on, you'll feel better.' The young woman got up and she and Charlie helped Tilly to her feet. Tilly lifted the hand still clutching the remains of the violets, stared at it and then at Charlie, her eyes filling with tears.

'Never mind them, Till,' he said quickly. 'You just sit down here and I'll run up and get some more. Is that alright Miss? Can you stay while I get some more of these? I'll be quick as I can.'

'Of course I can,' said the young woman. 'Don't hurry. I've got plenty of time.' She beckoned to the boy, who had been standing a few yards away watching with round eyes. 'Ernie, why don't you go with this nice man and get some flowers for us too?' The boy looked puzzled. They had already bought flowers and laid them on his brother's and sister's graves.

He was about to speak when he saw his big sister wink. She dug into her purse. 'Here you are. Hold out your hand.' The boy solemnly held out his hand and watched a sixpence drop into his palm. 'Two bunches.' She looked at Charlie enquiringly. 'Would you mind taking Ernie with you? I'm sorry, I don't know your name.'

'Oh,' said Charlie. 'I mean, no, 'course I don't mind, Miss. I'm Charlie, Charlie Downs. This is Tilly, my wife... Matilda, but you don't really go by that, do you, Till?'

Tilly shook her head.

The young woman smiled at them both. 'How do you do, Mr and Mrs Downs. I'm very pleased to meet you. I'm Annie Cappuccio and this is Ernie, my brother.' She didn't look any more than Tilly's age, but she had an aura of quiet confidence that made her seem much older and more mature than both Tilly and Charlie. 'There now, we're formally introduced, so we can be friends. Why don't you men go and buy some flowers, and Tilly and I will sit tight here.'

The two men needed no second bidding and set off along the path to the cemetery gates, the boy doing his best to imitate Charlie's longer stride and live up to the responsibility his sister had given him.

Annie Cappuccio and Tilly sat on the wooden bench in silence in the sun for a minute or so, Tilly staring down at the handkerchief crumpled in her hands, and Annie looking out across the cemetery. They were almost exactly the same size, small, slight young women dressed very similarly in long, dark, waisted overcoats and round straw hats, but Tilly felt acutely conscious of her shabbier coat and her tear-streaked face, and the other young woman seemed to sense it.

'Makes my blood boil to hear that kind of nonsense from the clergy,' she said sternly. 'He wanted to be away to his lunch! Prancing about in his silly get-up. He should be out there helping the poor if he's a good Christian. And that wife of his! She's a disgrace saying that rubbish to you.' She sucked air through her teeth and shook her head, then she looked sideways at Tilly and smiled. 'They deserved each other, didn't they? He looked like a long streak of misery and she looked like the back end of a tram. Good riddance to the pair of them.'

Tilly looked up at her, startled, then she smiled too and wiped her eyes again with the handkerchief.

'That's better,' said Annie. 'You know, I'm sure I've seen you in the shop, but maybe I've seen you here as well, since then. Might I have? Over the past few months? I come here every Sunday if I can leave my mum. We've got two buried in here, and I like to come and sit here for a little while.'

Tilly took a deep breath and sat up straighter on the bench, and poured her heart out. 'My little girl died a few days after she was born, back in April it was, in all that snow. Eleven days after. Six months gone but it seems like yesterday.' She smoothed out the handkerchief on her lap. 'I can't get over it. Not fit for anything. Can't do my job. Can't look after Charlie. Can't think of anything except my little girl...' She had to blow her nose again, hard, and crumpled the handkerchief up again.

'Of course you can't,' said Annie gently. 'Have you got any others? Was she your first?'

Tilly nodded. 'Yes.' She said it so quietly Annie barely heard her, and bent closer.

'Have you got anyone you can talk to? Your mum? Someone close?'

Tilly shook her head again. 'Not really. There's a neighbour downstairs who's been very good. Mrs Hoddle, but she just says the same as the church people, 'It's God's will' and all that. Charlie tries his best but he doesn't understand. Poor Charlie.'

'No one else at all? No other family nearby?'

Tilly shook her head. 'I don't have any family I know of. I didn't ever know my mum and dad. I lived in the girls' home at Barkingside ever since I can remember.'

They heard footsteps approaching and both women turned to see Charlie and Ernie walking back towards them. Ernie waved a bunch of violets and ran the last few yards to the bench.

He held up the bunch in one hand and a penny in the other. 'Look, Annie, they gave us a luck penny for buying three more bunches, and Mr Downs said I could have it. Can I?'

'That's very kind of Mr Downs. If he says so, of course you can, but maybe we could use it to buy a bunch for Mum?'

The boy looked so crestfallen even Tilly smiled.

Annie laughed and made a face at her brother. 'I'm just pulling your leg, Ernie. You keep it for birdseed and I'll buy another bunch for Mum on the way out.'

She turned to Tilly. 'I'd like to talk some more if you do? Have you got time to come and have a cup of tea with us? Which way are you going from here?'

Charlie gestured at the lodge and the gates where the flower sellers were camped. 'We were thinking of walking a bit, that way along Bridge Street back to where we live, wasn't we Till?' The thought of heading back to the gloom of Parfitt Court with Tilly after this latest upset made his stomach turn over.

Annie Cappuccio looked enquiringly at Tilly, who looked up at Charlie and nodded. 'We'd like that, wouldn't we, Charlie?'

Charlie beamed at the women. 'Yes! Yes, that's a good idea, thank you Miss...'

Annie clapped her hands on her knees and stood up. 'That's settled then, but you must call me Annie. We'll go and put our flowers where they belong, shall we, and then when you're ready we'll go and have a cuppa. When I only have Ernie with me we always go home by Single Street so Ernie can look into the bird shop, but first we'll go and have a cup of tea and a cake at the café on the corner there overlooking the canal. Whetherolds. Do you know it?'

They did know it. Charlie had always thought it was too genteel by half for the likes of him and Tilly, but he wouldn't mind braving it with this determined new friend.

'Yes, we know where you mean, Miss. Let's go there then.'

They all walked down the path back to the children's corner and separated to lay their flowers on the three small graves. Tilly knelt again next to Eliza's headstone and Charlie could hear her murmuring, but there were no more tears, and when he gave her his hand to lift her back to her feet, she smiled as she had at the gates earlier, and she kept hold of his hand as they walked back to where Annie Cappuccio was waiting on the path.

41

As the house party approached the archway that led into the stud courtyard, Lord Saltwood stopped and took his watch out of his waistcoat pocket. The gentlemen and the ladies would go their separate ways from here, he said, to Sid's surprise, and meet again in exactly three-quarters of an hour.

They would all return to the house for tea on the lawn at four o'clock. The Australian would much rather have spent longer at the stud and less time at the table. The six courses of traditional Sunday lunch they had only recently finished had lasted for two hours and Sid thought the amount of Mrs Courtenay's sensational roast beef he had eaten would have kept him going for about two days in the outback. It hadn't helped that he had been seated with the vicar's wife on his left, and this tiny woman had eaten so little that Sid had felt ashamed of his own intake.

He could say nothing, however, and he joined the other men while Lady Saltwood led Lady Whiteley, Philippa Prior, Bel Kidman and the girls onwards through the arch to see the mares and foals. All three of the Kidman girls walked behind their mother with the slightly slumped shoulders that even their father recognised as the body language of tragic disappointment.

Lord Saltwood turned away briskly with Sir Francis, Sid Kidman, William and Prior hurrying after him towards the stallion quarters on the other side of the lane that divided the two sets of imposing stone buildings.

Lord Saltwood spoke over his shoulder without breaking stride. 'I would like to show you the stallion first, Mr Kidman, then we can join the ladies briefly and look at the mares and foals.'

Kidman nodded energetically. 'Lead on Lord Saltwood. I'm keen to see how you do things here in England. I like to think I might breed a decent racehorse in Australia one of these days, but do you mind if I ask if the girls can come and see the stallion too? They're very keen on the horse side of my operation and they'd like to see him.'

If Sid had been surprised by the separation in the first place, he was even more surprised by the reaction his question provoked. Lord Saltwood stopped and turned to his guest with a look of blank astonishment.

'Ah...' he cleared his throat loudly. Sir Francis bent his head and looked thoughtfully at the gravel drive. William turned away to study the top of the hedge surrounding the stallion paddock.

Prior, as always, stepped into the breach. 'I'm sure you understand better than anyone, Mr Kidman, that we prefer to keep the ladies away from the stallion. He can be a little boisterous. I'm sure you'll appreciate the precaution.'

The Australian realised that Prior was tactfully skirting around the old grooms' belief that if by chance it was that unmentionable time of the month for any of the women in the party, the stallion was likely to react in the same way he would to a mare in season. A stallion sporting a two-foot-long erection was something his girls had inevitably seen before at his famous horse sales but he would have to admit he had been embarrassed the first time it had happened in view of his wife and daughters.

It had happened just once in public to Lord Saltwood, twenty years before, when he had been proudly showing off his Derby runner-up to a party of guests. He had instructed the stud groom to lead the young stallion down to the front of the house on a sunny Sunday just like this, so the experience had occurred in front of his mother, his wife, three wives of important guests and a handful of female members of staff.

It was impossible to find out which female was responsible for the stallion's sudden lust. If he could have pinned the blame on any of the maids he would have sacked her on the spot. But there was no escaping the evidence of Crecy's spectacular arousal, and it had taken two men to help the stud groom drag the snorting stallion out of sight, his pizzle swinging underneath him as though it was questing for a target.

The first Lord Saltwood, John Saltwood the ironmaster, the current Lord Saltwood's father, had married the daughter of a Bristol coal merchant for his money and not for her breeding, and the old dowager Lady Saltwood had actually saved the day by roaring with laughter at this display. Her son had not been amused at all and had vowed that he would never be humiliated in this way again, and from that day on, Chiddington stud had followed the prevailing wisdom that the fair sex should not be allowed anywhere within sight or scent of a stallion under any circumstances other than at the races, where it was unavoidable but the colts were otherwise occupied.

So it was only the men who admired the son of Crecy in his enclosure, held proudly by the stud groom.

Agincourt was a bright bay, the spitting image of his sire in the painting that Kidman had admired. There was a recognisable similarity in his colouring and the carriage of his head and his calm, confident character, but this living horse in three dimensions was even more the embodiment of equine perfection than his painted sire. The late morning autumn sunlight illuminated the dappled patterns in his polished bay coat and glowed along the curve of muscle down the crest of his neck and over his quarters.

Horse lovers talked of a specially fine horse 'filling the eye'. This one filled Sid Kidman's heart with pure joy.

'Agincourt,' said Lord Saltwood briskly as though he was reading from a catalogue. 'Foaled May 'ninety-nine. By Crecy out of a King Tom mare. He has Voltigeur on his sire's side and St Simon blood again from his dam sire. Finished fourth in the Guineas in 'oh-one and we had to withdraw him a week before the Derby in 'oh-two. He didn't match his sire on the course, but he is producing some very good offspring and I have a two-year-old in training that I hope might go one better than his grandsire next year.'

The horse's bloodlines didn't mean much to Sid and he moved sideways a couple of paces to admire the horse from a different angle. 'My word,' he said. 'I thought that hunting horse of yours yesterday was pretty close to perfect, but I reckon this one might be better. He couldn't be better presented.'

Lord Saltwood inclined his head. 'Thank you, Mr Kidman. I value your opinion, and I'm sure Nicholl here will value the compliment just as highly.'

The stud groom, Nicholl, touched the peak of his cap. He did value the compliment even though he had had nothing at all to do with the horse's breeding, racing success or good conformation, but Kidman's comparison of his thoroughbred charge to Lord Saltwood's hunter went a long way to spoiling it. He and Daniels, the head groom in charge of the domestic stables, detested each other.

The stallion sensed his sudden change of mood and moved, and the groom glanced guiltily at his employer. The horse had been standing in a textbook position. Trying to persuade him to put his feet back precisely in the right places would probably make matters worse, but fortunately for Nicholl Lord Saltwood had not noticed.

William was very well aware how the grooms felt about each other, but the two men were very careful indeed not to show their mutual animosity to their employer. In this instance, his lordship's eye was fixed firmly on his guest, and there was a glint of triumphant revelation in it. 'You may well compare the two, Mr Kidman, because they are both by Crecy. Agincourt is full bred, of course. Trafalgar is three-quarter-bred by Crecy out of a half-bred mare. All the Chiddington hunters are three-quarter thoroughbred, and I think you might be surprised by the other quarter.'

The stallion had had enough of the groom's surreptitious attempts to make him move his hooves back into perfect show position, and he lowered his head into the man's chest and butted him backwards. The groom murmured to him, 'Stand still,' and tugged gently on his lead rein. It was attached to a highly polished stallion bridle, and for a moment or two the pressure of the bit in his mouth persuaded the horse to do as the groom had suggested. But he wasn't going to stand all day and listen to the droning noises these curious creatures were making, and he shifted sideways again, eyeing the groom in a way his handler knew meant it was time to move on.

'Beg pardon, your lordship,' he said, and Lord Saltwood turned to him frowning. 'Beg pardon for interrupting you, your lordship, but may I move 'im away, sir?' Lord Saltwood glanced at the stallion briefly and then waved his hand. 'Yes. Take him back.'

The group watched the horse pacing away from them in his long, steel-sprung stride along the gravel path that led back to the high-hedged paddock and the cosseted, solitary life of the working stallion. He would be led out again on Monday to serve a mare in a violent, lunging explosion of shuddering lust, but the majority of his time he would spend alone.

As the end of his tail swung out of sight around the corner of the

245

building, Lord Saltwood turned back to Kidman and challenged him again to guess the missing ingredient in his favourite hunter's breeding. Sid Kidman had glanced across Sir Francis at William as Lord Saltwood watched his stallion disappear, and raised an eyebrow. William shook his head slightly.

'No,' said Kidman. 'You've thrown me.'

'Welsh pony,' said Lord Saltwood, smiling his tight smile. 'You may not credit it, but it's true. We introduced it fifteen years ago when my son George was eleven. He was hunting a fourteen two Welsh pony mare that went lame. She came into season and she was covered by a thoroughbred colt and produced a top-class filly foal. All the thoroughbred size and speed but tough as nails and quick as a cat on her feet. So I decided to put her to Crecy as a three-year-old and she threw the best hunter in England. I've been breeding Welsh pony into our hunter bloodlines ever since. It has been a great success, hasn't it, William?'

William looked at his father and not at Sid Kidman. He had listened to the head groom, Daniels, telling Kidman the same story at much greater length the previous afternoon as the three of them had toured the Park stables. Exactly the same story with the exception that Daniels had quite rightly taken the credit for suggesting the cross between the half-bred Welsh filly and the Derby-winning thoroughbred. It was a story William had heard many times from the head groom and several times from his father, and Sid Kidman knew from his face as he answered his father's question whose version he believed was true.

'Yes, sir, it has,' he replied quietly.

Lord Saltwood looked back at his guest. 'If you're taking breeding stock back with you to Australia, Mr Kidman, I recommend a Welsh pony or two. You won't regret it, I guarantee it. Charles Coltman is your man. I would be very happy to introduce you to him.'

Kidman nodded. 'I'd be grateful.' It rang a bell with the Bard of the Bush, he thought, and quoted out loud: '...*A touch of Timor pony, but three parts thoroughbred at least...*' That was the recipe for a top stockhorse in *The Man from Snowy River*. Lord Saltwood looked at his guest blankly for a moment and shook his head. 'Welsh pony is the thing, Welsh pony mare to a full thoroughbred or perhaps three-quarter bred but nothing less. Now we should join the ladies and see how they're getting on with the mares and foals. I daresay they will be petting them,' Lord Saltwood's eyes flickered very briefly towards his son, 'and it makes them unmanageable.'

Twenty minutes later the Park party emerged from the stud courtyard into the sunshine. It was just after three o'clock, and the party had split into small groups, strolling back towards the house along the drive.

42

'He's coming in tomorrow on the train, Jack. I don't think you're going to like the sound of him. I certainly don't.'

Sergeant Macdonald sniffed and shook his head. 'Things are changing, Jack, and they're leaving me behind, I can tell you.' As if to demonstrate just how far behind he was being left, the Springvale and District policeman was wearing his old blue uniform for old times' sake, it being a Sunday evening and he off duty, sitting in his own home with one of his oldest friends.

'Well Mack, you're moving on and up, aren't you? Off to the bright lights of Townsville next week and chasing real criminals rather than mustering up drunken ringers. I'm very sorry to see you go, you know that, but you're going on to better things, not before time. And you'll be with Rosemary.'

They were both holding glasses of Bundaberg rum and Jack Gallagher raised his to the sergeant. 'Health and happiness, Mack. I wish you weren't going, but you've done us proud and you deserve a much bigger step up.'

Macdonald sniffed again more loudly and grimaced.

'Thank you for those few kind words, Jack. Very kind, but sub-inspector second class? Pushing pieces of paper round a desk? Living with my mother-in-law? I'd rather stay a constable here in Springvale and die in my old boots out here in the bush, but there you are. Crack goes the whip and you know what the donkey does. I must tell you about the new man you'll be dealing with. The reports I've had from my contacts are not very favourable.'

They were sitting in squatter's chairs on the verandah at the back of Mack's small police house on the southern edge of the sprawling little town. It gave them a clear view down the low hill to the river, and to their left the railhead, stockyards and goods depot that were giving Springvale a new lease of life.

On a Sunday evening there wasn't another soul to be seen, but tomorrow morning it would be roaring with cattle being herded into the stockyards ready for loading as soon as the weekly Rockhampton train hit the buffers late in the morning. It would be a long train almost entirely made up of cattle cars, but there would be a goods wagon or possibly two full of supplies for the town and the district's farms and out-by stations. And there would be a single passenger-carriage that would bring Springvale's new policeman, and take Rachel, May and her mother away down to the coast and a long, slow onward journey to Brisbane.

'His name's Cleary,' said Mack gloomily. 'Hmmph. More bloody Irish. Just what we need here.' If he didn't know James Macdonald as well as he did, Jack thought he might have seen a glimmer of a smile behind the grey walrus moustache.

'I don't have anything against the Irish, as you know, Jack. There's one or too good ones among 'em. I've never come across a bad Scot, of course. You know where you stand with the Scots. They all have a grudge, and if they're drunk you know they want a fight about it. As for the English... enough said, but you have to admit the Irish, well, you're never sure where you are with the tricky ones, and this one's a tricky piece of work, right enough. You'll need to be careful, Jack.'

He leaned forward. 'You remember that enquiry down on the border two or three years ago? Cunnamulla way? Well, Cleary was mixed up in that, using the old native trackers on the quiet and notching up blackfellas on their rifle stocks. Wouldn't believe it in this day and age, would you?'

The sergeant had been policing the outback in Queensland for over thirty years and Jack knew the older man had seen everything there was to see in the long, grey history of conflict between white and black. In the Springvale district Mack had long since enforced a moderately fair peace, but now he was leaving and in any case Jack was well aware that even here you didn't have to scratch the surface very deeply to find a much darker story still unfolding. He remembered Rachel's words on the Warrigal verandah that had spoiled his supper three evenings previously.

'So he's a hard horse?'

'Aye,' replied the sergeant. 'Royal Irish Constabulary back in the old country. Came out of that no one knows why and emigrated in '02, joined the Rifle Regiment and then two years ago he was kicked out of that and joined the police. They hushed it up but my contact tells me he was shown the door with a boot up his arse.'

To the north of them, a single bell began to toll for Father Paul's evening service. The shadows were lengthening and the Capricorn dusk was already shading the western sky a deeper blue.

The two men sat in silence until the bell had finished ringing.

'Six o'clock,' said Jack. 'Another day almost done. Are you keeping an eye on Father Paul? He wasn't getting along too good earlier.'

'Aye, I am. He's a good man but he's drinking far too much and it's tickling up his gout something terrible. I wonder how much longer they'll expect him to carry on trying to hobble round this damned great parish.'

'Until he dies, I reckon,' said Jack. 'I don't think the church will want him cluttering up the place back down in Brisbane. Or Melbourne, God forbid. Can you see him among the bishops, sneaking a nip from his flask during Mass?'

Sergeant Macdonald shook his head. 'I'm sure he'll soldier on here. I don't know what he'll make of the new fella.'

'What did they chuck him out of the Rifle Regiment for? And how did he get into the police if the Rifles didn't want him?'

The sergeant looked at Jack seriously. 'Well now, that's a very good question, and the answer is the Irish seem to be taking care of their own.' He took another swallow of rum. 'You know as well as I do how the Irish mob works in this country. Off the record, Jack, I'm told it's probably the new Commissioner. Turns out they both come from the same part of Ireland and Cahill followed the same track when he was a young fella. Royal Irish Constabulary, Queensland Rifles, Queensland Police. So the word is, he's giving Cleary another chance, but they know he's a bad bargain so they've packed him off here because this place is settled and everybody gets along. They think he can't get up to much mischief, but he's not the sort of chap to stay out of trouble long and now he's going to be your problem, Jack, I'm sorry to say.'

Jack raised his eyebrows. 'A serious problem, you think?'

'Aye, well, this is what I've been told, and it comes from someone very senior. The man's a bully and as far as he's concerned he's always right. You know, one of those awkward sods who thinks if everyone else is putting the other foot forward, he's the only one marching in step. Why he left Ireland I don't know, but I do know he was thrown out of the Rifles for bullying.'

'Bullying? Bullying who? The blackfellas?'

Macdonald shook his head. 'No, not just blackfellas and drunks he can kick around without anyone complaining, but bullying his own men, the younger men and anyone under him. The minute he was commissioned in the Rifles he started throwing his weight around, and he wouldn't be told, even by his commanding officer. The men hated him so much the CO reckoned they'd shoot him first chance they got, so a transfer was arranged behind the scenes and the Commissioner took him on.'

'Good grief. Do we have to put up with him? asked Jack. 'Can we complain to someone?'

Macdonald shook his head again. 'Not until he's stepped over the line again, which he'll do sooner or later, or I'll eat my new hat and pay for another one. No, the Commissioner will want him to have a fair go, and maybe he's right. Maybe he's learnt his lesson, but from what I've heard he's not the sort to admit he's ever wrong. Apparently, he comes across all Irish charm and blarney when you first meet the fella, you know, nice as pie, but if he doesn't get his own way you get the real thing. My contact tells me he hates blackfellas. The only thing he hates worse is the English, and he'll favour an Irishman every time, right or wrong. So there you are, Jack, you'll be alright with him until you cross him, so I would recommend you avoid him whenever you can and watch him like a hawk when you can't. That's the best I can do for you, I'm afraid. Chapter and verse on Constable Michael Cleary, your new policeman. I don't need to tell you this is strictly between you and me, of course.'

Jack leaned back and looked heavenwards at the roof of the verandah. 'Strewth. Rachel wants me to report that fella squatting on Berrie Berrie to you for the way he's treating the blackfellas there, and I need to report him for duffing my cleanskins. Now you tell me your new man is going to love him because he's bog Irish and slap him on the back because he's beating the hell out of the blacks.'

'Aye, well, you'll just have to head that girl of yours off so she doesn't lock horns with him. She takes after her mother, doesn't she? Looks and spirit just the same. Stands up for what's right never mind the opposition and won't back down from a dust-up.'

Jack sighed and took a long swallow. 'You're right, Mack, she's Florence all over again. I look at her sometimes and miss Florence as badly as I ever did.'

The sergeant stared out into the deep darkness of the evening. 'I'll miss these evenings, Jack. I'll miss not seeing that girl of yours growing up into a very fine woman.' He looked across the verandah. 'Do you remember when you told me you were going to marry Florence? Must have been eighty-seven or eighty-eight?'

'Eighty-seven,' said Jack quietly.

'Eighty-seven it was. Twenty-one years. It doesn't seem so long ago, does it? What the hell happened to all those years? Aye, well, you told me and do you remember what I said?

Jack laughed. 'I do. You told me straight out if I was stupid enough to choose an Italian girl from Melbourne I should make bloody sure I was doing the right thing before I jumped in.'

'Aye, I did. I didn't want you to make the same mistake I had. I was four years married and I knew fine well I'd married the wrong woman. And then you brought Florence Perversi up to Warrigal and when I met her by God I envied you Jack. She was one in a million, wasn't she, and what she saw in you I don't know, but you were happier than a dog with two tails and somehow that made up for my mistake.'

Macdonald picked up the bottle from the verandah floor and leaned across to refill Jack's glass. He refilled his own and cradled the bottle in the crook of his left arm.

'They tell me there's a god, Jack, but I stopped believing in that the night you brought Florence into town and Father Paul buried her. There's no god I can believe in who would take a woman like Florence in her prime, take her away from you and Rachel. Anyway, I had a wife who knows everything so I didn't need a god.' He laughed.

'But lately I've been thinking. Maybe Rachel's a sort of second gift to you. I know it's been hard, losing Florence and bringing up Rachel on your own, sending her off to school and keeping her safe and out of trouble. Before I go I wanted to tell you I reckon you've done a pretty good job, Jack. She's a wonderful girl, just like her mother. Will you keep in touch and let me know how you're getting on? How she's getting on?'

He cleared his throat. 'Listen to me will you. Maundering on. Drink up Jack. We'd better finish this...'

From the far end of the town came the tinny brass braying of the Springvale branch of the Salvation Army, playing the first hymn of their Sunday evening street service outside Swanny Gosling's Stockman's Rest and Oyster Saloon. The two men could picture the three-man band, or rather, the one man and two women in their Sally Army uniforms, playing *'Onward Christian Soldiers'* to three scruffy dogs and possibly Jamie Jamieson's kangaroo.

One of the dogs began barking.

Jack grunted. 'Hah! There you go, Mack. That's what we need, the pair of us. Salvation.'

43

Ernie Cappuccio walked ahead with Charlie back along Bridge Street from the canal, telling him about the birds they would see at the dealer's in Single Street and still marvelling that his new friend was a real horse bus driver.

He'd been on holiday to Brighton once with his mum and Annie and his other older brothers and sisters before his mum became too poorly. They went in a carriage called something like a *broom*, he thought, with hampers full of food from his father's shop, pulled by two horses. No, he'd never been to the old Club Row bird market in Spitalfields and yes please! He'd have to ask his sister but he was sure she'd let Charlie take him. Maybe she'd come too, with Tilly.

Annie and Tilly walked together, half turned towards each other as they talked, discovering far more important things about each other in this first flush of friendship than two men would have discovered in a lifetime. Tilly couldn't remember ever talking to anyone as openly as this, and she felt that an enormous weight she had been carrying on her own was being lifted off her shoulders by this slight, bright girl she had known for barely two hours.

As they walked behind Charlie and Ernie along the canal towpath, oblivious to the other Sunday afternoon strollers, Tilly told Annie about growing up in a house with twenty-two other girls at the Barnardo's Village Home for Girls out in Barkingside, not so far from Romford. She knew her mother had died in the women's hospital in Whitechapel when Tilly was barely a year old, so she had the names her mum had given her, but she knew nothing much about her mum and less about her dad.

Then she had been offered a job as a maid with the Kennedys in their haberdashery shop in Stepney when she was sixteen, through Mr and Mrs Gilroy that was, who ran the bus company Charlie worked for out at Romford, then here in Stepney. 'They used to take us older girls on a picnic outing in the buses every year, and Mrs Gilroy always tried to find good places for the girls to work. She was very kind to me.'

'Is that how you met Charlie, then?' asked Annie.

'Well, sort of,' said Tilly, glancing along the pavement at Charlie's back view. He was leaning down to listen to the boy chattering excitedly alongside him.

'Charlie didn't start driving here until about two years ago. I think Mr Gilroy had told him he should look me up at Kennedys, but then Mrs Gilroy died all of a sudden, and it was just an accident, really. I got offered this job as a barmaid in the Mile End and he came into the pub one night just after I'd started there, and he introduced himself, and we got on like a house on fire. We were friends right away, you know, and we had a lot in common, and I thought he was kind... and handsome...'

'Perfect,' said Annie firmly. 'Just the way it should be. You have to be friends, I always think. Friends don't hurt each other, and kindness is the most important thing in a man. And there's not many of those about. I thought straight away Charlie was a kind man, and they're the best.'

She was intrigued by Tilly's career move from behind a haberdasher's counter to behind the bar of the biggest pub in Stepney. What a thrill. Wasn't it difficult for such a pretty young girl dealing with all those men getting drunk?

Tilly admitted that she had been nervous to begin with, but nearly all the men had been so complimentary, and the younger ones had been protective, gallant even. And then Charlie had turned up.

'Well,' Annie said quietly, 'you were lucky, Tilly. From what I've seen here in Stepney, not many women get any respect from men at all. Most women have a hard life and not much help from their menfolk. My mum always used to have as many women working for her as she could afford, when she was up and about, cleaning, helping in the kitchen, washerwomen coming once a week. Really poor women, you know, trying to feed a family on a few shillings a week, some of them widows, most of the married ones frightened of their husbands. Off to the pawnshop every Monday and in again to get their Sunday clothes and the kids' shoes back on a Friday night. It opened my eyes, I can tell you. My mum used to give them their dinner, make sure they ate properly, and she sat them down with us children at our table. We're all equal, she says, and we all have to stand up for each other. It's a man's world, Annie, she used to tell me. The men have got this world the way they want it, and we women have to stand together and stop them walking all over us.'

Her expression changed, and she looked much less sure of herself and much younger. 'My mum's really poorly now, but when she married my dad she had a bit of money of her own, so she could stand up for herself, and my dad's not a bad man, but she was right, you know. Even my dad has things all his own way.'

Back on Bridge Street they were startled by a sudden rush of noise, and stopped to watch a bicycling club rattle by, heading north east towards Bow and out into the nearby countryside. Twenty or more young men clattering past on the cobbles in a whirl of wheels, all wearing knickerbockers and a club shirt, and caps the same colour. They rang their bells at the two women, and several of them waved their caps and called out scintillating remarks such as, 'How do you do, ladies,' and 'Lovely afternoon, ladies,' as they sped past. One of them winked, and another twirled the ends of his moustache raffishly with his fingertips.

Annie laughed derisively and linked arms with Tilly as they walked on. 'There you are. The male of the species in all its manly glory, and not a woman in sight.' But as she spoke another, smaller bevy of bicyclists suddenly emerged from behind a slow-moving wagon and they saw that this was a group of ten or twelve women, bowling along as briskly as the men before them. Like the men, most of them seemed to be wearing what amounted to a uniform, but theirs consisted of small straw hats, waisted white shirts with ties, and all of them were wearing the new split skirts called *culottes*, widely condemned by starchy politicians, pop-eyed church leaders and most newspaper editorial writers as garments designed explicitly for the immoral purposes of titillation, temptation and entrapment.

Two of the bicyclists were wearing ties striped green and purple, and another had a ribbon in the same colours pinned to her shirt.

'That's better!' exclaimed Annie. She withdrew her arm from Tilly's and clapped the cyclists as they passed. 'Well done!' she called out. 'Hurrah for the Women's Union.'

All the cyclists pinged their bells loudly as they rode past and the two wearing striped ties waved and shouted, 'Votes for Women!'

across the road. The badge-wearer didn't trust herself to lift a hand from her handlebars on the cobbles, but she beamed over her shoulder and hurrahed back, and then they were gone, and Charlie was calling to ask if they were alright.

'Yes, thank you, perfectly alright,' Annie called back. 'We're coming.' She tucked her hand under Tilly's elbow again. 'That's more like it. Mum would have been out there with those Suffragists like a shot, if she was younger and she had her health. I don't hold with breaking the law, you know, like the Suffragettes do, but I've signed up with the union.'

They had nearly caught up with Charlie and Ernie now, but Annie stopped abruptly again and her grip on Tilly's elbow tightened. 'You do know about the Women's Union, Tilly? The Suffragettes and the Suffragists?'

Tilly shook her head. 'I've heard of them, of course, but that's all.' She felt embarrassed that she didn't know more.

Annie looked at her keenly. 'Well, you've had a lot on your plate to deal with, haven't you? I'm not surprised, but maybe it would help, you know. Come and see what's going on. Women standing up for their rights together, toffs and match-girls, all equal, campaigning to have a say in our own lives. You might like to join the cause.'

They caught up with Charlie and Ernie on the curb at the corner of Single Street, and then followed Ernie's lead down the narrow side road towards a line of small shops. On a sunny Sunday, one of the shops had a selection of second-hand furniture displayed on the pavement, and beyond that they could see birdcages hanging in tiers around the doorway of the narrow shop beyond. Ernie sped along the pavement, swerved around the furniture, and disappeared into the cage-hung doorway.

'I don't really like to see birds in cages,' said Annie, 'but Ernie does love them and the bird dealer is such a kind man, he lets Ernie feed the birds and then he does something really special for us. I think you might like it.'

Tilly didn't like the sight of the caged birds very much either and was quite happy to stay on the pavement with this unexpected new friend. The inside of the shop was dark, filled with the whistle and chatter of dozens of birds calling out of the gloom. Ernie would be deep in the back of the shop and its covered yard, Annie said, where the most expensive birds were kept warm by a stove night and day, parrots from Africa and the Amazon, cockatoos from Australia, and gorgeous birds-of-paradise from she wasn't sure where, poor things.

The cages suspended around the doorway held small songbirds, linnets, goldfinches and bright canaries in the main, but one held three pairs of drab, brown and dun-coloured London sparrows, and their captivity touched Tilly particularly. They seemed to be making the best of it. One of them was hunting busily through the litter on the floor of the cage. The others watched them intently from the perch above, and Tilly felt a pang of guilt that she had nothing to give them.

'Charlie took me down the market once,' she said to Annie. 'All those birds, hundreds of them, and the other animals squashed in those little cages.' She shuddered. 'Rabbits and squirrels and such, and all the kittens and puppies for sale. They were nice, but it was horrible seeing them all piled up along the street and people picking them up and poking at them and looking for a better one.'

'I couldn't agree with you more,' Annie said. 'Come on, we'll give Mr Schumacher a call.'

She leaned in through the shop door and called out, 'Excuse me there. Hello? Mr Schumacher? How much for the sparrows today?'

There was a pause, and then the dealer appeared, sliding out between the stacked cages as far as the doorway. He was very old and his bald head was fringed with a circlet of curly white hair that seemed to merge into his eyebrows and continue right the way round his head, like a hair halo that had settled on top of his ears. He put his hands into the long pocket on the front of the long, stained apron he was wearing over his Sunday suit and looked at the two young women over his wire-frame spectacles.

'Ah, that depents,' he said, in a surprisingly deep voice through a badger-grey moustache that entirely covered the lower half of his face.

'It varies.' He had an accent that could have come from anywhere in middle Europe. 'Depenting on how much I like you.'

Annie Cappuccio gazed at him for a moment, then she laughed. 'So how much do you like me today, Mr Schumacher?' The little man raised his eyebrows at them and then he laughed too. 'My dear Miss Cappuccio, you know I like you very much. You and Ernest are my favourite customers. But today I will have to charge you a whole halfpenny each for the seed, so that is... ,' he looked baffled and turned in the doorway. 'Ernest, I need you to tell me, if I am charging a halfpenny each for seed for six sparrows, what is the cost in total?'

Ernie pushed past him and jumped down the steps to the pavement. 'That's easy Mr Schumacher. That's thrupence. Annie, can we pay thrupence?' He looked at his sister intently, and she nodded. 'Of course we can. We've got thruppence to spare for a good cause, easy.' Her brother took the threepenny bit and skipped back up the steps to deposit it in the bird dealer's hand. 'There you are, sir. Can I do it? Can I do it, Annie?'

His sister looked thoughtful and glanced sideways at Tilly. 'Well... I think so. What do you think, Tilly?'

Tilly had no idea what they were talking about but she nodded. 'Of course, if you think so...' Before she had finished speaking the boy was kneeling on the pavement and flicking back the catch on the sparrows' cage door. The moment the little wooden gate swung open the six dowdy birds were out in a whirr of wingbeats. They all settled for a moment on the gutter of the house opposite, and then flickered away over the roofs in different directions, homing back to the places where they had been trapped.

To Tilly's amazement, the dealer smiled and nodded. 'Bravo, Miss Cappuccio. Bravo, Ernest. The songbirds, they give many people joy, but the sparrows should be free. The boys are bringing them to me every day. I tell them to stop but still they come, and I must pay for the birds so they come to no harm. You must come back next Sunday and liberate some more. Please bring your friends.'

'It's a deal!' said Annie emphatically. She looked at Tilly. 'What d'you say, Tilly? Will you come next week and set some more sparrows free? We could meet at the cemetery again and then we can come and see Mr Schumacher and maybe you'll come to the Women's Union with me?'

Charlie was standing behind the bird dealer watching this scene over the top of his haloed bald cranium. To his amazement, Tilly clapped her hands and laughed her old laugh. 'Yes, yes! We'll come, won't we, Charlie?'

44

As he always did, Lord Saltwood had set the pace back towards the house from the stud, walking ahead with his Australian guest, taking him by the elbow to propel him away from the others.

He looked at his half-hunter watch and steered Sid to the end of the track that led west alongside the walled garden and past the home farm, where Kidman and William had stopped the day before.

From where they were standing they could see the gate at the end of the track, and through the opening in the woods they could see fields rising away to distant woodland.

Lord Saltwood inclined his head down the track towards the grass pastures and the biscuit-coloured fields of wheat stubble. 'Prime agricultural land,' he paused. 'Probably the most productive in the world.'

Sid resigned himself to another lecture. It seemed to be Lord Saltwood's preferred mode of communication.

'I reckon it was the first thing that struck me when we arrived in England,' said Kidman. 'Bel remembered it. She was just a little girl when her family left Scotland but she remembered how green it is everywhere. Grass you could feed ten head an acre. There isn't anything like this back home in South Australia.'

Lord Saltwood nodded. It was not a compliment as far as he was concerned. Simply a matter of fact. 'Excellent land, yes, but even with land like this and the most scientific agricultural practices we can't produce the quantities of food we need for our workers. Factory workers. Miners. Navvies and so on. We can't produce enough and we can't produce it anything like as cheaply as the colonies. That's why we're importing more and more. Wheat from Canada. Mutton from New Zealand. Beef from Australia.'

He looked at Sid Kidman. 'Cheap, affordable, profitable beef from your cattle stations, Mr Kidman. Have you met the Vestey brothers yet?'

The Australian was slightly alarmed by the apparent non-sequitur, but he nodded casually. 'I met them in London about a month ago.' He knew exactly why Lord Saltwood had asked him, and he also knew that his host certainly knew that he had already met the Vesteys more than once during the course of his stay in England.

'I would be very surprised if the Vesteys had not taken a keen interest in you.' Lord Saltwood nodded. 'Clever men. Food merchants from Liverpool, originally. Now they're the biggest importers of meat in Britain, frozen beef and mutton, principally, but they don't mind what it is or where they get it as long as they make a profit. They've made money on beef from the Argentine and the Cape, poultry from Russia, eggs from China, believe it or not. We need a great many eggs to feed forty million people, but it's beef that keeps the wheels of industry turning, Mr Kidman.'

Lord Saltwood looked intently at his guest. 'The Vestey brothers struck the lodestone in Argentina. The ranchers in the Argentine used to sell the hides and the very best cuts of meat. They threw the rest away. Until they discovered the benefits of refrigeration. Refrigeration changed everything, as you know. It has internationalised the food industry. The Vestey brothers bought Argentine beef for next to nothing, and then they built cold stores, and then they bought land, and now they're shipping thousands of tons of cheap Argentine beef into Great Britain and they're selling it in their own shops on high streets in every city in England. It is making them a great deal of money.'

Here we are, thought Kidman. The bottom line.

'But they have a problem,' continued Lord Saltwood. 'Or rather, they have two problems. The first is that they have found a way to avoid paying any tax, which makes them richer but also irritates the government. The second is that the Argentine is not part of the British Empire.' Lord Saltwood smiled a predatory smile. He had turned Sid round so they were walking back along the track the way they had come, and steered him briskly along the curving drive away from the four young people who were now approaching them, talking and laughing.

'The British Empire favours its own markets, Mr Kidman, because we have invested heavily in them, and my friends in government assure me that new trade tariffs are going to make it difficult for competition from elsewhere here in our own back yard.' He looked intently at his guest. 'Do you follow me? There will be measures to favour Australian beef, and businessmen like the Vesteys are aware of that. They will be looking for opportunities to share in the Australian advantage, and the Vesteys will be looking for the lion's share. They prefer control to partnership.'

Sid Kidman wondered if Lord Saltwood realised that this was a prime case of the billy calling the quartpot black. His lordship's reputation for ruthless self-interest made the Vesteys look like the Cheeryble brothers. The governess Bel had engaged for their son was reading *Nicholas Nickleby* aloud with Walter, and Sid was avidly following every word of it. His host, he thought, had so far shown no signs of any Cheeryble kindheartedness. So was he being offered a warning, or an enticement, or a threat, wondered the Australian.

Lord Saltwood spoke quietly but forcefully as they walked. 'The British Empire is the biggest the world has ever seen. We control a larger area of the world's surface than Alexander or the Romans ever did.' For a moment Kidman thought he might be seeing a glimmer of poetry in the financier's soul, or at least a sense of history, but it didn't last. 'That makes the Empire the biggest marketplace that has ever existed, and when we met last week in London we were standing right in the centre of it.'

He stopped walking again and turned to face back towards the stud. They could see Lady Saltwood and Bel Kidman walking slowly together towards the church, deep in conversation. The two women stopped at the lychgate and they saw Lady Saltwood gesture towards the graveyard. The breeze stirred the ostrich feathers that curled over the crown of her ladyship's hat.

Lord Saltwood looked back at Kidman. 'Do you know how many ostrich feathers we import every year simply to decorate ladies' hats?'

Kidman shook his head. 'A pretty big pile, I reckon.'

'Four hundred tons,' Lord Saltwood told him flatly. 'Four hundred tons of ostrich feathers. I own sixty per cent of the company that imports them. There's a warehouse full of nothing else in the Pool of London. Very profitable. Have you visited the docks in London yet?'

The Australian was getting used to these crow hops in his host's one-sided conversation, but this time he was ahead of his lordship. He had found his hosts in England all too keen to show him the wonders of the home country, and he and Bel had spent countless hours being politely astonished at the scale and magnificence of everything from castles and cathedrals to water cascades and water closets.

The Thames cutter pilot who had given them a guided tour of the Pool of London's endless mercantile waterfront from the comfort of a shaded boat on a boiling day in August had left no corner unseen and no facts and figures unrecited, or almost none, apparently.

This was the treasure trove of the Empire, their guide had told them proudly, five miles of warehouses lining the Thames from Barking right up to the foot of Tower Bridge, the greatest storehouse of commodities the world had ever seen. He had opened his arms wide as though he was inviting them to take their pick. Spices from the east. Diamonds and gold from Africa. Gold and opals from Australia. Sandalwood and mahogany and ebony. Hundreds of tons of cinnamon and nutmeg. Thousands of tons of ivory. Cotton. Tea. Indigo. Cocoa. Rubber. Everything valuable and trade-able under the sun that never set on the dominions of a short, stout, asthmatic king emperor. The pilot had inhaled deeply as they passed a spice warehouse. 'There. You can smell the wealth, sir, madam. Gold dust!'

Ostrich feathers had been one of the few things he hadn't mentioned.

Lord Saltwood carried on. Kidman could see where he was heading.

'We dominate global trade partly because we control most of the world's sources of supply and the majority of its ocean-going trade, and partly because we are the richest nation on earth. We built the Empire on trade, but it isn't trade that maintains our position. Do you know what it is?'

Sid was confident he knew the answer this time. One of the other many guided tours he and Bel had endured during their visit had been an eye-opening excursion to an astonishing country house and estate in Yorkshire. Wentworth Woodhouse was considered to have the longest frontage of any single building in the British Isles, and the servant whose sole duty it was to keep all the clocks ticking did his tour of duty round the house on a bicycle. Sid had seen him in action, to his great delight. The house stood in an estate of many thousands of acres, but the money that paid for its owners' palatial lifestyle came from the coalmines worked by thousands of miners whose families inhabited the endless rows of blackened brick terraces a mile beyond the park gates.

Their guide on this occasion had been one of the two stewards who managed the estate, and he had told Sid with pride how important the Wentworth coal was to the national economic wellbeing. To the Kidmans, the 'model' pit village they had been shown looked like a vision of hell on earth, and the contrast to the big house just a mile away had rendered them both speechless.

'Coal?' said Sid.

Lord Saltwood looked carefully at his guest. 'Ah... Exactly, yes, indeed Mr Kidman. Coal. I hope you will forgive me for explaining all this to you, but I'd like you to understand the background to our venture and why I believe the time is right to make this commitment now. Timing is everything, as you know better than anyone. Getting the right commodity to the right market at the right price and above all at the right time.'

Lord Saltwood waggled his hand at the pastoral idyll of his estate. 'Land has always been seen as a measure of wealth and status in this country, Mr Kidman, but the real source of wealth for landowners today is the coal underneath it, and the iron and steel and industry that coal produces. High-quality coal is our single biggest export to the world, but even more importantly it is the fuel that has powered our industrial revolution, and it is industry that has made us and keeps us the most powerful empire in history.'

Kidman wondered if this might be something of a sensitive subject for Lord Saltwood. All the land they could see around them, the estate, the wealth and the title derived from the industry and ambition of a Saltwood grandfather whose hands were callused and tattooed with coal dust from wielding a hammer in his own ironworks just fifty or sixty years ago.

Lord Saltwood gave no sign at all of any personal sensitivity about his origins. 'Owning land in Great Britain has paid dividends in the past, Mr Kidman, and it may do so again in the future, but land is not generating anything like the wealth it used to here. Quite the contrary. We cannot compete with the scale of your production in Australia or

Canada, and food is becoming one of our largest imports. The returns on agriculture are declining every year. Land values are falling. Even landowners with coal under their fields are feeling the pinch. Furthermore, the government is now planning to tax land to pay for their damned dangerous tinkering with our natural social order.'

Lord Saltwood paused for a moment, and then they walked on. They had arrived at the junction where the drive curved left away past the church towards the Chiddington lane and right towards the front of the Park. They both turned to see where the others were, and they stood and looked past the rectory at the brown and bay mares and their foals grazing in the stud paddocks.

'We have always made the best machinery in the world here in England, Mr Kidman. The Germans and Americans are catching up with us but we still make the best steam engines and locomotives and ships, the best motorcars and armaments and spinning machinery. But we cannot grow enough here to feed the men who make and serve the machinery,' Lord Saltwood went on. 'Did you know there are more people living in London than in the whole of Australia?'

This was another thing Kidman did in fact know, because he had been obliged to hear it several times during the past six months from other supercilious Englishmen, but when he nodded his host simply ploughed on regardless. 'Four millions and growing. Millions more in Birmingham and Sheffield, Bristol, Liverpool, Manchester, Glasgow. Wherever there is industry there are workers to feed, and they want cheap meat. Coal is the fuel of our industry, and beef is the fuel of our working men. So we need the beef you produce to feed our workers, Mr Kidman. There is a major opportunity here just waiting for us to grasp it.'

Sid wasn't at all sure the workers and their malnourished families in the Wentworth Woodhouse pit villages ever enjoyed much in the way of beef, but he said nothing.

Lord Saltwood clasped his hands behind him and leaned forward, and Kidman could almost feel the force of the man's intensity vibrating up through the gravel under his feet.

'Our venture will enable us to sell them the beef they want at a price they can afford. We can secure a dominant advantage in beef exports from Australia to Great Britain *and* into Europe. The Vesteys are building a monopoly in the distribution of meat here, and they are looking for a chance to extend that monopoly into production and importation. We can beat the Vesteys to the jump, Mr Kidman. They are looking for land in Australia but they are looking to the west, and you and I both know that the future lies in the east of your country. I am offering to invest in you and your vision for the outback because I know we can control this market and we must grasp this opportunity now, while we can.'

Sid decided that Lord Saltwood's words were a warning, a threat and an enticement rolled into one, but the power of his conviction was compelling. He looked south across the green expanse of parkland, but he was seeing a very different country.

His own vision for the outback was to make the best of that vast, untamed, unforgiving place for its own sake. What made his eyes gleam was the sight of water flowing in a dry creek, and a thousand dark shapes with their heads down grazing at dawn on saltbush after rain. He loved the scent of a deal on a property that would add another stepping stone to his outback chain, and the sight of a big mob of bullocks kicking up a dust cloud on their way down the droving route to Adelaide.

There were other men building their own empires in Australia, but it wasn't a race or a competition. Plenty of room out there for any number of men with the guts and the luck to make a go of it. Sid wasn't in it to conquer the world, or primarily for the money either. Money was just the means to buy more properties and stock. But he had seen the possibilities of international trade and investment here in England, no doubt about it, and it was exciting. He'd been selling horses to the British army in India for years from his Kapunda saleyards, but the meat market here that Lord Saltwood was describing made that look like very small potatoes. It was a market that could help make his vision a reality, a profitable reality that would enable him to add still more to his outback vision.

Lord Saltwood's competitive compulsion was something else again. Sid stood on the manicured drive that connected the vast house to its only slightly smaller stud, wondering if he might be getting hold of a mickey bull by the tail.

Lord Saltwood looked at him sideways, perhaps conscious that his medicine might have been too strong, and then he nodded his head in the direction of the young people. 'May I ask if you have come to a view about William?'

The Australian recognised this as something of a defining moment. Whatever Lord Saltwood had said previously, he strongly suspected that if he declined to take William Saltwood back with him, he was also likely to take less of the financier's money too. That was not an insuperable problem, but on balance he had decided that William Saltwood had shown him enough to make the bargain work, in spite of Bel's deep reservations about the whole notion.

Sid looked at his host, and then back along the drive to his daughters and the young man whose future would be decided by what he said next. He took Bel's warning seriously, but on balance he believed he could call the tune back on his own territory and besides, he was beginning to see more potential in the son than he had expected.

'Well,' he said slowly, 'I don't reckon I've seen a better youngster on a horse in a long time.' Sid looked back at Lord Saltwood, whose face gave away about as much as the old stones of the big house behind him. 'And I reckon we might discover a few things in young William that might surprise us. I can't promise anything, but I think we should give him a fair go.'

Lord Saltwood's expression didn't change one iota, but his guest and future business partner saw a brief flash of ferocious triumph deep in his eyes. A moment later he thought he might have been mistaken.

Then Lord Saltwood smiled his tight, controlled smile, and the three Kidman girls and William Saltwood were puzzled to see the two men suddenly shake hands. Lord Saltwood gestured towards the stud. 'I would very much like you to take one of my Crecy mares back to Australia with you,' he said as casually as though he was offering his guest a bag of apples. 'I hope it would be a suitable symbol of my respect and ...ah ...my complete confidence in our venture.'

Kidman stared at him for a few seconds, then he laughed and slapped his thigh. 'Now horse-trading is what I do best, Lord Saltwood. That is a very fine offer, and I'd like to buy a couple of others if you let me, and we can start breeding racehorses on Milbourne again.'

45

Jack Gallagher had hoped to get Rachel away on the train on the Monday afternoon without encountering the new policeman. He wanted to meet him quietly himself so he could at least set their relationship off on an uncontroversial footing, even if Mack's warning suggested there was going to be trouble in the not-too-distant future.

The more Jack had thought of his old friend's gloomy prognosis during the course of the morning, the more it worried him, and knowing he couldn't share Macdonald's confidential information with anyone else made it worse.

He had done his rounds in the town, first to Westy's livery to check on the horses and look at the new wagon being built for Warrigal, then to Dalgety's to book the next shipment of cattle from Warrigal to the Brisbane auction yards. He had called in to say g'day to Bridget Plashey at her store because Westy, who admired her ardently but hopelessly from afar, told him she hadn't been looking quite herself lately, and finally walked back to the bank in a bleak mood for a meeting with Lucas Barrymore. Everything seemed as it always was, but with every step he took on his way round town, he grew gloomier.

Mack Macdonald had been the police constable in the Springvale district when Jack first took over Warrigal from his father, fizzing with big plans and energy, twenty-seven years ago. Lucas Barrymore had been assistant and then manager at the bank for the past twenty years. Now both of these trusted allies and friends were leaving the district, and in Mack's place he would have to deal with a new man who had all the makings of a serious irritation.

In particular, Jack worried about how he was going to deal with the big Irish squatter on the Milbourne outstation. There was no doubt in his mind that the man was occupying it illegally. The fellow was also undoubtedly duffing unbranded calves and probably stealing horses too from neighbouring properties, including Warrigal, and Jack wasn't at all sure how he could deal with that if he couldn't trust the local policeman to handle it properly.

In general, he worried about the blackfellas. It had been peaceful in the district for so long under Mack's benign regime that most people had conveniently forgotten the uproar only twenty-five years ago. The spearing of one white stockman had sparked a wave of white retaliation that had left twenty-nine Aborigine men, women and children dead, and another ten blackfellas carted off in chains to die in the Townsville jail.

The white stockman was well-known in the area as a bad drunk, and it was also known that he was speared for kidnapping and raping a black girl. But he was white, the district around Springvale was full of white miners fired up with hysterical tales of murderous black savages gathering all around them in the bush, and three prominent station owners had organised a muster and a massacre of every black human being who could not escape.

They had called it 'natural justice', and despite the young Constable Macdonald's best efforts, none of the perpetrators had been arrested and subjected to the white justice system that should have held them to account.

The three pastoralists who had led the retaliation were all still running their properties – or in one case, the son was. Some of the men who had pulled triggers and killed black children were still working in the district. On reflection, Jack had to admit to himself that Rachel was right. Not much had changed. The old rotten taint of white contempt for the blackfellas was undiminished.

Maybe it would always be there. Herb Heinemann had agreed with him as they ate lunch at the hotel. 'When was the last time you saw a blackfella eating in here? When did you see a blackfella riding his own horse along the street here? Do you know any blackfellas who own land?'

The front door was open and they could hear the faint echoes of cattle being loaded at the stockyards half a mile away. A cloud of dust from the yards was rising above the roofs of the buildings on the south side of the main street.

'Civilisation is a thin veneer, Jack. Always was. Same with the Jews. That's why my father came here from Austria and my grandfather went to Austria from Russia. All over Europe Jews were fair game. We were child killers. We were money-lenders. We looked peculiar. We prayed standing up. We weren't really human...'

Maureen Heinemann had come over to the table where the two men were talking and patted her husband's shoulder. 'You killed Jesus, Herbie. Don't forget that. You father always said that was the gentiles' best excuse.'

Heinemann rolled his eyes and shrugged. *'Oy veh!* So we did. We deserve it all. Am I complaining?'

Jack laughed despite himself. It was old man Heinemann to a 'T'.

It was nearly three o'clock by the time they had finished their coffee. Maureen Heinemann had jollied Jack into a brighter frame of mind, and he was laughing at another imitation of Herb's father when Rachel walked through the front door, followed by Sergeant Macdonald and behind him, the new policeman.

Rachel made a meaningful face at her father and Mack raised his eyebrows wearily as he took his hat off. Jack and the Heinemanns all rose to their feet and Maureen bustled across to Rachel. 'There you are! How's May? Are you excited? I'd give anything to be coming to Brisbane with you but somebody's got to keep the place going and Herbie's too busy yacking to your father.'

She turned to Mack. 'Good afternoon, Mack, how are you? Are you ready to leave us as well?'

The sergeant smiled at her and shook his head. 'Good afternoon to you, Maureen. Herb. Jack.' He nodded to them both. 'Not quite leaving you this minute. I am showing Constable Cleary round the town, and we bumped into Rachel, Miss Gallagher, on her way up from the Barrymores. So we came on in and I can introduce you to your new police constable.'

He shot Jack a look under his eyebrows, and then turned and stepped aside so that Cleary could move into the room properly.

Standing next to the older Sergeant, Cleary looked everything that a policeman should be and Mack didn't. He was immaculately turned out in the recently adopted khaki police uniform, and unlike Mack's it all looked as though it had been made to fit him. Curiously, it didn't look as though he had slept in it on the thirteen-hour overnight journey from Rockhampton, and Mack's did. Unlike Mack's sweat-stained headgear, the hat Cleary carried under his left arm looked unmarked, and his polished boots didn't look as though they had walked up the same dusty street as Mack's had very obviously trodden. He smoothed his light brown hair with his free hand and smiled. Maureen Heinemann said later that he was a good-looking young man with a very nice smile.

Mack introduced them. 'Constable Cleary, this is Mr and Mrs Heinemann. Mr Gallagher, Jack Gallagher. Herb and Maureen own the hotel, and Jack runs the Warrigal station. It's on the map of the district I showed you at the house.'

The younger policeman stepped forward and shook hands with the two men, then nodded to Maureen Heinemann. 'It's a pleasure to meet you, Mr Gallagher, Mr Heinemann, Mrs Heinemann. If I can serve you and the district half as well as Sergeant Macdonald, I will be doing my job very well indeed.'

Sergeant Macdonald raised his eyebrows fractionally at Jack again, and rubbed a hand over the lower part of his face in a gesture that Jack recognised as a mime for flannel. The sergeant turned towards the door.

'Miss Gallagher and Constable Cleary have been introduced, so perhaps we should leave you for the now and go on up the town.'

The new policeman didn't seem to be in such a hurry. 'It was a pleasure to meet you, too, Miss Gallagher. Do I gather you're on your way to Rockhampton this evening?' Cleary seemed completely relaxed, and Maureen Heinemann exasperated Jack later by telling him that the Irish lilt in the constable's voice made her go weak at the knees, even though she said she had knees of steel from running up and down stairs all day.

Rachel nodded. 'Yes, I'm going to Brisbane for a few weeks with a friend.'

Cleary looked sincerely regretful. 'I'm sorry to hear that, Miss Gallagher. I hope you have a very good journey and I will look forward very much to making your acquaintance properly when you return.'

Rachel's eyes flickered briefly to Jack and then to Maureen Heinemann. Cleary smiled at her.

'Perhaps you might be kind enough to show me round your part of the district? It will take me a while to get to know the whole area and I'll need a good guide.'

It was such a blatant piece of flirtation that Maureen Heineman had to cough to disguise a giggle, and Rachel flushed.

'I'm sure there will be no shortage of good guides who know the district better than me. But, of course, we'll do anything we can to help you settle in. We can show you some of the problems we think you might need to be aware of, can't we Dad?'

Jack met Sergeant Macdonald's stern look of warning for a second and then floundered in like a drunk trying to catch a barramundi in a billabong with his bare hands.

'Ah! Yes, you'd be welcome to come and have a look round Warrigal, constable, of course. Any time. Or at any rate, when you're ready. Or when we're there... But we must let you get on now with Sergeant Macdonald and we must get ourselves sorted out for the train, Rachel. Look at the time. Maureen, would you help Rachel?'

His friends did their duty. Maureen took Rachel's arm and turned her away from Cleary's admiring gaze. And Mack moved in front of the new constable and shook hands as he never used to do until that moment with Herb Heinemann and Jack Gallagher.

'You'll need to be in good time to get May on the train, won't you, Jack,' the sergeant said meaningfully. 'We'll not keep you any longer. Come on, Constable Cleary, we must get out from under their feet.'

Cleary also shook hands with the two men, but as he turned away to follow the Sergeant he glanced up the stairs where Maureen and Rachel were just disappearing onto the landing.

The two men stood looking at the wire screen door for some moments after it had banged shut, and Heinemann turned to Jack and winked. 'Now that's a man seeking a wife if ever I saw one. He seems a very presentable fella. How'd you like a policeman for a son-in-law, Jack?'

Jack stared at him. 'Not at all, in this case. I wouldn't touch him with a ten-foot forky stick.' A surprised Heinemann opened his mouth and Jack shook his head. 'Don't ask me why, but I need you to keep a bloody close eye on Constable Cleary.'

46

Shortly before the Kidmans were due to follow the Saltwoods London-wards in the second Rolls-Royce, Sid pushed his way through the green baize doors again after an early breakfast and paid a quick farewell visit to the stables behind the big house.

As he had hoped, Daniels was in the enormous yard, supervising the morning feeds and allocating duties.

Sid hailed him, and the head groom walked towards him across the yard, lifting his hat to the Australian in genuine respect.

'Good morning, sir.' He looked up at the sky. 'Not such a good morning as yesterday, I'm afraid, but good enough for your journey. We'll be sorry to see you go.'

'I'll be sorry to leave,' said Sid. 'You have been very kind, Mr Daniels. As soon as the women folk have had their breakfasts and made themselves ready, we'll be away up to London, I reckon.' He put his hand into a waistcoat pocket and pulled out a folded banknote. 'This is for you, Mr Daniels. You've been very obliging and I have enjoyed talking to you very much.'

Daniels shook his head. 'No, sir. That's very kind of you to offer, but it's been a pleasure to have you with us, Mr Kidman, and I can't take that from you.'

Sid laughed. 'You must have it, Mr Daniels. I reckon your boys might like a bit of it. Anyway, it's not a tip, it's a fee for everything I've learned here and a down payment on learning some more. I hope we'll meet again, perhaps here if I'm lucky. I'm keen to know more about the thoroughbred breeding and training side of things before I head home, and to be honest with you I'm not sure I rub along well enough with Mr Nichols over there.' He nodded towards the stud, visible through the courtyard archway.

Daniels smiled. 'No, sir. I'd be glad to help if I can.' He pocketed the note and was about to speak again but was interrupted by the sound of engines being started at the far end of the courtyard. Both men stood and watched as the Chiddington maintenance man, Purless, swung the starting handle on the first of the Saltwood Rolls-Royces. He stepped away as the engine caught, and moments later Lord Saltwood's chauffeur eased the car out of the carriage house and parked it facing out of the courtyard. The second Roller followed piloted by the under-chauffeur, and then Purless swung the handle to start the Whiteleys' Daimler, and their chauffeur joined the Rolls-Royces in a line of pristine, highly polished luxury motorcars.

Sid noticed that the tyres of all three vehicles had also been meticulously cleaned and shone with some kind of polish. Much like oiling a horse's hooves for the smartest turnout, he thought. Daniels sniffed and wrinkled his nose with disapproval. Even though the very slight breeze that morning was blowing from the west, they could still smell the sharp tang of petroleum right across the yard.

'You're going up to town with Brightwell, sir?'

'Yes, that's the plan,' replied Sid. 'Very kind of Lord Saltwood. We're all going by motorcar with Mrs Prior and our luggage is going back by train. Pretty good organisation, I'd say.'

Daniels nodded. 'Yes, sir. Then I think Master William will follow on in that green motor of his.' He looked at Sid with a hint of awkwardness. 'I hope you won't take it amiss if I put in a word for Master William, sir?'

Sid gave him his full attention.

'It's just that he doesn't always come across... well, he might seem... he might make you think sometimes that he's... ' The head groom was struggling and Sid did his best to help him out.

'He might give us the wrong impression?' They were more or less the same words Bel had used when she told him what Lady Saltwood had said on Saturday morning. Pleading her son's cause, was what Bel had called it. It suddenly dawned on Sid that Daniels probably knew about the plan to send William to Australia. Or at least he knew Sid had been watching the young man and judging him. It was another example of the bush telegraph he was getting used to experiencing. Servants in big houses somehow seemed to know what was going on above stairs almost as quickly as their masters, or even long before them in the case of Master William here. It was the same in their hotel. He had learned to consult the pageboys if he wanted to know where Bel and the girls or Walter were and what they were doing.

'Yes, sir, that's it,' Daniels said with relief. 'He doesn't always come across the right way, but he's a good boy, sir, and I hope you'll think well of him.' The head groom was looking more embarrassed with every word. He was trespassing well beyond the boundaries of proper servant behaviour, talking about the family to a guest.

'That's alright with me, Mr Daniels,' Sid reassured him. 'I can appreciate what you say.' The head groom was clearly anxious to say more

'Thank you, sir. He's not just a good horseman, Mr Kidman, he's a good boy. Pardon me for saying it. Things have not been the same here since... well, since Miss Marianna died. It hit them very hard, her ladyship and Master William specially, very hard, sir. It changed them. Changed everything.'

Sid nodded. 'My wife said Lady Saltwood talked to her about it. She was quite emotional, which isn't like Bel.'

'Miss Marianna was the spit of her ladyship. Spit of Master William for that matter, and as good a little rider as either of them. Brave wasn't in it. Just like her brother. Master William, that is.'

Daniels glanced at the house as if checking that no one was watching or close enough to hear. 'Her ladyship went out of her mind with it, sir. Maybe Master William did a bit as well, but he'd just gone off to school and I reckon he had to bottle it up. Not let it show. He was very different when he came back for the hunting at Christmas. Angry underneath, if you see what I mean. Ready to pick a fight all the time, specially with Lord Saltwood.'

To their left they could hear voices of grooms in the stables, and hooves on stone. Jim appeared, leading Lord Saltwood's hunter, and both men watched the chestnut horse walking calmly out to spend the morning in a paddock.

'He was just a two-year-old when Miss Marianna was killed,' said Daniels. 'We were breaking him that summer.'

Sid turned back to the head groom sharply. 'Killed? My wife said Lady Saltwood told her the little girl died of consumption? She said quite a few children round here died of it at the same time.'

Daniels looked startled, then stricken. 'Ah... I don't think her ladyship meant that, sir. There was a number of children did catch consumption around then, but Miss Marianna... '

The head groom looked utterly miserable, stranded out in no-man's land, knowing he had said far too much already but he would have to explain more to the big Australian guest. He looked at Sid for a moment and then made a decision.

'I'd like to tell you what happened, Mr Kidman, because it shows you how the land lies, but it's forbidden for us to talk about it here. If Lord Saltwood found out I'd be sacked, and so would my lad and the rest of my family that works for his lordship.'

Sid considered the implications of this in silence, then he nodded. 'It's up to you, Mr Daniels, but I can promise you that Lord Saltwood won't hear anything from me or my wife, and Bel's the only person I would tell. Unless it's a police matter, of course, and if it is I reckon you should tell them, not me.'

Daniels shook his head. 'No, no. It all went on the record with the medical examiner. It's just Lord Saltwood's orders so her ladyship won't be reminded, and I'm sure his lordship doesn't like being reminded neither.'

They heard another set of hooves emerging from the stable building and the young groom, John, Daniels' nephew, emerged leading the old grey pony.

'Well, there you are then. That's what started it, sir. Old Pegotty was Miss Marianna's pony. They got along famously together. That was a sight to see the pair of them flying. Quicker over a furlong than most of those racehorses, that old pony in her prime.' He jerked his head contemptuously towards the stud. 'She was twenty years old back then but she could jump like a good'un. Getting well on now and prone to founder so we have to keep her off the grass mostly, but she has to have a bit of turnout and sun on her back, poor old girl.'

They watched the pony, almost white in the bright morning light, disappear out for her short spell of grazing on the clipped verges.

'She had her first touch of founder that backend, just as the cubbing started. Late August it would be. Poor Miss Marianna was beside herself for the pony, and missing the cubbing, and missing Master William too. Missing him badly when he went away to school.'

The cars began to move away from the other end of the yard, chugging one at a time through the archway on their way round to the front of the house.

Daniels looked at Sid. 'I mustn't keep you, Mr Kidman. You'll be getting ready to leave in a minute, sir.'

'It'll be a while, I reckon,' said Sid. 'Unless someone's cracking a stockwhip in there. I've never known my girls to be ready to go anywhere on time.'

The head groom smiled briefly. 'They waste a lot of time, the young, don't they, sir? And by the time they're old enough to realise how it flies by, it's too late.' He sighed. 'Miss Marianna didn't waste time. Maybe she took after Lord Saltwood that way. She didn't want to waste the cubbing neither, so she asked if she could have another pony, and Lord Saltwood said if she wanted to go cubbing she must ride Master William's new pony while he was away.'

He was looking back ten years, and Sid noticed that the head groom was rubbing his forefinger and thumb together compulsively through one of the buttonholes in his tweed jacket.

'Lady Saltwood said it was too strong for her, she was only eight and Master William's pony was fifteen hands, but Lord Saltwood said she could manage, and Miss Marianna, well, she would ride anything and she was so proud to be riding Master William's hunter. Anyway, they were all three out the day it happened, just over by Lessed the hounds were, and about two o'clock hounds were running and the Master, Mr Lavery, you know, he jumped a big wall out of a farmyard. His lordship told Miss Marianna to go through the gate with Lady Saltwood but he jumped after the Master and Miss Marianna's pony, Master William's new pony that is, took a hold and followed him.'

The head groom was speaking quietly and Kidman leaned closer to hear him. 'Master William had got him jumping like a stag but he slipped going in and they turned over and the pony came down on top of her. They brought her home in a carriage with the doctor, but she never came to and she passed away three days later. I was bringing second horses up, sir. I saw it happen.'

The head groom's eyes focused on Sid Kidman again. 'It was a very bad time, Mr Kidman. Her ladyship was at death's door herself, she took it so hard, and Master William, well, when he came home he couldn't stand to see his mother like that and blamed Lord Saltwood for putting his sister up on his pony and not allowing that Miss Marianna wouldn't be strong enough to hold it. And he blamed himself as well because it was his pony, and he was away at school so he wasn't here to prevent it, which had nothing to do with it, of course, but there you are.'

A footman appeared at the back door of the house.

'You must go, sir.' Daniels looked away towards the archway, framing the old pony and the young groom holding her as she picked her ration of grass. 'Lord Saltwood wanted to have the old pony shot but I got word to Lady Saltwood in the house and she begged him not to. But he had Master William's pony taken to the kennels. Shot and fed to the hounds, you know. Wasn't his fault, of course. When he came home at Christmas Master William used to spend all the time he could out here with me. Said he wouldn't be in the same house as his father. He was just turned thirteen. Lady Saltwood never rode a horse again after, but she told Master William he must carry on. She said his sister would want him to. Lord Saltwood still hunts, too. Never mentions it. So there you are, Mr Kidman. I'm sorry to go on like this. I haven't told a soul any of this for ten years. It's a relief, really. We don't want to lose Master William, but I'll be easier in my mind now you know why he comes across badly sometimes. It will be good for him to get right away and make his own life. He won't think so, but it will, and he'll turn up trumps. You'll see, Mr Kidman, I guarantee it.'

The footman was approaching them across the yard.

Sid held out his hand. 'Thank you, Mr Daniels. I appreciate what you've told me and I can guarantee you no one except Bel will ever hear me repeat any of it.'

Daniels shook hands, and Sid started to walk towards the footman. He stopped and turned. 'I'll see you again Mr Daniels, I'm sure of it. We're not going home until March. If I don't see you this visit, I'll be back in a couple of years, and if you ever fancy coming to have a look at how we go along in Australia, you'll find a place with me any day.'

The footman had reached him. Sid raised a hand in salute to the head groom and strode off towards the back door.

47

Just after noon that day, Will stopped the Napier outside the front door of Polly Brockenden's house in Soho Square. He swung himself out onto the pavement, jumped the two steps up to the door and tugged twice on the bell-pull.

It was clouding over and there was a noticeable chill in the air after the warm sunshine of the weekend, but he divested himself of the driving duster, hat, goggles and gauntlets he had worn for the journey up from Chiddington, and then watched the comings and goings across the square while he waited for his call to be answered.

A motorised pantechnicon was moving away from the front of the Crosse & Blackwell offices on the north side. A Catholic priest, distinctive in his caped black soutane, emerged from St Patrick's Church on the corner of Sutton Street, and a group of young nurses hurried into the new Women's Hospital on the corner of Frith Street to his right just as the clock of St Giles' church began striking noon.

The unusually plain red brick Catholic house of worship looked across the square at an unusually ornate French Huguenot church on the other side. Polly had told him gleefully that on Sunday mornings the supporters of these bitter enemies stalked stiff-legged around each other like two packs of strange dogs, but the Papists had the last laugh. Their ancient catacombs, hallowed by generations of faithful Catholic bones, spread under the square like an enormous warren right up to and possibly under the Huguenots' front door.

The complexities of local religious conflict were of no interest to William, but he did know that Soho Square had long since ceased to be a fashionable address for a respectable gentleman. But then Polly was neither of those two things, thought William, respectable or a gentleman.

He pulled the bell handle again, hard, but it was several minutes more before he heard the sound of bolts being drawn on the other side and the door was opened by Leighton, Polly's butler. He stood swaying slightly in the doorway and said nothing.

'Good morning, Mr Leighton,' said William. The old man's gaze focused slowly on William's face. 'Mr Brockenden is not at home to visitors this morning,' he said carefully. The butler looked rather pleased with himself for managing this announcement and belched almost silently behind a very grubby white-gloved hand.

'Glad to see you're still upright this late in the day, Leighton.' William raised a hand and waved. 'It's me, William Saltwood. Friend and ally of your esteemed master, who will certainly be at home to see me.' William pushed past the butler into the hall, taking care not to breathe in as he eased by, and stopped at the foot of the grand staircase that led up to the first floor.

He turned to see the butler still standing motionless in the open doorway. 'You had better close the door before a bailiff sneaks in here.'

Leighton closed the door with exaggerated stealth and then turned slowly and walked past William through the hall with all the precarious dignity of a bishop who had finished off too much communion wine before he gave the final blessing.

William trotted up the first flight of stairs and stopped on the half-landing as the butler negotiated a left turn into the dining room below him. From halfway up the stairs he could see the scurfy pink and brown-blotched bald patch on the top of the butler's head as the old man made his way to the sideboard. He stopped in front of three covered chafing dishes still standing where they had been left on the warming plate for breakfast at least three hours before William had arrived.

Leighton stood looking down at the dishes for a few seconds, then, instead of clearing them away as William expected, he lifted the lid on the nearest. From the landing, William could see that it was half full of scrambled eggs. The butler stared into the dish, then pulled off one of his gloves, reached his hand into the dish and scooped out a large lump of congealed egg with his fingers. He tilted his head back and dropped the egg into his mouth, wiped his mouth with the glove, and replaced the cover on the dish.

William took the remaining stairs two at a time and strode along the landing to the first bedroom door that opened off it. The door was slightly ajar. The room behind it was entirely dark. William pushed the door open and a voice from the darkness groaned. 'Go away, Leighton, and shut the door behind you.'

William walked across the room and paused by the curtains. 'It's me, Polly, you slug.'

Another, louder groan came from the far side of the room. 'Dear God, William Saltwood, you know I love you but do not open the curtains...'

William opened the heavy velvet curtains no more than six inches, and a shaft of dust-laden light sliced a narrow gash across the darkness, across the swathe of evening clothes scattered on the floor, and lit a large, dishevelled, medieval four-poster bed which had at some point lost the top half of three of its four posts.

'You heartless beast,' said Polly Brockenden's muffled voice from under the bedclothes. 'I thought you were a friend, but you have come here to torture me.'

'Put a sock in it, Polly, if you aren't wearing them,' said William briskly. 'I gave you until midday and look at you, weltering in your squalid pit. It isn't civilised. Wake up, brace up and get up, in that order.'

He walked across the room to the bedside table nearest where he judged his friend's head must be, picked up the empty wineglass standing on the table and sniffed it. 'Polly, this is laudanum, isn't it? You aren't taking laudanum again are you, you worm?'

A hand emerged from the bed and cautiously pulled the bedclothes downwards enough to reveal a tangle of long black hair and one half-open eye. 'It was just a very small nightcap, I promise you.'

William shook his head and replaced the glass on the table. 'Don't be a bloody idiot, Polly.'

'Don't moralise, dear boy, and please don't shake your head at me like that. It makes me feel sick.' Brockenden pulled the bedclothes down another couple of inches and opened his other eye. He smiled at William. 'Come on in and have a rest, my dear old thing. Relax. Take no notice of the busy old fool.'

William pushed his hands deep into his pockets and sucked his teeth in a good impression of Daniels assessing a new horse at Chiddington. 'What on earth are we going to do with you, Polly? You are a pitiful specimen.'

Brockenden closed his eyes and winced. 'I know I am. You know me too well, dear William. I don't know why you bother with me.'

William laughed. 'That is a question I frequently ask myself. Pity, I suppose. Or habit. But you can't be using laudanum again after that last episode, surely to God?'

Brockenden opened one eye again and squinted up at William. 'I need it to sleep, dear William. If I don't take it my demons get the better of me in the dark and the goblins come hunting for me.'

William looked down on him and decided not to press the point. His father had not needed to tell him that Brockenden's finances were teetering on the edge of a cliff. He had known since they had met as twelve-year-old boys at Eton that Polly had inherited an estate mortgaged to the hilt at the age of seven, and nothing he had done since then had made the situation anything but worse.

Will had suggested to him only a few months earlier that he should consider selling the shabby mansion in Soho Square and renting somewhere smaller and more convenient. Polly had shrugged and smiled and done nothing of the kind.

He was smiling at William now, which William found irritating.

'Lying in bed doesn't help, you know. You're in a hole but you must do something about it. You could start by selling the lease on this place and moving.'

Brockenden closed his eyes again and shook his head.

'Yes, Polly. *Do* something. Sell the lease and move somewhere smaller until you can sort out your finances. You rattle around here like a pea in a drum anyway, paying servants you can't afford who are too old or too drunk to look after you properly. Leighton is getting worse, you know, if that's possible. I've just seen him helping himself to your breakfast with his fingers, for God's sake. You'd be better off without him.'

Brockenden shook his head again and heaved himself slightly further up his pillows.

'I don't think I've actually paid him at all since he came here.' Polly put his hands behind his head and yawned. 'We prop each other up and he entertains me. I like his notoriety. Anyway, the only place he could go from here is the poorhouse. No one else in England will have him. I give him sanctuary, with bed and board, of course.'

'And whatever was left in your wine cellar. But that's beside the point. Leighton's welfare is not your concern, Polly,' said William. 'Your concern is to sort out your own muddle. Why don't you get up and we'll get a grip of this business together. Make another plan. Starting with a swift exit stage left from Soho Square.'

Brockenden lifted his head slightly and shook it. 'I've told you before, dear boy. The lease might be worth a bob or two, but it's mortgaged to the last sooty brick, like everything else, you know it is. If I sold it, there would be no money for me, and I wouldn't be able to rent anything bigger than a dog-kennel in a backyard.' He waved a hand languidly in the air. 'Anyway, the trustees seem to be covering the costs of this place somehow. I have no idea where it comes from, but my allowance does appear regularly, inadequate though it is.'

William jingled the change in his pocket. 'Well, Polly. We will just have to move to Plan B or C. Or possibly D or E in the light of my own recent change of circumstances. I'm afraid it's not good news.'

Brockenden raised his head higher. 'Would you be very kind and take Polly's cover off first? He's been consigned to outer darkness since three o'clock this morning, and he will be very miffed.'

William walked across the room to a tall, indistinct shape standing against the wall under a large, homoerotic painting of one semi-naked Spartan soldier gazing languidly at another lounging on a dishevelled bed. He took hold of a corner of the dark drape that hung in folds from the dome of the object, and turned it upwards and away with a flick of the wrist to reveal a large birdcage, occupied by a multi-coloured parrot that had plucked the whole area of its chest entirely clean of feathers.

A cold, reptilian eye regarded William for several seconds, then the parrot shook itself and bobbed its head twice.

'Laaavely boy,' it said.

'Hello Polly, who's a lovely boy,' said Brockenden.

'Fucking laaaavely,' said the parrot dispassionately. 'Pretty Polly. Lovely boy. Pretty boy.' It bobbed its head again and whistled loudly. 'Hello Polly. Fucking laaavely...'

'If you put his covering back on half way he may shut up,' suggested Brockenden.

William scooped the drape off the floor and dropped it over the half of the cage facing into the room. A prolonged, inarticulate squawk greeted this, followed by the shrill, paperboy whistle, then a perfect imitation of a distant telephone bell and a faint voice answering it. 'Brockenden residence. Fucking laaavely...' Then there was silence.

'I don't know why you keep that damned thing, Polly,' said William after a few moments waiting to be sure the parrot was going to keep its peace. 'It's even more horrible than Leighton. Doesn't it remind you of school?'

'Polly is my closest living relative, you know that. I keep him because he's one of the few certainties in my life and he needs me. What happened at that dreadful place wasn't his fault, you know that too.'

William looked down at his friend. 'Yes, of course I know it wasn't his fault but I would have thought you might prefer not to be reminded of it every day.'

Polly shuddered theatrically, and William laughed. 'To hell with the hellish dump. We have a more immediate problem. A financial problem. Lord Saltwood has stopped my allowance.'

Brockenden sat up in bed, awake and alarmed. 'What? Why? Are you pulling my leg, William?'

'No, Polly,' said William, 'I'm afraid I'm not. I was involved in a slight fracas on the way back to my college after our dinner the other night, and to cut a long and tedious story short I was sent down for good and Lord Saltwood has taken his usual dim view. Much worse than usual in fact. My allowance has been stopped and the drawbridge pulled up with me on the wrong side of it. All my usual allies have been warned off. This is a sticky one, Polly. For one thing, it means I won't be able to buy my half of the Napier from you.'

Polly uttered a moan of anguish. 'Oh William, don't say that!' He fell backwards onto the pillows and put his hands over his face. 'I was depending on it *utterly.*' He sat up again suddenly and looked suspiciously at William. 'Please tell me this is one of your awful little jokes. Really. Don't tease me, dear boy. It isn't funny.' His face crumpled as William looked down at him, and he slumped back again with a louder wail of despair, pulling the bedclothes over his face.

From the covered cage came an almost identical drawn-out moan, but this one rising with a note of something other than despair.

William clouted the cage hard. 'Shut up, you bloody vulture.'

There was a loud sqawk of outrage and one final, 'Laavely boy...'.

'Polly, if you go into a theatrical decline I will leave now.' William took a few steps towards the door and Polly whipped the bedclothes away again and raised his head. 'Don't go, Will. I will be sensible, I promise, but this is a disaster.'

William turned back to the bed and sucked his teeth. 'Well, it's a tight corner, I can't deny it. Lord Saltwood has made an appointment for another interview this evening and I suspect he's got some sort of a devious plot brewing, but for the moment I'm on the ropes. So I can't help you any more until I know where this is all leading.' He kicked the foot of the bed. 'Anyway, Polly, you can sell the Napier to someone else. You won't get as much for it as I was going to pay you, but you can still raise a hundred and fifty. I still for the life of me cannot understand what possessed you to buy the wretched thing in the first place.'

Polly raised himself on his elbows and made an apologetic face. 'I haven't exactly paid for it, but I really was relying rather on that two hundred....' He smiled. 'Forgive me, dear William, I am such an unfeeling, selfish brute. There you are in the wars, and I'm moaning about my dreary little problems.'

He looked suddenly anguished again. 'Oh my God, it's my fault!'

'Of course it isn't your fault, Polly, you cloth-head,' said William briskly. 'What do you mean you haven't exactly paid for it?'

Polly slumped backwards yet again, and waved the question away. 'It is my fault, it is! You wouldn't have been out of the college late if I hadn't come down to see you. You wouldn't have been sent down and your father wouldn't have cut you off without a bean. It's all my fault. Oh God!'

He sat up again on his elbows and looked with sudden interest at his friend standing at the end of the bed. 'What happened, dear William? What did you do to get sent down and disinherited?'

By the time William had recounted the sequence of events in full, Brockenden was clutching his head and laughing, echoed by the invisible parrot, but the conclusion reminded him that the consequences for both of them were entirely serious.

'Good Lord, dear Will, I'm so sorry. You make it sound so

amusing, but of course it isn't. What on earth will happen now?'

William grimaced. 'I have absolutely no idea. I can't guess what Lord Saltwood has in mind, but I know for certain it isn't going to be much fun. Some sort of penance. I suspect he's going to make me work off my debts somehow in one of his wretched businesses, but God knows what that will entail.'

48

After a late lunch with Bel, the girls and Walter, Sid sat down in the Langham's writing room to draft a letter to his business manager, Bel's half-brother, Wally Will.

Although Bel had taught him to read and write competently in his early twenties, he much preferred to talk, and his rare letters were famous for all the wrong reasons.

Sid had explained once to Bel that his main difficulty in writing letters was knowing where to start, how to carry on and how to finish, and the first two sheets of barely legible scrawl were discarded.

The third attempt wasn't much better, but Sid wanted to get this torture over and done with while things were fresh in his mind. He looked closely at his pen to make sure he hadn't damaged the nib with all his scratching out and then bent over the hotel's expensive letterhead.

Dear Wally,

~~You may be~~ I am writng to you from ~~Langam~~ The Langham Hotel here in London as you will see. ~~You will nev~~ We have been at a place called Chidington with a chap called Lord Saltwood who ~~is one of the richest~~ men in England keep that bit Wally He wants to put ~~big~~ alot money into my Stations. ~~He has~~ Lord S has also got ~~some~~ mobs of top horses Wally he is has given me a ~~mare~~ first rate thorobred mare I can hardly keep my eyes off her I have bought ~~some~~ other ~~exepp~~ sevral very good horses and poneys and 2 stud bulls here you will not believe them By the way ~~the~~ Victoria River Downs ~~deal~~ is sold to a conseortiom here. There is a big profit in it I will keep a 16th share but get over £50,000 The ~~way Bel and the girls~~ cost here in London is very high I am going to need it. At the zoo we saw a camel pulling a grass mower. ~~There was~~ It reminded made me think of home althogh ~~it also~~ made me think of the high transport costs in the bush ~~as well~~. I will be glad I will ~~get~~ reckwest the agent to send you more details Wally. It is a fortune we could buy a hat full of stations. They have Milbourne in

Queensland ~~Lady Saltwood has it now~~ near to Warrigal. Tell Jack G not galloping Jack if he can manage it as well that wold be good. ~~They~~ Lord S wants there son to come back with us Bel is not keen at all you know Bel. Anyway the son William ~~is his name~~ may dig ~~in~~ his heels in I think he could make good ~~if he is he~~. Well Wally there ~~is~~ are going to be a lot of detales to work out. Lord S owns a bank and their is more money than you or me could shake a stick at ~~is their~~ if we want it. ~~I hope evryone are all well Give my regards~~ I hope the house has not caugt fire again. Do not tell Bel I ~~said~~ wrote that. At the AustriaIiasia club I herd cattle prices are up ~~a height~~ in Adelaide which is good as the hotel bill is getting big as the Carandotta bullock. If they go up a lot ~~tell Art~~ make sure ~~that old fellow~~ George Whitaker from Tipparee butchers gets a ~~nock down~~ real good price if he buys my ~~cattle~~livstock he ~~is~~ was on his uppers when we left. Give my regards to all Wally. I trust you are well we are all well here.

Yours sinceerly
Sid

Kidman cast his eye over his work and was moderately satisfied he hadn't disgraced himself or Bel too badly. He would dictate a much lengthier version to the agent's secretary if and when a deal was agreed but he wanted Wally Will to be aware and on his toes as soon as possible.

He sealed the envelope and addressed it to:

Walter Will Esq
Kidman Office
Adelaide
South Australia

He dropped it into the hotel's collection box, knowing that it would be stamped by the hotel and the Empire's postal service would deliver it to the right door in a matter of just six or seven weeks' time.

We live in remarkable times, thought the Cattle King as he left the writing room. He wondered what remarkable times the next few weeks might bring and headed back up to their suite. The girls had taken their younger brother out to a teashop to make a fuss of him, and until now Sid had had no time alone with Bel to tell her what he had learned that morning in the Chiddington Park stableyard.

49

William stood in the library of the Grosvenor Square house, staring at his father and mother. Lord Saltwood stood with his feet apart and his face set, one hand on the back of the Chippendale armchair where Lady Saltwood sat looking down at the crumpled lawn handkerchief she held in her lap.

His older brother George stood on the other side of his mother's chair.

'Australia!' said William eventually. 'You cannot mean it...'

Lord Saltwood frowned. 'Of course I mean it, William. I am offering you a chance to do something useful with your life. This is the perfect opportunity for you to change your ways and set a new course, clear of your debts. Your mother and I agree that this is the right thing for you to do.'

Lady Saltwood looked up at her son and nodded imperceptibly. 'It is a wonderful opportunity for you, my dear. I would be so happy to know that you are going to rebuild the property for me.' She glanced up at her husband and then back to her younger son. 'It will be yours one day, and you will restore its fortunes, I am sure. That would be a wonderful thing to achieve, William.'

William stared at his mother for several seconds. He felt as though someone had landed a haymaker on the side of his head. 'But you can't want me to go to Australia, Mama! Surely you can't seriously want me to spend the next two years in *Australia*? Two years! It's a prison sentence...'

Of course his mother didn't want him sent to the far side of the world for two years. He knew that. Lady Saltwood was doing what she had been told by his father. Doing her duty. This was entirely Lord Saltwood's idea.

He looked into his father's dark grey, almost black eyes. 'I know I have made a mess and I deserve to pay for it but this is unfair, sir. This is not an opportunity. It's a damned unfair punishment.' He remembered Sid Kidman's words suddenly, that remark the

Australian visitor had made when they were riding at Chiddington.

'This is part of some deal you are making with that Australian cattle fellow, isn't it?'

Lord Saltwood's eyes narrowed, but William was beyond caring. 'You've concocted this with Kidman! What am I supposed to do? Spy out the land for you? Marry one of his blasted daughters? That's it, isn't it, you want me to marry one of those Kidman girls? Just like brother George...' He gestured at the third figure standing to one side of the fireplace, resting a hand on their mother's chair.

George Saltwood took a step forward and pointed a warning finger. 'You mind your tongue, William. And don't drag me into this, or Adela. My marriage has nothing to do with your stupid behaviour or this or anyone but me.'

The Honourable George Saltwood took after his father in looks if not in force of personality, but he was the heir to the Saltwood empire and he did what he was told to the best of his ability, including limiting his choices of a wife to a shortlist of girls with dowries and business connections his father approved of. That spring he had picked the daughter of a leading American industrialist, an attractive, affectionate girl he and Lady Saltwood genuinely liked, who would bring to their marriage next summer a breath of fresh Atlantic air and a father with a huge fortune and excellent connections in the booming American oil industry.

George had returned to London that morning after a weekend staying with his fiancée at the country house where his future father-in-law was enjoying breaking as many holy English traditions as possible in the shortest possible time, and been summoned to add his negligible influence on his younger brother in this family conference.

As he always did, Lord Saltwood waved away his older son's intervention. He stood squarely in the middle of the fireplace, with his own father's portrait staring down over his shoulder, bouncing slightly on the balls of his feet.

They all heard his fist smacking into his other palm behind his back. 'I suggest you remember who you are talking to and concentrate on the matter in hand, William. You are not in a position to indulge in childish tantrums. I am leaving this house in ten minutes to vote in the House of Lords, and you must make your decision now.'

Lady Saltwood looked up at her husband and put a hand on his arm.

'My dear, your offer is so generous but this is a very big decision. Will you allow William a little more time? Let me talk to him a little longer.'

Lord Saltwood looked down at his wife and put his own hand on hers. Then he looked up at William, and his eyes hardened again. 'For your mother's sake, I will leave this until the morning. I cannot imagine why you need more time to consider this. I am giving you an opportunity that most young men of your age could only dream about.'

William looked helplessly from his father to his mother.

Lord Saltwood rested his hand firmly on his wife's shoulder. 'The House may take all night to finalise this bill, Eleanor, but I will be here at breakfast and we can resolve this matter then.' He looked at William again. 'I will see you here at half past eight tomorrow morning. I trust that for once in your life you will make a sensible decision. Your future depends on it.'

Lady Saltwood, George and William remained silent, looking at the library door as a footman closed it behind Lord Saltwood, listening to the subdued voices in the hall, the front door closing, and the sound of the Rolls-Royce engine receding as it left the square, heading for Westminster.

George shook his head at his brother. 'You just don't learn, do you? You've brought this on your own head and you don't have any choice. I'd say Father is pushing the boat out for you a damned long way further than you deserve...'

'Of course you'd say that, George. You wouldn't say boo to a bloody goose, never mind say no to Lord Saltwood. That's why you spend your life running around like a glorified office boy, trying to keep up.'

George took a step forward and Lady Saltwood stood up quickly between them. 'William, that is completely uncalled for and really very unfair. Please apologise to your brother. George, this is very difficult for all of us. Please don't lose your temper.'

George shook his head at his younger brother and then moved away towards the door. He turned. 'Don't apologise to me, William.

Apologise to Mama for all the pain you cause her. All your damned life you've expected Mama to defend you and bail you out of trouble every time you've landed on your backside. But not this time, boy.' He walked to the door and opened it. 'Time to pay the bill, William. Good evening, Mama.'

He closed the door behind him. Lady Saltwood sank back in her chair and shut her eyes for a moment. 'Oh William. He would have tried to help you. He has tried in his own way since you were a little boy, and now you have been so unkind.' She sat up straight. 'Sit down my dear, please, and let us see if we can make something sensible come out of this.'

William sat on the arm of the same leather armchair he had occupied just four days previously. He rested his elbows on his knees and his head in his hands.

'I'm sorry for what I said to George,' he said quietly. 'I know he's stood up for me before. But he's toeing the line, Mama. He's even more under Lord Saltwood's thumb than me. Or you. I do apologise to you.'

'William, there is no need to apologise to me. Neither George nor I are under your father's thumb, as you put it, and I do wish you would not refer to your father as Lord Saltwood. He is your father, and if he is a little... well, severe with you sometimes, you must admit that you have tried his patience. He has given us all a wonderful life...'

William stood up abruptly. 'Mama, Lord... my father has made us all live precisely the way he wants us to live. He rules every single minute of our lives with a rod of iron, and woe betide any of us who puts a foot out of line. He has treated me like a badly behaved puppy all my life, and George too. He's kept me on the shortest possible rein, do this, do that, nothing ever right, nothing ever good enough. I don't think my father actually likes me much, and he certainly doesn't approve of anything I do.'

Lady Saltwood reached for his hand and held it in both of hers. 'Now that is not true, William. Please, sit down my dear.' She let go of his hand and waited until he had perched again on the armchair. 'Your father is the head of this family and he has always wanted the best for you, but you know he has the highest expectations of you too. He has achieved so much himself, and he expects his sons to do the same.

This is hard for you and George, I know it is, but can you understand his point of view? Can you see how your... your escapades upset him?'

William raised an eyebrow at his mother. 'Upset him? I certainly can see how my *escapades* upset him. I get a monumental dressing down and another damned unpleasant lecture on my very obvious shortcomings. Exactly like the beaks at school. The only thing he doesn't do is thrash me like a dog. I'm not a son, Mama. More like a useless employee in the family firm. If he could, he'd sack me.'

'Please, William, you mustn't exaggerate like that, and you must realise that you have overstepped the mark many, many times, and it does seem sometimes as though you do it deliberately to antagonise your father. And your father has been forbearing, you must admit.' Lady Saltwood smoothed her handkerchief on her knee.

'Until now.' She had not dressed for dinner yet, and the plum-coloured silk of her long skirt showed dark through the white lace trim of the handkerchief.

Because the staff were aware that a family crisis was underway in the library, and at least two were listening intently in the hallway, none of the servants had come in to close the curtains. They remained open, gathered in their silk rope loops, and through the fine muslin inner curtains the new electric street lights glowed in the darkening square. A cab passed, and William unconsciously registered the slight irregularity in its trotting hoofbeats that told him the horse was not completely sound.

On the wall in the shadows above an escritoire hung the painting of a white, wooden, Queensland homestead.

William dropped to one knee in front of his mother and took her hands in his. 'I can't agree to this, Mama. This is just part of another business deal Lord Saltwood... my father is doing. It's not about me or my future, it's about money, it always is. All the time, all my life, there he goes, the son of the money-grubber.'

Lady Saltwood freed her hands and put her palm on her son's cheek. 'I know it has been hard for you, William, and you know that it has hurt me too. The world can be an unkind place, and many people resent your father's success, and his money. But perhaps it will be good for you to go to a country where your father's reputation won't overshadow you. Somewhere you can be yourself and make your own life. Doesn't that appeal to you?'

William stood up and plunged his hands in his pockets. 'No, Australia does not appeal to me. Nothing that Lord Saltwood has planned for me appeals to me. Just the opposite.' He sat down on the edge of the club chair opposite his mother. 'I've had enough of it, Mama. It's unbearable. There I was at the Park like a stupid pawn being lined up in whatever game Lord... my father is playing with this Kidman fellow, and I had no idea.' He jumped to his feet again. 'And you must have known, Mama! Good God, you must have been in on this too!'

Lady Saltwood rose to her feet too with her hands clasped in front of her and took a step towards her son. 'William, please, I knew nothing of your father's plans with Mr Kidman until he told me before dinner on Friday.'

William stuffed his hands in his pockets again and glared at his mother. 'What! He cooked up the whole idea on the spur of the moment?'

'No. He had spoken to me months ago about the possibility that you might go out to Australia to learn how to restore and manage the property, the Milbourne property, but that was not to be until you had finished at Oxford. Then Mr Kidman appeared here in London in the spring and your father began to explore the possibilities of investing in his business in Australia, and then you were sent down the very weekend the Kidmans were due to spend with us at Chiddington, and your father put two and two together, my dear, and here we are.'

It was warm in the room, but Lady Saltwood shivered and turned to the fire. 'It was a coincidence, my darling, but as far as your father is concerned it was a perfect opportunity to kill two birds with one stone. No, not that, but you know what I mean.'

'Killing two birds is exactly what I think Lord Saltwood is trying to do. I'm sorry for being angry with you, but why couldn't you have warned me? You might have told me what was in the wind.'

Lady Saltwood smiled rather forlornly at her younger son. 'My dear, your father forbade me explicitly from telling you, and also from giving you any financial help. He wanted Mr Kidman to meet you first and... well, he wanted Mr Kidman to see for himself whether he would take you to Australia with him.'

William looked at his mother with astonishment. 'You mean Kidman was *vetting* me! Vetting *me?* I can hardly believe this! This whole weekend... and you didn't warn me!' He slumped back onto the chair.

Lady Saltwood covered her eyes with her hand for a moment. 'Your father has also had enough, he says. He is adamant, William, and it is my duty to support his view in this. Regardless of what I myself feel.' She sighed. 'Believe me, my dear, your father has made his decision, and you know that nothing I can say will alter it.'

William was well used to the steely resolution of his father's decisions, but none of them up to this point had affected or altered the course of his life so drastically.

Lady Saltwood pulled herself upright. She could feel the beginning of a headache growing behind her eyes, but she willed herself to be positive. 'I don't want you to go to the other side of the world, my dear, of course I don't, but I do very much like the idea that you will be involved in restoring Milbourne. You know your great uncle left it to me entailed so that it must pass to you. He wanted you to have it, William. No one else.'

William laughed. 'That must have been a sour one for my father to chew on. I don't think Great Uncle Teppermoor liked my father much, did he?' He looked up at the painting of his grandfather, John Saltwood, the belligerent, bullet-headed first Lord Saltwood. 'Or my grandfather. Trade, Mama, the money-grubbing bloodline.' He was smiling but his voice had a ragged edge of deep bitterness. 'Bloody business. Always business. Money over everything.' He looked down at his mother.

Lady Saltwood was looking down at her hands, and William felt a sudden stab of guilt.

As the eldest daughter of an impoverished earl and one of the most beautiful debutantes of her day, Lady Eleanor Baylsley had effectively been offered up to the highest bidder on the marriage market the moment she was presented at court. The twenty-seven-year-old John Saltwood had wanted her for her beauty and her title from the moment he first saw her, but it was the first Lord Saltwood who had secured her for his son in return for taking over the mortgage on the run-down Baylsley estate in Dorset, paying the bills for urgent repairs to its rambling and badly leaking house, and buying the young couple their own country estate in Berkshire, Chiddington Park.

It was common practice for the sons of hard-up dukes and earls to marry wealthy heiresses regardless of where and how their fathers made their fortunes, but Eleanor Saltwood understood better than anyone the personal and social slights inflicted on any woman who was sold the other way across the frigid chasm between old aristocracy and new money.

There was a discreet knock on the library door.

'Come in,' said Lady Saltwood. The door opened and Sugden, the butler, took a step into the room, one white-gloved hand still holding the polished brass doorknob.

'I beg your pardon, your ladyship. May I ask if you require dinner to be delayed?'

Lady Saltwood looked up at the ormulu clock ticking on the mantelpiece and stood up hurriedly. 'Thank you, Mr Sugden, but we mustn't trespass on Cook's patience. We will dress now and you can tell Mrs Malvern we are looking forward to her always wonderful cooking.'

'Very good, your ladyship.' Sugden inclined his head to Lady Saltwood and withdrew from the library without at any time having looked at William.

'Is it Sugden who reports our movements to Lord Saltwood from this place, Mama?'

'Now, William,' said Lady Saltwood, with a slight frown and a nod towards the door. 'Let us go and dress and then you and I will have dinner together and we can talk about the Milbourne property and what's to be done.' She walked towards the door and William moved past her to open it for her. Just before he reached it, his mother stopped and said quietly, 'You must make up your mind before breakfast tomorrow, my dear. I hope very much that you can accept your father's offer. I am not sure I can bear the alternative.'

50

Charlie caught himself whistling on his morning walk down the Mile to the stables on Monday morning. The weather was turning colder but he was feeling more cheerful than he could remember at any time during the past six months.

The previous evening, they had climbed into their sagging bed together in the dark, and then when he had whispered, 'Good night,' to her, Tilly had reached out and stroked his face.

'You're a good man, Charlie Downs,' she whispered back. 'I love you, you know...' She shifted closer to him and he kissed her very gently at first, waiting for her to pull away, but she didn't.

She kissed him back, locking the fingers of one hand in his hair and pulling his body towards hers with the other. In all their explorations of each other before the baby had been born and lost, she had never shown this fierce urgency. She had been more than willing but shy and tentative at first, knowing nothing. Charlie had very little experience to draw on himself, limited to a few brief, backstreet encounters and the shockingly embarrassing advice to be gentle and patient that Ellie Gilroy had given him on his wedding day, shortly before she died. He had tried to take it. He had led the way and Tilly had followed, learning what he had wanted, delighted to please him.

Now she was biting his lip and tugging at his nightshirt so hard he could feel it tearing. He was terrified of breaking the spell of this miracle, but he whispered, 'Easy, Till,' and freed himself a moment to pull his nightshirt up under his arms, sitting up to rip it over his head, feeling Tilly pushing it away and then her hand slipping up the inside of his thigh and gripping his erection so hard he winced.

She let go, but only to throw the bedclothes off the bed and kneel beside him, pulling her own long nightgown up and dropping it on the floor. For a second she was looking down on him, and in the faint light from their curtained window he could see the curve of her hip and shoulder, and then she leaned down to kiss him again, ferociously, her hair cascading across their faces and her hands reaching for him again.

Charlie pulled her down onto the bed beside him and she turned onto her back, lifting her hips and pulling him inside her, locking her arms and legs around him frantically. Her fingernails were digging into the long, rigid muscles of his back, and she was bucking under him like a wild animal, biting into his shoulder.

And then there was an angry voice roaring in the court and she froze and stiffened and was Tilly again, distraught, pulling away from him, pushing him off her. 'Oh no, Charlie, stop. Oh no. We can't... we can't...' She went limp, and then threw her arms around his neck and lifted her head to kiss him passionately again.

Charlie could feel tears on her face and lips, and he had just enough self-control to restrain himself. Just enough, oh Christ.

'Easy Till. Sorry girl.'

She hugged him tighter, her lips so close to his ear her words seemed to be whispered inside his head.

'I'm sorry, Charlie It's me. I'm sorry, Charlie, please don't be angry with me. I'll come right, I promise.' She pulled away again so she could look into his eyes. 'I'm getting better, aren't I?'

Charlie freed a hand and stroked her hair away from her forehead. He stroked her face and whispered reassurances back. ''Course you are, Till. We'll get through it alright. We're getting along at a good clip now, you and me.'

He held her until she slept, not daring to move in case he woke her, silently cursing the shouting drunk and the laughing woman in the court, feeling a great warm tide of love and care spreading like a blanket over them both.

Tilly had hugged him again and raised her face to kiss him when he said goodbye in the morning, and he had run down the stairs into Parfitt Court feeling as though he'd won the Derby sweepstake.

He waved at a puzzled cart driver and wished good morning to the three souls he passed on the street before turning down White Horse Lane. He bid a cheerful good night to Ruski Dimitri, the nightwatchman, who was heading out of the yard on his way to a truckle bed warmed by the previous occupant in his common lodging house, and he clapped a startled Ringer Bell on the shoulder as he dodged round the enormously fat farrier to get to the drivers' clubhouse door.

It was only when he was in the room that he remembered Tommy Crawfurd would not be coming into the stables again, and he laughed out loud.

From the yard he heard the farrier asking, 'What the 'ell's got into him? Monday morning and he looks like he's on his fuckin' 'olidays.'

Which was true. He felt as though their chance meeting with Annie Cappuccio the day before had transformed his life and his view of the future. Tilly *could* be her old self again, or something much more like it. She *could* get over the loss and the grief, and maybe one day she would agree to trying a new life with him. Maybe in Australia.

He'd learnt enough recently not to broach that subject again the previous evening. He knew how fragile Tilly still was, and he knew he would have to bide his time. But this morning the dread was replaced with optimism, and a growing confidence that the dream was not dead.

Charlie might not have grinned at Davey quite so sunnily as he strode across the yard to see his team being hitched up if he'd seen Tilly sitting hunched in her chair in front of the tiny fire she had lit to boil the kettle.

Almost as soon as Charlie left, the cold realities of her life stripped away the warm remnants of the previous day's good feeling. The crushing weight of grief landed on her like a ton of broken bricks, and with it a sodden cloud of guilt. Her baby was dead. How could she have walked away from her grave and poured her heart out like that to a new friend? How could she have laughed at the bird dealer and the sparrows? How could she have been excited by the idea of visiting the Women's Union? Most crushing of all, how could she have risked becoming pregnant with Charlie the night before. The ultimate betrayal.

It was the noise of the kettle that forced her to haul herself out of this overpowering misery. It must have been boiling for some time because when she got up and lifted it off the fire there was no water left to make her tea. It must have been hissing at her for minutes but she'd been lost, back down at the bottom of the well.

She realised that she was desperate for a cuppa, so she took the kettle to the cracked sink and filled it again from the single, cold tap, and while she was doing that she remembered the tea she and Charlie had sipped from china cups in the posh teashop near the canal.

Annie Cappuccio had insisted on paying for the tea and the cakes.

What an extraordinary woman she was. The same age as Tilly, she had discovered, but a world older in experience and confidence. She'd told Tilly that she'd been training to be a teacher but had given that up to stay at home, running the house and nursing her invalid mother, looking after at least six brothers and sisters, tending the graves of two more, supporting the fight for women's right to vote, and sparing a whole Sunday afternoon to mop up a weeping stranger.

Tilly wished with all her heart that she could be more like Annie Cappuccio. But at least she could be *with* Annie Cappuccio, and she would need to be worthy of this friendship or she would lose it. She had to stand up for herself and be a woman like Annie. She couldn't wait to see her again next Sunday. Six days.

She wiped her face with the dishcloth, took a deep breath and started to make herself ready for work.

51

By the time she kissed her younger son goodnight, Lady Saltwood was feeling the first sharp warning flashes of a migraine. As her maid shut the bedroom door silently, Lady Saltwood lay in the dark and prayed that she had done enough during their dinner together to persuade William to agree to his father's plans.

But in the morning she remained confined to her darkened room after a sleepless night, exhausted and blinded with pain, so she was not present in the library after breakfast when Lord Saltwood stood in front of the fire in exactly the same spot he had occupied the previous evening, and demanded an answer.

Lord Saltwood clasped his hands behind his back. 'I hope that you are going to tell me that you are accepting my offer and doing your duty by your mother, William. I cannot believe that even you can have come to a contrary decision. Be quick about it. I am leaving in six minutes.'

The debate he had attended in the House of Lords had not come to a vote until nearly two o'clock in the morning and it had not gone the way his lordship had wanted.

William clenched his jaw and told himself to stay calm for his mother's sake, but his father's aggressive impatience undid all Lady Saltwood's loving diplomacy in a split second, and despite his best efforts all his resentment boiled towards the surface.

'This is not a fair choice, sir. Surely there must be something else I can do to make amends... there must be some other way I can pay my debts and put things right?'

Lord Saltwood stood very still and looked coldly at his son for a few moments. 'You do not understand, do you, William? You have no choices except those I give you. I will repeat them. If you go out to Australia with Kidman, learn to manage your mother's property and help to restore it, commit yourself to this for two years and take responsibility for your actions as you should, I will clear your debts here in England and I will support you and your career in Australia during those two years and thereafter.'

He leaned forward and continued more softly. 'If you choose not to accept this offer, then you will leave this house and find your own way to deal with your debts. You will receive no support from me or from your mother, or any other member of this family. Those are your options. They are not negotiable.'

Above and behind his father, the portrait of his grandfather looked out at William with the same expression of confident power he could see on his father's face. Like father, like son, in their case, anyway, but not in his.

He took a deep breath. 'I understand that I have made a serious mess of things, sir, but I don't understand why I have to go to Australia to put things right. Why Australia? Why won't you let me do something here to pay off my debts? You might as well send me to the North Pole.'

His father regarded him again with the same cold, dispassionate gaze. In the silence between them they could hear the quick, light footsteps of a maid crossing the tiled hall to the front door. Lord Saltwood half turned and glanced at the clock on the mantelpiece. It showed four minutes to nine o'clock. On a normal day, Lord Saltwood would have been in his office in the City or at Chiddington Park for at least an hour by this time in the morning.

'I am leaving here in four minutes' time, and I feel disinclined to explain your position to you yet again or my reasons for giving you this choice, but in this case, I will.' He raised his left hand with the fingers spread and ticked off his points one by one with his right forefinger.

'Firstly, there is nothing you can do here in England that would enable you to pay more than a fraction of your debts. You have no skills or qualifications and no opportunities to earn anything approaching half of that amount of money within the next two years.'

He tapped a second finger. 'Secondly, without your university studies to attend to, I am certain that your behaviour and quite possibly your spending would become even more irresponsible than it is already. You appear to be incapable of keeping respectable company or behaving properly and legally here in London. You will not find the same distractions in Australia, and you will be fully occupied learning how to run your mother's property.'

There was a discreet knock on the library door.

'Wait,' said Lord Saltwood. 'And thirdly, your mother wants you to take this course. She wants you to try and make something of this place, and of yourself. You will, after all, inherit it. For once in your life you will be doing something useful for your mother, and for the family, and for your future. Not pleasing yourself with yet another costly display of juvenile delinquency.'

William's blood was up by now. 'That's it, sir, isn't it? Money. This has nothing to do with my mother or my future. It's all about money, I know it is. It's always about business, and somehow for once I am useful to you in your business, whatever plan you are hatching with that cattle fellow. Well, I won't be part of your blasted business plans, and I won't help you to make yet more blasted money...'

Lord Saltwood's eyes narrowed and he leaned a little more towards his younger son.

'You have a contempt for money that you cannot afford, William. It embarrasses you that I make money as a businessman? But you are more than willing to spend it, are you not? As much of it as I allow you and far more. Where do you expect this money to come from? Without the money I make, you would not be living in this house, or hunting at Chiddington, or attending the best school and the best university in the world, or paying for Champagne for your useless cronies to swill down. It is time you grew up, William, and recognised the real world and your place in it.'

William stared at his father, but Lord Saltwood was checking the clock and walked past his son without a glance on his way to the door. 'If you change your mind,' he said without turning round, 'you can stay here and tell me when I return this evening. If you persist in a childish fantasy that you can sort out your financial mess yourself, then you must leave this house today and inform Prior when you have found somewhere to live. He will provide you with a full record of your debts, and he will inform your debtors that they are to deal directly with you. You will discover what money really means. Or more accurately, what the lack of it really means.'

Lord Saltwood raised his voice slightly. 'Door.' The door was opened as he approached it, then closed behind him by an expressionless footman as his lordship walked briskly across the hall.

William remained where he was, seeing Sugden in his mind's eye helping Lord Saltwood with his coat, handing him his perfectly brushed silk top hat. The front door opened by the footman. The Rolls-Royce waiting at the foot of the six steps. He heard the front door close, and then the thump of the car door shutting and the rising note of the engine pulling the big car away from the kerb, and fading as it disappeared towards the City.

He stayed where he was for several moments looking blankly at the fire burning in the centre of the monumental marble surround. He looked around the library as though he was a visitor, at the formal ranks of books in their glass-fronted mahogany cases, the Persian rugs, the silverware and the Dresden china ornaments, the leather armchairs, the paintings on the papered walls. His eye rested briefly on the painting of Milbourne, half hidden by the fronds of a large potted palm, then moved on to the fireplace and the image of his grandfather staring down at him.

'To hell with both of you,' he said. 'I am not a Saltwood and you won't make me one. I am a Baylsley, not a bloody commercial traveller, whatever you and Lord Saltwood the second thinks.'

When he turned away he could almost feel his dead grandfather's implacable, unblinking, black-eyed gaze boring down between his shoulderblades, but he didn't look backwards. Nobody opened the library door for him, so he did it himself. Then he walked briskly across the hall, ignoring the footman and, for the second time within a week, made his way upstairs to pack.

On the landing at the top of the stairs, his mother's maid, Violet Parsons, was waiting to intercept him. 'Lady Saltwood would like to see you, Master William.' She had told him at breakfast that his mother was still prostrate, lying in her darkened bedroom and unable to bear any light or sound. But Lady Saltwood would put up with anything to know that all was well with her younger son.

William felt a stab of guilt, knowing that he was about to cause his mother even greater distress than she was suffering already, but he knew he must tell her himself and he followed Miss Parsons along the wide corridor that led to the principal bedrooms towards the rear of the house.

Miss Parsons asked William very softly to wait while she checked that his mother could still see him. She slipped through the door and closed it noiselessly, and then reappeared moments later putting a finger to her lips and beckoning William into the room.

William moved into the bedroom as quietly as he could. He knew the layout of the room but in the almost total darkness he lost his bearings, and he flinched when Miss Parsons placed a hand on his arm to guide him to the side of his mother's bed.

'Please be as quiet as you can,' she whispered. 'If you could kneel by her ladyship's pillow? Just here.'

In all the years that Lady Saltwood had suffered these crippling headaches, beginning in the first, dreadful Christmas holiday home from Eton following his sister's death, William had never been present in his mother's room during one of her migraines, and it shocked him to realise now how badly they affected her.

As his eyes adjusted to the darkness he could make out a pale shape resting on the bedcover that must be his mother's hand, and he placed his own hand very gently over it. His mother's hand turned and grasped his.

'William?' Lady Saltwood's voice was no more than a sigh. 'I'm so sorry, my darling.' Her words were slow and slightly slurred, and William could smell the same faint alcoholic hint of laudanum on his mother's breath as he had in Polly Brockenden's bedside glass.

'I'm so sorry I could not be with you this morning,' whispered Lady Saltwood. 'Have you agreed with your father, my dear?' He heard the faint rustle of Miss Parsons' dress beside him as she carefully replaced the damp cloth across his mother's forehead.

William hesitated, trying desperately to choose the best way of minimising the bad news, and finding none. 'Mama, I cannot accept Lord... my father's terms.' The pale shape of his mother's face turned towards him on the pillow and she gave a soft moaning cry that cut William to the heart. 'Oh my dear William. Don't tell me this. I cannot bear it.'

William tightened his grip on his mother's hand and leaned closer to the ghostly face framed by her long hair. 'Please, Mama, don't worry about me. I will make good, I promise you, but I will not let my father ruin my life with this scheme.' His voice had risen and he saw his mother wince. Behind him he heard her guardian maid ssshhing him.

'Master William, please lower your voice...'

William dropped his voice to a whisper. 'I'm sorry, Mama. I am truly sorry for putting you through this, but I can manage, really I can. I'm going to stay at Polly's and I will send you a note in a few days. We can meet somewhere and talk about this, can't we?'

Lady Saltwood groaned again and William saw the shine of a tear escaping from the corner of her eye. 'My dearest, you know that nothing will incense your father more. Please William, you do not know your father... Please do not try and fight him...'

Miss Parsons moved forward and bent beside William. 'You mustn't upset yourself, your ladyship. I will arrange everything with Master William. Please, Master William, you must leave now. Hush, your ladyship, please...'

William raised his mother's hand and kissed it. 'I'll talk to you in a few days when you're well again, Mama,' he whispered. 'Don't worry, we'll make a plan.' He rose to his feet and tiptoed towards the faint line of light that marked the bottom of the door, and let himself out.

William walked to his own room with a surge of red anger rising in his chest. Fight his father? No, he wouldn't fight his father. But he would fight Lord God-damned money-grasping Saltwood every inch of the way.

Australia?

He'd see him in hell first.

Coming next

THE SONG OF THE BUTCHER BIRD

BOOK II

SOHO SQUARE

October 1914

POOR BUGGER ME

The short, middle-aged American woman sat on her bed in Darwin's best hotel, which wasn't saying much, and double-checked the final details in the document that would confirm her employers as one of the most detested landowners, cattle producers and meat processors in Australian history.

She was a very long way in every respect from the one-horse town on the Nebraska prairie where she had grown up, but tropical heat and tundra cold, distance and deterrents were all the same to this indomitable woman, and the employers who had made her the highest paid woman executive in the world trusted her implicitly to maximise their interests in the deal she was about to sign on their behalf.

With her usual unfussy, brisk deliberation, she left her hotel and walked along the shaded side of the main street, bang on time for what she hoped would be her final meeting with the government official responsible for the allocation of Crown lands in the top end of Australia.

She took absolutely no notice of the murmurings beginning to circulate that the official had been playing his own strange game in the negotiations that had begun many months earlier down in Adelaide. Whether that was true or not, he had certainly agreed astonishingly generous terms with this matronly, implacably reasonable woman, gifting her British employers control over twenty million acres of northern Australia for a pittance.

It didn't matter to them or to their troubleshooter that this extraordinary deal would make her employers' name a curseword for everything the Australians hated about the British, and everything the blackfellas hated about the whitefellas. All that mattered that afternoon was the document that nestled safely in the large handbag that swung gently on Miss Brodstone's arm.

The blackfellas up in the top end didn't know what to make of her. She was a whitefella, obviously, so they assumed she was up to no good, but she was a tough one, no doubt about that. Small and not so young neither, but always cheerful, even after twelve weeks riding round the bush on a camel.

The stock and station agent who sent Sid Kidman a full account of her visit grilled the big blackfella who had been picked to guide her around the vast area of northern Queensland and the Northern Territory that she was engaged in securing, and passed on his views more or less verbatim.

'She said she come here to do us some good. Make all this into cattle country for her boss in England. Give us jobs, maybe.'

Long Tom had been educated at the mission in Normanton and worked for station owners and drovers all his life, and he was picked for his English as much as his knowledge of the bush. Possibly for his size, too. 'They said if she got lost she could look around and spot me. I'm a pretty big fella. Bigfella blackfella. That's a good joke for a whitefella.'

She was alright though, he told the agent. 'She talked to me a lot in camp. She reckoned I knew the country a lot better than those whitefella bushmen and that government fella. She was right there. Bugger me we saw a lot of country, way out past my place. My people are Wunamara, but we went out west into Bularnu territory, Wurrumungu, Jingili, Mudburra.'

He had admitted to her that out that far west he was almost as much a stranger as she was. 'I only been that way once before with Mr Arbuthnot, drovin', pickin' up a couple thousand bullocks comin' across out by Camooweal from Wave Hill.'

Her boss already bought that place a couple years back, she had told him. 'Is that right? Wave Hill's a big run, that's for sure. Gurindji land,' said the black stockman. 'Those blackfellas was pretty fierce on the whitefellas just a while back. I hear they do what they tell 'em now. All got to live on the station and get what they given.'

'I don't think we'll have any trouble,' the small American woman had said confidently. 'We'll take care of them.'

'I reckon she will,' Long Tom told the agent. 'You'd have to be up early to muster that one into the mob. Went walkabout round all that territory on a camel about three months, looking at everything, askin' questions all the time about water and feed, how many cattle it would carry? What's that called? What's this called? Where's that? How d'you make this camel go faster? Yes sir, tough as the hide on an old blackfella's backside.'

'Anyway,' Long Tom told the agent, 'we was so far out bush this time the whitefellas was scared they'd get speared and end up bush tucker. Well, maybe a few years back. The blackfellas is scared shitless now. They know the black police are gonna come and get 'em if they hurt any whitefellas. Bad buggers, them native trackers. We heard they been at it again down in Gudjal country not long before Miss Brodstone come here. Killed a mob of blackfellas for knockin' one whitefella on the head.' Bush telegraph. Quicker than wire any day.

The news of the massacre five hundred miles to the south had put the wind up the bush blacks as far north as the Gulf, the agent reported to Kidman, but Miss Brodstone had reassured them her boss would see them right.

'Give 'em good jobs and good tucker,' was how Long Tom put it.

Back in town after Miss Brodstone's departure, the two whitefellas who had reluctantly travelled with them told the black stockman her boss was going to buy all that territory they had seen and make one big station out of the whole lot, or maybe a few big stations.

'I reckon they reckoned they'd get good jobs too. Maybe managers, but I didn't reckon much to them. Couldn't find their way out of their own swags, those blokes. When they had a drink or two after in the pub, they brought me out a drink of rum round the back and they said she got the government fella roped. Must have got some deal goin' so her boss would get all that country for just a few quid, millions of acres, and maybe the government fella was getting a few quid for himself, they reckoned. All sorts of talk was goin' round. I dunno.'

That was the crux of it as far as Sid Kidman was concerned. Miss Brodstone's English boss had bushwhacked him while he was facing the other way, concentrating on the war effort. He wasn't surprised.

'Didn't look back when she walked away off home but she done a good job for her boss in the home country. She said she was doin' all this business for her boss to help the war against the other whitefellas. Send back tucker for the soldiers on her boss's ships.'

The black stockman looked dubiously at the agent. 'Make her boss plenty money, that's for sure. Maybe the blackfellas would get a share of that. What d'you reckon, boss?'

The agent shook his head and shrugged.

When Long Tom relayed it all to the old blokes in camp, they were pretty certain they knew the answer.

'She said they was goin' to do us some good, eh? Never works out that way when whitefellas tell us they goin' to do us some good. They do theirselves some good alright. Won't do the blackfellas any good, I reckon. Same old story, whitefellas grabbin' the blackfellas' land.'

There was a low murmur of weary anger around the fire.

'Why isn't this bossfella in England payin' us blackfellas for the land?'

'I was thinkin' that but I didn't say it,' said Miss Brodstone's faithful guide.

'Our land, eh?'

'They'll bugger it all up.'

'They always do.'

October 1908

1

It was nearly a month after their first encounter before Charlie saw Sid Kidman or heard from him again, and his glowing optimism was drying up and dying like the leaves that were beginning to gather in the gutters along Stepney Green.

Then Kidman reappeared, riding on the driver's seat of the last London General horse bus of the day on the Liverpool Street Station to Limehouse route.

By this time on a weekday evening the daytime flood of equine, wheeled and human traffic had subsided to a manageable stream and Charlie had an uninterrupted view of the other bus across the junction. It was only when the driver raised both hands in a comic salute that Charlie realised the driver himself was leaning on the corner of the guard rail on the upper deck behind his usual seat, and someone else was holding the reins. A second later he recognised the man who had brought the London General bus to a standstill at the Duke Street stop. It was the Australian Cattle King.

Charlie knew the official driver, one of the few nearly as young as himself, and he called out, 'Evening Mr Stoker,' using the sardonic formal courtesy the drivers extended even to their rivals.

'Evening Mr Downs,' replied the London General driver cheerily. He shifted an elbow onto the side rail, drawing Charlie's eye to the smart Dewar's whiskey advertisement that ran the whole length of the LGOC bus's upper deck. That was another twist in the downward spiral for the small bus companies. Big outfits like the London General, operating on the best and busiest routes through central London, could charge big advertisers big fees for their mobile hoardings. His own bus sported a small and grimy banner extolling the virtues of Carson's Extra Refined Clear Lard.

The Australian's voice cut through the gloom. 'G'day, son,' he called across the street. 'Just you hold hard there a minute.' Sid Kidman stood up and pushed the reins back into Ernie Stoker's hands, clapped the London General driver on the shoulder and disappeared down the far side of the red bus.

Charlie put one hand up beside his mouth and called across. 'You going to Australia then, Ernie?' The other driver had clambered over the rail, settling himself on his seat and tucking his apron across his knees. He gathered up the reins and shouted a reply over the top of an empty carrier's van rumbling between them. 'Nah. Got a job driving for Young's, down Richmond way. Two and a half quid a week and all the beer I can drink. Ha Ha Ha! What about you?'

For a moment, the other driver's good fortune took all the wind out of Charlie's sails. To find any horse-driving job at all was a huge slice of luck, but driving a dray for London's biggest brewery was luck on an inconceivable scale. Brewery dray drivers could expect at least half a pint of their employer's best at every public house on their round. They claimed it was the perfect way for the brewery to keep tabs on the quality of their landlords' beer-keeping, and the drivers took their responsibilities seriously. It was not unknown for an experienced team of dray horses to find its own way back to the brewery at the end of a hard day's quality control, with the unconscious driver and his mate snoring together in the back of the wagon.

Then as the tall figure of the Australian came loping across the street between pools of gaslight shed by the streetlamps, Charlie's spirits lifted again. If this man was true to the newspaper reports, here was his way out, an option as good as Ernie Stoker's and far more exciting. He wasn't going to finish his days as a fat old drunken drayman.

Charlie raised his whip to Ernie Stoker and called a cheerful farewell as the London General driver clicked his horses forward. 'See you tomorrow, Mr Stoker.'

'Not if I see you first, Mr Downs,' came the time-honoured reply.

The Australian in his wide-brimmed hat jumped up the stairs at the back of the bus and strode along the upper deck, rocking the vehicle on its ancient springs. Charlie slapped the reins gently on Samson and Delilah's backs. 'Away we go,' he called out to them, and they needed no second bidding to start again towards their stables.

As soon as the bus had gained enough momentum to allow the horses to settle into a steady trot Charlie turned anxiously to the figure leaning over the rail next to him. 'D'you remember me, Mr Kidman? You give me your card a few weeks back.' He slapped his pocket. 'Did you mean what you said in the papers?'

The older man grinned back at him. 'I remember you well, son. You saw the papers did you? I meant every word of it. You want a job in Australia? I'll give you one. Come and work for me. I'll see you right.'

The Australian rode with him all the way back to the White Horse Stables, hallooing a cab at the next stop to send a scrawled message back to his wife at their hotel. He told the cabman to return for him or send a night cab to collect him at midnight, and then he quizzed Charlie all the way back onto the Mile End road, up to the turn-off and under the flaking archway into the dimly lit yard.

Charlie introduced him to Gilroy, who pumped his hand delightedly until Charlie suggested that the old man should show the visitor round the stables while he made his final inspection of his own horses, and the remaining buses came rattling into the yard as the route closed down for the day.

At half past ten Charlie sent a message home to Tilly with the last conductor to leave the yard, who lived two streets north of Parfitt Court, and would tell her Charlie would be late, not to wait up. Then he followed the Australian and Gilroy into the drivers' room. Two of the other younger drivers came with him, but the majority of older men shook their heads when they were asked if they wanted to know more about Australia and Kidman's offer of jobs. 'Not for me,' said Arty Lockinge promptly. 'I went to Southend once for a day by the seaside and that's as close to that much water as I want to get. If I was his age,' he jerked his head towards Charlie, 'I would think twice, but not now. But thanks for the offer, Mr Kidman.' Arty shook hands with Kidman again respectfully and then bid them all goodnight in his normal cheerful fashion. 'See you all in the morning if we don't all die in the night.'

It was nearly eleven o'clock, and as the nightwatchman, Ruski, swung the yard gates closed behind the last stablehand, a hansom rattled to a standstill and the driver called, 'Cab for Mr Kidman.'

Sid stopped just as he was about to step into the driver's room. 'Yes, that's me, I ordered a cab, but not until midnight. Will he wait, if I pay him for his time?'

'I've never known a cabbie who won't wait till kingdom come if you pay him,' said Gilroy. 'Let him in the yard, Ruski, and give his horse some hay if he wants it. He can sit in the feedhouse with you and get warm.'

The old man ushered Sid to the best chair by the fire in the driver's room, and sat down heavily opposite him. The three younger drivers drew chairs closer to the older men, leaning forwards so their faces caught the firelight, and listened while Kidman and Gilroy drank tea and swopped yarns about the pleasures and perils of the coaching road. The old man offered their guest a brandy, but Charlie warned him not to accept it, and the Australian claimed he'd rather drink tea any day. 'Never had much use for hard drink, myself,' he said. 'I've seen too many men lose most of their money and all their good sense with it. I saw a man kill himself drinking moonshine when I was a lad, working at German Charlie's grog-shop. Mind you, it was shocking stuff and he did drink about a gallon of it.'

He listened keenly to Ted's lament for the passing of the old world with its flying mail coaches and their caped drivers, Gilroy's father and Charlie's grandfather among the last, and now the unstoppable onrush of modernity.

With his coaching experience, Kidman understood precisely how the life had been strangled out of Gilroy's business. Overheads spiralling relentlessly upwards and fare prices heading inexorably in the opposite direction, squeezed down by the big companies as the bigger, faster, cheaper motor buses barged and blared their way onto the most profitable routes.

'They've bought up all the good times, you know, the good routes,' said Gilroy wearily. 'We can't compete with them. They've got the money to pay for all these new knick-knacks as well.' Gilroy waved his hand at a broken ticket punch lying on one of the unused chairs. 'It's all more cost and less profit, all the way along the line. The sums didn't add up any more, concluded Gilroy, sadly. The General had nailed him in the end.

Sid watched him keenly and nodded sympathetically. He'd thought he'd seen it all in Adelaide and Melbourne, he told them, when it came to horse-drawn transport, but he'd never seen anything like the sheer scale and complexity of London. 'How many horses are there on the streets every day, do you reckon?'

'Two or three hundred thousand, maybe, and twenty years ago they say there was half a million horses working in London,' said Gilroy, reflectively. 'Maybe more in the good old days. And half of those were bus horses.'

'I believe it,' said Kidman. 'One of the big companies showed me round a building on Tuesday that had seven hundred horses stabled in it, right in the middle of the city!' Gilroy and Charlie both nodded. 'Four floors of stalls! Four jolly floors! Ramps up and down. I have never seen anything like it in all my life. And that's just one of their yards.'

The four British men had never heard anything like it either when Kidman told them stories about his own coaching days. They listened mesmerised by the images of moonlit stages along scarcely defined tracks that snaked across the endless outback, with Kidman falling asleep at the reins in the hot night. Or swimming a ten-horse team across a roaring flooded river with the overloaded mailcoach bobbing drunkenly behind them in the swirling currents like a miniature galleon. 'We had to swim the passengers across too. The old biddy I took across jolly near drowned me, and then she set about me with her hat for getting it wet.'

Kidman told these tales as though they were comical everyday trifles. He described harnessing a bucking, unbroken colt into a ten-horse team to replace a lame horse, and the same colt steady as a veteran by the end of a thirty-five-mile stage that nearly killed Kidman and several of his terrified passengers. 'I reckon we did about half of it off the track and all over the paddocks. We took out about two miles of fencing but missed the trees, thank the Lord, and he was like a lamb by the time we finished that run. What you might call a kill or cure education for both of us.'

He looked at the three bus drivers and laughed. 'There you go, boys. Come and swim a team across a South Australian creek in full spate. You haven't lived until you've done that.'

Sid put his hands on his knees. 'Well, there you are, you young fellas. Time for you to be getting some beauty sleep, but I can come back again and talk to you if you're interested.' He nodded at the three drivers. 'I'm offering a proper job to any of you who wants to try it, for as long as you want it. Good wages, a decent life, and who knows what opportunity you'll find out there when you've got your feet under you. Passage out paid, of course, and I'll pay both ways if you don't like it and want to come home.'

Gilroy slapped his root-hand on his knee and leaned towards the three drivers. 'There you are. Chance of a lifetime Mr Kidman's offering you. Just the ticket for young men like you.'

He caught Charlie's eye and shook his head. 'It's the womenfolk you're up against, Mr Kidman,' he said. 'Same for Charlie here. But maybe Charlie's got a better chance with Tilly, seeing as they...' he stopped and glanced at Charlie again awkwardly. 'Well, not so many ties, maybe. Ain't that right Charlie?'

Charlie was saved from replying to this by a knock. It was the nightwatchman.

Kidman jumped to his feet, pulling out his pocketwatch. 'My word,' he exclaimed, 'look at the time!' He shook Gilroy's hand, and the old man tipped his head towards Charlie. 'Charlie's keen to go with you. Desperate keen.' Charlie nodded. 'I'd go tomorrow, Mr Kidman, but my missus won't hear of it. She won't entertain the idea at the minute, but I'm not giving up. I'll keep on trying.'

Kidman turned to Charlie and regarded him for a few seconds in silence. They heard the St Dunstan's clock strike the quarter. 'Don't push too hard, young fella. Give her time. I'm not heading home until next March. And maybe it would help if she could meet Bel and me, and the girls as well. Would that help, d'you think?'

'Yes, sir, that could change her mind. She'd see you were straight up. She would listen to you, I'm sure she would.' He grabbed the Australian's hand and shook it fervently.

Gilroy slapped Charlie on the back. 'There you go, Charlie boy. Don't you give up. Mr Kidman's going to fix it for you. But now you better run home. You've got to be back here in a few hours and out on the route again.'

2

When he had at last managed to extricate himself from Lord Lonsdale's domineering patronage at the boxing exhibition in Covent Garden, William Saltwood hurried to the corner of King Street and found a cab to take him to his assignation with Clara.

As requested, the cabbie urged his tired horse to get a move on along Upper St Martin's Lane and West Street, slowing to a walk as they emerged into the throng spilling across Cambridge Circus from the Palace Theatre.

The ornate brick frontage of the Palace was blazing with electric light, illuminating a steady stream of men hurrying into the big, circular urinal that dominated the centre of the Circus, and sauntering more comfortably out of it. But the crowd was dispersing slowly towards the restaurants still full with late supper clientele, and the cab picked its way more easily round onto the head of Shaftesbury Avenue and then stopped behind the theatre in the shadows cast by the stage door lamp onto the cobbles of Greek Street.

The cabman whistled to the doorkeeper, and pointed downwards to his passenger with an exaggerated nod and wink, and two minutes later Clara emerged from the stage door, wrapped tightly in a hooded silk cloak that did nothing to disguise the curves of her figure. The doorkeeper escorted her and handed her into the cab. He murmured the address and the cabbie nodded and winked again.

Doubly loaded now, the cabhorse managed to raise a slow trot along Greek Street, turned left on Bateman Street, south on Dean Street, and disappeared into the narrow mews lane behind Old Compton Street.

The mews were lit by a single gas lamp, but the cabbie clearly knew where he was going and drew the reins to halt the cab opposite a plain door with a small, iron-barred opening at eye height. When the cabbie whistled softly, the glint of an eye showed briefly at the grill, and a second later the door was pulled inwards and a man's head appeared through the opening.

He peered into the cab and then nodded to the cabbie. There were glimmers of light showing behind the building's heavily curtained windows, and in that faint light the two figures in the cab emerged, William first, and then Clara, who waited for him to hold her by the waist and then jumped down into his arms and kissed him. He murmured something into her hair and she laughed, a deep gurgle of relaxed pleasure, and he guided her through the door with a hand on her hip, letting his hand fall to trace her behind with his fingertips.

A door opened in the building just as they reached it, spilling a brief wash of candlelight and a tantalising smell of food into the night, and Clara laughed again as she pulled William by the hand through the door.

The door closed discreetly behind them, and in the darkened alley the cabbie stuck his tongue out and waggled it at the doorman.

'Lucky young bastard. Wish I was getting a lick o' that.'

The doorman had almost closed the gate, but he stopped and grinned. 'Know who that is then?'

The cabman shook his head.

'That's Lord Saltwood's youngest, the Honourable William. Lord Saltwood the banker. Richest man in England. He's not the only one she brings here, though.'

The cabman laughed shortly. 'Ha. Hope he gets the clap and crabs to go with it. I'm off home. Not to a doxy like that, mind. Lucky little sod.'

The gate closed and the cabman clicked his tired, hired horse along the alley. He turned back towards Cambridge Circus on the off-chance of a lawyer needing a ride north east to Lincoln's Inn, but no one hailed him, so he shook the reins and headed to the jobbing livery stables in Cock Walk Yard, a sway-roofed relic tucked away in time behind the Fleet Street advertising and commission agents and newspaper representatives and the chaotic, ink-spattered, whiskey-sodden, tobacco-reeking offices of the *Dublin Daily Express*.

In the soft light and scented warmth of their very private room, William discarded his tails and his white waistcoat, shrugged his white braces off his shoulders and helped Clara to unwrap herself from her cloak. She kissed him again and he ran his hands slowly down her back, unfastening the hooks on her stage costume, and as it loosened he tried to pull her towards him, but she smiled and stopped him with the palm of one long-fingered hand on his chest, and moved away behind a screen.

He heard the splash of water as she stepped into the copper bath that had been filled with hot water for her, and she sighed ecstatically as she slipped into it.

Patience was one of the first things Clara had taught William nearly three years earlier. Take your time. Enjoy it. We have all night... Try this...

She had taught him a lot more since then, including the surprising fact that putting the woman's wishes first was infinitely more fulfilling than bulling your way to self-gratification and collapsing in a heap on top of her.

So he pulled his white tie undone as he waited, sitting patiently on the edge of her bed until he heard her low, amused voice calling him softly to come and hold her bathsheet. It was a blissful necessity to bathe like this when she came from an evening in the theatre, she said, to wash away the heat and the lights, and the smell of lust rising to the stage like bad breath from her audience of middle-aged men.

Now she was his and his alone, and they were here together in the private luxury of her dimly-lit rooms. She was rising out of the water and William delayed as he always did, transfixed by her naked, confident body as she turned slowly away from him in mock modesty and invited him to cover her again.

He was so absorbed in the moment that he failed to hear the quiet knock on the door. She laughed at him gently. 'Will, the food is here. Don't let it get cold.' Reluctantly he dragged his eyes away from the sway and swell beneath the damp bathsheet, and moved to the door. This was part of their ritual, another prolonging of anticipation. It must be midnight, and right on cue, he heard the chiming of clocks, one somewhere in the building, another ringing the hours on a church tower some way across the city.

On every monthly assignation he spent with Clara here, a servant would arrive at their door exactly at midnight with a bottle of Champagne and a tray of food – roast chicken *à la Française* from the Main d'Or on Old Compton Street, asparagus drowning in melting butter, peaches. They would eat in front of the fire, teasing each other, drawing closer, kissing more seriously, her tongue flicking between his lips, flavoured with strawberries.

Unusually, this evening, there was another, louder knock on the door and he opened it with quick irritation to find that there was no servant with a tray waiting on the other side. Instead, there was a suited, clerkish figure holding a sheet of papers, and behind him, hovering discreetly, the burly doorman.

The suited figure was extremely apologetic and begged forgiveness in a confidential whisper for his intrusion, but he was the manager of the establishment and he must have a word, please, just to clear up a small problem with the account? The man glanced across the landing anxiously and bobbed his head towards Clara's room. 'Perhaps it would be best if we could discuss this privately, Mr Saltwood,' he whispered.

'What the hell are you talking about?' William was blocking the doorway, but then Clara appeared behind him, tying the sash of a silk robe. She put a hand on William's arm.

'Hello Mr Arnold,' she said. 'Come in, but just you, I think.' She drew William back into the room and when the manager followed she closed the door before the doorman could move across the landing.

'What is this?' asked William angrily. 'Surely this could wait until the morning, man? Who in the name of hell are you, anyway?'

The manager winced and shook his head regretfully. He shuffled the papers he was holding and pulled one of them out, cocking his head to check it was the one he wanted.

'My name is Arnold,' he said, 'and I am responsible for the running of this establishment, and the management of the accounts.' He held up the papers. 'I regret to have to inform you that these accounts for your visits here over the past six months have been returned to us, unpaid.'

'What?' William snatched the papers out of the manager's hand and held them up to the light of the lamp nearest him. 'This is outrageous...' He turned to Clara, who had moved away and was looking down into the red coals of the fire. 'Clara, can you explain this? What on earth is going on?'

William was not stupid or naïve, and he had understood from the moment he had been introduced to the variety hall performer by his older brother that money was involved in their relationship. Clara gave every sign that she enjoyed his company, but their assignations had been organised on a business footing from the start.

But he had understood that these rooms were Clara's lodgings, and when he had tried to ask her how he should 'contribute to her costs' she had laughed and put a finger to his lips, and in a number of other intimate ways distracted him from the subject. It was all dealt with, she had breathed into his ear. Just a trifle to pay for the Champagne. He mustn't think about it again. What about this...?

So he hadn't. He had asked George once how it was all dealt with, and George had also brushed him off. 'Put it down as part of your education.'

George had not told William that he himself had enjoyed the same education in Clara de Beauville's rooms, or named any of the other privileged boys who had passed into manhood through the Old Compton Street school doors. William had done what was suggested and enjoyed every minute he had spent with one of the most sought-after theatrical courtesans in London.

Until now. He stared at the figures on the accounts, itemising his last six evenings down to the last spear of asparagus. Champagne charged at five guineas a *bottle*! Four guineas for the rent of the rooms. So these were not Clara's rooms. But *four* guineas for a night? Hot water and linen charged at two guineas. Charges for crockery and cutlery and service. And at the foot of the list, a figure of thirty guineas for 'Fees' that hit him like a punch in the solar plexus.

The bill for each of the six evenings came to over fifty guineas, which even to William's fairly cavalier sense of values was eye-wateringly extortionate.

He looked up and met Clara's gaze, and she smiled and shrugged sympathetically. 'I'm sorry, Will. A bit of a shock, isn't it? But I hope you think I was worth it.'

The manager coughed into his hand. 'I beg pardon, Mr Saltwood, but we must ask you to settle your account with us, fully and immediately.'

Wlliam turned back to the man and stared at him. 'What?'

'We must ask you to settle your account, sir. It comes to three hundred and thirty-six guineas...' he shuffled through the papers,

'...eight shillings and tenpence.'

There was silence for a moment. William ran a hand through his hair. 'This is ... good God, man...' He looked at Clara again but she only smiled again, regretfully. 'I... who was paying for this before, for God's sake? Why have they not been paid now?'

He knew before the manager spoke. 'The accounts were dealt with by someone at Lord Saltwood's bank, sir...' He peered at a letter on top of the papers.

'Prior,' said William.

'Yes, sir, that's it. Mr Prior advises us that Lord Saltwood has instructed him to return the accounts, and that we must present them to William Saltwood for immediate payment...'

Fact and Fiction

The Song of the Butcher Bird is a work of historical fiction, mixing real history, people, places, issues and events with imaginary events and characters. One of the things I hope readers might enjoy is trying to spot what is fact and what is fiction, and where this story might connect with yours.

Sid and Bel Kidman and their children were real, and many of the events I have described in *Bigfella Kidman* happened, or events very like them. Many of the people they met on their visit to England were also real, and later in the story they will meet more. There are several real key players in the story in England and Australia, and I am acutely aware that many of these real people have living descendants, and possibly lawyers. So I have been as careful as I can be to ensure that my descriptions of these characters and their actions are as truthful as possible, and based accurately on published material that is in the public domain.

Most importantly, I have tried very hard to get Sid and Bel Kidman right, and I would like to thank Sid's biographer, Jill Bowen, for all her help in keeping me true to this extraordinary man. If you would like to read more about him you can find Jill's biography online: *Kidman. The Forgotten King*. Many thanks also to Kathleen Richardson for her memories of travelling from Adelaide to England wth Bel Kidman in 1938 – and almost immediately back again when war broke out.

It has been fascinating doing the research for the story. I am sure I have missed or misrepresented a great deal but I have tried to capture the reality of life in England and Queensland in the last days of the Edwardian age. The world was changing at a bewildering speed. Trains like the Cheltenham Flyer were thundering at over seventy miles an hour through countryside that still moved through the seasons with the same, measured walking pace of shire horses pulling a plough or cows coming in to be milked by hand. Sporty new motorcars were matching the Flyer for speed, and the internal combustion engine was beginning to dominate the roads, particularly in London, as the principal form of horsepower. Men were beginning to take to the air in powered flying contraptions. People were being frazzled regularly by state-of-the-art but lethally uninsulated household electrical appliances. Telegraphs could wing messages around the world in minutes, and the telephone was creating the first universal form of social media.

On the other hand, there are a lot of horses in my story because in 1908 horses still played an absolutely fundamental and essential role in our economic and social lives, in transport, leisure and in war, in Britain and even more so in Australia. They will continue to crop up in large numbers all the way through the story until some of our characters take part in the last great cavalry charge by the Australian Light Horse in the World War I Middle East campaign to eject the Turks from the Holy Land. There were tens of thousands of horses working in London in 1908, and a handful of small horse bus companies were fighting a rearguard action against the London General. But they were disappearing fast and Sid Kidman really did offer any horse bus drivers who wanted jobs a chance to emigrate and work for him in Australia. Thank you to the London Transport Museum Library, formerly of Covent Garden, for all your help in giving me so much background on the horse buses.

By the time my story starts in 1908, the migration of the great majority of the British population from rural to urban working life was complete. Most lived and worked in conditions of poverty and hardship that are almost impossible to credit a century later, paid subsistence wages, their livelihoods threatened every day by disease and accident, unprotected by anything much in the way of health and safety regulations or any support in times of trouble except charity or the ultimate shame of the dreaded Workhouse.

In those conditions and the onrush of scientific progress, millions of workers were turning away from the church and towards the unions to make their claims for a better life here on earth now, never mind later in heaven. The red shoots of the new political Labour movement were sprouting in all the major industrial centres. In the last years of Edward VII's reign, tens of thousands of miners were marching and striking, and railwaymen, dockers and factory workers followed their example. The Suffragists and Suffragettes of the Women's Union were on the march, too, lobbying, protesting, flourbombing and hunger-striking to break the chauvinist stranglehold on every aspect of their lives. It was a period of profound social and political agitation, a watershed between the age-old certainties of the feudal, patriarchal status quo and the new age of democracy where everyone would, or should, have a fair go – or at least, a fairer go.

There were growing fears among the establishment that Britain's working classes were being dangerously infected by the communist and socialist firebrands flocking to London from all over Europe. The new Liberal government was bowing to the will of the masses and Lloyd George was preparing to hit the rich with higher taxes in his 'People's Budget'. Many among the old, conservative plutocracy believed Britain was heading towards revolution, and they were beginning to plan how to defeat it. When he wasn't drinking, scratching his boils, chasing his housekeeper or sponging money off Engels, Karl Marx had managed to complete the first part of his communist manifesto, *Das Kapital*, in the British Library, and in the very early 1900s Lenin spent much of his exile from Russia in London. He held the second annual conference of the Russian Social Democratic Labour Party in an old chapel on Tottenham Court Road, and in 1908 he wrote *Materialism and Empirio-criticism* in that hotbed of anti-imperial revolutionary ferment, the British Museum Reading Room.

Britain was the only country in Europe (including Russia) where these leading revolutionary thinkers could live, write, congregate and fight each other without being arrested on sight and jailed or disappeared by the authorities. To be fair, imperial London gave Marx and Lenin plenty of inspiration for their critique of capitalism. In the winner-takes-all heyday of Edwardian Britain, the social and business elite were making hay while the sun never set on the British Empire. But the elite was changing. This was a time when business tycoons made huge fortunes on the bent backs of the workers, and when Liverpool food merchants or cotton machinery manufacturers in Accrington could send their sons to Eton to polish their manners and their accents, buy them an estate and a title, and leap in just two generations from the factory or shop floor to the dizziest heights of the landed aristocracy. Lord Saltwood is a fictional example, but there were dozens of real cases where this happened. Aristocrats also lost fortunes, through wild overspending, blind bad management and sometimes gambling. William Saltwood's debts are comparatively modest, but given that £1 in 1908 was worth approximately £50 today, he has still managed to rack up a student debt of £150,000 on an allowance of £50,000 a year.

There were also many examples of principled industrialists who tried to improve their workers' lives, and Stepney seemed to attract more than its share of wealthy philanthropists, including the banking super-rich such as the Rothschilds and the Coutts, who were funding hospitals, schools and new housing. Dr Barnardo began his mission to scoop neglected boys and girls off the streets in Stepney, and a young solicitor called Clement Atlee was managing the Haileybury Boys' Club in Stepney too – one of many such clubs opened across the East End after the Boer War by the major public schools. Mostly, though, the toil of millions of miners and factory workers was funding a golden age of hedonism for the privileged few – vast country houses and sporting estates, shooting parties, hunting, and the delights of the summer season: racing at Ascot, yachting at Cowes, lavish fancy-dress balls and Henley Regatta, all governed by rigid social protocols and much of it blessed by the patronage of the short, portly, pop-eyed king-emperor, Edward VII.

I have tried to describe the real lifestyle of a fictional, super-rich aristocratic family as accurately as I can, and anyone who has watched *Downton Abbey* will get the picture. I've also explored the streets of Stepney and Whitechapel to understand the location of the Mile End pub and Gilroy's Municipal Omnibus Service, and the lives that Ted, Tilly and Charlie would have led there. Thanks to the Ordinance Survey maps of London of the time, I have been able to locate Gilroy's stables in the real White Horse Lane. The maps show that there was a Scottish Laundry on the Mile End Road. There was a home for Lady Deaconesses at Stepney Green, and the Lady Deaconess in charge really was Miss Mary Cock. Tilly ate for two in King's Eel Pie Shop and Café, and Miss Batt ran a dressmaking business from her house in Beaumont Terrace. There was a very real Annie Cappuccio as well, and I hope any living members of her family will forgive me for taking liberties with her life and bringing her into the story to rescue Tilly from the despair of losing her baby. Annie was a wonderful woman who will feature more in the next stage of the story. Many thanks to the

Tower Hamlets Local History Library and Archives in Stepney for so much background detail, much of it photographic.

Babies, children and women in childbirth really did die in sickening numbers in Edwardian England, especially in the backstreets of the poorest areas where hygiene and medical care were virtually unknown. They also died in big houses and in the countryside, carried off by TB or typhoid, accident, sepsis, whooping cough, pneumonia or measles. In the outback, white children and women died like flies, just as the livestock died in the drought, hundreds of miles from any possible help. Nowadays it's so rare that it makes the news. Then, virtually every family followed a small coffin to the cemetery at least once. Bel Kidman did lose two of her six children, and she lived in relative civilisation near Adelaide.

Then there were the sons that didn't come back from the wars. More than 22,000 British soldiers died in the two Boer Wars that ended in 1902. You can find memorials to those who died for the British Empire in these embarrassing and unjust wars all over Britain, and many more scattered throughout South Africa, Canada, Australia, New Zealand and even India. So the obelisk on the edge of Chiddington village green would not have been unusual, and the statistics are about right. Only one in three of the British fatalities were caused by enemy action. The other two thirds died of disease. Eighty-six British soldiers were killed or injured by lightning and one was eaten by a crocodile. Six years after the second war ended, the scars of these conflicts were still quite raw in Britain, and even more so in South Africa, where 26,000 Boer women and children and up to 20,000 black Africans had died of disease in the concentration camps the British herded them into. Later in the story, of course, these losses will be dwarfed by the First World War, when nearly ten million humans and eight million horses were slaughtered, and between fifty and a hundred million died in the global flu pandemic that followed it.

The treatment of the Aborigine peoples in Australia by white, mostly British colonialists is even more shameful than the British treatment of the Boer families and indigenous African people. There is no getting round this, and it's one of the main themes in this story.

Sid Kidman believed in the Australian principle that everyone deserves a fair go, but he was rare in extending it equally to the

Aborigines. Sid had worked as a teenager under the wing of an Aborigine stockman called Billy, and all his life he credited Billy with teaching him most of what he knew about the bush. He employed Aborigines on his stations and insisted that his managers and stockmen treat them with fairness and respect. It was an approach that will bring him and some of our fictional characters into conflict with the many white station owners, politicians and policemen who take an opposite view in this story. He was ultimately given a knighthood by the British government, but the blackfellas of South Australia conferred a higher honour on the whitefella they called Bigfella Kidman King of all Adelaide.

There are many instances in this story where the original Australian peoples are referred to as 'blackfellas'. It does not seem to have been a term that implied disrespect or worse when used by a white fellow. The Aborigines used it to describe themselves when they spoke English in the same way they referred to the whites as 'whitefellas', and I have used both in that spirit. Sid Kidman used it himself, and he certainly didn't use it in a pejorative sense any more than the Aborigines meant to insult him when they called him Bigfella Kidman. Although six inches shorter than his older brother Sackville, Sid was a big fella, well over six feet tall. When other whites wanted to show their contempt for the Aborigines they used names that are nowadays unspeakable by white people. You will find them in the mouths of some of the characters in this story because those were the words that were used at the time, and it would be ducking the issue to pretend otherwise. The Aborigines had their own insults for white people in their own languages, and still do.

Today, the consensus seems to be that the indigenous peoples of Australia prefer to be called Aborigines, rather than the generic Aboriginals. Two hundred years ago, there were an estimated 700 to 750 distinct Aborigine familial groups, tribes or peoples in Australia and Tasmania, each with their own language or dialect. Today, just over a hundred languages remain alive, and fewer than twenty are still in use. In *The Song of the Butcher Bird* I am using Gudjal as a representative language of central, eastern Queensland, with many thanks to William Santo's Black Ink Press primers for my first lessons. As in most other parts of the British Empire, for all their supposed intellectual superiority, the whites relied on the blacks to learn English. Very few whitefellas managed to learn more than a smattering of their local blackfellas' language.

Then there's the boomerang. Thousands of years before the white west applied the principles of aerodynamics to flight, the Aborigines were carving sophisticated delta-wing weapons that returned to their hands if they didn't hit their targets. And around the time my story begins, a brilliant Aborigine inventor, writer and teacher called David Ngunaitponi was drawing plans for an 'antigravitational device' that was essentially a boomerang-winged helicopter. You can see his likeness on the Australian fifty-dollar note.

The record of the relationship between white colonialists and black indigenous peoples makes very uncomfortable reading for a white European. Just as there was in the bitter debate about slavery in Britain a century before this story, there were whites who stood up for the rights of the black minority in Australia. As with slavery, however, it may be impossible for a white person today to comprehend what it must have been like to be dispossessed of your land and your children, hunted, massacred, exploited, segregated, and systematically betrayed and abused in every conceivable way, as the blackfellas have been by the whitefellas in Australia.

It shouldn't have been this way, and it wouldn't have been if the white colonialists who followed Captain James Cook out to *Terra Australis* had also followed his example. If he had been a horse, old Sam Downs would have described James Cook as a 'Scholar, a Christian and a Gentleman'. In his early voyaging around the world he exemplified the Royal Society's ethos that every human being encountered anywhere in the world should be treated with equal respect, and Cook behaved towards the peoples he encountered in the South Pacific and on the great 'undiscovered' reaches of the east coast of Australia with the same courtesy he would extend to his neighbours on the few occasions when he was home in Stepney.

In 1908, Aborigines were still being hunted down and killed with impunity by whitefellas in the less 'settled' areas of Australia, including the north west, the Kimberleys and the 'Top End' of the Northern Territory and Queensland. Whitefellas were also being speared in these areas by blackfellas who resented the intrusion into their tribal lands not only of the arrogant whitefellas themselves but also of the hundreds of thousands of cattle, sheep and horses that obliterated many traditional forms of flora and fauna the Aborigines relied on for food. The vicious circle of violence escalated until the whitefellas organised punitive expeditions and in many instances massacred large numbers of Aborigine men, women and children, with the tacit or sometimes overt collusion of the authorities.

The most recent date I can find of a recorded massacre is 1928, when a party of whitefellas led by a police sergeant ambushed an Aborigine camp at night in Western Australia and killed about 200 men, women and children. Not one of the white perpetrators was punished, although the policeman may have been demoted.

This happened just 90 years ago, but I am getting ahead of the story. There's a lot more to come, and I hope you will want to follow it. Even better, if you have a connection to any part of this story, please join in.

You might have a connection to characters real or fictional. You might be related to the Kidmans of Suffolk or the Downs of Essex or to Annie Cappuccio. Your family tree might include a horse bus driver who went to Australia, or didn't, a philanthropist or a Suffragette. You might be connected to Stepney or Adelaide, or to one of the dozens of stations that formed the Kidman & Co empire until the last of them was sold recently. There are many sideroads on a journey from London to Queensland and beyond, and many lives glimpsed in passing that catch your eye and make you wonder.

You might be surprised to find that this story, or their story, touches your story, and you can follow the story, find more background, diversions and blogs, and keep in touch at **www.yellamickey.com**

Thank you to Rick and Susie, Hugh, Nicky, Mary, Angus and Tim for your patient support. To Ken, John, Jossy, Di, Freda and Eddie for your professional help. And to Alice, Nicky, Hattie, Georgie, Jos, Hugh, Mark and Bea for reading, weeding and encouragement.

All shortcomings are entirely mine.